James Nelson has served as a seaman, rigger, boatswain and officer on a number of sailing vessels. He is the author of the five books comprising his *Revolution at Sea* saga, as well as *The Guardship*, the first book in his *Brethren of the Coast* saga. He lives with his wife and children in Maine.

His website can be found at www.jameslnelson.com

D1324746

Also by James Nelson

THE GUARDSHIP

and published by Corgi Books

THE BLACKBIRDER

Book Two of
The Brethren of the Coast

James Nelson

CORGI BOOKS

THE BLACKBIRDER
A CORGI BOOK : 0 552 14842 3

First publication in Great Britain

PRINTING HISTORY
Corgi edition published 2002

1 3 5 7 9 10 8 6 4 2

Set in 10½/12pt Galliard by
Kestrel Data, Exeter, Devon.

Corgi Books are published by Transworld Publishers,
61–63 Uxbridge Road, London W5 5SA,
a division of The Random House Group Ltd,
in Australia by Random House Australia (Pty) Ltd,
20 Alfred Street, Milsons Point, Sydney, NSW 2061, Australia,
in New Zealand by Random House New Zealand Ltd,
18 Poland Road, Glenfield, Auckland 10, New Zealand
and in South Africa by Random House (Pty) Ltd,
Endulini, 5a Jubilee Road, Parktown 2193, South Africa.

Printed and bound in Great Britain by
Cox & Wyman Ltd, Reading, Berkshire.

*To those millions of people stolen from Africa
and upon whose long-forgotten backs this
country was raised to greatness*

Pirate – a sea-robber, or an armed ship that roams the seas without any legal commission, and seizes or plunders every vessel she meets indiscriminately, whether friends or enemies.

Privateer – a vessel of war, armed and equipped by particular merchants, and furnished with a military commission by the admiralty, or the officers who superintend the marine department of a country, to cruise against the enemy and take, sink, or burn their shipping, or otherwise annoy them as opportunity offers. These vessels are generally governed on the same plan with his majesty's ships, though they are guilty of many scandalous depredations, which are very rarely practiced by the latter.

– William Falconer
An Universal Dictionary of the Marine

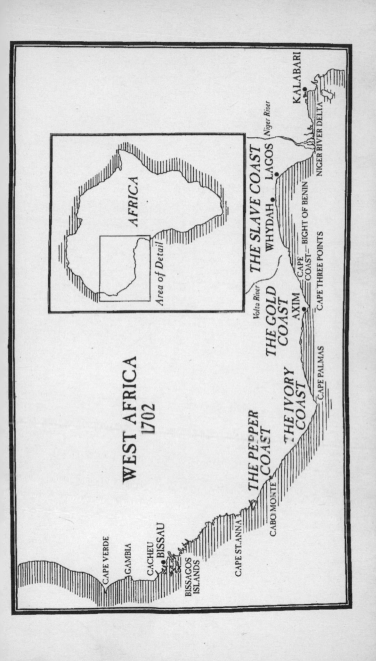

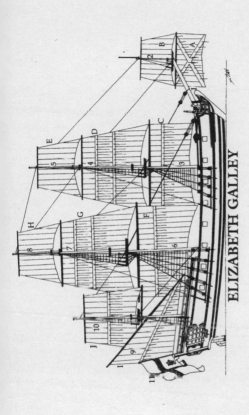

ELIZABETH GALLEY

SAILS

A. Spritsail
B. Spritsail Topsail
   (pronounced *tops'l*)
C. Foresail or Fore Course
D. Fore Topsail
E. Fore Topgallant Sail
   (pronounced *t'gan's'l*)
F. Mainsail or Main Course
G. Main Topsail
H. Main Topgallant Sail
I. Mizzen Sail
J. Mizzen Topsail

SPARS

1. Bowsprit
2. Spritsail Topmast
3. Foremast of Fore
   Lower Mast
4. Fore Topmast
5. Fore Topgallant Mast
6. Main Mast of Main Lower Mast
7. Main Topmast
8. Main Topgallant Mast
9. Mizzenmast
10. Mizzen Topmast
11. Ensign and Ensign Staff

THE BLACKBIRDER

CHAPTER 1

The church was all heat and white sunlight, dust and the smell of dry grass and manure pushing in through flung open doors. Flies swirling, lighting, black specks on white painted pews.

Sunday. June 14, the Year of Our Lord 1702.

In the pulpit the preacher droned, on and on.

Marlowe shifted, felt the sweat running under his heavy coat and waistcoat and shirt. Realized he had had no thought for . . . how long? No thought, just consciousness. Like an animal.

The preacher waved his arms, entreated God.

The air was close, oppressively hot. The church was nearly twenty years old, built when the now-burgeoning Williamsburg was still a backwater called the Middle Plantation. People crammed in like hands of tobacco prized into a cask. A blessing in winter, a misery in summer.

Marlowe looked at his shoes, then over at Elizabeth's legs, the outline of her thighs just discernible through layer upon layer upon layer of silk and taffeta. She had to be even hotter than he was. But she would remain proper, because she needed to feel proper after her many years of secret impropriety.

Propriety was why he was there in the first place, in his own pew. Not in front of the communion table; those pews had been sold long before to the first families of Virginia. Their pew was behind the vestry, which was still perfectly respectable. The important thing was that everyone, today's newcomers and yesterday's, knew they *could* afford a pew in front of the communion table, were one available.

Marlowe had purchased the pew – at no little cost – because Elizabeth did not wish to jeopardize their place in Virginia society. She did not wish to risk losing this new life they had carved for themselves in this new land. They had position now in tidewater society, and people with position spent Sundays in their own pews.

As a merchant seaman, Marlowe had had Sundays off. He'd had no duty, save standing watch, unless the ship was run by some petty tyrant who could countenance no idleness among those to whom he paid wages.

What had it meant when he was on the account, among the Brethren of the Coast?

Nothing. As often as not they hadn't any notion of what day of the week it was. It did not matter to the lawless and the godless, whose hours called them only to slothfulness and debauchery.

Marlowe realized his legs were cramped. He stretched them out full length, flexed the muscles, savored the relief. Stole a glance at his friend Francis Bickerstaff, seated on his other side. He was dressed in conservative, unadorned clothes. He held a Bible in his lap, sat rigid, his eyes intent on the preacher. He looked as if he might have been a preacher himself.

16

Bickerstaff was a pious man, after his own fashion. A former tutor, fluent in Latin and Greek and all those things that the overeducated and underemployed seemed to know. He appeared to be absorbing every syllable of the preacher's harangue.

But the preacher was, to Marlowe's certain knowledge, a fool. He doubted there was anything the man could say that Bickerstaff would find enlightening. He concluded that Bickerstaff was as far removed from the sermon as he himself was, but that Bickerstaff, as usual, was better at hiding it.

Three years. Three years they had been coming to that cursed church.

He lowered his head, hoping it made him look pious. It had not been so bad before, with the old Reverend Hathaway, who was a good man, godly and thoughtful, and could spin a sermon that was not so oppressively dull. But he had taken fever and died a year back, and the Right Reverend Ezekiel Trumbell had taken his place. What the congregation had done to deserve him, Marlowe could not figure.

His thoughts wandered away from those considerations as his eyes wandered to the hem of Elizabeth's dress, then slowly up her leg. He pictured her thighs under all that cloth, the smooth white skin, the flat, lovely stomach, the curve of her hips, the way she looked lying naked in their big bed.

He felt himself becoming aroused, had a vague sensation that that was not appropriate in church And then the warm sensuous drowsiness lapped over him and he felt his eyes close, felt delicious sleep pulling him down . . .

Felt a sharp elbow in his ribs that jerked him back to church.

'Stop that, Thomas,' Elizabeth hissed, never taking her eyes from the preacher, her expression of pious attention never wavering.

'What?' Marlowe felt himself flush. He wondered, did she mean his falling asleep, or had she guessed at his salacious thoughts?

'I do believe Reverend Trumbell is speaking to you, dear.'

Marlowe straightened and focused on the Reverend's words. Trumbell's head was turned in their direction, and his eyes flickered toward the Marlowe pew, like fingertips testing a hot griddle, then pulling away fast before they are scorched.

Oh, God. Will you not even look me in the eye, you little worm?

It was the speech about the danger of free Negroes again. Dressed up with some nonsense about Cain and Abel, but at its heart it was the same old speech. Marlowe wanted to curse out loud.

'And the precursor to Cain's sin of the blood? Was Adam's failure to obey God's command to keep dominion over all the beasts of the field, yea, all the living creatures.

'And so today, like Adam, are we not commanded to have dominion over all the beasts of the field, and all the heathen creatures, be they man or beast, who have not the benefit of knowing God? It is our duty as Christians to prevent the wicked idleness into which man must fall if the Godly do not keep dominion over them. We fail in our duty if we do not hold the reins tight. And most especially must we keep dominion over those poor children of Africa, whose childlike innocence . . .'

'Oh, God, I pray, preserve me from such

blather . . .' Marlowe said, a bit too loud. A few heads turned, Elizabeth's sharp elbow struck home.

It was his slaves, of course. His former slaves, actually, the ones that had come with the plantation he had purchased from the estate of Elizabeth's late husband. He had freed them all and then employed them as wage labor.

It was not a popular decision in the tidewater.

Marlowe saw Trumbell's attention shift from his pew to those in front of the communion table and he followed the Reverend's gaze. In the second pew back sat Frederick Dunmore, arms folded, listening with great care to the words. He had the entire pew to himself. He had no family that anyone knew of.

Of course, Marlowe thought. Check with Dunmore, the Lord and Master, make sure you're delivering the speech the way he told you. How had Bickerstaff put it, from one of his plays? 'Speak the speech, I pray, as I pronounced it to you . . .' That was Dunmore.

He was dressed in white, as he always was: white silk coat and waistcoat, brilliant white breeches and socks, a great white river of ringlets from his periwig cascading down the front of him. He blended into the pew like a deer blends into an autumn field. He looked as if he were trying to dress like God himself.

'You dog . . .' Marlowe muttered, and then to Bickerstaff whispered, 'It is that dog Dunmore that is behind this blather, you know.'

Dunmore was a newcomer to the colony, late of London and just turned plantation owner. In the year he had been there he had wormed his way into the House of Burgesses, had somehow arranged that enviable pew. It took a vast sum of money, spread judiciously and thick, to achieve all that.

Marlowe sighed, purposely loud, leaned back, arms folded, and thought of old Reverend Hathaway. He had been a man of his own mind, a man who led his congregation and would not be its puppet. In fact, he was one of the only men in the tidewater, he and Bickerstaff, who supported Marlowe in his decision. He believed it was God's will that the blacks be free – the same reason Trumbell was now using to insist on their bondage.

Dunmore carried his support of Negro bondage with missionary zeal. When he heard what Marlowe had done he had gone apoplectic, had been waging a silent war on Marlowe ever since. He had seen to it that the laws concerning Negroes carrying firearms – laws that had been hitherto rarely enforced – were strictly adhered to.

He hired minions to keep up a loose surveillance of Marlowe House, hoping to find some cause for complaint, some clear breach of the law. Marlowe knew that Dunmore was investigating the legality of his freeing, then hiring, his former slaves, was considering bringing suit.

And, of course, Dunmore had convinced Trumbell to speak from the pulpit on that issue. He had somehow arranged to have his own opinions flow from the Reverend's mouth.

Cowardly little bastard, Marlowe thought. His anger was a smoldering thing, a glowing spot in a pile of coals, not the hot flash that made him act without thinking, that led to so much trouble.

But what could he do? He would have happily called Dunmore out and put a bullet through the man's head or a sword through his chest – Dunmore's choice – but Dunmore always maneuvered his way around blatant offense, like a lady stepping carefully through a stable. He was clever about never doing anything that would give Marlowe cause to demand satisfaction.

People were standing now, shuffling out of pews. Marlowe looked up. It was over, thankfully over. His thoughts had carried him through the end of the service, had put one more torturous Sunday morning in his past. He stood, stretched, and smiled the first genuine smile of the morning.

'Come, my love,' he said, extending a hand to Elizabeth, 'let us have dinner and then get us down to the river. I am with child to see her with her topgallant gear sent up.'

'You saw her yesterday morning.'

'But then she did not have her topgallant gear sent up.'

'Thomas, you are insufferable,' Elizabeth said, but the end of the service and the prospect of the sight that awaited him at the river were making Marlowe giddy, reckless.

'And you, my love,' he said in a voice so low that only she could hear, 'are so beautiful I wish nothing more than to give your arse a good squeeze, right here.'

'If you do, I shall cut your throat in your sleep,' she said with the sweetest of smiles as she brushed past him and stepped down into the aisle between the long row of pews.

Marlowe followed docilely behind his wife as she wound her way out of the church, flashing white-tooth smiles to those she passed, receiving smiles

21

back from the women, appreciative glances from the men.

Appreciative but furtive glances, a quick up-and-down and then eyes averted. No man in Williamsburg wanted to offend Thomas Marlowe. Men who had done that had died. Men who had once tried to bring him down by bringing Elizabeth to shame had died brutally. His fellow gentlemen-planters viewed Marlowe as a pet tiger: tame, domestic, but still wild inside, dangerous and unpredictable. He knew it and encouraged it.

Elizabeth led them to a side entrance, not through the main doors where Trumbell was greeting the parishioners as they made their exit. They stepped out of the little Jacobean-style brick building and into a small garden that served as a buffer between the church and the dusty Duke of Gloucester Street.

Marlowe squinted against the brilliant sun. It blazed in a clear blue sky and bounced its light off those patches of granite not shaded by the small maples lining the arbor. He savored the smell of jasmine baking in the sun. A cardinal flashed by, a streak of red, calling with its odd liquid voice.

He breathed deep, taking the warmth and the jasmine into his lungs. The heat felt good, not the close-pressed heat of a packed church but the full, honest warmth of a perfect summer day in Virginia.

'Hey, Marlowe, there you are!' Hartwell Page pushed his way between two saplings and came huffing up, his round face red with the heat, in startling contrast to the white sculptured wig that sat on his head.

He wore a brocade coat with an intricate pattern, the weight of which was causing the sweat to run down his cheeks. Under his left arm he carried his hat, which would never have fit over his wig. With his right arm he worked a walking stick as if it were the bilge-pump handle on a sinking ship. He was built like a cannonball and carried himself with as much subtlety.

'Thought I'd catch you here, Marlowe, didn't reckon you'd wish to shake hands with that rascal Trumbell! Beating around the bush this morning, about your Negroes, eh? Not going right at it like last time, the dog. He's as mad on the subject as that Dunmore! Ah, Mrs Marlowe, charmed!' He bowed as much as his ample waist would allow, just as Mrs Page struggled up behind him. She was much the same shape as her husband, though quiet, as if she were forever bowled over by Hartwell's effusiveness, as, indeed, most people were.

'Well, I reckon Reverend Trumbell is entitled to his opinion, as is any man,' Marlowe ventured.

'Oh, balls, Marlowe, beg your pardon. Wasn't a man of the cloth you'd have put a bullet through his head by now, eh?' He gave Marlowe a suggestive jab of the elbow. Page seemed to enjoy the proximity to danger that being with Marlowe suggested.

'If he wasn't a man of the cloth he would probably keep his mouth shut,' Bickerstaff said, squinting off at some distant point. 'But the greater coward is Frederick Dunmore, who puts the words in his mouth and makes great speeches when Thomas is not about. I don't know what is more craven than cowering behind a collar. Cowering behind a woman, perhaps?'

23

'Well said, Bickerstaff, well said!' Page gave Francis the elbow jab.

'This is a new thing for you, Francis,' Marlowe said. 'You have been quite reserved in your judgment of the Reverend and his handler before now.'

'Let us say just that my cup of tolerance runneth over.'

'Right, well, now,' said Hartwell, tiring of that line of talk, 'reckon I know where you're bound, after dinner.'

'I was thinking to head down to the river . . .'

'Course you were, course you were. But I must insist that you dine with me and the wife. Have 'em laying out a feast for the king himself down to the tavern. Pray, bring your lovely wife here and the good Dr Bickerstaff and join me.'

Bickerstaff had told Page on at least three occasions that he was not a doctor of any kind, but Page either could not recall or could not be convinced.

'We would be delighted, I believe,' said Marlowe. Page was a bit much, but he could be amusing, and he did not exaggerate the quality of food he would have ordered up. The straining of his waistcoat against his midriff bore silent testimony to his proclivities where food was concerned.

But, of course, accepting the invite would mean . . .

'And after dinner, then, Marlowe, if it ain't too much bother, I'd be honored if I might accompany you down to the river. Haven't been down since you stepped the masts. But even then, magnificent! Navy could never do the like. She ain't another *Plymouth Prize*, I'll warrant.'

Marlowe thought of the decrepit, half-rotten

Plymouth Prize, his former command. 'No, she ain't the *Plymouth Prize*.'

'I've a mind for something along those lines myself . . .' Page added. 'So, what say you? Dine with me?'

Why not? It was hard to refuse Hartwell Page's invitation, which he gave with such force.

'Delighted. And we should be pleased to have you along afterward, Hartwell. I would welcome your advice.'

'Ah, Marlowe, you are a lying dog, but I thank you. You know I'll give advice, whether I know a thing or not.'

And advice he gave, through a protracted dinner of hominy, hashed beef, squirrel, asparagus, red herring, and sallet, advice on everything from plantation management to growing tobacco to Marlowe's current enterprise.

And Marlowe and company listened, ate, laughed, drank, enjoyed themselves thoroughly. Page was one of those few who could pull off an hour of running monologue without being insufferable.

That fact aside, it was still a relief when the two parties took to their separate carriages for the seven-mile ride to Jamestown and the docks that thrust out into the James River.

They settled in their seats, Marlowe, Bickerstaff, and Elizabeth, the first private moment they had had since morning, and Bickerstaff said, 'I am sorry, Thomas, that you must suffer that idiot Dunmore. And of all things, for freeing your slaves. I have said it before, it is the most decent act you have ever committed.'

'I thank you, sir. I know that you suffer no

delusion about why I did it. Purely selfish reasons, didn't care to live surrounded by a great crowd of people – clever people, and stealthy, you know, can come and go as they please – who wish to cut our throats in the night.

'I think it no exaggeration to say that our people love us for what we did, paying them, treating 'em like human beings. We're the only plantation owners in the tidewater that don't lay awake nights worrying about an uprising. I know from my . . . former days . . . what men in bondage are capable of.'

'Well, whatever your motives, it was a decent thing. Though it seems to greatly offend this Dunmore, the upstart little bastard.'

There was no more that needed saying on that subject, so as they rolled south Marlowe and Bicker-staff talked of preparedness, of future plans.

Elizabeth participated a little in the talk, then fell silent, looking out the window at the green fields and patches of oak and maple and yellow pine.

Marlowe glanced her way a few times, but she did not notice. Whatever was troubling her, he would hear about it before he slept that night.

And then they were there. The coachman gave a shout, a command in some African tongue, punctuated by a flick of the reins. The horses stopped and Thomas and Elizabeth rocked forward and the loud clatter of hooves was replaced by the whine of insects and the ringing of a single hammer.

That would be King James, Marlowe thought. King James, former prince of the Kabu Malinke, former slave, now Marlowe's majordomo, captain of the *Northumberland*, the plantation's river sloop, which he could see tied to the quay.

King James. His comrade in arms. No day off for him. He would be too impatient to get to sea to observe the Sabbath.

Marlowe was on his feet and out the door, anxious for an uninterrupted look, anxious to take her in before Page struggled out of his carriage and began talking.

He strode forward, toward the dock. Heard Bickerstaff behind him, giving Elizabeth a hand down from the carriage. Doing his office. He would apologize later; she would understand.

Thomas stopped, breathed deep. Jasmine, pine, brackish water. Fresh-cut wood and tar and new cordage. Paint drying in the hot sun.

She lay tied to the dock, floating on a perfectly even keel, the slow-moving river breaking around her bows and sweeping aft, giving the illusion that she was already under way.

Marlowe's eyes moved up, slowly up, sweeping along her lofty rig, now rising to its full height with topgallant masts in place. Her spars were tapered like a woman's leg, her masts raked at a jaunty angle, as if she were fully aware of her beauty and did not feel the need to flaunt it. Marlowe made a low, guttural noise in his throat.

She was eighty-four feet on her waterline, one hundred and twenty-three feet sparred length, from the end of her bowsprit, on which sat the little doubling of the spritsail topmast, all the way aft to the big lantern that stood proudly over the taffrail.

The black muzzles of guns, eight along each side, jutted audaciously out of their gunports, gleaming in the sun. Fore, main, and mizzen masts rose from her decks, bright oiled wood crossed by black spars.

27

Gangs of thick black shrouds sprouted from the doublings and ran down and aft, terminating at their deadeyes with symmetrical perfection.

One hundred and eighty tons of fighting ship, laid out to Marlowe's specifications under his oppressively watchful eye.

The *Elizabeth Galley*. His savior, financially, spiritually. His private man-of-war.

CHAPTER 2

Old King Charles was dead. He had missed ruling over Spain's greatest era by two generations, had weakened his country further with his relentless fighting with Louis XIV of France. And now he was gone.

It seemed odd to Marlowe that the death of one old man he had never met, in a city that he had never seen, could have so profound an effect on his life, but there it was.

King Charles had died leaving behind no offspring, no one to occupy that place on the throne of Spain on which his royal arse had sat for the past thirty-nine years.

But in his last days he had declared Louis XIV's grandson, Philip, his heir Philip, great-grandson to Spain's Philip IV. Philip, a Frenchman and a Bourbon.

With that one declaration the old man had ended years of maneuver and haggling by the nations of Europe, dashed the ambitions of the House of Hapsburg in Austria, shown England the frightening visage of France and Spain united under Bourbon rule.

It was unacceptable. It meant war.

For thousands of officers and gentlemen from England, from France and Spain and the Netherlands and Bavaria and Savoy and a handful of others it meant glory, promotion, the majesty of leading men in a noble fight.

To those people who stayed at home and dealt in weapons, cloth, and food, it meant high prices for guns, uniforms, and barrels of salt pork and salt beef.

For the tens of thousands of men who filled the ranks of the armies it meant mud and hunger and disease, bitter nights and mornings of terror and death in distant countries for causes they only vaguely understood.

And to Marlowe, standing in the bright sun, two thousand nautical miles away from that unholy quagmire, in a land which, on a day such as that, was as close to Paradise as one might find on earth, it meant privateering.

It meant venturing forth on the great ocean, his element. An end to the monotony of domestic life, the possibility of great riches. Action. It meant a letter of marque and reprisal, a license to play the pirate against half the shipping in the world.

Before him was the ship. On the morrow he would receive the letter of marque. In a week he would be at sea, stalking the fat merchant ships, as he had so many times before. But this time it would be legal. Patriotic, in fact.

'Damn me, damn me!' Thomas felt Page's meaty hand slap him across the back; it made him stagger forward a step. 'Lovely, Marlowe, damned lovely, this ship!'

'Thank you, Hartwell. Will you come aboard, allow me to show you around?'

'Delighted, delighted. Mrs Page will wait in the coach. But look, son, you see to your little lady there, reckon you've put her nose out of joint. None of the old flourish tonight, hey? Hey?' The elbow struck home. Page walked toward the gangplank, chuckling all the while.

Marlowe turned, too late to help Elizabeth down from the carriage or across the broken ground, Bickerstaff having served those functions.

In the past she had forgiven him these lapses, but as the moment of his sailing approached she was becoming less and less understanding. He could see from her face that he had misjudged her present mood.

'Pray, forgive me, my dearest one. In my enthusiasm I have quite ignored you,' Marlowe said, as obsequious as he could be.

'Quite.' It was a humorless response.

'What think you of your namesake? Is she not beautiful enough to carry your name? The most beautiful ladies in the New World, both Elizabeths and both mine.'

Such silly flattery would not move Elizabeth Marlowe in the best of times, and it did not now. 'I know little of such things If you say she is beautiful then I take your word on it.'

'Will you come on board? Allow me to show you her finer qualities?'

'No, Thomas, I think not. I shall go and keep company with poor Mrs Page, who has been so heartlessly abandoned by her husband.'

With that she turned and walked quickly back to the carriages, leaving Marlowe and Bickerstaff alone on the dusty landing.

'Well, Bickerstaff, it is you and me alone again. Let us go aboard before Page is able to do too much damage.'

They stepped up the gangplank and through the gangway into the waist of the ship. The new-vessel smells overwhelmed the competing scents from the land and the river, marsh and warm pine needles yielding to tar slush, pitch, resin, and varnish. It was a welcome change. Marlowe preferred those scents over any that God and the land could provide.

He paused, leaned back, looked aloft. A reflex action, the first bit of business when coming on deck. Meaningless, really, with the ship tied to the dock, the sails lying in great bundles on the quay.

Still, his eyes ran up the masts and along the yards and down the black standing rigging, looking for some flaw, something that needed correcting – running rigging led wrong so it might chafe through, deadeyes not perfectly aligned, any bits of rope hanging loose – but there was nothing. Just as there had been nothing the last time he had engaged in that exercise, early morning of the day before.

'Very good, Marlowe, very good!' Page came stamping up. 'Tell me again where you found her. Boston?'

'New York. She was a merchantman, of course. Named *Nathaniel James*. Owned by a merchant of the same name who got a bit overextended. Invested in some fool pirating nonsense to Madagascar, or some such. In any event, lost nearly everything. This ship had been dockside for two years, something of a wreck from the gunnels up. But sound, you know. In her heart, sound.'

'Shame you couldn't have started from scratch. Man-of-war built from the keel up.'

'Ah, Hartwell, I am not so rich as you that I could do that!' Marlowe said, though it was a lie. He could have, had considered doing so, but big-ship building was largely unknown in America, and all but non-existent in Virginia.

That meant England, which would have taxed his resources too greatly. At thirty-six years old, or thereabout, he was not so reckless as he had been a decade before. He might gamble most of what he had, but he would not gamble it all.

What was more, Marlowe did not care to linger around London's waterfronts, with the chance of being spotted by one of his old associates, or, more dangerous, one of his old victims.

'She is sturdy, nonetheless,' Marlowe continued, leading Page to the bulwarks. 'Stripped her down to the frames from the waterline up, redid it all with live oak, two and a half inches thick. Now she is all predied for a fight. Should do for what I have in mind. We'll not be fighting the French navy, you know. Fat, slow, underarmed merchantmen are what we are after.'

'Marlowe, you make me sick, sick, sir, with envy. Oh, the adventure of it all, not to mention the damned money you shall make! You'll be back within the year and you'll buy us all out, make yourself king of Virginia!'

Marlowe laughed. But the idea had merit.

Page slapped the barrel of one of the guns, grown hot under the insistent sun as if it had been fired again and again in some sea battle. He squatted, sighted down the gun, grunted as if he had gleaned

33

some information from that exercise. 'Salvaged off the wreck of the *Plymouth Prize*, are they?'

'Indeed they are.' The *Plymouth Prize* was Marlowe's last command, his first legitimate one. She had been the guardship on the Virginia station, sent there by the Royal Navy to protect the colonies against pirates. Governor Nicholson had asked Marlowe to replace her corrupt and incompetent captain.

The cat, as it were, asked to guard the canary.

In fact, the cat had tricked the governor into giving him that enviable assignment, but that truth had never been discovered.

Marlowe's foray into command of a Royal Navy vessel, decrepit as she was, had ended the year before, when the *Prize* and the pirate she was fighting had both blown apart like twin volcanoes, fire touching off their powder magazines.

Less than two dozen men had come through the explosion with their lives. Marlowe had been one. Had come through not just with his life, but with his reputation and fame secured for the bold act of fighting and beating the pirates who had laid waste to the countryside. Less publicly known, he had come through with a fortune in loot, secreted away in his Jamestown warehouse, taken from the sea robbers he had arrested.

It had been a successful year. He was eager for more of the same.

'How'd you raise them?' Page asked. 'Grapple for 'em?'

'No, I had my people dive for them. Some of them are prodigious great divers.'

'Your Negroes?'

34

'Yes, indeed, my Negroes. They were able to slip harnesses around them, and we hauled them up.'

'Don't know how you manage it. They're terrified of the water, those Negroes, most of 'em. Pagan African water gods live there, or some nonsense. I don't reckon I could get any of my niggers to dive like that with all the whipping in the world.'

'I shouldn't imagine you could,' Bickerstaff interrupted. Such talk annoyed him greatly. 'But if you treat them as men and pay them wages commensurate with the danger, you would be surprised what they might do.'

'Well . . . indeed . . .' Page's voice trailed away into a cough.

'Nicholson's let me have the guns on loan – still government property, of course. Reckons it official thanks and all that.'

'Damned hard to come by, great guns. I imagine I'd be privateering myself, but for want of great guns.'

The hammering, to which their ears had grown accustomed, stopped and a moment later King James stepped up through the hatch at the forward end of the waist.

He was dressed in a sailor's loose pants and linen shirt, with a leather jerkin over that. His shirt and the waist of his pants were soaked through with perspiration; it looked as if he had been standing in the rain. The thin material clung to his chest and arms and the small of his back and accentuated the bold lines, the curve and ripple of muscle, the only benefit he had derived from years of heavy forced labor in the fields.

In his right hand he held a five-pound maul. With his left hand he wiped the sweat from his face, ran his hand back over his short cropped hair, took a chestful of the fresh air.

'Here's that buck, King James!' Page exclaimed. 'Might have guessed it was him doing all the pounding away, the eager dog!'

James looked over at the three men, noticing them at last. 'Ah, Captain Marlowe, good day, sir. I didn't hear you come aboard. Misser Bickerstaff, Misser Page.'

'James, what are you about, pounding away, and on the Sabbath, no less?' Marlowe asked.

The black man smiled, a conspirator's grin. 'Jest setting a few drifts to rights, Captain. Under way by week's end and it all gots to be done by then.'

'Well, in that case I forgive your irreligious activities,' Marlowe said. For the past three years he had been taking James along as a seaman. He would ship aboard the *Elizabeth Galley* as boatswain. He had already proved his worth as a fighting man.

James was as eager as Marlowe to get under way, to plunge into that life again.

'I do not know as Reverend Trumbell would forgive you, though, James.' Marlowe continued his ribbing. 'He did not sound overly forgiving at sermon this morning.'

'Don't matter. Reverend Trumbell listens to that Dunmore, and that Dunmore don't think a black man got any more immortal soul than a rock. When I sees him praying for a rock's salvation, then I'll listen to what he gots to say to me.'

Page was beginning to wander off, and Marlowe, aware of his social obligations, said, 'I will leave off your soul for now, James. I must show Mr Page the rest of the ship.'

With that he led Page and Bickerstaff forward, under the overhang of the foredeck, where the big brick oven housed gleaming copper pots, just abaft the foremast. They poked through bosun's lockers and sailmaker's stores, and then climbed down to the lower deck, where even the five-foot-four-inch-tall Page had to stoop a bit to avoid striking his head on the deck beams.

They made their way aft, stopping to peer down through the main hatch to the hold below. Marlowe showed his guest the tiny cabins of the minor officers who would sail under him, the spirit room, the pantry where the private stores of officers and captain would be kept. Three years as a gentleman planter had dulled his taste for rotten meat packed in casks of salt and for bread crawling with weevils.

It was with evident relief that Page allowed his host to lead him up the scuttle to the great cabin aft and offer him a seat on a plush velvet cushion atop the lockers under the aft windows.

Sunlight glanced off the river below and threw undulating patches of white light across the sides and overhead of the cabin. The windows, propped open, let in the smells of the warm riverbanks, the gurgle of water, the occasional thump of the rudder as it was pushed side to side by the current. It was a sleepy, peaceful moment, quite at odds with the violent raison d'être of the *Elizabeth Galley*.

Bickerstaff went to the wine rack, perused the bottles. 'Claret? Yes? Let us enjoy this now, it will soon be damned hard to come by, what with this war against France. I do not foresee a quick end to it.'

'Those are words to gladden a privateer's heart,' said Marlowe, accepting a glass.

'But not a tobacco planter's, Marlowe, and you are still that as well,' Page reminded him. 'We'll lose all the markets in Europe with this damned war. England cannot begin to buy all the crop we grow. Prices will plummet. I fear we shall all be ruined.'

'I fear you are right,' said Bickerstaff, who was more knowledgeable and interested in such things as agriculture and world markets than was Marlowe. This, despite the fact that, strictly speaking, Marlowe was the plantation owner and tobacco farmer, and Bickerstaff merely his guest.

'And to make matters worse,' Bickerstaff continued, 'the planters in this country are redoubling their crops. They hope to make as much as they can by selling twice as much, but the prices are falling fast as a result. Less money for more work.'

'Yes, well . . . don't know what else might be done . . .' Page mumbled, with a defensive tone. 'Hey, Marlowe, how are you manning this ship? Sailors are damned scarce in these parts. Can hardly man the tobacco convoys, and them merchantmen need less hands than you will.'

'Sailors will be drawn to money like filings to a lodestone,' Marlowe said. 'I cannot say that it has been an easy thing, manning the *Galley*, but there is such a potential for profit that I have attracted enough hands. I shall fill the crew with some of my people. King James, of course, and a few others. The difficulty is that such men are impatient for results. If we have no success early on I might well find myself in some port or other with not enough men to win the anchor.'

'From what I have seen of your abilities, and your

luck,' Bickerstaff offered, 'I do not envision that happening.'

A knock on the cabin door, and King James swung it open, leaned inside. 'Beg pardon, sir, but the wind's fair and tide just ebbing now so I reckoned I'd best be getting under way.'

It took Marlowe a moment to understand what James was talking about. Under way?

His new acreage. Now it came back. The acreage he had purchased a month before, just north of Point Comfort at the mouth of the James River. He was sending the sloop with a hold full of supplies – food, tools, lumber – down to the new property. His men, already there, would begin clearing the land, for cultivation, perhaps, or perhaps a shipyard or whatever else might seem a profitable venture. In the excitement of fitting out the *Elizabeth Galley* he had entirely forgotten.

'Very well. Bon voyage.'

'Thank you, sir. And, sir? Lucy coming with me, if you be so kind as to remind Mrs Marlowe?'

Lucy was Elizabeth's personal servant – like James and all the former slaves at Marlowe House she was free – and James's wife.

'I'll remind her, though her memory is not nearly as far gone as mine. And I will recall you to your duty, James. This is not a yachting holiday, Lucy or no. Down and back, as fast as wind and tide allow.'

James smiled. 'You have no fear, Captain Marlowe. As fast as wind and tide allow.' With a good-bye to Bickerstaff and Page he was gone.

Marlowe leaned back in his chair, sipped his claret, took in the wide cabin, the fresh paint, the fine furniture. Velvet cushions on the settee; a rack of expensive English muskets and pistols, brass-bound and engraved; portrait of his beautiful wife on the forward bulkhead; an enviable selection of wine.

Marlowe had seen squalor aplenty, had lived and sailed with the pirates, a base existence, and he did not care to live like that anymore.

And since he was now a wealthy planter and privateersman, he did not have to.

A fighting ship, rebuilt to his own specifications, under his own eye, an all but full complement of experienced seamen.

Tomorrow, a letter of marque and reprisal. By week's end a privateering voyage.

He smiled. There was nothing else he could do.

CHAPTER 3

King James watched the breeze ruffle the surface of the wide river, felt it cool the wet fabric of his shirt. His eyes swept along the river, noting the strength of the current in the angle of the reeds, predicting the coming steadiness in the wind from the cat's-paws that spread shivering ripples over the brown water.

Jamestown. The James River. King James. All three of them named for some long-dead monarch, all connected, intertwined, running together like the dark rivers of Africa searching for the sea.

He stood on the river sloop's quarterdeck, all the way aft by the taffrail. His bare foot rested on the head of the rudder post that thrust up through the deck. It twisted underfoot, as if trying to shake him, as the tiller swung side to side within the confines of the beckets that held it amidships.

Lucy was hurrying along the road, making for the sloop, a basket on her arm. She was young, James doubted she was above seventeen, but of course most of those who had been enslaved had lost track of the passing years; and she was beautiful, with her soft black curls spilling out from under her mobcap, her skin the color of cocoa with cream.

At another time James might have let his eyes linger, might have teased himself with the sight of his wife. But at that moment he was in command of the *Northumberland*, and his inspection of Lucy as she hurried toward them became just a part of his overall assessment of the vessel and her people.

King James was more mariner than husband. He understood that, did not necessarily see it as a flaw.

His gaze moved past her, inboard, to the six men on deck. Cato and Joshua, casting the last of the lashings off the foresails, were sailors. They had been part of the sloop's crew for nearly a year now.

William, Good Boy, and Quash were passengers. Good Boy and William were carpenters, natural talents with wood, and Quash an experienced blacksmith. Along with material, James was transporting the skilled people who would transform Marlowe's new wilderness. They were strong and smart young men, all somewhere around twenty years old, all former slaves like himself, freed by Thomas Marlowe.

He felt like an old man around them.

It would have been worse, were it not for Sam, the only white man among them. Once a blue-water sailor, Sam now considered himself too old for deep-sea voyaging and was happy making short trips around the bay.

James loved the sloop, every inch of her, the sweep of her sheer, the elegant curve that the bulwarks made as they met at the bow, the mast, straight, solid.

Sometimes in the curve of Lucy's hips he saw the *Northumberland*'s tumble home, in the taper of her bare leg he saw the bowsprit jutting out over the water.

The little ship was freedom and the dignity of command. In making the sloop his, he had met and defeated the horrors of his first taste of the sea and ships, the Middle Passage.

'Come along, woman, we'll miss the tide!' James called out as Lucy came huffing up to the dock.

'Wouldn't be so late if one of you was a gentleman, would help a lady with her things,' Lucy called back, but she was smiling and James was smiling. It was just banter.

'Forward there!' he called out as Lucy was helped aboard. 'Let's go.'

No more needed saying. They had been sailing together for three years, two of those years under James's command. Cato and Sam clapped on to the jib halyard and hauled away. The sail jerked up the forestay, flogging slightly in the breeze.

'Stand by that bow fast, there,' James called out as he slipped the becket from the tiller with his foot.

And then, from forward, Lucy's voice, shrill, with an edge of panic. 'No!'

Everyone aboard the sloop froze. Lucy was standing in the waist, her eyes wide, staring at nothing. She took a step back, toward the rail.

'What, Lucy, what is it?' James hurried forward.

Lucy shook her head in mute protest.

'What?'

'I got a bad feeling. Something ain't right.'

'What? What you talking about?' There was nothing wrong that James could see, and if there were, he would certainly notice it before Lucy did.

'Something ain't right . . .' Lucy said again. It was the best she could do, by way of explanation.

'Girl, you are being foolish. Now get aft and stop this nonsense.'

'No, I ain't going!' She turned and stepped up onto the rail and onto the dock before James could stop her. 'I ain't going and if you was smart you wouldn't neither!'

James scowled at her. This was insane. Lucy could be flighty at times, but he had never seen anything like this.

'Goddamnit, girl, get back on this boat!' James shouted, but Lucy only shook her head and backed away. He glanced forward. The others were watching, wide-eyed. Losing an argument with his wife was not helping his authority.

Worse still, he could see that his men were getting spooked by all this. If they believed whatever premonition Lucy thought she was having, then soon he would be without a crew.

'Fine, then, you walk back to the damn house and we'll talk about this when I gets back!'

He spun around and walked aft, head up, and his men avoided meeting his eyes.

Joshua slipped the bow fast off the piling, pulled the line aboard and coiled it down.

The forward edge of the sail came taut and Cato and Sam sweated the last bit of slackness out and belayed and Joshua hauled the canvas out by the sheet. The breeze caught it and the bow of the sloop swung away from the dock and out into the river.

James stamped aft, swung the tiller out to starboard. Joshua jogged after him and slipped the stern fast off the piling. A minute later the sloop was on her way downriver, leaving Lucy behind as she stood on the dock, watching.

Damned foolish, foolish woman. But in fact James was spooked too, by her fear, so clearly genuine.

A minute later and they were passing down the larboard side of the *Elizabeth Galley*. Through the quarter gallery windows James caught a glimpse of Marlowe, leaning back in his chair, feet up on the mahogany table. The table that cost more than half a year's worth of the wages that Marlowe paid one of the black men that worked for him.

But James could no longer be angry with Marlowe. The anger at his enslavement was still there, of course, the knife edge of rage, fast and lethal, but it was no longer poised to strike.

Marlowe's releasing him from bondage had not released him from the anger as well. James had not believed Marlowe's words about freeing his people and paying them. He had not been impressed when Marlowe spoke to them in the patois of the African coast.

It had not occurred to the others that Marlowe might have learned that language as a slaver himself, but it had occurred to James.

His rage had not been quelled by Marlowe's keeping his promise, or Marlowe's making James majordomo of the household. A white man's trick to exact the best labor from the best people. And it had worked.

It was the *Northumberland* that had done it at last. Pushing James to the challenge of learning seamanship, setting him aboard a ship, a cursed ship. Giving him responsibility. Giving him weapons and asking him to fight aboard the guardship, side by side with white men. It was treating him like a man that had done it at last.

He understood Marlowe now, knew the real reason that Marlowe had freed his people. Knew that Marlowe had fought side by side with black men during his days as a pirate, that most egalitarian of communities. The only rich white man in the tidewater to ever have called a black man an equal.

James loved him more because of his history, his motives. Marlowe freed his people for pragmatic reasons, not for some lofty intellectual ideal such as Bickerstaff might espouse. Now James wanted nothing more in life than to plunge into battle again, at Marlowe's side.

The *Northumberland* was gathering way, carried by the tide and pulled by the breeze in the jib. At the base of the mast the crew tossed off peak and throat halyards and made ready to raise the big mainsail.

Five minutes later the mainsail was set and drawing, the halyards faked out on deck for running, and the sloop settled down for the short, pleasant trip downriver. The *Elizabeth Galley* and the bright spot of color that was Lucy, standing on the dock watching them, and what was left of Jamestown fell astern, and then were lost from sight as the *Northumberland* swung round Hog Island and James turned her more southerly for the reach downriver to Hampton Roads.

It was there, just below Hog Island, that the *Plymouth Prize* had fought to the death with the pirate LeRois. The governor had unknowingly set a thief to catch a thief when he had sent Marlowe after that murderer and sea robber.

The charred remains of the two ships were still visible at low tide. James had got to know them well

46

during the past months as he oversaw the salvage of the cannons from the wreck.

Marlowe called the divers 'his people,' called all the blacks 'his people.' But they were not King James's people. They were Congolese, a tribe more accustomed to the water than were the Malinke. The distinctions were blurring, but they were still real.

The river was huge, over three miles wide, and the *Northumberland* ran easily downstream. Cato ambled aft, took the tiller from James.

'Favor the north shore,' James instructed the young black man. They would need the room to leeward when they passed Newport News and swung round into Hampton Roads.

James stepped up on the low bulwark, steadied himself with a hand on the backstay. Past the tall reeds, the fields ran up easy slopes to the big plantation houses along the shore. The seabirds wheeled around the topmast head and the ducks made their little flotillas along the banks.

The sun beat down on the deck, warm, even hot, but not oppressive. James could feel the soft caulking that stuck to the bottoms of his feet. He felt the sloop heel to leeward in response to a gust from the shore, heard the note of the water rise a bit in pitch.

He ran his eyes along the deck, looking for something that needed attention. There was nothing that he could see. His sloop was perfect. He felt his anger with Lucy subside, his disquiet brought on by her fear fade away.

He was happy, and that emotion still seemed like a stranger to him, like something from another place. There was his boyhood in Africa, a life of princely

47

indulgence, and then the long, long black nightmare of slavery. And now, so many years after going to sleep, he was awake again.

Three uneventful hours later they turned north-easterly and ran across the wide mouth of Hampton Roads. There were a few ships anchored there, and the sun, now inclining toward the west, burnished the roofs of the buildings that made up the town of Hampton.

James had lived in Virginia for twenty years now, five more than he had lived in Africa. He had watched the extraordinary speed with which the settlements had sprung up, taken firm root, spilled over and taken root in half a dozen places further out, spreading over the countryside.

He had never been to England, but he pictured the shoreline there crowded with people, mobs, hundreds deep, waiting, jostling onto the ships that brought more and more immigrants to be absorbed by this new land.

The wind was from the northeast and freshening. They left Point Comfort in their wake and stood out into the wide Chesapeake Bay. They would have to make a few miles of easting at least before they could tack up-bay and fetch the landing at Marlowe's new property.

Off the starboard side, the mouth of the Chesapeake opened up, and beyond it, the Atlantic Ocean. Acclimated as he was to having land all around, the wide, endless space between the capes gave James an odd feeling, like hanging over a precipice, like being in a house with only three walls.

'Do you see that?' Cato asked, breaking into James's reverie. 'The ship?'

'Yes.'

He had seen it three minutes before. It was his job as captain to be more alert than anyone else on board.

'Something ain't right . . .' Cato offered.

James grunted in reply, unwilling to offer an opinion. But he had been thinking the same thing as he watched the ship struggling along, nine miles or so to the south. She was too far off to make out any detail, but there was something in the way her sails were trimmed, something in her plodding motion, as if she were dragging something, that raised an alarm in James's head.

He picked up the sloop's telescope and trained it on the distant vessel. The image in the lens yielded no more definite information, but neither did it lessen James's conviction that something was wrong with her. He could see foresail and mainsail lashed to the yards – they could not have been called furled, with the great ungainly folds and lumps of canvas – merely tied up out of the way. The mizzen yard and its lateen sail seemed to lie across the quarterdeck. Heaps of gray cloth were just visible. James thought he could see some bits of rigging swinging loose.

And then, a puff of smoke, a flash from a muzzle. A cannon fired, not at the river sloop, but from the other side, to leeward. A few seconds later, the muffled report, like the sound of someone beating a rug. A gun to leeward. A universally accepted sign of surrender or distress.

'Let's run down on this fellow,' James said to Cato, then, as the helmsman eased the tiller to weather and the *Northumberland*'s head turned more southerly, he called out, 'Joshua, Sam, see to them

49

sheets. We're going run down on yon ship, see if she needs help.'

The *Northumberland* moved fast with the wind over the quarter and soon she had halved the distance. Through the glass James could make out the ensign, the British merchantman's ensign, flying from the masthead, upside down, another distress signal.

The ship was sagging off to leeward, the wind setting her down on the beach, and while she was in no immediate danger of taking the ground, it was clear that she would have to come about, and soon.

The *Northumberland* was no more than two miles away when the merchantman tried to tack, swinging up into the wind, slowly, her sails beating in disorderly array. Her bow came up, up, and hung there, unable to turn further, like a dying man making one last feeble and useless attempt to save himself.

And then she fell back again, having missed stays, her sails in a shambles.

James watched through the glass. One by one the yards came sailing down as halyards were let go. No topmen racing aloft to stow them, the clews and bunts were not even hauled up. The sails just hung there, as if letting the halyards run was all the effort those on board could manage.

A flash of white under the bow and James knew they had dropped the anchor. They would go no further. Now that they could see help was on the way, they would anchor and wait rather than struggle on.

'You keep to windward of them,' James growled at Cato, and Cato replied, 'Windward, aye.' James wanted a look at these people first before he laid his sloop alongside of them. He had seen enough of pirates' deceptions to be wary. They would stay safely to windward until they were certain.

One mile, then half a mile, and they could see more and more of the frightening condition that this ship was in. Shrouds and backstays hung loose, great gouges were shot out of the bulwarks. Strips of torn sail fluttered aft in the breeze. Those, and the inverted ensign, were the only bunting showing.

'What the devil happened to you?' James muttered to himself.

'What do you think?' asked Joshua, standing by the main sheet.

'I do not know . . . Attacked, maybe, or caught in a gale, short-handed. Plenty out there can do that kind of damage.'

James studied the ship as they approached, and there was nothing about her that said 'pirate'. She was armed, of course, but no more than any merchantman would be in those dangerous times. There were none of the rough-cut gunports of hastily rearmed ships, no forecastle or quarterdeck cut away to make a flush-deck vessel, as one often saw among the Brethren of the Coast. No, this one looked to be just what she appeared: a merchant ship in dire trouble.

They were only a few hundred yards away when the smell reached them.

Had they been downwind of her they would have noticed it miles before, but with the fresh breeze, it required they get much closer than that.

James felt the foulness wafting into his nose, his mouth, his lungs. It made his hands clench, his stomach convulse like ingesting some airborne

51

poison. It set the anger and hatred racing through him like fire on a powder train before he even understood why.

'Dear God,' he heard Sam behind him muttering. 'A blackbirder.'

A blackbirder: slave ship. And the smell, that of human beings packed in and battened down. Piss and shit. Blood. Pleading, desperate fear. The unknown. Worse, far worse than quiet death.

Not for twenty years had James smelled that stink, but with one breath it all came back to him, and all the rage he had locked away in some small cage of his soul came tearing free again.

The *Northumberland* was charging down on the slave ship, making right for her bows, and if something was not done immediately she would smash headlong into her.

Someone was standing on the slaver's bows, waving. A warning or a plea, James could not tell.

He pulled his eyes from the battered vessel, pushed Cato from the tiller, grabbed it, swung it a bit to larboard. The sloop turned until she was on a heading to run down the blackbirder's leeward side. The wind came over the sloop's transom, the mainsail by the lee, fluttering, the boom right on the edge of sweeping across the deck in a great destructive arc, but James did not care.

They passed under the blackbirder's jibboom, just missed fouling the sloop's shrouds on the spar, and passed down the ship's side. Now, to leeward of the vessel, the smell enveloped them entirely, like a fog, so strong it seemed they should be able to see it. And from the hold – muffled and quiet – the screams, the cries, the rattling chains.

James pushed the tiller harder over, swinging the sloop away from the slaver.

'Damn it, James, be careful, you'll jibe the damned . . .' Sam started, got no further.

'Shut it! Shut your gob!'

James felt a wild anger, an anger that did not care what it destroyed, that tried to cause some destruction, some injury, if just for the release.

And then, just as the big mainsail was ready to jibe and tear the sloop's rigging apart, he swung the tiller back the other way. The sloop described a great arc, swinging back toward the slave ship, turning up into the wind, the sails flogging. She came to a stop at the base of the slaver's boarding steps.

James pushed his way through his gawking men to the bulwark that bumped against the high-sided blackbirder. A white face with equal measures of soot black and filth brown looked down at him, a man standing at the slave ship's gangway. Clothes torn, hair wild, streaks of blood on his filthy shirt. Pistol in his belt. The face of a man who could not recall his last rest. But more defiant for it.

James stopped, looked up. The man looked down. Then the man said, 'Where is the captain of this sloop?'

'I am the captain.'

They held each other, stare for stare. James could see the narrowing eyes, could hear the debate in the man's head.

A nigger? A nigger coming to our aid?

'Cast off,' the white man said. 'Leave our ship. It is no concern of yours.'

Nigger.

And then another man was there, just as haggard,

but with the defiance beaten out of him, and the other man said, 'For the love of God, Captain, let them aboard if they can be of some help.'

The captain turned, shoved the man with more force than James would have thought he had in him, screamed, 'Shut your mouth!' and James was on the boarding steps, scurrying up, Cato and Joshua and Sam right behind him.

He stepped through the gangway onto the deck, met the captain's loathing with hatred of his own, looked around at the destruction.

Lines lay strewn about the deck, great tangles of rigging draping off the pinrails and lying in heaps in the scuppers. One of the small cannon amidships, aiming down into the hold. Smashed bits of grating, smashed bits of rail, smashed barrels, bottles, crates of cabin stores torn open, their contents scattered around.

The doors to the binnacle box were half torn off their hinges, hanging open, swaying with the rocking of the ship. There was a wide black scorched circle on the deck where someone had apparently built a fire, an inconceivable thing on a wooden ship.

Black patches on the deck, swirled into bizarre patterns, marking those places where people had thrashed and bled their lives away. Chains. Netting full of stone, bent to fathoms of rope, ready to carry the bodies, living or dead, to the ocean floor.

James's hands were trembling. A film of sweat covered his body. He could smell its unhealthy odor, even over the stink of the slaver. His jaw ached from the pressure with which he clenched his teeth together.

James turned slowly to the slaver's captain and the

five white sailors who stood behind him. At the gangway stood Cato, Joshua and Sam, William, Good Boy, and Quash.

'What happened?'

One of the sailors replied, addressing his words to James. 'We was took by pirates. They used us horrid, for days. Killed half our men. Took two dozen of our nig . . . Negroes, and before they left, set the rest loose. Stood off in their boats, watched us fighting to . . . to get them down below again.'

James breathed, loud, panting, trying to get control. He could see it before him, like a play, the desperate blacks pouring out of the hold, not knowing what to do because they did not understand enough to form a plan, just wanting to be free of the hold.

And then on deck meeting guns, cutlasses, cannon. The cannon blast down through the hatch, canister shot tearing men, women, children apart in the darkness, the dead and wounded left below. Too dangerous to open the hatches. Wounded on deck thrown overboard. Retribution taken, a lesson for those listening below, and then over the side.

The trembling had turned into shaking, King James's arms and hands vibrating like a luffing sail. A keening sound formed in his throat. James realized that he had no control over himself, like a sleep-walker, some part of his mind was in control but he had no control over it, some dark part that he did not know was there.

He heard Sam saying, 'James, James, get ahold of yourself, this here is for the Court of Admiralty . . .'

He met the captain's eyes, saw no sorrow, no remorse, only malevolence there.

'Get off my ship, nigger.'

James stepped across the deck, moving on the captain. 'Nigger?'

'I said get off my ship!' the captain shouted, and as James advanced he jerked the pistol from his belt, pulled back the lock with his palm.

James's hand fell on the handle of his sheath knife and before he could think, the steel was clear of the sheath and he was advancing into the barrel of the captain's gun.

'Nigger?'

'Draw a blade on me? You'll hang for this, you black bastard!'

They were a yard apart. Two men motivated by hatred alone, neither able to think beyond the moment.

The captain raised the gun higher, the round hole at James's head. James took a great stride, grabbed the barrel, twisted it. The gun went off, the bullet tore through James's shirt, thudded into the deck, and the knife shot forward and plunged hilt deep into the man's chest.

Then, screams, shouts of rage. The white men behind their captain surged forward. James felt hands grab him, a fist strike the back of his head, but he could not take his eyes from the haughty captain's face, the wide eyes, the blood erupting from his mouth.

A cutlass flashed over him and James gritted his teeth and waited for the deathblow but then his men were there, the crew of the *Northumberland*, surging into the slaver's crew with fists and sheath knives. They were all fighting – his men, the blackbirder's men – slavers and former slaves locked into it. A gun

56

went off, steel clashed on steel, someone screamed. A great brawl was taking place around him and James knew he had to stop it.

'Enough! Enough!' James shouted, and the volume and authority of his voice made the fighting men step back, weapons lowered, glaring at one another but not moving.

It was silent, save for men gasping for breath or moaning in agony.

There was a dead man at the tip of King James's knife. A white man, a ship's captain. James had killed him.

And in this way he had ended his own life as well.

CHAPTER 4

The battle had lasted no more than a minute.

James let the body of the captain slip from his knife. It stared up, wide-eyed, from the deck. It seemed surprised. James could not imagine why.

Aft, two of the slaver's crew were dead, another cut badly across the shoulder. Armed though they were, those exhausted, half-crazed slavers had been no match for the *Northumberland*'s men.

The three living men of the blackbirder's crew sat on the deck, hands up in surrender. One was weeping, sobbing, tears running down his stubbled cheeks. Around them, James's men held them at bay with their own weapons.

They thought they were finally safe, James reflected. Thought they had come through it at last, reached the safe embrace of the Chesapeake, and then this. Death at the hands of black men.

James took a breath. The anger was gone, it had dissipated with that one cathartic thrust. But now he had to think, because everything that he had come to know and depend upon was over, for him, for his men, for every person aboard that tortured blackbirder.

'What the hell have we done? What the hell have we done? They'll fucking hang us for this.' Retching. It was Sam, puking with abandon. He was smeared with blood, his coat and shirt torn in the melee.

Under it all, under the noise of the sobs and the retching and the shouting, was the sound from the hold; clanking, screaming, moaning.

And despite those many layers of noise whirling through his head, James could see the essential truth of Sam's words.

They *would* fucking hang them for this.

The black men; himself, Cato, Joshua, the others – all would be lucky even to live that long. No jail would hold them until a trial. They would be dragged from their cells and beaten to death. A warning.

God, he had to think.

'James . . .' Cato now, the tone of that one word pleading.

'Get them people up from below. Break open them hatches, get them people on deck.'

It was something to do. Forward motion, the next step, and it gave James a moment to think while the others were occupied, allowed him to think without a dozen eyes boring into him, as if trying to peer through his skin and find an answer that they thought must be there.

'James . . .' It was Sam now, his eyes wild with panic. 'I don't blame you for what you done, don't blame you, but this ain't my fight, you see? I didn't want no part of this . . .'

'Go. It ain't your fight, so just go. Take them' – James nodded toward the three surviving members of the slaver's crew – 'take them aboard the sloop and go.'

'Take the sloop? But how . . . ? What about you?'

'We ain't going back. Not to Virginia. Nowhere in America.'

'You're going to sail this blackbirder? She's near a wreck, food and water's probably gone . . .'

'It don't matter. We gots no choice. Whatever condition she in, we gots to go.' He had not decided that so much as understood it. They could never go back, not if they wished to live to week's end.

Lucy. Dear God, had she seen this coming? Some premonition? He had heard of women having such things. He had called her foolish. Now he might never see her again.

And then William was at his side too, tugging on his shirt, his dark eyes wide. 'I don't want no part of this neither. I ain't gonna hang for this.'

'You got no choice, boy.'

'I didn't have nothing to do with killing them people,' William protested, which might have been true. James had not seen the fight. 'I don't want no part of this.'

'It don't matter,' James said. 'They'll hang you just for being here, and you a black man. Don't you see that?'

'I ain't staying.'

James looked at him for a long moment. The kindest thing he could do would be to chain William to the deck, make him come. But he had no reason to think that the fate of the men on the ship would be any better than what waited for William back home.

'All right. Go with Sam.' James turned from William and addressed the former deep-water sailor. 'Tell Marlowe what happened. Tell him the truth.

Gonna be a lot of stories told, but I want Marlowe to know the truth.' That was important.

Sam nodded and he and James looked at each other, neither man sure of what to say.

'God speed you, King James,' Sam said at last.

'And you.'

Then Sam turned to the white men at his feet and James turned his attention forward and both understood that that had been their last meeting on earth. James could think of no other words, not with the raging confusion, the terror, and the uncertainty in him.

He had not felt such things for twenty years, not since the last time he had walked the deck of a slaver, iron manacles on his wrists and ankles.

King James left Sam to his business and walked forward to where Joshua and Cato and the others were using belaying pins to knock out the wedges that were holding the tarpaulins over the main hatch gratings. Cato's hands were trembling and he fumbled the pin, dropped it to the deck, swore, snatched it up again.

This was his moment to think, but nothing would come, no solid ideas, only swirling impressions and overwhelming desperation, and he was drawn instead to whatever horror lay beneath the heavy canvas.

'Here,' Cato said, 'grab hold there.' Joshua grabbed on to the larboard corner of the tarpaulin as Cato grabbed the starboard. From below the cloth the sounds from the hold were muffled but loud, a vast array of voices in tones of anger and fear and sorrow to the point of abandon. James recognized the cadence of African languages, but he could not make out any of the words.

Now and again the sound was punctuated by a wailing, or a screaming or what sounded like a loud entreaty to God. The people in the hold would have heard the anchor cable running out, would be able to sense that the ship was no longer under way. They would know something was about to happen, and their experience would tell them that any change meant some fresh misery.

Cato and Joshua looked at each other, apprehensive. But the thing had to be done.

'Go,' James called, and the two men walked forward, peeling the tarpaulin back off the hatch.

The stink rolled up over the deck and enveloped them, and James was staggered to realize that what they had smelled before had been but a watered-down taste of what the hold contained. It was more than just the smell of bodies and waste. It was festering wounds, rotting human flesh. Death and decay in that closed, hot, sweltering hold.

'Oh, dear God!' Quash exclaimed. Good Boy retched and vomited on the deck. James clapped his hand over his mouth, took shallow breaths, tried to keep himself from vomiting as well. Joshua and Cato dropped the tarpaulin, staggered away.

The cacophony from the hold rose in pitch. Pleading, wailing, and still James could understand no word of what they said. Slavers, he knew, purposely mixed people from distant tribes in their ships so that they would not be able to communicate, to organize and plan. What if none of these spoke Malinke? How would he talk with them? And did he himself remember enough Malinke? It had been more than two decades since he had used that tongue with any frequency.

Dark fingers reached up through the holes in the grating, like tiny arms reaching out, beckoning help. They had to get those people out, but now James's men were too revolted and too terrified to approach that black hole.

They were saved the trouble. From below a voice cut across the wild jumble of sound, giving an order in some language foreign to James, and with an organized effort the fingers grabbed ahold of the grating and pushed it aside.

James's men were silent, staring at the hatch, which seemed to move of its own accord. And then from below a black figure emerged, stepping carefully up the ladder, clearly unsure of what was waiting on the upper deck. He blinked and squinted and shielded his eyes from the dim evening sun, looked around. He stepped over the combing, still in a half crouch, ready to move if attacked.

James stepped forward, hands up, palms out. The man looked at him, looked around the deck, seemed to relax a bit as his eyes moved from black face to black face.

He looked back at James, straightened his stance. He was a big man, six feet tall at least, powerfully built and well proportioned. Handsome. He smiled with big white teeth set against dark skin. Held up his hands. Addressed James with words that James did not understand.

James stared at him, shook his head. The man said something else, it sounded like a different language, and James shook his head again.

The man squinted at him, looked closer, and then spoke again, slowly, and the language was Malinke. Slow, uncertain, but clearly Malinke. James's native tongue, at once familiar and foreign. Images of his father, of his village, swam before him as he heard the words: 'I am Madshaka. Are my people safe to come up?'

James nodded, then spoke slowly, finding the words deep in his memory. 'Yes. You are safe. Tell them to come up.'

Madshaka turned, looked back down the hold. He called something in the first language he had used, then the second, and then repeated the order in two more languages. One by one the people came up from the hold, frightened, confused, broken. They squinted, like Madshaka, though the light was fading fast in the west. They spread out across the deck, looking carefully around, not trusting the reality that greeted them: freedom, safety.

Madshaka stepped up to James. He was naked, save for a cloth around his hips. All of the Africans were dressed that way. The stink of the hold clung to him.

He looked down at James, but despite his overwhelming size he appeared subservient, almost cowed. He said in James's native tongue, 'You are the chief here? You are Malinke? What is your name?'

'Yes, I am Malinke. Was Kabu Malinke, from the House of Mane.' His name? That was not so easy to answer. 'Once I was known as Komdaka, prince of the Malinke. Now I am King James.'

'King James?' Madshaka said, trying the words out, working his tongue around them. 'What of the ship's crew?'

'Dead. Captain dead, some others dead. The rest sent away.'

Madshaka looked at him and his eyes grew wide and a look of astonishment, of gratitude and near worship spread over his face. He sank slowly to his knees in front of James, grabbed his hand and kissed it. James felt himself flush, cleared his throat, tried to work out the words in Malinke to tell Madshaka to stand.

Then Madshaka released his hand and looked up into James's eyes and spoke, and the words were English.

'Thank you. Thank you, King James. You set us free from hell.'

James took a step back. He could not have been more surprised if Madshaka had burst into song. He thought of all those languages the man had called down the hold. African tongues. But how could he speak English?

Madshaka got to his feet with a fluid thrust of the legs, smiled down at James, spoke again in English. 'I was a *grumete*, a boatman. I am of the Kru of Bassa, the most skilled boatmen. I was a merchant, interpreter. Traveled the whole coast, from Gorée to Congo. Carried many people in my boat. Learned many tongues.'

The two men regarded each other. Madshaka was Kru, from Bassa. King James was Malinke, from Gambia. They had most likely been born within six hundred miles of each other. But now James was a man of the New World, and the gulf between them was as wide and as deep as the Atlantic.

'Are any aboard Malinke?' James asked. He did not know why. It just seemed like something he should know.

'No. Ship from Whydah. There are people from many places, all mixed up. Ibo, Yoruba, Awakam, Aja, Bariba, Igbomina, Weme, Za. No Malinke.'

James nodded. A polyglot group, but all from within the arc of the Bight of Biafra and the Bight of Benin, two thousand miles from where he was born.

Behind them, more and more people were coming up out of the hold, standing in small clusters, huddled together as if for warmth, men, women, and a few children looking around, pointing, talking in their odd, lyrical voices.

The *Northumberland*'s crew were in their own group, looking at the freed slaves with as much curiosity as they themselves were being watched. Cato and Joshua had been born in Virginia, as had Quash and Good Boy.

James pointed at the gaping hold, the destruction all around. 'What happened?' he asked.

Madshaka looked around, shook his head. He was silent for a moment, as if trying to put the chaotic tale in some order. 'We at sea many weeks, many weeks. Very little food, very little water. Sometimes they let us up here, mostly keep down there.

'Then, a week ago, we attacked. *Boo-con-eers.* Pirates. They take the ship, steal some of our people. They on ship two, three days. Much drinking, much devilment. When they leave they set us all free. We try to take the ship from that bastard captain but the white slavers, they have guns, swords, and we, nothing. They drive us down again, shoot down into us with cannon. Close up the hole.

'They afraid to open hole, afraid we fight them again. So for week we sail, they don't give food, no help to the people hurt in fight. They die, just left down there. Dead men, women, children. They open up a little place, give some food, some water, but only a little. Many die.'

King James shook his head, tried to imagine the horror. There had been dead enough on his own voyage to the New World, sometimes left for days before their bodies were hurled overboard. He had thought no horror on earth could match that which he had experienced, and here was Madshaka making him realize that he was wrong.

'Kusi!' Madshaka called across the deck, and then in a language that James thought to be of the Aja territory he addressed the man who turned. The man nodded, hurried away from his cluster, stood by Madshaka's side.

'Him Kusi, Fante, from Great Popo. He *grumete* too. Not so good as Kru. He speak many languages.'

Kusi nodded. He was a slight man, shorter than James and older by ten years at least. His face was lined and he bore the traces of ritual scarring, but he had an honest look. 'I speak English too, and other tongues.'

'Well,' James began. He stopped himself, framed his words in Malinke, and said, slowly, haltingly, 'It is good you both are here. We have much work. You must translate for me. We will have to sail the ship.'

The two men nodded, as if they were already resigned to the fact that they would have to put to sea once more.

The last of the captives climbed up from the hold and stood shielding their eyes from the sun, dazed, staring around. There appeared to be eighty or so in all. James was sure that there had been far more than that when the ship had sailed from Africa.

Madshaka turned toward the clusters of freed Africans and addressed them in a loud voice, a

67

commanding tone that made them all fall silent and listen.

He spoke in animated tones, repeating himself in several tongues and the people nodded. James could not follow the words, but he saw eyes darting toward him. And then Madshaka pointed at James, his finger like the barrel of a gun, and along the deck the people sank to their knees, their wide eyes locked on him.

'He tell them you are their great savior, a great king come to free them,' Kusi explained.

'Oh, for the love of God . . . Madshaka, tell them . . .'

But Madshaka turned, as if he did not hear, and in a half dozen great strides was back on the quarter-deck. He snatched up a cutlass that had been discarded there, raised it over his head. He gave a cry, a battle cry, a wild, corkscrew of a sound, and in one stroke severed the dead captain's head from his body.

Against the rail Joshua turned away, puked with abandon over his clothes, on the deck.

Madshaka snatched up the head by the hair and held it aloft, dripping blood from the ragged neck, dead eyes rolled back. He shouted something several times in several languages, and the people bowed further. Then with barely a flick of his wrist he flung the head overboard.

'You are great man to them, savior,' Kusi said.

Savior. A savior would not have allowed that barbaric display. But it was done, and maybe it would even do some good.

Think, think. Thoughts struggled like a drowning man, kicking for the surface, desperate for air, but they could not rise.

Savior. If they were taken now, then their fate would be much worse than what it might have been on a tobacco plantation. He had condemned them all with his uncontrolled fury, and now they looked at him to carry them to safety.

Think, think, but he could not. They had to go, that much he knew. They had to leave the Chesapeake, leave America, go somewhere. Then perhaps there would be time to think, to organize his mind, to hit on the solution that, like the sky through the surface of the water, he could see, dimly, but could not reach.

'Madshaka, Kusi, come here. You must translate, tell the others what to do.'

And then slowly he began to explain to the men, in the simplest terms, how they would cut the cable and set once more the slaver's flogging, limp topsails.

She stood across the bedroom, leaning against her vanity. 'Oh, dear God, Thomas, pray do not insult me with this rubbish!'

Her arms were folded across her breasts, her long, blond hair untied, hanging down her back and over her shoulders, one wisp half across her face. She was wearing only her shift and the thin fabric did little to hide her body underneath.

Men had fought and died for that body. And well worth it, Marlowe thought.

Lord, but she looked fine. Angry like that, standing defiantly upright, lips pressed together, a slight scowl. She was beautiful at any time, but when she was angry there was a quality that Marlowe could not define, but which he found utterly alluring.

He had made the mistake of telling her that once,

69

when she was angry. Thought it would soften her mood, make her more pliant. He had rarely been so wrong in his judgment.

He wanted to bed her, not fight with her. But fighting was all she was up for that night, and for something so irrational. Damned women, could never understand a thing.

'Listen, Elizabeth, I shall say it again. Tobacco prices have been falling for a year and more, and you know it. And this war will make it worse, much worse. Francis reckons half the plantations will go under, or their owners will have to take on huge debts, and you know what that means. We discussed this venture, agreed it would be a good chance to save us from all that.'

Elizabeth sighed, closed her eyes, threw back her head. A damned patronizing gesture. Much more of that and Marlowe reckoned he would not wish to bed her at all.

'Listen, Thomas, for I too shall say this again . . . no, wait. I won't. You do not listen in any event. Just . . . just for a moment, think about your ship. Picture the second that she came into sight from the carriage, the moment that you leapt out, quite ignoring Francis and me. Have you pictured that? Now, tell me that this damned privateer is just about money.'

Marlowe scowled, remained silent. Damn her, the insensitive bitch. He glared at her, wanted to leave the room, slam the door, tear it from its hinges. Felt the uncomfortable sensation of looming truth.

He had been thinking for two months of the feel of a heaving quarterdeck under his feet, the insular world of a ship long under way, the thrill of sighting a strange sail, the brace and leap of boarding some prize.

He had never once thought of the money he might earn, the booty he claimed might save Marlowe House. Did not even know how much he would need to keep the place running, or how much he already had.

'We cannot survive the season without I bring in some money from this venture,' Marlowe said slowly.

'Oh, indeed? And how long can we now go before we must borrow? Tell me, how long can we continue to pay our people before the money is gone? Or are we broke now? Pray, tell me.'

Marlowe was silent once more. Elizabeth kept the books, Bickerstaff ran the plantation. He just rode around, lord of the manor. Hadn't a clue what was going on, because he didn't give a damn about such things as farming and bookkeeping. And so he could not answer that question. He knew it, Elizabeth knew it. Damn her for doing this to him.

They were silent for a very long time, eyes locked. Two very stubborn people, two people who had learned from hard use never to yield an inch.

And in Marlowe's mind, the heaving quarterdeck, the leap over the rail.

He knew that Elizabeth was right. He was bored. He had spent well over a decade as a pirate – an extraordinary amount of time for that profession – and half of it just to get himself to the place he was now.

He closed his eyes. Opened them again, gave her a weak smile. 'You are right, my love. You are right.'

'Thomas, do not placate me . . .'

'I am not, truly I am not. I want to do this thing

because . . . I want to do it. I do not know what more to say, what I can do to make it better.'

He saw her anger, her stubborn unwillingness to yield, melt away just as his own had done. She was across the room and in his arms, her head tucked under his chin.

'My love, my love, I am sorry,' he said.

'Don't be, Thomas. I understand. You would not be the man you are if you could stay happy at home. I just . . . I . . . you must understand. Understand yourself why you have to go.'

They embraced, and after a minute Elizabeth spoke, her face buried in his chest, her voice muffled. 'I am just selfish. I can't stand seeing your joy at something besides me, and our home. I hate that ship because it is a part of your life that is not a part of mine. It will take you away from me.'

Marlowe did not know what to say to that, so he said nothing. They just stood there, in each other's arms, rocking slowly, enjoying that heightened affection that follows an argument, like the bright blue skies that come on the heels of a cleansing storm.

And then a pounding from belowstairs, an insistent fist on the front door. They both looked up, ears cocked to the sound.

'What the devil . . .' Marlowe muttered. It was well past midnight.

The pounding came again, and then quiet, and then again. Marlowe released Elizabeth, and stepped quickly for the door, Elizabeth just behind him. Out of the bedroom and down the hall, his slippered feet silent on the rug that covered most of the oak floors. At the top of the wide stairs that flowed down to the front entry Marlowe saw Caesar, the aging house servant, muttering and hurrying toward the door, dressed only in his nightshirt, a flickering candle in his hand.

Marlowe bounded down the stairs, Elizabeth still behind him, quite ignoring her immodest appearance. Caesar stopped on seeing him, glanced at the door, awaited orders. The pounding resumed.

'Pray, open it, Caesar,' Marlowe said.

Caesar grabbed the doorknob, twisted, swung the door back. In the light of his candle stood Sam.

His clothes were torn, his face and shirt smeared with blood and vomit, his eyes wild. And even before he spoke, Marlowe knew that everything had changed.

CHAPTER 5

Governor Nicholson huffed, cleared his throat, moved objects around on his desk. Squinted and frowned at something on the wide cuff of his coat, picked it off, flicked it away.

Nicholson generally came right to the point of a matter. When he did not care to, he engaged in the elaborate ritual he was now enacting.

Marlowe, seated before the governor's desk, crossed his legs, adjusted his sword, gave a little cough. He looked at the swirling pattern in the flocked canvas covering the walls, ran his eyes up to the ceiling high above, the intricate walnut crown molding that ran around the juncture of wall and ceiling. A lovely room, he had always thought so.

Nicholson had insisted they meet in his office, the office of the governor, because this was a matter that required such formality.

The governor's office was in the Wren Building of the College of William and Mary, a block of rooms that, to College President Blair's dismay, Nicholson had commandeered until the Governor's Palace was completed. It was only a few months earlier that Blair had managed to get the whole House of Burgesses out of the Wren Building and into the not-yet-finished Capitol.

Williamsburg, it seemed, was rising up from the earth, buildings growing between the stakes and strings that cut the open countryside into various lots and parcels, like a garden laid out and waiting only for things to sprout.

In an upright, slipcovered chair against the wall sat Frederick Dunmore, all but glowing in his white suit of clothes, all vestiges of his Boston Puritan heritage gone. A neat, trim man of no great size. Just the hint of a knowing smile on his face. No need for overt gloating, not when one has been proved so profoundly right.

His chair was in line with the end of the governor's desk, not quite in front, not quite behind. A careful choice, Marlowe was certain. Made himself look like he was Nicholson's right-hand man, without exposing himself to the possibility of the governor asking him what in hell he was doing, sitting beside him.

'Yes, well, Marlowe, a letter of marque . . .' the governor began at last. 'Don't really see how we can do that now . . .'

'Governor, there has been a terrible incident, I am certainly aware,' Marlowe said in his most reasonable tone, 'but I don't see how that alters the situation. Slaver or no, there is still the war with Spain . . .'

'War with Spain?' Dunmore burst in. 'We have troubles greater than that, sir, and in a good part thanks to you.'

Marlowe turned his head slowly, held Dunmore's eyes just long enough to make it clear that his comments were not welcome, and then turned back to Nicholson. 'My men, the ones who returned with the sloop, told me of the horror they found on the slaver. I do not know what King James was thinking, but whatever it was I am in no doubt that he had ample reason for doing what he did.'

That was not true, of course. Marlowe had a damned good idea of what James was thinking, of the rage that led him to slay the white crew. But of course he could not say that.

'I am hard-pressed to imagine any situation that would justify killing half of a ship's crew, particularly one in so weakened a state—' Nicholson began, only to be interrupted by Dunmore.

'There is no circumstance, sir, that can justify a black man killing a white. It can never be justified. If we find excuses for this, then we undermine the whole structure of our society here in the tidewater.'

'Our' society? Marlowe thought. Who the hell are you, you bloody Yankee bastard? Marlowe had been in the tidewater three years, was a hero in Williamsburg, and he still felt like an outsider.

He turned to Nicholson. 'What is this son of a bitch doing here?' Turned back to Dunmore, dared him with his eyes to demand satisfaction for that affront.

'Marlowe, I know you are not happy, but there is no call for that.' Nicholson pulled Dunmore from the fire. 'Mr Dunmore is here as a representative of the burgesses.'

Marlowe wondered how he had managed that, how he had got the more reasonable faction to let him be the representative at this meeting. Favors called in, debts written off. Dunmore would have done anything in exchange for this moment, the moment when he could sit there and watch Marlowe squirm because he had freed his slaves.

'There is another concern, Marlowe,' said Dunmore, smug in the governor's protection. 'This example you have set, it puts us all in great danger of our Negroes rising up against us, do you see? And again, there is the war with Spain, which you mentioned. The guns on your ship are property of the crown, and I do not see how under these circumstances we can allow you to keep them. We need them now just to protect ourselves from the danger to which you yourself have exposed us.'

Marlowe felt the hot flash of anger. Ten years before, Dunmore would not have made it through that speech, would have been begging for his life before he had uttered two sentences.

But Marlowe was a gentleman now, he reminded himself, and should not kill men but in affairs of honor, and even then it was frowned upon.

He clenched his fists, and with the last rational part of his brain congratulated himself on his self-control.

The guns, oh God, they were going to take the guns! They could never be replaced! All of the planning, all of the expense, for nothing. James, damn your black hide, why did you do that?

'I'm sorry, Marlowe. I know you've gone to great expense already.' Nicholson rearranged the silver writing set, moved a stack of papers three inches to the left. 'There is one thing I had thought of, one last shift that could solve this whole thing . . .'

Marlowe leaned back, took a deep breath. He doubted he would like what came next, but how could it be worse than his present circumstance?

Dunmore uncrossed his legs. This was apparently something new to him and he looked concerned.

'Dunmore is right, you know, this is a bad example . . .' Nicholson held up his hands to ward off Marlowe's protest and Marlowe sat back again, silent. 'I know King James, know that he's a good man. Bit of a hothead, but a good man. But still, this sort of thing cannot be countenanced, not by black men or white.

'I think the best thing over all, Marlowe, would be for you to keep the guns and go after these renegades, bring them back here. I can guarantee they'll get a fair trial, get justice. If they are innocent, then they can go free.'

Marlowe leaned back, let his eyes wander over the muskets and pistols mounted on the wall behind the governor. Heard Dunmore give a grunt at the governor's suggestion but he said nothing.

Marlowe wanted to sink his head in his hands, wanted to scream in frustration, wanted to put a sword in Dunmore's belly, and King James's too, for getting him into this corner.

Of course they would not go free. Sam had described the whole thing in nightmarish detail. Marlowe understood exactly what James had done, knew why he did it, could taste the rage in his own mouth, knew he would have done the same. But that truth would save no one from the gallows. He would be bringing them back to die, or kill them in trying.

And if he refused? What of that place in society that Elizabeth so coveted?

He had been so sure of himself, setting his slaves free, despite the tidewater's better judgment. Any number of planters had their slaves working river sloops, but Marlowe had set free black men aboard his. Men who had their pride restored. Men who were no longer cowed, who would no longer suffer any abuse, as long as it came from a white man. Hell, perhaps he *was* to blame.

There was a great deal of anger directed at Marlowe, he had already heard rumors.

And the guns, and the letter of marque. Gone. It would be fiscal ruin for him.

He would stand accused of protecting killers. Black killers, of his own making. It would strip them both, him and Elizabeth, of all the layers of respectability that they had accumulated, strip them back to their most basic selves. A pirate and a whore.

Damn you, James, damn you for this.

He could not do that to Elizabeth, she was his first loyalty, and damn King James for forcing him to make this choice.

'Very well, I shall go after them.'

'Governor,' said Dunmore, 'I hardly think that Mr Marlowe is to be trusted with—'

Nicholson held up his hand to stop Dunmore, but not before Marlowe was on his feet, two steps toward Dunmore, saying, 'Do you call me a liar, sir? Do you dispute my honesty in front of the governor?' No patience for this now. Give me a reason, you bastard, Marlowe thought, pray, give me a reason . . .

'Marlowe, please, take your seat,' Nicholson said, and Marlowe did so because the governor was a man to be respected. 'Dunmore, hold your tongue. If Marlowe says he will do a thing, then he will do it. I'll countenance no insults to his character.'

Dunmore grunted again.

'Governor, I shall need some kind of official order

from you, something with your seal authorizing me to do this.'

'These people are outlaws, Marlowe, you need no official permission to hunt them down.'

'Sir, I must insist. Official orders, with your seal.'

Nicholson considered this, could find no reason to object. 'Very well, if you insist.' He picked up a small silver bell and rang it. It had a silly, tinkling sound. From a side door the governor's secretary appeared, bowed to Nicholson. The governor told him what was needed and the man nodded, then disappeared again.

'So,' Nicholson said with a weak smile, 'damned dearth of rain we've had of late, what?'

The horse moved down the familiar road at his own pace, just fast enough to satisfy Marlowe and stave off a nudge of boot heel in the flank. He needed no direction; they had traveled that way nearly every day for two months.

For Marlowe, perched in the saddle, it was not a pleasant trip, not like before. No eager anticipation now, just apprehension. No rapture at what the old, decrepit *Nathaniel James* had become, but rather fear for what would become of her now.

He stopped at the point where the road curved around to the dock and afforded him the first complete view of his ship, sat there regarding her while the horse found some new grass on the edge of the close-packed dirt road.

It was a sight to bring joy to a shipowner's heart. The full complement of seventy-five men was aboard; not so many as Marlowe would have liked, but enough, and as many as he could ever hope to find in that place where seamen were in damned short supply. They were swarming over the ship, hauling away on the stay tackle and easing the stores down through the main hatch, laid out on the yards bending sail, reeving off running gear, caulking and paying the last of the seams on the quarterdeck.

They were nearly all of them prime seamen, all eager for a little privateering.

'Well, damnation, let's do it, then . . .' Marlowe muttered, gave the reins a jerk, got the horse under way.

His approach did not go unnoticed, as he reckoned it would not. All hands aboard the *Elizabeth Galley* would be aware of what their bosun had done, of their captain's meeting with the governor, of the potential consequences.

Indeed, it was the talk of all Virginia. Marlowe doubted there was anyone in the tidewater above the age of five who had not heard of what had taken place and already discussed it at length. High talk would have been flying through the rigging all morning. They would want answers, and because of the paucity of seamen they knew they could demand them.

One by one, as Marlowe approached, the men set aside their tools or eased off the lines they were hauling or slid down backstays to the deck, until by the time he reined to a stop at the gangway they were gathered like a mob waiting on the verdict of a trial.

'Captain Marlowe!' It was Griffin, the bosun's mate, an unpleasant fellow, face like one of those small, ugly dogs. Marlowe reckoned he had appointed himself bosun after the news of King James's departure.

'Captain, we was all wondering, did you fare well with the governor? We on for our voyage, then?' Griffin, assuming the bosun's role as crew spokesman. Marlowe did not care for it, not a bit.

First, the stick.

'See here, Griffin, all of you!' He had their attention now. 'My dealings with the governor are my concern alone, do you hear? This is not a damned pirate ship. I'll countenance no questions, no votes, no inquiries into my business, is that clear? If any have a problem with that, leave now! Leave now!'

To Marlowe's vast relief no one moved.

He reached into the haversack slung over his shoulder, pulled out the governor's orders, the ones he had insisted upon. Glanced around for Bickerstaff. His friend was on the quarterdeck, overhauling the ship's pistols. An expert with firearms and edged weapons, not from soldiering but from his days as a tutor instructing young gentlemen in their use.

He was a good fifty feet away, listening, cleaning firelocks. He would not be able to see much from that distance in any event.

Now the carrot.

Marlowe unrolled the governor's orders and held them up. An impressive document, with great scrollwork and the huge glob of a waxed seal. Nicholson could be counted on to do nothing by half.

'As you can see, the governor has issued us a letter of marque and reprisal, just as promised.' He rolled the parchment back up. 'I wish to be under way at the first of the ebb on the morrow, so turn to. We've much to do.'

A moment of silence, and then Noah Fleming, first mate, a steady and unimaginative man, just what Marlowe liked in an officer, shouted, 'Three cheers for Captain Marlowe, then!'

The men belted out their huzzahs, and with genuine gusto, Marlowe was pleased to see.

What they would be doing in a week's time remained to be seen.

Ten minutes later, Bickerstaff joined him in the great cabin, waited silently while Marlowe poured a glass of wine, guzzled it, poured another, and finally turned and said, 'Wine with you, Francis?'

'Thank you, yes,' said Bickerstaff, taking the glass, sitting in his familiar chair. 'The governor gave you a letter of marque?'

'He did. Damned reluctant, but he did. That bastard Dunmore was there as well. Lucky he did not get a bullet through his head.'

'I commend you on your restraint, sir. We are to leave on the morrow?'

'Yes. There is one other thing. Didn't tell the men, didn't reckon they'd be so happy about it.'

Marlowe paused, slugged down the wine, poured another glass. He was not so happy about it himself. Miserable, in fact. Had not realized how miserable until that moment, the moment he had to explain himself to Bickerstaff.

'We must go after King James, bring him back.'

Bickerstaff stared at him, silent, for what seemed quite a long time. 'You agreed to this?'

'What else could I do? But look, there is every chance that we will never find them.'

'And if we do, you'll bring James back to be hanged like a dog?'

'I shall try. I imagine James or I will be killed in the trying. I don't reckon we'll both be coming back.'

'James would not come back alive.'

'I have no choice in this, Francis, please understand. There would have been no privateering without I agreed to this.'

Bickerstaff shook his head. 'Privateering? We are talking about betraying a friend.'

'Betraying?' Marlowe was getting angry and trying not to. 'James betrayed me, putting me in this position.'

'You know why James did what he did. You would have done the same.'

'Indeed I would have.' Marlowe leaned back, his mind weaving through the maze of arguments. 'And I would have been an outlaw as well. See here, Francis, you are the one forever harping on the law, the rule of law. Recall how Wilkenson took the law into his own hands, burned our tobacco crop? Well, how is what James has done any different? What law gives James the right to murder a ship's crew, as detestable as they might be, eh?'

Bickerstaff thought on that for some moments, long enough for Marlowe to consume two more glasses. Finally he said, 'You are right, Thomas. It grieves me to say it, but you are right, in a philosophical line. I cannot deny that you are morally justified in trying to bring James to trial. But of course you do not believe a word of your own argument.'

'Not even the first syllable of it.' Marlowe closed

his eyes, took a deep breath, tried to drive the misery away. 'But I must do this thing, because if I do not, then Elizabeth loses everything dear to her.'

He opened his eyes. 'And I must justify it to myself, or I shall never sleep again.'

CHAPTER 6

Twenty-four hours since they had cut the black-birder's cable and gone, riding the northeasterly wind through the capes and back out into the big sea. Twenty-four hours and that innate human reflex to find order began asserting itself.

The eighty or so Africans still alive, some just barely, had organized themselves into clusters, by family, by clan, by common language, the men talking and planning, the women tending to their families, the children emerging slowly from their trauma, looking about, exploring the world within arm's reach of their mothers.

The ship – James did not know her name and did not want to know – was drifting, the sails brailed up and banging in great folds, the light airs pushing them along more sideways than forward.

He knew where they were, or close enough. James had learned to dead-reckon, had sailed the *Northumberland* in fog enough times to under-stand about noting speed and heading and drift, if it could be figured, and to deduce from that where the ship was. He had found a chart, had pricked their position hourly. Knew that it would be important, once they had decided what they would do.

He was on the quarterdeck, alone. He had no clan, save for Cato and Joshua, Good Boy and Quash, and they were forward, knotting and splicing and fixing those things that needed fixing for the ship to function.

King James sat atop the nearly wrecked binnacle box, surveyed his command. The people. The family. The clan.

The pumps were the only work that needed doing, and they needed a distressing amount of attention, as the ship was taking on quite a bit of water. Madshaka had organized gangs who relieved each other at the turn of the half-hour glass. The creaking of the pumps, the gush of water, were the leitmotif under the babble of talk on deck.

James looked forward, and saw Madshaka emerge from the hold, his head and big shoulders rising up from the dark as he mounted the ladder, his face grim, set. None of the other people had by choice gone back down there after Cato and Joshua had unbattened the hatch, and James doubted that they ever would.

Only those dozen strong young men chosen by Madshaka had gone down, gone back into the pit with Madshaka and James to clear away the bodies, the parts of bodies, and throw them overboard, to light brimstone fires and replace the stink of death with the stink of hell. Hell burnt clean.

It had taken hours. Among the worst hours in James's life, and the competition was fierce for that distinction. Now it was time for the next step.

'Madshaka, pray, a word.'

Madshaka trotted aft, his big bare feet making no

sound on the planking. Madshaka was a blessing to James, a natural leader, like himself, invaluable in bringing order, second in command by tacit consent.

'Yes, Captain?' Madshaka said, with his big smile quite at odds with the somber look he had had coming up from the hold.

'We have to figure what we will do next. We can't drift forever. We must decide.'

'That true. That true.' Madshaka screwed up his face, as if framing a question, began, paused, and then said, 'Captain James, you know much about them pirates?'

James knew quite a bit about pirates, in fact, having fought them at Marlowe's side aboard the guardship, having learned of their ways from Marlowe, who knew from firsthand experience.

'Yes. Some.'

'When the pirates aboard this ship, I listen. They aboard a long time, and I listen, but I don't understand. They have no chief, I think. Each man have a say in what they do. And black men too, black men among the pirates and they have a say. Is that right?'

James nodded. How to explain those nefarious people? He hated pirates, those robbers, murderers. He had killed many of them with his own hands. And yet, and yet . . .

Madshaka was not wrong in what he perceived. The men who turned pirate were the world's downtrodden, and they would no longer suffer such abuse. Each man had a vote, each man received an equal share. Total equality. The color of their skin was not an issue, only their courage and devotion to the brotherhood.

Marlowe was the first, one of the few white men to

treat James as an equal. He had gained his color blindness among the pirates. How to judge such men?

'The pirates pick their captain, their chief. But he is only chief when they fight. Other times, they all choose what they are to do, where they go. Every man gets an equal share of what they steal.'

Madshaka nodded, raised his eyebrows. 'That is very fair, I think, very just.' He paused, looked around the deck at the various clusters of people. 'You could tell them what to do, and they would listen. I could tell them, and they would listen to me. But maybe, we do like the pirates? Maybe we vote on captain, on where we go? It seem . . . most just.'

James nodded as well, uncomfortable though he was with modeling any part of himself after the pirates.

Still, Madshaka had a point. It could not be up to him, or any other one person, to decide what they would do. They must vote.

It was with some small sense of relief that he called Kusi over and explained what he and Madshaka had decided, told Kusi what to tell the others.

They would vote. It would not be on James's shoulders. The group would decide. He would do their bidding.

For a moment, at least, the weight was gone.

Kusi and Madshaka went from group to group, explaining, hearing suggestions, conferring. There seemed to be quite a bit of organizational talk, but James had no idea because he could not understand a word of it.

For two turns of the glass the tribes carried on an animated debate within their groups.

Good Boy, Cato, Quash, and Joshua left off their work, came aft. 'What's acting?' Cato asked.

'Madshaka and I was talking. Reckoned we got no business telling all them people what to do. Reckoned we'd vote on it, what we's to do, where to go.'

The four young men nodded thoughtfully but they did not look so sure. James imagined they would be happy to let one man – him – make the decisions for all. They would have been happy to be relieved of all responsibility in that regard.

At length men from each of the tribes stood and came aft and sat cross-legged on the deck in a semicircle around the binnacle box. Madshaka and Kusi stepped up, flanked King James. Madshaka spoke.

'Each of the clans, they send three men. The men talk for the tribe. Easier that way, not so many men.'

James nodded. It was a sensible thing to do. Each individual tribe would be expected to hang on to the hierarchies that the pirates had shunned.

'I . . . Kusi and me . . . have told them what we decide, that we all vote where we go, what we do.'

'Good, good. We best talk on it then, and then we vote.'

Madshaka and Kusi turned to the assembled men, began talking, fast, in the odd and incomprehensible languages of West Africa. James leaned against the binnacle box, arms folded. Hoped that he looked calm, in control. He was in fact quite uncomfortable. All this talk, and he understood not a word.

Heads nodded, men spoke to one another, the translators moved on to the next group. Twenty minutes of this and they were done, and the deck was filled with the babble of discussion, debate. Madshaka and Kusi stepped back, flanking James once more.

One man sitting near the mizzen fife rail leapt to his feet, held James's eyes, spoke loud, passionately. In James's ear, Kusi said, 'He say you the captain, when we fighting, just like Madshaka say the pirates do.'

James nodded. Kabu Malinke prince to slave to freeman to pirate. Royalty to outlaw.

Kusi continued. 'He say we must go back to home . . . he mean Africa . . . must take all the people back to their homes.'

Madshaka translated the words for the others, switching from one tongue to another, and heads nodded and voices rose and one did not need to understand the words to catch the tones of agreement and assent. Africa. They would go back to Africa.

James's clan did not look so sure. 'Africa?' Good Boy said. 'What we do in Africa?' James imagined that Good Boy was, at that moment, as far from Virginia as he had ever been in his life.

'I don't know,' James said, talking low. He did not want Madshaka and Kusi to overhear him, though he was not sure why. 'We got to do it, for these people. Then, I don't know what we do. We think of something.'

The four men muttered agreement. It seemed more like resignation.

More fast talk, translated arguments, hands waving, impassioned speech. Madshaka said, 'They argue over where in Africa to go.' He turned back to the group, called out something, the men were silent.

He called out again, one language at a time, and the men of each tribe in turn responded. Voting, deciding. James felt entirely removed from this process, as if he were something less than a member of the group.

At last Madshaka turned back to him. 'We go to Kalabari. It is decided, we go there, and these people go home, upriver, overland.'

Kalabari, in the heart of the Niger River Delta. Far from the slave factories of Whydah and Popo and Sierra Leone. There the people could use the great Niger River to carry them into the heart of their lands, and from thence over the savannahs to their homes. It was decided. James had not even understood the debate.

'Very well . . .'

Africa. The name whirled around in James's head. Africa. He never thought he would see it again.

A prince when stolen, what was he now? He did not even know if his city was still standing, if his people still existed. He had not seen either for twenty years. The Malinke might have been wiped out years before, for all he knew.

Twenty years, and all that time he had fantasized about this moment, when he would return to Africa. And now that that dream was taking form and substance he did not know how he felt about it, did not know what if anything there was for him now in his motherland.

'We gots to get the boat sailing,' Madshaka urged him, gently.

James nodded. 'Yes, we do.'

He would think about Africa later. Right now they

had to get under way. For more reasons than the others knew.

James knew, had realized it even as they were voting on their destination. It had dawned on him as he had wallowed in his regret at missing the chance to go privateering aboard the *Elizabeth Galley*.

They would blame Marlowe for this, those people in power in Williamsburg. There would be no letter of marque, not for a man who had brought this terror on the colony of Virginia.

There would be only one way for Marlowe to regain his precious place, and that would be to hunt the black killers down, to bring them back. He would not want to do it, would recoil from the thought, but in the end he would agree because he would have no choice. He would do it for Elizabeth.

'Get them men together.' James turned to the *grumete*. 'Madshaka, get them in three groups, we'll organize them by mast. Cato, Joshua, you each go with a group, show them how to do what I say. Madshaka, Kusi, you all translate what I say. If we going to live we got to start learning these people how to sail this ship.'

They had to get the boat sailing, the half-rotten, festering, leaking tub. Because in their wake would come the *Elizabeth Galley*, new, fast, well armed, determined.

CHAPTER 7

Elizabeth knelt on the lawn at the edge of the flower
beds, sunk her hands in the moist dirt. She could feel
the dampness creeping through her skirt and wool
stockings, but it felt cool and good, with the sun
beating on her back and her wide straw hat.

She picked up a spade and scooped the loose dirt
out until she had a hole ten inches deep. Then she
carefully, lovingly picked up the little rosebush and
set its roots in the hole before pushing the dirt in
around it.

Playing at agriculture. Sometimes that bothered
her. All over the tidewater people broke their backs
working the soil, slaves and freemen alike, just to eke
out a living or to make someone else rich. But she
just played, like the noblewomen in France who
found amusement in pretending to be simple country
girls.

But those were just minor concerns, because she
loved to work in the gardens, loved to make Marlowe
House a more beautiful place. More her own.

She had lived there since coming to the New
World with Joseph Tinling. But the house had not
been her home, it had been merely a place to endure

Master Tinling's brutality. After his death she had sold it to Marlowe, then a newcomer to Virginia, had moved to town, happy to be shed of those echoing rooms and their horrible memories.

But after she and Marlowe wed she had moved back, and now she was exorcising those demons of her former life, remaking the wretched Tinling House into the Marlowes' ancestral home. New furnishings, new carpets, new portraits, fresh paint.

The gardens were a big part of that, Elizabeth's chief contribution, because unlike the furniture or the paintings, which were just items to be purchased, the garden was something that she could do herself, something pure and organic. Coaxing beauty and nourishment from the earth.

It was midmorning but she had been at it since just after sunrise. She needed the garden's cathartic influence, the release of tension that comes with physical labor.

She had seen Thomas and Francis Bickerstaff off in the predawn hours. Before, she had been angry about his going off privateering, abandoning her. She was angry that Thomas had grown bored with the home she was trying to make.

But that all changed the moment Sam blurted out his awful story.

It was a very different departure from the one she had envisioned. There was none of the suppressed excitement, none of Thomas's feigning disappointment in leaving when in fact he was aching to be under way, none of the footloose buccaneer that made Thomas so equally loved, hated, feared, and appreciated in the tidewater.

Rather, it had been a somber moment, and

Thomas had been genuine in his desire not to go. But go he must, they both knew that.

And Elizabeth, who was no fool, was not insensible to the fact that he was going after James more for her than for himself. Thomas could have told Nicholson to sod off, but for her sake he had told the governor 'Yes, sir.'

She worked her shovel in the dirt, spacing the plants three feet apart. In a few years they would be great thorny bushes, spilling over with brilliant small red flowers, like drops of fresh blood on mounds of green.

And then a shadow fell over the turned earth and a man's voice, loud and full of delight and surprise, said, 'Lizzy? Could that be you?'

Elizabeth wheeled around, gasped in surprise, squinted against the sun. The man was standing no more than five feet away, had approached over the grass so she could not hear him.

She stood, slowly, and threw her spade down like throwing a knife. It stuck in the dirt and quivered. She wiped dirty hands on her apron, leaving arched brown streaks on the linen, folded her arms across her chest. 'Dear God . . .' she said.

'Oh, no, Lizzy, none of that. Well, certainly, there are some women think I am a god, but not you, surely?'

She held him in her harsh gaze, then at last she had to smile and shake her head. 'Billy Bird. I had never thought to see your face again.'

'Ah, like a bad penny,' he said, swept off his cocked hat, a big plume trailing astern, bowed elegantly at the waist. He wore white silk stockings and white breeches bleached so bright that it hurt to look at them in the late-morning sun. Under a red coat with neat embroidery around the pockets and cuffs he wore a red waistcoat and a calico shirt. A buff leather shoulder strap ran diagonally across his chest, the silver buckle winking in the sun, a heavy sword hanging at his waist. He wore no wig, and his hair was long and clubbed, as the seamen wore it.

'You look like a damned peacock, as usual, Billy.'

'And you . . .' He straightened, held out his hands. 'Is this what has become of the beautiful Elizabeth Sampson, late of Plymouth and London? Working in the dirt like some pickaninny?'

She did not know if she wanted to hug the man or stick a knife in his guts. She never did. She and Billy Bird went back many years. 'My name is Elizabeth Marlowe now, Billy, and it gives me great pleasure to work in the garden of the home of which I am mistress.'

'Ah, great pleasure! And you know there is no one who can give you great pleasure like old Billy Bird, my darling.'

'Billy, lay one hand on me and I will cut your balls off and stuff them down your throat. You know me capable of it.'

Bird chuckled at that. 'Yes you are, yes you are. But how about a hug for an old friend?' He held out his arms again, and after a second's hesitation Elizabeth stepped into them and gave Billy Bird a hug. He held her to his chest, gently, affectionately. He smelled faintly of perfume and tobacco smoke and tar. They squeezed each other and then stepped back again.

'It's been . . . three years at least,' Elizabeth said. 'Where have you been?'

'Rhode Island, mostly. Boston, New York. And off on the far-flung oceans of the world.'

Elizabeth nodded. 'Well, you shouldn't have come here. Governor Nicholson has no love of pirates. He has hanged any number of them already.'

'Pirates! Oh, Elizabeth, really! I am an honest merchant, and besides I have never committed anything that smacks of piracy against a Christian. That I know of.'

'Indeed. I am sorry to say that you just missed meeting my husband, speaking of people you should not cross.'

'Oh, have I really? I am sorry to hear that.'

'Uh-huh,' said Elizabeth. Bird's timing would not be an accident. Everyone in Williamsburg and Jamestown knew that the *Elizabeth Galley* had sailed on the tide that morning.

'Though in fact I believe I have met your husband . . . Thomas Marlowe? In Port Royal, some years back. But his name was not Thomas Marlowe then, and he was something less than an honest man of the soil . . .'

'You are mistaken, I am sure. But whatever you think, I am certain you can keep it to yourself, just as you are certain that I'll tell no tales about you.'

'I am the soul of discretion, ma'am, you know that.'

'The soul of discretion.' But for all his loud-mouthed boasting, Elizabeth knew that Billy Bird could keep his mouth shut when he had to, and she trusted him. 'What brings you to the tidewater? Are you staying?'

'I have taken up lodgings at the King's Arms. Just temporary, of course.'

Just until Thomas returns, Elizabeth thought.

'I've some small business here,' Billy continued, 'and my ship is down at Norfolk, fitting out. Ship, I say. She is a brig, in fact, just a little thing. Lost my last ship off Madagascar. I will tell you all the unhappy details, but first I think you should invite me in for a cup of chocolate.'

'Do you?' Elizabeth folded her arms, cocked her head, regarded Billy Bird. Plymouth, London, Williamsburg. Since she was fourteen years old she had known Billy, and he always seemed to pop up again, wherever she was. They had been friends, had enjoyed the occasional roll in bed. And here he was again.

She could well imagine what he was hoping for now. He would be disappointed, but he would get over it. A cup of chocolate, however, was within her newfound moral boundaries.

It was a still morning, little wind, and the insects were just starting in with their buzzing. Elizabeth was about to ask Billy in when she heard the horses, a long way off. She paused, lifted her head, and listened.

There was more than one, not galloping but not walking either. The sound grew louder as the riders approached. She looked down the long, tree-lined road that ran up to Marlowe House.

She couldn't see anyone, so she knew they were still a ways up the rolling road that connected their plantation to Williamsburg in one direction and Jamestown in another.

Men on horses, riding fast. That was never a good thing. All these men, racing around on their great animals, always off on some important duty,

99

inflicting some misery or another on someone. Like a pack of wolves. Chasing down fugitive slaves, chasing down pirates, chasing down threats to their beloved property.

'These would be friends of yours?' Bird asked.

'I doubt very much friends.'

They listened for a moment more. The riders grew closer. 'I say, Lizzy, I never care to be conspicuous when there are men, no doubt armed men, charging about the countryside on horses. So if you do not mind terribly, I shall just duck into your house, perhaps indulge my eye with your exquisite taste in furnishings. You always did know how to spend a man's money.'

'As ever, the soul of discretion.'

Billy Bird gave another of his elaborate bows. 'Your servant, ma'am.' Then he straightened and trotted off toward the porch.

'Caesar!' Elizabeth called out, and then again, louder. 'Caesar!'

Behind her she heard the main door open, heard bare feet on the wide front porch.

'Ma'am?' said Caesar. He was a former field slave, now head of the household. Past fifty, a gentle, soft-spoken man. No great demands were made of him. Marlowe figured that he had earned his rest, his easy duty.

He looked with only vague curiosity at Billy Bird, who brushed past him with a friendly nod and disappeared into the cool interior of Marlowe House.

Elizabeth climbed up to the porch, scanned the road again from that higher vantage. She could see a cloud of dust, a mile or so away, kicked up by the approaching riders.

'Do you hear those horses coming?' she asked.

'No, ma'am.' Caesar's hearing was not all one might wish.

'About half a dozen, I should think.'

'They gots to know Mr Marlowe ain't here. What you think they want?'

'I don't know.' That was true, but she could guess. Marlowe's free blacks were the topic du jour in Williamsburg. This visit would involve them in some way. She did not think it would be for the black people's benefit.

'I don't imagine that whoever is coming is going to do us any favors,' Elizabeth said, and Caesar nodded. 'Round up all the people in the house and hurry out back and tell everyone working in the fields to lose themselves. Do you think you can all hide yourselves until these people go?'

Caesar nodded. 'If they's only six of them, and no dogs, we can hide so they don't find us.'

'Very well. Go.'

With that, Caesar disappeared and Elizabeth stepped slowly down to the lawn. In the far distance, on that part of the rolling road visible from Marlowe House, she could see the riders, small, bobbing specks against the green fields. She only hoped she had heard them in time.

They turned onto the road running up to Marlowe House, seemed to pick up their pace for that last charge down to the plantation. Halfway there, two hundred yards away, and Elizabeth could see the white coat and breeches of Frederick Dunmore at their head.

And I thought I would be lonely with Thomas gone, she thought.

Hurry, Caesar. Pray, hurry.

They reined up in front of her, their great, sweating, panting beasts pawing and shaking heads, twisting around under their riders, as if anxious to be at it. Dunmore, foremost, in his white coat, filmed with dust, the locks of his long white periwig flung back over his shoulders, twisted and tangled like Medusa snake-hair. Sword, brace of pistols in his crossbelt, musket thrust through a loop in his saddle.

Behind him, three more plantation owners, and behind them, deferential, Elizabeth recognized the overseers from those plantations. Professional slave handlers, men whose earnings were commensurate with their ability to enforce discipline, their measured brutality.

'I am sorry, Mr Dunmore, but I am afraid you have missed my husband,' Elizabeth said.

'Didn't come to see your husband, ma'am. We come for your niggers.'

'I'm sorry, you've what?'

'We've come for your niggers. Threat to the tidewater. Too bad that innocent white men had to die before anyone would listen to me. We'll hold them until the burgesses figure out what to do with them.'

Elizabeth held his eyes and he held hers as his horse shifted and worked under him. She hoped her expression could convey even a fraction of the contempt she felt. 'Had you come yesterday you might have discussed this with Mr Marlowe. Now you will have to wait for his return.'

'No waiting. No time for that, and nothing to discuss.'

'Damned convenient, sir, that you did not get around to this until this morning, when you knew

Mr Marlowe had sailed. One might think it . . . cowardly? Craven? What word might one use for a sneaking, crawling puppy such as yourself?'

Dunmore's face flushed, to Elizabeth's satisfaction, but his demeanor did not change. 'I shall deal with Mr Marlowe, depend upon it.' He wheeled his horse, shouted, 'We've no time for this nonsense! Let us go!'

With a dramatic wave of his hand he led the men off, around the house, off between the barn and the tobacco sheds, off to the former slave quarters – now the homes of Marlowe's free laborers – and back to the fields where they worked.

Mr Marlowe shall deal with you, depend upon it, she thought. Deal you out a bullet through your head.

Elizabeth had never been a great supporter of Marlowe's freeing his slaves – formerly Tinling's slaves – whom he had purchased along with the Tinling plantation. But she loved the people, cared for them in a maternal way, and knew they were no threat. She had to agree with her husband that Marlowe House had none of the volatility of other plantations.

And now this. This bastard Dunmore, a Boston man of all things, taking it upon himself to keep the tidewater safe from such abominations as free blacks.

Oh, Caesar, please, please have warned them all in time.

'Do you know, Francis,' said Marlowe, breathing deep, patting his chest, 'one could almost forget one's woes, in these circumstances.'

'Almost.'

The two men stood leaning against the weather bulwark on the *Elizabeth Galley*'s quarterdeck, all the way aft. The wind had filled in once they had cleared the capes, and now they were enjoying fifteen knots over the larboard quarter. The *Galley* was bowling along with all plain sail set, making nine and ten knots with every cast of the log. There was not a cloud to be seen, nowhere on that unbroken, three-hundred-and-sixty-degree horizon.

Marlowe turned and leaned over the rail, peered astern. The wake was arrow straight, deep blue and white furrows under the counter that faded away as it stretched back toward the land. To the north, but well behind them now, was Cape Charles, to the south Cape Henry, the gaping entrance to the Chesapeake Bay, like monstrous jaws from which they had just narrowly escaped.

And before them, nothing. Just the wide, blue Atlantic. No impediments, considerations. No politics out here, just seamanship and gunnery.

Below them, the ship, tight and yare, well armed, well manned. She felt solid underfoot. It was always a source of wonder to Marlowe that something that heaved and rolled and pitched could at the same time feel so solid and unyielding. A trick of the mind, no doubt. It didn't matter. The *Elizabeth Galley* was everything one could wish in a ship, just as her namesake was everything one could wish in a woman.

He was about to say as much to Bickerstaff when he was jerked from his contentment by a crack, like a pistol shot, and for that instant he was back aboard some fetid pirate ship where the winner of a quarrel was the one who snatched his gun and fired the quickest. He wondered if his men were looking to their pistols already, and if so, who had killed whom?

All that he thought in the instant between the crack like a gunshot and the banging and flogging of canvas that had broken free of its restraints.

He whirled around and his eye was drawn to the chaos aloft.

Something had snapped and now the weather clew of the main topsail was free and the entire sail was slamming and twisting and flogging itself to death. Marlowe could see it wrapping around the main topmast forestay, dragging itself across the heavy rope, shredding itself against the gear aloft. Streams of canvas blew away like bandages coming undone.

At the base of the mast, Griffin, looking up, shouting. Not orders, not instructions, just cursing, useless filthy invectives spilling from his mouth, directed at the sail.

Useless man. In the rush of getting under way fast Marlowe had neglected to replace him as bosun.

He pushed past Bickerstaff, raced forward, ready to give the orders himself to get the big sail under control when Fleming burst out from under the quarterdeck, shouting orders as he ran. 'Clew up! Clew up! Come along, you lazy bastards, lay into them clews! Ease away the sheets there, ease away, handsome now! Mr Griffin, mind your duty!'

Half a minute more and the sail was subdued, hauled up to the topsail yard by its clews and bunts while all the time Griffin kept up his pointless and useless cursing.

The ship was quiet again, the men attentive, and Fleming ordered the main topgallant sail in and the yards lowered into their lifts and hands away aloft to unbend the topsail. The crisis had lasted no more than three minutes, but it had been enough to shatter Marlowe's fine mood and force him back to the unhappy reality of the moment.

Fleming stood at the base of the mainmast, examining the frayed end of a long piece of cordage that lay strewn over the fife rail and the main hatch. He squinted aloft, then dropped the rope and stepped up the quarterdeck ladder and aft. 'Looks like the topsail sheet chaffed right through. Must have had a bad lead,' he announced.

'Indeed. We'll have quite a few such kinks to work out, I wouldn't wonder,' said Marlowe. 'Let us hope we get it all straight before we have a real situation. And well done, Mr Fleming.'

'Thank you, sir,' said Fleming, embarrassed. He coughed, mumbled something about seeing to the new topsail, and disappeared down into the waist.

'Good man, Fleming,' Marlowe observed.

'Indeed,' said Bickerstaff. They were standing just forward of the mizzenmast now, out of earshot of the helmsmen aft and quite ignored by the men below them in the waist, who were busy with the new topsail. 'Now Thomas, forgive me, but I must ask. You have not yet said anything to the men about hunting down King James and the others aboard that wretched slave ship. Are you intending to tell them?'

'Of course I am,' Marlowe said, pleased with his genuine sincerity. 'Of course I am,' he said again. 'But it is a delicate thing, you see. They won't be happy with it; quite a lot of risk and no reward, save for my reputation.'

'These are not pirates, Thomas. You do not need their approval.'

'No, but they ain't man-of-war's men either. Privateers are tricky business. Push them too hard one way and they take French leave of you, and there you are, stranded in some port with no crew. Push too hard the other way and they chuck you overboard and turn pirate. In truth, I am in charge only as long as they all agree I am in charge. I suppose they are like the pirates in that, except that it's a bit more of a fuss for them to depose me.'

'But it is still your intention to hunt James and the others down?'

'We are hunting them now. It is just that you and I are the only ones who know it.'

'Hunting them how? How can you guess where they are?'

'James and Cato and Joshua were the only ones who know any bit of seamanship, and Cato and Joshua know only the sloop, really. James's experience with square rig is limited to the *Plymouth Prize*, and though he is a capable fellow there is only so much he can do with his untrained people and his own limited knowledge. Right now I should think they are running for it, downwind. They would not try and shape a course to windward, not now.'

'But they might later?'

'Perhaps. Once James has trained them a bit.'

'They will go to Africa.' It was a statement.

Marlowe was silent for a moment. 'Yes. I had thought of that. That is why we must catch them now. These men' – he gestured toward the waist – 'will not care to go to Africa to hunt them down. And do not think it has not occurred to them that they need only knock me and you and Fleming on the head and suddenly they are equal partners in the finest pirate ship afloat. They lack only sufficient motivation. And if it has not occurred to them, you can bet that little bastard Griffin will point it out.'

The two men were silent, watching the hands forward bundling up the new topsail in readiness for sending it aloft.

'Beware, beware, the Bight of Benin . . .' Marlowe muttered.

'Pardon?'

'Oh, just some old sailor's nonsense. One of these warnings set to a bit of verse. "Beware, beware, the Bight of Benin. One man comes out for each forty go in." The Slave Coast is a deuced unpleasant place. Deadly to white men.'

'One might think that Divine retribution.'

'Perhaps. Whatever it is, let us pray to all that is holy that we do not have to plunge into that dark place.'

CHAPTER 8

Twenty minutes after Dunmore and his men had disappeared behind the house they were back. Angry, scowling, driving their horses hard, taking their frustrations out on the animals.

Once again Dunmore reined up in front of Elizabeth, blocking her way with his horse, as if he were cornering a runaway slave.

'Where are they?' he demanded, his voice like a spade in gravel.

'Who?'

'Don't come it the innocent with me! Your niggers! Where are your niggers?'

'Were they not all standing in a line, waiting for you to clap them in chains?'

Dunmore scowled at her. His eyes moved up to the house. 'You have them in there? Hidden in there?'

Elizabeth stepped forward until she was just a few feet from Dunmore. The smell of the horse was strong in her nose, its breathing loud. 'Do not think for one moment you will go uninvited into my house. You may come sneaking around here when Mr Marlowe is gone, but he will not be gone forever, do you understand? He has been more than tolerant of your insults thus far, pray do not seek to find the limits of his patience.'

Dunmore had not yet arrived in the tidewater when Marlowe shot Matthew Wilkenson in a duel over Elizabeth's honor. He had not been there when Marlowe fought and killed the pirate LeRois. But he would have heard the stories, would understand the potential danger in pushing the man too far.

His horse spun around under him and he had to swivel his head to keep his eyes locked on Elizabeth's.

'You'll not hide them forever, your bloody murdering niggers. You and your precious Mr Marlowe will not put the entire colony in jeopardy with the notions you are putting in the Negroes' heads, is that clear? I will be back! I will be back with dogs, with guns, with more men! I will be back!'

He spun around again, called to his band, and they rode off before Elizabeth was able to get in another word.

She watched them as they rode away. The overseers might agree with Dunmore, but ultimately they were just following orders. The other planters she knew socially. They did not support Marlowe in his decision to free his people, she understood that. But they had lived with it for three years now, had never before uttered more than the mildest of protests.

It was Dunmore. He was the one getting them worked up, had been for some time, quietly agitating. And now this thing with James and the slave ship. The spark in the powder magazine.

Why did Dunmore care so much?

'Bloody unpleasant man.'

Eizabeth turned. Billy Bird was standing on the

110

porch, watching him ride away. 'He does seem damned interested in your business.'

'You heard that?'

'Yes, yes.' Billy came down the stairs, hopping from one down to the next. 'Watched the whole thing from the window, right up there.' He pointed with his thumb.

'That would be my bedchamber.' Elizabeth tried to make her voice icy.

'Ah, so it would. Recognized the ambience, got damned randy just stepping through the door. In any event, yes, a thoroughly unpleasant fellow. What is his name?'

'Dunmore. Frederick Dunmore.'

'Hmm. I recognize him, know him from somewhere. Had a notion of that when I saw him leading that ugly business last night, but I am certain of it now.'

'What . . . ugly business?'

'Well, they pulled some poor Negro fellow out of the jail there in Williamsburg. A whole crowd of them, but that Dunmore was the one egging them on. Can't miss him, in all his white kit. Looks like a bloody ghost. Pulled this poor bastard from the jail, beat him good and hanged him, right there on Duke of Gloucester Street. Sheriff tried to stop them, I'll give the man credit, but he never could. Big mob, torches, the whole thing. Quite a show. If I'd known Williamsburg was so exciting a place I would have come sooner.'

Elizabeth closed her eyes, fought down the growing dread. 'Do you know who it was, at all, that they hanged?' She knew the answer even before she asked the question.

'Someone said his name was William. Involved in some kind of murder aboard a slave ship.'

Elizabeth nodded, eyes shut tight. William, you poor, poor boy. Why didn't you flee with the others?

'Does this have anything to do with your people?' Bird asked. 'Your beloved Mr Marlowe?'

Elizabeth opened her eyes, breathed deep. 'It does indeed. Damn that man.'

'Damn who? Marlowe?' There was a hopeful note in Bird's voice.

'No, Dunmore. Why the hell couldn't he have stayed put, why did he have to come here?'

'He is not from this country?'

'No. He arrived a year ago. Less, I should think. Came from London, I understand, but he is from Boston originally.'

'Boston . . .' Billy said thoughtfully. He frowned, looked down at the ground. 'Boston . . .'

'Do you know something about this?'

'Well, now that you say he is from Boston, I do seem to recall something. Yes. Yes.'

'What? What of it?'

'I don't know.'

'Billy, damn your eyes . . .'

'No, truly. I recall him now. Saw him around town on a few occasions. But mind, I was not in Boston long, dreadful place, all full of Puritans and their somber nonsense. Anyway, there was something about him . . . what was it?'

Elizabeth wanted to scream, wanted to slap Billy, to make him blurt it out before she could change her mind and tell him not to. She hated rumor, vicious stories, had been nearly brought to ruin herself by them. She didn't want to hear any more.

But Dunmore, some vile thing about Dunmore, that was different, was it not?

'Never you mind, Billy Bird. I don't want to hear any of your vicious gossip, even if it is about that bastard. I promised you some hot chocolate and you shall have it and then you shall be on your way because I have not a moment to lose.'

James sat on one of the small cannons on the quarterdeck and looked down the length of the flush-decked ship. The people had worked hard and they were hungry.

They were gathered in their clans, little clusters of people dressed in whatever they had been able to find in the great cabin, in the crew's dunnage. A woman had wrapped herself in one of the curtains pulled down from the great cabin windows, had managed to make the cloth look like a respectable garment.

The men, dressed out in the former crew's clothes, the contents of the slop chest, were beginning to look like proper sailors. They were becoming acclimated to their surroundings and initiated into the mysteries of square rig.

Children, with the resilience of their age, were starting to wander away from their mothers, to play. Squeals and laughter cut across the deck, that former killing field.

They had worked hard for the past two days. The men at sailing, under James's command, under the tutelage of Joshua and Cato, as translated by Madshaka and Kusi. They had organized by mast, and those with knowledge of such things had explained in rough terms how a big-wind ship was sailed.

Young, strong men. Those were the ones the slavers took, and those were the people who made up the crew now, to their great advantage. James had led them aloft and out along the yards, had shown them as much as they needed to know to set and furl and reef sails.

They were agile, fearless aloft, natural sailor men. And Madshaka and Kusi, the *grumetes*, were accustomed to the water, familiar with ships, having made careers bringing white men and cargo in their boats through the huge surf that pounded the African shore.

It had gone better than James would have dared hope. He had seen some of God's greatest idiots become tolerable sailors, and these men were far above that class.

He had seen the pirates – filthy, depraved, subhuman – but sailors to the bone. These African men could learn.

The women had cleaned the decks, had set things to right, had seen to the family units. They cleaned in order to make the ship their own, to purge it of what it had been, for the same reason that James had lit brimstone in the hold.

They had to remake it in their way, otherwise they could not stand to remain aboard.

The sun was disappearing toward Virginia. They were on a broad reach, foresail, topsails, and topgallants, braced about just a bit. The leaking, weed-covered hull was able to make five knots, no more. But they were making progress, leaving the New World farther and farther below the horizon.

James had a vague idea that they should be making more northing, that the sailing route to Africa was that way, a great arc up through the north Atlantic and down, following the winds, but he knew little about offshore navigation.

He did understand leadership, however, and knew that they had to do something, had to make some progress, even in the wrong direction. Without progress there was no hope, and where hope was gone, terror and despair were sure to come.

And he had problems bigger than navigation. By now Marlowe would have passed through the capes, would be out there, somewhere, in their wake. Marlowe was a cunning bastard, and though it would seem an impossible task for one ship to find another on the great ocean, James did not think it unlikely that Marlowe would find them.

And he had problems bigger even than Marlowe.

Food: there was little of it. He and Madshaka and Cato had searched the ship, from great cabin down to the keelson, had taken note of everything that was aboard. Madshaka told them the people had been half starved, and now James saw that it was not merely capricious cruelty. There simply was not much food aboard.

On the deck was a portable stove; a fire sparked up with firewood from the galley and the doors of the binnacle box. Around it the women gathered, cooking the meager rations for their families, just as they had done thousands of times in their far-flung villages. The men sat on the deck, leaned on the rails, rested from the day's exertions, talked about what they would do next.

Madshaka came ambling down the deck. There was the suggestion of power in his loose-limbed stride, the potential of power, like a man holding the

115

bulk of his strength in reserve. He held two of the wooden plates they had found in the galley, carried them easily in his big hands.

'Captain, I bring you some food.' He held out the plate and James took it with a grateful nod. He was terribly hungry. A small piece of salt pork and a little clump of dried peas from the sailors' stores, some of the thin porridge for the slaves. James ate it all greedily.

'Thank you, Madshaka.'

Madshaka nodded and was silent while he ate and James ate. Then he said, 'We got food for two, three more days. We need more.'

James nodded. He had been thinking the same thing. But where to get it from?

There was only one reasonable answer, but James did not care to think of it.

'We got to take it.' Madshaka said it for him. 'We got to stop another ship and take it. I know you don't want to do it, I don't neither, but these people will starve if we don't.'

James was silent for a long moment. Madshaka always addressed him in English, never Malinke. Somehow it seemed the African tongue would have been more appropriate. Madshaka no doubt thought him more comfortable with English. 'You're right. You're right. We got no choice.'

Pirates. They were running the ship with that rough pirate democracy. Now, raiding on the high seas. But there was no choice, the thing had to be done. 'We'll take food, just food. And not all that's aboard.'

'Just food,' Madshaka agreed.

'There's shipping here,' James explained, 'this way,

116

between the Caribbean and the American colonies. Good chance we see something tomorrow, the next day.'

'All these men we got, good, brave, strong men,' Madshaka added. 'No problem. We go alongside, jump on other ship, take her, no problem.'

'No problem,' James agreed. No problem in terms of the tactical situation. The morality of the thing was another question.

But it was just food. His people had to eat. James was suddenly very tired.

'Madshaka, I must rest. I think the wind is steady, should stay like this through the night, I reckon. No need to trim the sails or change course. Things should be—'

'Captain, Captain,' Madshaka interrupted. 'You go sleep. I look after things here. The people need you, you no good to them if you too tired to think. You go down to the great cabin, you sleep.'

James nodded, gratefully. Sleep. Nothing had ever sounded so good to him as sleep did at that moment. The physical activity alone would have been enough to exhaust him. The concerns over preserving the lives of the people aboard had pushed him well beyond his limit.

'I thank you, Madshaka. If anything happens, change in wind or weather, a light is seen, you get me.'

'Of course, of course. Never to worry.'

James made his way below and aft. The great cabin looked as if it had once been a fine affair. The smashed furniture was polished walnut, the cushions, now shredded and pulled apart, were a rich red damask. Among the many empty bottles scattered

117

about and rattling across the deck with each roll of the ship James recognized labels he had seen in Marlowe's well-stocked cellar.

The condition of the great cabin did not matter. The torn settee cushions looked as inviting as any feather bed. He sat heavily, felt the motion of the ship under him, the hypnotic rhythm of the vessel's rise and fall, the gentle side-to-side motion that set everything swinging in little arcs.

He swung his legs up on the settee, letting the sleep come over him, warm and seductive. He felt his whole body pulled down into the torn cushion like it was wrapped around him and then he was asleep.

In his dreams James was floating above the ship, looking down on it, on the people on the deck, swooping ahead to make certain the way was clear, flying over the jungles that ran down to the pounding surf of the African coast, then back to the ship.

And then someone on the deck saw him and screamed, ran in panic, and then another and another and all of the people were terrified to see him flying over them.

His eyes fluttered and opened. The screaming was still there, the rushing of feet, but overhead now.

The screaming was real, not a dream. Something was happening on deck. James's head felt thick, he had no notion of how long he had slept.

He launched off the settee, tripped on the broken carcass of a chair on the deck, kicked it aside and raced out the door, bouncing off the cabin doors along the alleyway as the roll of the ship tossed him side to side in his race for the quarterdeck.

Up and out the scuttle, the sliver of moon and the stars giving his eyes all the light they needed to see the chaos on deck, men running here and there, lines cast off, people tripping in their rush. His eyes moved automatically aloft but the sails were still set, still drawing perfectly, the wind still on the same quarter.

'Madshaka! Madshaka!' He grabbed the big man's arm as he rushed past, turned him around. 'What? What is it?'

'Man go overboard!' Madshaka shouted.

'Heave to!' James shouted. 'We must heave to! Get the men to the foremast braces!' Shouts flying around the deck, orders in half a dozen languages. 'Go! Get them ready on the foremast! Where the hell is Kusi?' They needed order. They needed to talk to one another, to all hear the same commands.

Madshaka ran forward, James aft. The helmsman, confused and terrified, was staring at the compass, keeping the ship exactly on its prescribed course, not knowing what else he might do. James wanted to tell him to round up when the fore braces were cast off, but he had no way of telling him that, so instead he took the tiller in his own hand and pushed the helmsman aside.

He eased the helm to weather, looked down the deck, waiting for the foreyards to brace around. He had no idea how long the poor bastard had been in the water, how much distance they had put between themselves and him. With the steady wind, they had to have traveled a good cable or two just since he had come on deck.

'Brace the foreyards! Come on, man!' James shouted down the deck. It was total confusion. All of their carefully practiced drills seemed to be coming apart. Madshaka, for all his calm efficiency during

119

their earlier maneuvers, seemed to be in a frenzy, shouting this and that, waving his arms. Men ran in all directions, responding to his orders. Where in damnation was Kusi? He was half of the team, it was all going to hell without him.

'Brace the—' James yelled again. It was pointless. Madshaka was the only one who could understand him and he was too busy bellowing orders to even hear.

He put the helm down, began to swing the ship up into the wind.

The weather leeches on the square sails curled and then collapsed and the sails began to flog as they turned edge to weather. The ship continued to turn, carried by her momentum, up, up into the wind. The sails came aback, fell silent, and then the ship stopped.

She was not hove to. Her sails were in disarray, her rig threatening to come down around their ears, but at least the ship was stopped. She was no longer moving away from the man in the water.

'Madshaka!' James shouted with all his considerable voice, and finally Madshaka looked aft. 'Get the boat over! The boat!' He pointed to the jolly boat perched on the booms amidships. Madshaka followed his finger, nodded, and began to yell orders in one language, then another and another. Men left off what they were doing, cast off stay tackles and boat falls, hooked them to the jolly boat.

James handed the tiller back to the helmsman and raced forward. Madshaka was a *grumete*, a boat handler. He should go with the jolly boat.

James arrived in the waist just as the boat was lifting off under Madshaka's directions. Up and over the side it sailed, and then down into the water and the boat crew scrambled down after it.

'Madshaka, you go!' James said.

'Yes, you stay with ship!'

'Where the hell is Kusi?'

'We find him, you don't worry. He *grumete*, good swimmer.'

James felt his eyes go wide, his stomach convulse. He spun around, looked aft, realized how ridiculous that was.

'Kusi! It is Kusi gone over?'

'Don't you worry,' Madshaka said, and there was genuine reassurance in his voice. He trotted to the rail, swung down onto the ladder. 'I get Kusi, don't worry.'

CHAPTER 9

King James stood at the rail, watched Madshaka drop easily into the jolly boat's stern sheets, watched the bowman push off. With a word from the *grumete* the oars came down, pulled together, up again, pulled again. The men of the boat crew were from those coastal tribes that bred boat handlers, and they worked as a unit as well as any unpracticed crew could.

James watched the boat claw swiftly past the ship. It was just disappearing from his sight under the counter when Madshaka opened the shutter of the lantern he had brought, held it low over the water. James heard his big voice ring out, 'Kusi! Kusi!' and then he called something in Kusi's native tongue. James cocked his head aft, listened, strained to hear some reply from beyond the taffrail, but there was only the slap of water, the bang of gear aloft, and then Madshaka's loud voice again.

Cato and Joshua, Good Boy and Quash were hovering around, as they did when James was not too distant to approach. He turned to them. 'How did Kusi fall overboard?' he demanded.

The four young men exchanged glances, shrugs. 'I

didn't see it,' said Good Boy, and that was followed by murmured concurrence from the others.

'We was up for'rd,' offered Cato. 'Kusi was all the way aft, I reckon. I didn't see him. Didn't even hear nothing. We was just talking and then that Madshaka started in yelling something to them others. We couldn't understand none of it. Didn't even know what was acting, at first.'

More nods from the others. 'Right,' said James. From overhead came a *whap whap whap* as a fluke of the breeze caught an edge of sail and flogged it against the mast. He leaned over the rail. From out over the dark water he could see the bobbing light, could hear Madshaka's voice, distant now, still calling out Kusi's name.

'We best get this rig sorted out,' James said at last. 'You men, get with your watches and we'll see what we can do.'

They moved forward, the five of them, calling out in English and waving and gesturing, and by that means got the sail trimmers to their stations. James stood on the main hatch, looked aloft, looked at the men lining the pinrails, the women keeping out of the way and holding their children back from being trampled in the mysterious goings-on of the men's work.

With pointing and pantomime James managed to communicate what it was he wanted, and the foresails were hauled around until they came aback and the helm put over and at last the ship was hove to properly, balanced there on the surface of the water. Lines were belayed, coiled down, and then there was nothing left but the waiting.

James walked aft, past the motionless helm. He

leaned on the taffrail. The jolly boat was no more than a prick of light out in the blackness, dimmer even than most of the stars overhead and going up and down with the swells. He could not hear Madshaka's voice but imagined he was still yelling. He shook his head. It was not good. If they had not found Kusi yet, James did not think they would.

Men began to sit at their stations, to talk quietly, but only a few. James could feel the ship's company overcome with that somber mood that follows a burst of excitement, the rush of an emergency. When people can do nothing in a crisis but wait, their spirits are dragged down to some low place, and only slowly do they climb up and out.

He had no notion of how long the jolly boat had been gone. They had never bothered with bells and half-hour glasses. Little grains of sand creeping through glass tubes were meaningless to Africans who ran their lives by the natural progression of dawn and noon and sunset. There was no mark of passing time, but still it seemed it had been quite a while before they finally heard the creak of the oars, the quiet drip of water from the blades.

James watched over the taffrail as the light from Madshaka's lantern grew brighter. Cato and the others crowded around, watching as well, and behind them word spread among the Africans and they too ran to the rail, looked into the night.

At last the boat was close enough to see the men at the oars, Madshaka aft, his big hand on the tiller.

'Kusi ain't there,' Quash said.

'Oh, damn, damn,' said Good Boy. A buzz ran through the others, and James imagined they were saying in their own way the same thing that the young Virginians had said. He remained silent. There was nothing to say. And he was not in the least surprised.

All that way across the Atlantic, and partway back, and the sea had finally swallowed poor Kusi up.

From behind, a wail, a shriek of anguish. James turned, saw the woman dressed in the curtain fall to her knees, tears streaming down her face. She fell forward, as if in supplication, and her back heaved with her sobbing.

Kusi's wife? His sister? James did not realize that the woman had had some special connection to the *grumete*. Why hadn't he known that? What other relationships were at play here, about which he was unaware?

The jolly boat passed below then; Madshaka's eyes stared ahead, never looking up at the many faces looking down at him. James turned and walked slowly to the gangway, reached that place just as the boat was pulling up below. Madshaka stood and stepped forward and scrambled up the boarding steps as if he had been shot upward from the boat. Stepped through the gangway, somber, frowning. He met James's eye, shook his head.

'We couldn't find him.' His voice was subdued, hoarse from the shouting. 'We searched, back and forth, a mile back . . .' A catch in his throat and then from his big, dark eyes, tears, and he said, 'We looked, Captain, God bless us, we looked as much as we could.'

'I know you did,' James said softly. Silence on the deck as the boat crew climbed up and through the gangway. There was nothing more to say. On the quarterdeck the woman still sobbed with abandon.

'Let us get this boat back aboard and get under way,' James said. Madshaka nodded, turned to the others, gave orders in a quiet tone, and the men shuffled off to their several tasks.

James stepped aft, watched Madshaka handle the swaying in of the boat. Kusi. He had hardly known him, of course, had known him just long enough to like him. James pictured his strong, dark body floating down, down, farther than he could imagine.

The boat came in over the rail and settled down on the booms, and with a few quick words from Madshaka men scrambled in and unhooked the boat falls and the stay tackle.

Kusi had been half of King James's link to the others, but now he was gone. It occurred to James that he could never again know what anyone aboard the ship was saying, only what Madshaka told him they were saying.

There was no reason that that should make him uncomfortable, but in a vague and undefinable way it did.

The men of the *Elizabeth Galley* were sweating, streaked with grime, their eyes white holes in smoke-blackened faces. Most were stripped to the waist, neck cloths tied around ears. But they were smiling, genuinely happy.

For the two hours since dawn, as they sailed before a steady quartering wind under topsails and top-gallants, with courses hanging in their bunts, the men had drilled at the guns, the former *Plymouth Prize*'s guns. For an hour they had run in and out in dumb show, pretending to handle cartridges, pretending to ram home, pretending to load with round shot, pretending to stand clear of the recoil.

They had been fast to begin with: the men were all seamen and all seamen had some experience with great guns, and they had grown faster still in an hour's work. So after that first hour Marlowe had ordered the powder up for some drilling in earnest, live firing by broadside and gun by gun. There was nothing that inspired the men to a fine, fighting mettle quite as much as the concussion of the muzzle blast, the gun flinging itself back against the breeching.

The men were ready for blood and riches, and they were in good form to garner both.

An hour of blasting away, expending precious powder and round shot, military stores that Marlowe had purchased with his own coin, and he figured that was enough. 'Well done, men, well done,' he called down to the grinning, eager crew. 'House your guns and I will turn you over to Mr Bickerstaff's good offices.'

The men swabbed out and leaned into train tackles and hauled the guns up to the gunports and lashed them in place. Then Bickerstaff, well versed in training gentlemen in swordplay, stepped down into the waist, drew a cutlass from the barrel, and told the others, those designated to boarding parties, to do the same.

He arranged them in long lines, ignored their silly grins, their snide muttering, and began to instruct them in sword work. First position, second position, third position, the men moved awkwardly through the drill. It seemed pointless to them, but they followed directions.

It had once seemed pointless to Marlowe as well, who knew the unsubtle slash and hack of hand-to-hand combat along a ship's deck. But Bickerstaff had almost bested him once with a sword, the only man to come that close since Marlowe had mastered the blade, somewhere around his twenty-first year.

Since then Bickerstaff had taught him the subtleties of swordplay, had made him an even better swordsman, along with teaching him to read and write, to move in proper social circles.

Once Marlowe had said, while reading through one of Bickerstaff's folios, 'Hoa, Francis. Hear this. "I pitied thee, took pains to make thee speak, taught thee each hour one thing or other. When thou didst not, savage, know thine own meaning, but wouldst gabble like a thing most brutish, I endowed thy purposes with words that made them known." That sounds like us, don't it?'

'Humph,' said Bickerstaff. 'You a Caliban to my Prospero? No, I think not. Not entirely, in any event.'

Not entirely. But still Bickerstaff had helped Marlowe become the man he was, transformed him from a pirate most brutish. That, after Marlowe had saved Bickerstaff from death at the hands of the pirate raiders – Marlowe's fellows – who had overrun the ship aboard which he sailed. In one manner or another they owed each other their lives. Their friendship ran deep now. It pleased Marlowe to be able to provide Bickerstaff with the time and place for his intellectual pursuits.

Why Bickerstaff continued to go to sea with him was a mystery.

The clash of cutlasses forward. Bickerstaff had the

men facing off in pairs, thrusting, parrying, slow and methodical. Their ardor that had been sparked by the great guns had not cooled, and Francis was having to keep them in check, making them go slow, lest someone be accidentally slashed thanks to his partner's enthusiasm.

Spirits were high. That was good. They would need spirit in reserve.

'Sail, ho!'

The cry from the lookout at the main topmast crosstrees, and all sound, all motion on deck ceased, every eye turned aloft.

'Broad on the starboard bow, and just hull down! A Spaniard, maybe!'

Don't give me your buggering opinion, Marlowe thought. He scowled, looked down at the deck. A buzz ran through the men in the waist. They ran to the rail, peered over, but they would never be able to see the distant ship from the deck.

Forward a few hands had the audacity to leap into the shrouds, start scrambling aloft. 'Forward, there! In the fore shrouds! What the hell do you think you're about?'

The men froze, looked back at Marlowe. He could see their sheepish expressions down the full length of the deck. He was about to call for Griffin to take their names when he saw the acting boatswain was leading the men aloft.

'Mr Griffin, what in the hell are you about? Get out of those damned shrouds, all of you! This is not a damned bloody pirate ship, do you hear me? You do not go aloft without my orders!'

Slowly the men climbed down again, trying inconspicuously to glance at the horizon before they

129

lost their vantage. Marlowe looked outboard, muttered curses. He had overreacted to the men in the fore shrouds, but this was a damned awkward situation, and his temper was short.

'Sir?' It was Fleming, standing before him, saluting. 'I beg your pardon about that, sir, they was in the rigging before I even seen them.'

'Not your fault, Mr Fleming, never think on it.'

'Sir, would you like me to take a glass aloft? See what I can of this fellow?'

'No, no. Good of you to offer, but I will go myself.' He shed his coat, slung the big glass over his shoulder, and pulled himself into the main shrouds and headed aloft, the familiar feel of thick cable-laid shrouds in his hands, thin ratlines underfoot. He was less accustomed to making this trip with shoes, and as the shrouds grew closer together near the masthead he had to squeeze his toes against the soles to keep from stepping clean out of them.

Boots, he thought. I must wear boots, or no shoes at all. He clambered up over the futtock shrouds and up onto the main topmast shrouds, leaving the round maintop below him as he climbed.

Perhaps I shall roust out a pair of slop trousers, he thought.

He was taking pains not to think about what he might see through the glass, what he might do about it.

He arrived at last at the main topmast cross-trees. The lookout had already shifted himself to the larboard side to give Marlowe the favored vantage. Marlowe nodded, planted his feet on the crosstrees, an arm through the topgallant shrouds, and ran his eyes along the horizon.

She was there, broad on the starboard bow, just as reported. Topsails, topgallants, a glimpse of courses on the rise of the swell. Ship rigged, of moderate size, perhaps a bit bigger than that. Sailing roughly the same course as they were. All that he knew without looking through the glass, which meant the lookout knew it as well.

At last he lifted the glass to his eye, twisted the tube until the horizon was sharp, and swept it along until the sails jumped in the lens. Now a whole new world was revealed to him. On the rise he could see gunports, but not so many of them. Oiled topsides, glinting every now and again in the morning sun. Spritsail, spritsail topsail, everything shipshape, but not man-of-war fashion.

No, he would not have taken her for a man-of-war, even if she had not been flying the French merchant-man's ensign off her ensign staff.

A French merchantman. She's bound back to France, no doubt, he thought, her hold bloody well loaded with goods traded from their new allies, the Dons, and all their bloody rich colonies to the south.

A fat prize. He could make their whole voyage that morning. If he was a privateer with a letter of marque.

'Hmmm,' he said gravely. 'Spanish. Frigate or perhaps a two-decker, hard to tell. But a man-of-war, to be certain.'

He took the glass from his eye, glanced at the lookout. There was disappointment on his face. Resignation. That was it, as far as Marlowe could see.

'Damned luck, eh?'

'Aye, sir, damned luck.'

Marlowe slung the glass back over his shoulder, grabbed the shrouds with both hands and swung outboard, then with his foot found the ratline on the futtock shroud and stepped down. Less than a minute later his feet hit the caprail on the quarterdeck. He stood there, balancing with one hand on the main shrouds, looking down at the men in the waist.

'What of her, sir?'

Griffin. Damn that man. He was done.

'Spaniard. Man-of-war. Frigate, I take her for, but could be a two-decker.'

More buzzing through the crowd of men forward, and Marlowe did not think it was all concern for their possible capture. The Elizabeth Galleys were experienced enough seamen that they would think to wonder why a powerful man-of-war did not seem interested in them, why they weren't tacking and coming in pursuit, and what a Spanish man-of-war was doing knocking around the coast that far north in the first place.

'Helmsman,' Marlowe called, hoping to distract them. 'Let us make our head more northerly, two points. Mr Fleming, I'll thank you to see to the braces.'

'Aye, sir! Come along, you lot, hands to the braces!'

They went, but they were not happy about it, and Marlowe could see glances shot back his way. The high spirits of the morning were gone, replaced by something more sullen.

God, if I get away with this, I shall not be able to do it a second time, Marlowe thought.

He had to find James and come to grips with him

and end it. Then back to Virginia, his good name restored, and the proper papers for a privateer.

He thought of that fat French merchantman, an easy run south of them. They all might have been wealthy, with a morning's effort.

Oh, Lord, if I do not end this soon I shall find myself pirating again, like it or not.

CHAPTER 10

Elizabeth invited Billy Bird in, led him into the kitchen, made a pot of chocolate herself, since there was no one left in the house to do it for them. They sat at the big table in the kitchen – somehow it seemed appropriate to entertain Billy there rather than in the more formal sitting room or drawing room – and she poured out their cups.

Over the steaming brown drink Billy told Elizabeth in some detail (and, she guessed, some augmentation to the truth) about his last voyage to Madagascar, his wrecking his ship on the reefs off that island coast, while sailing the Pirate Round.

Billy Bird had a true sailor's knack for yarning, and Elizabeth listened to the tale with interest, but her mind was mostly elsewhere.

'So I said to the fellow . . .' Billy paused. 'Lizzy, are you attending at all? You seem quite distracted, and this a tale the likes of which you will not hear again soon. I do hope you are not thinking on your precious Marlowe. I'll warrant he has not had half the adventures that I have.'

'Faith, Billy, there is no one could be more interesting than you. But, yes, I am distracted.

Thinking about my people. Wherever could they have gone?'

'Ah, your African is a crafty one, can take to the woods and disappear whenever they choose. Can't find them unless you have dogs. The people here think these Negroes are docile and broken, but that is a dangerous mistake.'

'No, Billy, I fear you are wrong. Perhaps those natives in the jungle are of such a kidney, but our people here are like children, sometimes. I fear they cannot shift for themselves. What if now they have lost themselves in the woods?'

Billy shook his head. 'I have sailed with many black men, you know, and they are as fierce as any. More so, in fact, because if they are caught there is no chance of pardon. It's the gallows for them, between the flux and flood of tides.'

'Thank you, Billy. You put my mind at ease.'

'Forgive me, dear Lizzy. I meant only to say that you should not worry. Your people will be fine.'

Then, as if in answer to this prediction, a knock on the kitchen door, just a light rap, and then the door swung open enough for Caesar to stick his head warily through.

'Mrs Marlowe? You all right?'

'Yes, Caesar, yes!' Elizabeth said, jumping to her feet, greatly relieved to see the old man. 'Come in, come in! Wherever did you go? Where are the others?'

'We went into the woods, ma'am. They can't find us, without they have dogs.'

'I should not be so sure. And in any event, they will be back with dogs, and soon, I fear.'

'That's right,' Caesar agreed. He couldn't have

heard Dunmore's threat, he just seemed to accept this as a given. 'Some of them others, they down at the houses, gettin' their things together. I come back for mine, and Queenie and Tom and Plato is outside. Poor Lucy's still in a state. Queenie says she'll get her things as well, if that's all right with you, ma'am?' Queenie was the cook for Marlowe House, Tom and Plato the occasional houseboys.

'Of course, let them come in.'

Caesar opened the door, beckoned to the unseen people, and a moment later Queenie and Tom and Plato shuffled in, sheepish, apparently unsure of their reception.

'Oh, Queenie, boys, I am so relieved to see you,' Elizabeth said, and that seemed to go far to ease their minds.

'I'm sorry, ma'am, for all this trouble—' Queenie began, but Elizabeth shook her head, interrupted, saying, 'It is never your fault. It's that bastard Dunmore, has been him all along. But whatever are we to do?'

'Well, ma'am . . .' Caesar began, glanced at the others for encouragement. Queenie nodded her head.

'Well, Mr Marlowe always said we was free, so we reckoned we'd head to the woods, hide out until we can come out safe again. Ain't like we're running, 'cause Mr Marlowe, he always say we can go if we want . . .'

None of the freed slaves had ever tested this promise. None had wanted to, and they understood as well that there were not many places that they could go.

Caesar was clearly unsure of how their plan would be received.

'Of course. There is nothing else for it,' Elizabeth said, to the others' obvious relief. 'First we shall need food . . .'

'Beg pardon, beg pardon . . .' Billy Bird stood, wiped his mouth elaborately with his napkin. 'Pray, forgive me, but these are intrigues I do not need to hear. By your leave, my dear Lizzy, I shall be off. I am at the King's Arms for another fortnight or so, should you need my services. Until then' – he stepped around the table, took up Elizabeth's hand and kissed it with a flourish – 'I say adieu!'

He grinned, nodded to the others, and was gone. Elizabeth did not think he was gone forever.

'Food, ma'am?' Queenie brought her back to the present.

'Yes, yes. Take whatever you can. You know better than me what is in the pantry. Plato, run down to the slave . . . your quarters there and bring back five or six more men. We shall take all the guns and swords and such from the drawing room, and the extra powder and shot from the cellar.'

'Guns, ma'am? Mr Marlowe's guns?'

'Yes, the guns that belong to Mr Marlowe and myself. Do you not see a need for them?'

Caesar and Tom exchanged glances. This was a largesse they had not expected. 'Oh, yes, ma'am,' said Tom. 'We surely could use them, if you could see fit to part with them.'

'Of course. Now let us round these things up and be gone. I do not know when Dunmore and those other sodding bastards might be back. There is not a moment to lose.'

Elizabeth felt strong, in charge of the situation, and it was a good feeling. Things could not proceed without her to organize them, to issue orders; these poor people would be in an utter state of confusion. She understood how Thomas felt, standing on his quarterdeck, seeing things happen in reaction to his spoken word.

Queenie and Caesar turned their attention to the pantry and the cellar. Elizabeth led Tom to the drawing room where a majority of the guns were kept, everything from battered old muskets to lovely fowling pieces and matching braces of pistols. Edged weapons too: swords, cutlasses, hunting knives. Thomas had taken the best weapons with him on the *Elizabeth Galley*, but he had amassed enough of a collection over the years that there was still an impressive arsenal remaining.

They stacked the weapons up on the fainting couch. Soon Plato joined them, leading a half dozen men from the former slave quarters who gathered up the weapons in strong arms, the food as well, and packed it all in sacks they had brought with them.

Elizabeth raced up to her dressing room, stuffed her warm cloak and other clothes into a pillowcase, then hurried down the stairs again and out back where the others were waiting.

'Very well. Let us go,' she said.

Embarrassed silence, looks shot back and forth. Then Queenie said, 'Bless you, ma'am, you ain't figuring on coming with us?'

'Of course I am.'

'This ain't your problem, Mrs Marlowe. Ain't no reason you should suffer this.'

'Of course it is my problem, it is all of our problem. I most certainly am coming with you. Now let us go.'

138

More looks, a few shrugs, and then the men hefted the sacks of food, slung muskets over shoulders, jammed pistols in belts and they all headed back toward the former slave quarters and the woods beyond.

Elizabeth could not have let them go alone. Billy Bird's assurances aside, she knew that they could not survive without her. These simple people needed her to show them the way.

They took to the woods, hiking hard along trails that Elizabeth could not even discern. Her skirts caught on the brush, and she found herself tripping over obstacles half hidden by the bracken, but she pushed on, keeping pace, unwilling to let her people face these hardships without all of the help she might be able to offer.

They came to a clearing, an open place in the woods where the grass grew waist high over a half acre or so. 'This looks a fine place to stop,' Elizabeth suggested. 'Set up some sort of camp right here?'

'Well, Mrs Marlowe, you right, no doubt,' said Plato. 'But maybe we best get a little further from Marlowe House. We ain't but a mile or so, and easy tracking through them woods.'

'A mile?' Plato had to be wrong about that; they were three miles at least, but Elizabeth did not want to argue. 'Very well, let us go on.'

It was almost dark, twilight after the long daylight hours of summer, when they came to another clearing, not unlike the first. Where they were in relation to Marlowe House, how far they had walked, Elizabeth had not a clue.

But her people obviously did. It was not an empty

139

field that greeted them, but one with a few crude tents already pitched, and firewood stacked up in a ring of stones. Four or five of the plantation's former slaves were there already. Three horses were staked out near the edge of the woods.

There were greetings all around, hugs, kisses, and from those who had come ahead, somewhat disingenuous enthusiasm at finding that Elizabeth had joined them.

And once it was full dark, once smoke could not be seen over the trees, the fire was stoked up and there was roast chicken and corn bread and potatoes. Elizabeth ate with an appetite she had not felt in some time. Her feet were raw and swollen and when she surreptitiously pulled off her shoes and stockings she saw that they were bleeding.

She could feel the muscles in her legs cramping up. It was not the distance, she did not think, however far they might have walked, but the hiking over broken ground that she was unaccustomed to.

Queenie came over, asked how she did, piled up some sacks filled with some soft thing for her to lean against. Took Elizabeth's feet in hand and rubbed them with a pungent ointment. Elizabeth wanted to protest, to insist that she not be treated like some lady of the manor, but Queenie's ministrations felt so good, and her feet hurt so much, that she kept her objections to herself.

'How is Lucy?' Elizabeth asked.

'Not so good, ma'am. She's terrible worried about King James. Had a notion something would happen, and now she blames herself for not stopping him.'

'I'll come and see her.'

140

'That would do a power of good, I reckon.'

Elizabeth stood, hobbled across the field to where Lucy lay in her tent. Her eyes were red, swollen from crying. She looked a wreck.

'Lucy?'

'Oh, Mrs Marlowe!' Lucy got to her knees, threw her arms around Elizabeth's neck. She began to sob again.

'Lucy, Lucy . . . James is a clever one, you know that, he'll get through this . . .'

'Oh, Lord, Mrs Marlowe, why ever didn't I stop him? I knew something was going to happen . . .'

'Now, Lucy, come along. You know you could not have stopped him. James is too proud to listen to anyone's warnings, you know that. Especially a woman's.' It was true. Nor was James alone in that. James and Thomas, two of a kind.

The people – thirty or more, in all – were circled around the fire, the orange light dancing off dark skin. Someone began to sing, soft, a rhythmic tune, words that Elizabeth could not understand. In her dumb fatigue it took her some moments to realize it was an African song, the words in the language to which the singer was born.

Lucy let off her embrace, sat back down on the blanket spread on the ground, and watched with Elizabeth, sniffling now and then.

The singing went on, high and clear, and at certain places the others would join in, a chorus, all their voices coming soft together, the beat steady and hypnotic.

They all knew it, though to Elizabeth's certain knowledge they were not all of the same tribe. Indeed, some of the younger ones had been born in

141

the New World, had never been to Africa at all.

Extraordinary, Elizabeth thought. They had already created some kind of an organized home, there on that grassy patch of wilderness. She imagined they were well versed in this, creating community fast, making a home wherever they landed, after the experience of being torn away from their real homes and villages.

She closed her eyes, let the warm sleep creep over her, felt herself being carried away with the rhythm of the singing. She began to understand, on some level deeper than conscious thought, why Thomas felt it was too dangerous a thing to try to hold such people in bondage, why Bickerstaff felt it was an abomination before God.

King James heard the lookout aloft sing out, and then Madshaka grinned wide, said, 'He say he see another ship, away, away.'

Madshaka turned and called down the deck, rapid bursts of language, one after another. Looks of relief, looks of anticipation, gratitude at the approach of salvation, fore and aft.

'I tell them, we see another ship. Get more food now. They very happy.'

James nodded. He resisted looking over the side, knew that they would not be able to see the ship yet.

Instead he looked aloft at the baggy sails, the shrouds and stays where the tar had worn away and the cordage shone white in patches like dried bone. This was a tired old ship. Chase was not possible. She could never run another ship down. The strong and brave men on her crew might overwhelm a victim, might take her easily enough, but the trick would be in getting close enough to board.

James turned without a word, began to pace quickly up and down the quarterdeck in an unconscious imitation of Thomas Marlowe. Think, think, think. Whipping his thoughts into some order, like turning a rabble into a ship's crew.

Priorities.

First, was this a ship worth attacking, was it a ship they might hope to carry? Was it a man-of-war, a slaver, a merchantman?

He stopped pacing, turned to Madshaka, who was waiting patiently for instruction. 'I am going aloft, see what I can of this ship. You get the heads of the tribes together here. Tell them what we talked about, how we take this ship for the food, just the food.'

'I tell them. But they want to vote on it, you know. Like the pirates do. Like we talk about.'

James paused, scowled. Anger sparked like a flash in a pan. Damn it all, damn their hobbling votes.

But, of course, Madshaka was right. He had been happy to have the full responsibility lifted before, when he did not want to make a decision. Now that he knew what course he wished to take he was not so happy to have his authority questioned.

So damn me too, for a false bastard.

'You right. You tell them what we talked about, make them understand we got to just take food. They can vote, but you try and see they vote right.'

'I tell them,' Madshaka assured him.

James stepped toward the shrouds, paused, turned back. Met Madshaka's eyes. 'You tell them.'

'I tell them.' Madshaka was not smiling now.

James held his gaze for a second more. 'Good.' He picked up the one remaining telescope and climbed into the main shrouds and then up aloft.

He gained the crosstrees and looked south in the direction that the lookout was pointing. They were in an area where one might expect ships of all kinds. Just the day before, James had thought he had heard gunfire to the west of them, broadsides and single guns going off. But it had been very faint, too faint to be certain. It had lasted about an hour and then there had been nothing more.

He had not bothered to mention it to the others.

Now he had the distant ship in sight and he raised up the telescope and looked through. It was not a very powerful glass, and there was a crack in the object lens, which was no doubt why it was left behind, but it did give James a somewhat improved view.

She was three or four miles away, downwind, but not directly. Ship rigged, about the size of the tobacco ships that sailed from the Chesapeake, perhaps a bit bigger. But a man-of-war? He really did not know. Climbing aloft he had thought that it would be obvious, but now looking at the ship he realized that he could not tell.

He lowered the glass, continued to stare south, his mind working on this new problem. Attack or flee? He pushed his thoughts into order. Either this ship was a man-of-war or it was not, and he could not tell one way or another.

If they attacked the ship, there was a chance they might all be killed.

If they did not get food in a day or so, then people would most definitely start to die.

The options were possible death versus certain death. There really was no decision. He stuck the telescope in his shirt and headed down again.

CHAPTER 11

King James poured a little trail of powder in the cannon's touchhole, stepped back, and gestured to the men on the train tackles to haul away. They pulled; the gun rumbled up to the gunport.

They were small guns, four-pounders, and of all the men aboard, James alone had any experience in loading and firing such weapons. He had not bothered training the others. It was pointless. They would never win a fight with guns.

He gestured for the ad hoc gun crew to stand clear, and when they were out of the way he brought the match down on the powder train. A hiss, a spark, and then the gun went off, blowing smoke out over the empty sea. It was not an attack. It was a signal. A cry of distress.

James looked aloft. The sails were hanging half in their gear, sloppy, flogging in the wind. The ensign was flying upside down. The ship looked very much as she had the first time he had seen her, coming through the capes. But this time the black men were not chained down in the hold. This time they were armed and crouching out of sight behind the bulwarks.

146

He looked at Madshaka, wondered if he himself looked as foolish as the *grumete* did. Madshaka's face and hands were painted white, with paint they had found in the bosun's locker, as were James's. They were wearing bits of the officers' clothes that they had collected from those men who had been wearing them: coats, waistcoats, breeches. Like the paint, it was enough to give the right impression from a distance.

James felt like an idiot, painted up in that way. But it had been his idea, and he could think of no other.

He looked up at Cato, stationed as lookout high up on the mainmast, could see he had nothing to report.

'Tell them to haul the gun in,' James said to Madshaka, and Madshaka repeated the words. An unshotted gun did not hurl itself inboard like a loaded one. James picked up the wet swab, thrust it down the muzzle, ladled powder into the barrel once more, then rammed wadding home and gestured for the gun to be run out again.

Once the distance between the two ships had closed, there would be no mistaking their ship for anything but what she was. All the scrubbing and brimstone in the world would not wash away the stink from a blackbirder.

If a blackbirder were to run down on a strange vessel, she would immediately arouse suspicion. If an approaching merchant ship were to see black men on a slaver's deck, they would haul their wind and bear away. No ship, save for a man-of-war, would knowingly approach a vessel that had suffered a slave uprising.

They had to get their victim to come to them.

More powder in the touchhole, the glowing match, and the gun went off again. The blast was still ringing in their ears when Cato called down. 'Hauling her wind, James! Here she . . . here she goes, staying now!'

'What he mean by that?' Madshaka asked.

'She turning, coming up to us. I guess she believe we a ship in distress.'

Madshaka smiled again, wicked, piratical delight. Translated James's words to the others, and they smiled as well.

'Tell them to get out of sight, behind the bulwark. We get aft, on the quarterdeck.'

The two men went aft and stood beside the lashed tiller, waiting, waiting. Tension undulated around the deck like heat from a furnace. The women and children were down below in the great cabin and the smaller cabins along the alleyway. They would not go back in the hold.

When the approaching ship's topgallant sails were visible from the deck, James called for Cato to come down. 'I think we set the foresail, you and me,' he said to Madshaka. 'That don't look wrong, that shouldn't scare them. Then we can close faster, get down to them.'

Madshaka nodded and the two men went forward, all eyes following them, not knowing what they were about. The yards were not braced perfectly, but close enough. They did not want to look perfect in any event.

James cast off the buntlines and the foresail tumbled down into a big, flogging sack of canvas, the lower corners still held up by the clewlines. He spun the weather clewline off the pin, let it run through his hand, and Madshaka took in the sheet as fast as he could.

The wind filled that half of the sail, bellied it out, and Madshaka could pull no more. James clapped on to the sheet and together they hauled away. They pulled together, in a steady rhythm, falling naturally into the work. Madshaka was a head taller than James, but both men were powerful, and soon they had the sail sheeted home despite the breeze's trying to tear the line from their hands.

They crossed the deck and did the same on the leeward side. The bow of the ship began to turn, her bowsprit pointing toward the ship coming up with them. James unlashed the tiller, brought it amidships, steadied the blackbirder on a course to intercept the Samaritan that was speeding to their aid.

Coming to our aid indeed, James thought. In a way you will never guess. 'You told them, we only going for food?' he said to Madshaka. 'And we ain't going to kill no one unless we have to?'

'I told them.'

The distant ship tacked and half an hour later tacked again, and by then she was hull up, no more than a mile away. With the foresail set and the blackbirder running with the wind between two sheets, the distance was dropping away fast.

Through the cracked telescope James could see figures moving around on the deck and he instructed Madshaka to wave his arms over his head, as if trying to attract their attention. There were not many people on the other ship, as far as James could tell, and he did not see very many guns. He did not think she was a man-of-war.

'Madshaka, tell them just a few minutes more,'

James said, and Madshaka hurried forward again, along the bulwark, speaking to the men crouched there.

A quarter mile from them the other ship rounded up into the wind, foresails aback. She was heaving to, as James had guessed she would. A moment later he could see a boat lifting off the booms. They would want to find out what the trouble was before committing themselves. If it was fever on board, for instance, the aid they would offer would be limited to floating supplies down to them in a boat.

The boat pushed off, pulling for them, and there was no alarm that James could see. By the time they realized that the blackbirder was not going to heave to it would be too late for them.

The blackbirder was making a good three knots with just her foresail set. She swept past the yawl boat with never a word to its confused crew, her bow aimed at the merchant ship one hundred feet away.

On the merchantman's deck, men were running like roaches, flinging off lines, but it was too late for them. Their foresails were bracing around, filling with wind, when the blackbirder struck, amidships, with a great rendering crash, smashing down bulwarks, snapping her own spritsail yard, sending a shudder like an earthquake through both ships.

The blackbirder was still driving herself into the merchant ship, the grinding, crunching, snapping still loud, when Madshaka wheeled his cutlass over his head and charged forward. He was screaming – it did not sound like words of any language – but the meaning was unmistakable.

From behind the bulwarks the waiting men sprung to their feet, raced after Madshaka, down the blackbirder's deck, up onto the bowsprit, out along that spar for a dozen feet, and then down onto the quarterdeck of their unhappy victim.

James ran too, as fast as he could, more angry with Madshaka for charging off than worried about the fight. There were no more than a dozen white men on the merchant ship's deck, terrified men, looking with wide eyes and gaping mouths at the black host, fifty strong, coming from the bowsprit above them and dropping to the deck, swords, cutlasses gleaming, all of them screaming in their alien and barbaric tongues.

James tried to push his way to the point of the attack but he could not get through the press of Africans racing for the bow and over onto the other ship. He leapt up on the foremast fife rail, craned his neck to see what was happening. Screams, white voices and black, blades raised overhead.

He leapt down again, raced around the larboard side of the bow, and clambered up onto the bowsprit that way, pushing his own men aside to gain his place. Up along the spar, hand on the forestay to balance him.

It was a slaughterhouse on the deck below. Madshaka was leading the charge aft, swinging his heavy cutlass like it was a twig, hacking away at any white man in front of him.

One of the crew threw aside the handspike with which he was defending himself, fell to his knees, arms raised in surrender, and Madshaka brought his cutlass down like an ax, catching the man right on the collarbone, all but cleaving him in two. He fell away and Madshaka jerked the weapon free, looked for the next man.

151

'No! No! Stop!' James shouted. 'No!' His voice could just be heard above the screams of the warriors, the shrieks of their victims, but it did not matter because not one of the men, black or white, could understand him.

He leapt down to the deck, hit the planks with his bare feet, took the shock with his legs. Warm, wet, he was standing in a pool of blood. There was blood everywhere, great splattered patterns shot along the white deck, pools, sprays of blood against the deck furniture.

Running, screaming, chaos, swords hacking at anyone who lived. James leapt forward, eyes on Madshaka's wide back. Madshaka's arm lifted again, cutlass in hand, and James grabbed it, spun the man around, his own sword under Madshaka's chin.

'Stop it! Tell them to stop it, or I kill you here!'

Madshaka's face was terrifying, subhuman. White paint and red blood and dark skin swirled together, and through it those eyes, dark and bloodshot and utterly wild. He was heaving for breath, and he looked at James with no spark of recognition.

But James too was just hanging on to control, and the fury in which he had killed the captain of the blackbirder was gathering against Madshaka. The shaking in his hand was transmitted through the steel of his sword. The point trembled an inch from Madshaka's Adam's apple.

The big man moved his arm, a quick jerk, and James almost drove his sword through his throat.

Then Madshaka let his arm drop and his whole body seemed to relax. He smiled. 'Yes, yes,' he said. He turned and addressed the men, shouted out, his voice commanding, cutting through what din was still echoing around the deck. He grabbed a cutlass-wielding African as he ran past, checked him, pushed him back against the bulwark, shouted something in the man's language.

Fore and aft weapons were lowered, voices silenced, and soon the only sound was the groan of the dying, the crunch of the two ships still locked together.

And in James's mind, he could see nothing but Madshaka's face, smiling through the paint and blood. It was the most hideous sight he had seen on that hideous day.

'Congratulations, Captain.' Madshaka was looming over him again, his face a mask of humble admiration.

'You bastard!' James hissed. 'I told you to tell them no killing unless we had to! You butchered them! You bloody butchered them!'

Madshaka frowned, shook his head. 'I told them. I told them many times, like you say. They go crazy.'

'You led them. You led them and you started them on this!'

Madshaka took a step forward so he was looking down at James, his voice low, little more than a growl. 'Look here, King James. You been too long with the white men. You don't remember how much these people hate. Maybe I go crazy too. I just get stolen from my home, remember. I just come across the ocean on the death ship. You just try to remember how you feel, twenty years ago.'

The two men stood, eyes locked. Madshaka said, 'When you kill the captain of that slave ship, I think then you remember.' He turned quickly away, moved down the deck, shouting orders in one language then another.

James stared out over the ocean. Madshaka was right, of course. Twenty years before there would have been no stopping him until every white man before him was dead. It was that same rage that had driven him to stick a knife in the slaver's captain, to make them all outlaws, pirates.

Here he was cursing Madshaka when it was his own lack of control, his own fury, that had led to their being at that place, adrift on the trackless sea.

He would not have balked at slaughtering slavers, plantation overseers. Was it because these men were sailors, merchant sailors, that he felt differently?

He shook his head. So much to do, so many considerations still before him. So much blood on his hands already. How he longed for the *Northumberland*, his little crew, the simple freedom of plying the Chesapeake Bay.

I am getting old, he thought.

Madshaka was rounding the men up, gathering them together aft. There was talk now, quite a lot of talk, vigorous arguments with hands waving and fingers pointing around, men shouting back and forth, heads nodding in agreement, faces screwed up in expressions of incomprehension.

James felt like he had no part of it, like he was not a part of the crew. But that was not right, he goaded himself. He was in charge, he was their leader, and until he had taken them to safety he could not abandon that.

He walked aft, stepped up on the carriage of a small gun, and shouted, 'Quiet, quiet!' Held his hands up over his head, and even though they could not understand him, the power of his voice, the commanding presence of a Malinke prince, brought the discussions to a halt.

'Madshaka, here.' The big man ambled over. 'Tell them they fought well, they should be proud.'

Madshaka translated and heads nodded, faces looking not joyful but satisfied.

'We have done what we needed. We have food now, and water, enough to get us home.' There was no need to mention the pointless slaughter. It was done, there was no changing that, and they would not be attacking any other ships.

'We have work to do now—' James continued, but one of the men cut him off, shouting out a question that met with murmured concurrence from several others.

James turned to Madshaka. 'He say, "Why don't we take this ship now? Why we go back in the death ship?" '

Why indeed? Before James could formulate a response that might make sense to that man, Madshaka translated the question to the others, and James could see more nodding heads, more agreement.

Why not? It was piracy, robbery on the high seas. But what would that mean to these people, who had been stolen from their homes and sold into bondage? They were victims of the most depraved kind of robbery. They were Africans, what did they know or care of the Europeans' customs and uses of the sea? Why should they ever think it was wrong to take a ship from white men, most of whom were dead?

Now Madshaka was talking again, addressing the assembled men. 'Madshaka!' James cut him off. 'What you telling them?'

'I telling them what you said.'

'No you ain't. What you telling them?' His fury was met by Madshaka's defiant eyes.

'I telling them they can vote. They can, can't they, or you calling yourself king now? King James?'

James held his eyes, did not let his expression waver, did not let his face reflect the raging inside. They could vote, he had agreed to it. In a moment of weakness he had said they would run things in the way of a pirate ship, and for his sins that was what they were doing.

Madshaka turned back to the men, delivered a few quick, clipped sentences; heads nodded all around, and then every man on the deck raised his hand.

Madshaka turned to James, gave him a hint of a smile. There was no need to translate the results.

'Very well. Tell them to go collect the women and children and whatever they want from the old ship. But first we throw these dead ones over.'

Madshaka gave the orders, pointed here and there, and men lifted corpses out of the sticky puddles of blood and carried them to the leeward rail and heaved them over the side. A dozen white men, slaughtered.

James closed his eyes. His head sunk to his chest. The nightmare went on and on and on.

It was with a great sense of relief that Thomas Marlowe stared through the glass at the ship, the battered wreck of a ship, drifting a cable length away. Relief, tempered with anger, regret, self-loathing, self-pity. A mixed brew, a rumfustian of emotion.

She was a mess, her spritsail yard broken, just the courses and fore topsail set. The smell told him she was a slaver. Reasonable deduction told him it was King James's.

She was flying her ensign upside down, was firing guns to leeward as a signal of distress, but Marlowe was not buying it. It was just what he would expect James to do, to lure them in. But he would not be fooled.

Now there would be an end to it, one way or another.

He could hear the muttering. The men at the great guns and the men at sail trimming stations and the men with pistols and cutlasses at their sides, ready to board, all murmuring, all expressing that discontent for which sailors were deservedly famous.

'What's the good of taking yon wreck, then? Bloody risk our necks for flotsam, not worth a sou.'

'It's them niggers, and Marlowe using us for his own good.'

'Ain't what I signed on for.'

'Nor me. Signed aboard a privateer, and Marlowe leaving off whatever he thinks looks like a man-of-war, and attacking some hulk.'

'It was Billy Hood was aloft then, said it didn't look like no man-of-war to him.'

They had too much time to think. Sailors would always get into trouble if they were given time to think. But in ten minutes' time they would be into it, some bloody work, and then it would be over.

The *Elizabeth Galley* had come up with the ship that morning, closed with her. Now she was hove to a cable length to windward. Marlowe would beat King James into submission and be done with it.

'We will not board?' Bickerstaff asked.

'We will not. Those freed slaves could be the death

of us, fighting hand to hand. They understand there is no quarter for them. Fight to the last man. But I reckon they know little of fighting with great guns. We'll stand off, give them a cannonading, hope they see fit to surrender.'

'You just said they would not call for quarter in fighting hand to hand. Do you think they will surrender under cannon fire?'

'No.'

'I do not see any but two men aboard, and they look to be white men.'

They did look to be white men, and the view through the glass only strengthened that impression. They waved, beckoned, but Marlowe stood firm, did not make a move one way or another. He could picture the hordes of armed black men crouching behind the bulwark, waiting for them to board.

He would let King James take the first shot, and then he would decimate them.

Ten minutes passed, and no one other than the two white men appeared on the deck. At last they seemed to realize that Marlowe would not be sending any aid, or laying his ship alongside. They disappeared down the leeward side of the blackbirder, and a moment later came pulling under her counter in a yawl boat, making for the *Elizabeth Galley*.

'Some of you men with small arms, come with me.' Marlowe stomped forward to the gangway, armed members of the boarding party behind him. He could not imagine how the two men in the yawl boat were part of some trick, but he would never, never be caught unawares.

The yawl boat pulled up below the boarding steps

and the two men scrambled up the side, not asking permission to board, not even bothering to tie the boat to the chains. It drifted well clear of the *Elizabeth Galley*'s side even in the few seconds that it took them to come aboard, but they seemed entirely oblivious, as if gaining the *Galley*'s deck was the singular goal in their lives and nothing beyond that mattered.

They stopped short at the gangway and looked around at the armed men, the row of guns, Marlowe and Bickerstaff. Their eyes were wide, bloodshot. Their hands were trembling. Marlowe had seen that look on men's faces before. It was how they looked when the pirates were done with them.

'Who are you? What ship is that?' Marlowe asked, but the men just looked at him, dumb.

'What ship is that?' he asked again.

One of the men uttered a sound. It was not a word that anyone could tell, but it seemed to break the impasse in his throat and suddenly sentences were spilling out. But they were not English. Marlowe shook his head to indicate that he did not understand; the man kept on talking.

And then Bickerstaff interrupted, talking the same language, and Marlowe realized it was French. The man turned to Bickerstaff and continued his explanation. At last Bickerstaff turned to Marlowe.

'You were right. This is indeed James's slaver. Or was, in any event. These men are from a French merchantman. They were attacked by black pirates, he says, from this ship.' He nodded toward the slaver, drifting away downwind. 'The whole crew was butchered, save for them, because they were in the yawl boat when the attack took place. I must say,

James is a man of some passion, but I am hard pressed to see him killing unarmed sailors in cold blood, white though they may be.'

'As am I. But I was surprised to hear of his sticking a knife in the blackbirder's captain, so it is hard to know what he is capable of.'

Bickerstaff turned and asked the French sailor a question, nodded as the man made a lengthy reply, and then turned back to Marlowe.

'They abandoned the slaver, which is in a wretched state, and took the merchantman. They carried away the merchantman's chief mate, who was also in the yawl at the time of the attack.'

'Oh, God!' Marlowe threw his head back, let out a long sigh of aggravation that built into a frightening shout as he tried to vent his pent-up anger. Then he turned to the first officer.

'Mr Fleming, pray see that the Frenchmen have some rum and some food. These poor bastards need some drink, some strong drink, I should imagine. Mr Griffin, clear the longboat away and tell off a boarding party.'

The slaver, her sails all aback, had drifted a good distance downwind from the *Elizabeth Galley*. An hour later she was safely to leeward when the fire that Marlowe and the boarding party had built in her hold worked its way through the main deck and up the rigging, turning the entire stinking affair into a great pyre.

James and the others had tried to clean it. Marlowe could see the signs: the recently scrubbed decks, the faint trace of sulfur in the hold where they had apparently lit brimstone to drive out the even more horrid smells of people locked down for weeks.

But he could imagine that all the cleaning in the world would not wash away the horror that that ship carried aboard. They must have been glad to be rid of her. In her state she would not have carried them back across the ocean.

Now he and Bickerstaff stood together on the *Elizabeth Galley*'s quarterdeck, all the way aft, out of earshot of the helmsmen or any of the crew. In the gathering dark they watched the bright column of flame that rose above the hated vessel and danced across the ocean swells.

Damn that ship, Marlowe thought. He hated her as much as James must have. Damn her, she was the cause of all this.

Burn, you whoreson villain.

'Ah, Francis,' he sighed. 'It was all so much simpler once. Being a barbarous pirate has its advantages, you know. When one operates beyond all morality, then one never suffers such a thing as a moral dilemma.'

Bickerstaff sniffed. 'Neither does a frog or a maggot concern itself with moral considerations, but I couldn't recommend the life. But let me ask you, Thomas, why were you so distraught to find they had carried off the chief mate? It did not seem to be from concern for his safety.'

'No, faith, it was not. The damned annoying thing is now they have someone who can navigate. If it had just been James I reckon he would have tried to beat to the eastward against the trades – he would not guess at any other way to fetch Africa. We could have run him down easy, put an end to this. As it is we are but a day or two behind them.

'But now they have someone who knows the sailing route. Now they can sail to Africa and we have

161

to follow and I have to convince these dogs forward that we're doing it all for their greater glory and riches, or who knows what they will do.'

He stared at the flames. They were all he could see now, with night having come full on them while they talked.

CHAPTER 12

Frederick Dunmore wheeled his horse around, took in a three-hundred-and-sixty-degree view of Marlowe House, the big white plantation house, deserted, the barn that waited for that season's harvest, the row of slave quarters, abandoned.

But not slave quarters at all, of course. Houses for free Negroes. All trim and neat with paint and shingles bought with the wages that Marlowe paid and laid out in the circular pattern of an African village. Some were white, some were crazy colors, reds and blues. Some had African symbols painted on their walls. It was the most egregious kind of effrontery. He spun his horse again, could not bear to look on it.

Twenty or so men – well-to-do planters, their overseers, indentured servants, even some common mechanics and laborers – had now joined him in hunting down the escaped Negroes. They were gathered on the big lawn that stretched away from the back of the house, relaxing, waiting. The dogs raced all around the grass, barking, howling, tearing up this and that.

Between his legs Dunmore could see the wide

163

black smudges from his saddle that stained his white breeches. Mud was splattered over his white socks. A constellation of little back holes spread across his dust-covered coat where sparks from the pan on his firelock had floated down and burned through the fabric.

But the clothing did not matter. He was happy to see the hard use it was getting. It was evidence of the great effort he was exerting in routing out this plague on the colony.

The people were starting to listen to him. They were starting to listen to reason.

Dunmore wanted slavery gone, abolished, made illegal. He did not wish to ever see another black man in America. Could not understand how the others failed to see that they were importing a plague, paying good money to bring into the land the means of their own destruction. Soon there would be more blacks than whites. And then, agitation, more and more liberties for the Negroes.

And then, with the lower sort of whites, inbreeding. Inbreeding. It was intolerable.

He turned again and looked at the Negroes' houses. Neat, even comfortable and homey. Unbelievable.

Sailing to London, years before, his ship had been caught in a storm, midocean, a wild, disorganized blow with the wind boxing the compass and big seas rising up from all directions, knocking the ship first here and then there. Lightning from every quarter. It was a black, freezing madness.

Dunmore had never forgotten that storm, coming as it had mere weeks after his own steady life had been blown to ribbons. It seemed then such a perfect physical manifestation for the rage that ran wild in his head, coming from all quarters, overwhelming him from directions in which he was not even looking.

'You men!' he shouted 'Those niggers' houses! Burn them!'

Glances back and forth, questioning looks. The storm in Dunmore's head raged harder. 'They built these houses with money that was not theirs, by law! I say burn them!'

A few of the men, the overseers and mechanics, got to their feet. They would do it, willing or not.

Oh, I am so very brave while Marlowe is off to sea, Dunmore thought. Man enough to burn his property, threaten his wife.

Coward!

But what other approach? What good could he do if Marlowe put a bullet through his head? Who would carry on with his mission? Had to be done that way, most effective, doing it for his race, a greater good.

The storm raged, lashed at him.

'Hey! Here comes Powhatan!' someone yelled, and everyone stopped and turned. Those men that were lighting torches for burning the Negroes' homes dropped the materials, stared out toward the woods.

A single Indian was approaching them, dressed in buckskin, musket in hand, moving at an easy trot. His name was not Powhatan, of course, but no one knew what his real name was, and rather than ask, everyone just called him after that long-dead chief. He never seemed to object.

He was a sometimes scout, sometimes guide.

165

Dunmore had finally broken down and engaged him for this business.

They had been hunting the Negroes for a week, forging out into the woods with dogs and horses, charging over trails and slashing through bracken, but they had found nothing. The dogs had picked up trails, sure enough, had set up great choruses of baying, had raced off like they had a fox treed, but it had always come to naught.

The damned Negroes had been leading them astray. Dunmore finally smoked it. They were sending a few of their men out to lay false trails, doubling back, splashing through streams, creating long meandering trails that dead-ended far from wherever it was the rest of them were hiding.

It was pointless. Hire a savage to catch a savage, Dunmore had concluded at last. Those Africans and their jungle ways. Perhaps a Red Indian could find them. He had all but given up hope that white men and dogs could.

He spurred his horse and rode toward the Indian, as did some of those others on horseback, wealthy planters who by tacit understanding were part of the decision-making cabal. They reined up around Powhatan and the red man looked up at Dunmore, and Dunmore alone, because Dunmore was the one who had put the gold in his hands.

'They about three miles from here. In a meadow. Tents, fire. They have scouts out in the woods, maybe what you call pickets. I can show you. But no dogs. That is why you don't catch them. They hear the dogs, lead them away from the camp.'

'Damn it!' Dunmore said, and almost added 'I knew it!' but since the dogs had been his idea he did not. 'Very well. We will leave two of the more useless ones back with the dogs. McKeown, that lazy Irishman, and that big fellow. Let's get the others ready to go.'

'And no horses,' Powhatan said, 'we not surprise them with horses.'

The other men on horseback, wealthy planters all, looked at one another, uneasy, and Dunmore knew that they did not wish to go on foot. Three miles in and back was a long way for men used to riding. And being on foot put them at the same level as the laborers and mechanics. It actually gave the Indian, practiced woodsman that he was, a certain superiority.

'No, we need the horses. Can't hunt them down without the horses. The speed they give us, and the fear they bring to these Negroes, will more than make up for a want of surprise.'

Powhatan shrugged and leaned on his musket. It occurred to Dunmore that the red man probably did not care one way or another about this fight. That did not matter, as long as he played his part.

Ten minutes and they were ready to go, Powhatan in the lead, the lower sort on foot following him, and then the men on horseback, feeling like the crusaders of old.

A crusade indeed, thought Frederick Dunmore. A God-given mission to rid this New World of a terrible and growing plague. A chance to murder my own demons.

It was amazing. Elizabeth could hardly believe how the people settled into their new life out in the woods, living like Indians, hunting, gathering edible plants, tending fires. Less than a week after fleeing Marlowe House and it seemed as if they had been living in that clearing for a year or more.

She tried to help. She wanted to be a part of it, in a useful way, but the other women seemed to feel it was their job to take care of her, to not let her expend any effort.

And she quickly discovered that there was precious little that she could do in any event that would have been of help.

She was not without skills; she could write a neat, round hand, could organize a formal dinner with the skill of a field officer, could lay out, plant, and tend a gorgeous garden. She kept all the books at Marlowe House with great accuracy. She could satisfy a man in any way he might wish – intellectually, socially, carnally – but none of those skills found a practical application there in the Virginia woods.

It was embarrassing. Even more so when she recalled how she had been certain these people could not get on without her.

All this she considered as she walked back up the now-worn trail from the stream to the camp. In her hands, two buckets, the water sloshing over her skirts and soaking through to her skin. It felt good in the heat of the summer morning. The smell of the pines was pungent. Birds flashed by, here and there, no longer concerned by the presence of these new creatures of the forest.

From the fields, the peal of children laughing, women singing at their work.

'Here, Mrs Marlowe, let me get that.' It was Plato, stepping up behind her, easing the buckets out of her hands even as he spoke.

168

'Plato, no, I am perfectly capable.' She held tight to the handles, tried to pull the buckets back. Water spilled over the rims.

Plato pulled against her. 'Please, Mrs Marlowe, it ain't proper . . .'

'Plato, damn it . . .' At that, the young man let go of the buckets, just at the moment that Elizabeth had redoubled her efforts at pulling them from him. She stumbled back, knew she was going down, tried to retain her dignity in that instant when her balance was lost, but it was too late. She landed hard on her posterior, the buckets tumbling over, soaking her completely.

'Son of a bitch!'

'Mrs Marlowe, Lord help me, I—'

'Never you mind, Plato.' She struggled to her feet, fending off Plato's help. Her wet, heavy skirts clung to her legs. She kicked one of the buckets out of her way, ignored the pain that shot through her toe.

Plato looked miserable, desperately unhappy about what he had done, quite at odds with the Plato of a few moments before, strutting around the camp on guard duty, one of Thomas's best fowling pieces over his back, a brace of pistols thrust in his belt.

Awkward as he might be in rendering domestic help, Elizabeth was impressed with the skill he had displayed in the kind of Indian-style warfare that they had been carrying on with Dunmore and the others.

It was a war that she and the other women had only heard about. It took place miles from the camp and involved not fighting so much as leading the searchers and their dogs on wild-goose chases.

'Here, let me fill those for you again,' Plato said, bending over and grabbing the buckets. Elizabeth

169

had been about to do the same, and if she had not anticipated Plato's move they would have knocked heads. She was grateful that she had seen it coming; slamming their skulls together would have been the end of it for her.

Plato grabbed up the buckets, smiled, and was heading for the stream when they heard a commotion at the far end of the camp, something happening. He dropped the buckets again and he and Elizabeth trotted off, Elizabeth holding her skirts up from her ankles, much encumbered by the heavy, wet cloth wrapping around her legs.

Two of the scouts were back, Wallace and George. Ashanti. Skilled woodsmen. They could move like deer through the thick bracken, disappear into the undergrowth. They had been a big part of keeping the white searchers away.

Now they came trotting into the camp with an urgency that they had not displayed before, waving the others over to them. They were already talking when Elizabeth reached the edge of the crowd.

'They coming again,' George said. 'No dogs. Saquam is leading them.'

A murmur ran through the crowd gathered around the scouts.

'Who is Saquam?' Elizabeth asked Plato.

'An Indian. A scout. The white people call him Powhatan.'

'Why is he helping Dunmore?'

'Don't know. Money, I reckon. Saquam has friends who slaves. He's helped some escape, but he'll do pretty much whatever someone will pay him for.'

Caesar spoke up. 'Body of me! Saquam will find us,

all right. Dunmore and them others couldn't, with their dogs, but Saquam can.'

'That right,' Wallace said. 'We go, try to lead them off, but you get ready to move. Get ready to move fast.'

The scouts turned and headed back for the woods and the group surrounding them broke like a flock of birds taking flight. People ran to their tents and began knocking them down, began gathering up supplies, loading up the few horses they had. Amazing, to see the speed and coordination with which the camp was broken. Elizabeth had never felt so useless.

'Queenie, Queenie.' She stopped the former cook. 'Where are we going?'

'No wheres, I hope. Maybe them men can lead that Dunmore away again, and we can set back up. But if we gots to move fast, well, we ready, and we have another place, higher up in the hills, about six miles. We can keep going, right back into Indian country.'

Elizabeth watched the former slave as she lashed her tent into a tight bundle. They were being pushed further and further back. Was this the answer, to keep retreating? Could they just live like this forever? She certainly could not. And if these people went to the woods for good, then for all practical purposes Dunmore would have achieved his goal of eradicating them.

Something had to be done, some new route explored. But what?

And then, a muffled shout, a swirl of activity at the far end of the meadow. George, racing across the tall grass, waving his arms, pointing toward the far woods.

'They coming, a mile away, or less. We ain't gonna fool them, Saquam know we here, he's leading them right along! We gots to go, go!'

Then Tom was standing on a pile of tents, calling, 'Them with muskets, come here! We set up for them, drop them when they come into the clear, slow them down some!'

'No!' Elizabeth pushed through the people until she was standing next to Tom. 'No! No killing! Listen to me, you have done nothing wrong, and when Mr Marlowe gets back you will be able to go back to your homes. But if you shoot white people, you will never be able to return!'

Murmuring voices, glances exchanged back and forth. Would they think that this was the limit of her dedication, that when it came to killing those of her own race she would no longer side with them?

If some did think that, they were not the majority. Someone yelled, 'Let's go! No ambush!' and heads nodded and the people dispersed.

Tom met her eye, gave her an angry, distrustful look.

'It is better this way, Tom. I gave you the guns to hunt and defend yourselves. An ambush is not a defense.'

He held her eye a moment longer, then turned and walked off.

Plato came running up, a sack over one shoulder, a canvas roll balanced on the other. It took Elizabeth a moment to recognize her own tent and clothing. She was not even aware that someone had packed it. 'Mrs Marlowe, we gots to go.'

The field was nearly deserted, more than half the people had already melted into the woods, heading in-country to some new, prearranged destination. Those who remained were gathering up the last of their possessions: cookware, food, scraps of clothing.

From the woods, not so far away, the pounding of hooves on the soft pine needles of the trail. A charge at the camp, an attempt to catch them before they disappeared again.

Elizabeth and Plato turned, ran toward the woods, toward the barely distinguishable trail carved through the undergrowth by animals or Indians or both.

Into the dark woods, the cool woods, nearly blind in the shadows after the brilliant light in the field. Plato just ahead of her, running with confidence, moving as if he were bred to woodcraft, Elizabeth with skirts hiked up, running, trying to watch Plato, the trail ahead, the hazards underfoot.

Behind them they could hear the horses. They had reached the meadow. She could hear voices, loud with outrage. 'They are getting away, they are goddamned getting away!' A gunshot, at what she could not imagine, perhaps fired into the air in impudent anger.

Further into the thick wood. She could hear the stream to her right, quite a wide stream, could see the gap in the trees that its passing made. They were moving up a gentle hill, not too steep, but Elizabeth's breath was coming fast. She wondered how long she could maintain that pace.

And then her foot came down on some imperfection in the trail, a hole left by an animal, perhaps, or an overturned rock. She felt her ankle wrench to one side, twisting beyond where it was meant to twist, and the pine needles and the young ferns coming up at her as she fell.

'Uuff!' The breath was knocked from her as she hit the ground, her ankle, still caught in the hole, twisting harder. 'Ahhhhhh!' She clenched her teeth, muffled the building shriek of agony.

Plato was ten paces ahead when he realized she was no longer behind him. He whirled around, ran back down the trail. 'Mrs Marlowe, Mrs Marlowe, you all right?'

'Yes, yes, I am fine. Help me up.' She could run on the ankle, she was sure. It would hurt, but she could do it.

Plato wrapped a strong hand around her arm, lifted her. Not so far behind they could hear orders shouted across the field, instructions for the hunters to fan out, to head into the woods. Elizabeth stood on her good ankle, the twisted one held just off the ground. Not so bad. The pain was going away already.

'All right, all right,' she said, more to herself than to Plato. She put her wounded foot down, slowly, eased her weight onto it. Lightning shot through the bone. The pain rushed up her leg, wrapped itself around her brain, made her head spin, drained the strength from her body like pouring water from a bucket. She felt herself twisting as she fell, the muscles in her arms and her legs no longer responding to her wishes.

Plato eased her down and she leaned back on her elbows, gulping air. Her ankle was throbbing, thumping like a drum, but as the weight came off, her mind cleared and she could think again.

Plato looked back toward the field, his eyes wide, afraid, his face filled with indecision.

'Go, Plato. Go,' Elizabeth gasped.

'No, I can't leave you . . .'

174

'I'll be fine. They don't want me . . .'

She didn't know if that was true, actually doubted that it was. They would have her in jail for something – harboring runaway slaves, giving guns to Negroes, something – but at least they would not drag her from jail and hang her, she did not think.

Plato looked down at her, clearly unconvinced. He lifted the canvas tent from his shoulder, tossed it into the woods, flung Elizabeth's dunnage after it. He reached down and grabbed her under the arms and, in one deft, powerful move, hefted her up and draped her over his shoulder and headed up the trail.

Her ankle hurt unbearably, and for a moment the pain masked Elizabeth's pure outrage, but not for long.

'Son of a bitch! Put me down! Put me down right now, you bastard!' she hissed, but Plato wrapped his arms tighter around her thighs.

'I'm sorry, Mrs Marlowe, I'm sorry, I'm sorry,' Plato kept repeating, his genuine contrition quite at odds with the manner in which he was carrying her.

She could not recall a more humiliating moment, and she had had some fine ones in her short life. Her ankle screamed in pain with each jar from Plato's long gait, her blond hair dragged on the trail and was kicked up by Plato's heels as he ran. It was like the Rape of the Sabines. She could just picture her arse sticking up in the air right next to Plato's face.

She thought about Thomas, how he would react if he saw this. Wondered whether he would laugh or beat Plato to death.

He would laugh, the son of a bitch, damn his eyes.

Plato moved off the trail, slowing as he threaded

through the trees. The low branches and under-growth tugged at Elizabeth's hair. And then the stream came into sight from Elizabeth's odd perspective. She craned her neck up, looked back in the direction from which they had come, but thankfully none of their pursuers were there.

Plato forged into the stream, his feet kicking water up into Elizabeth's face. She sputtered, spit, wiped her face. Across the deeper part, the water up to Plato's knees, and then up against the stream. Plato was moving slowly now, fighting the current. It was cool and quiet, but for the sound of the water, and in the far distance Elizabeth could hear the hunters once again.

Up and up the stream, around the larger rocks that parted the water as it ran down to the piedmont. It was slow going. Elizabeth's hair dragged in the water. Her ankle was growing numb.

She was aware of Plato's breathing, his gasping breath, his slower pace as he plunged uphill, up-stream. He slipped, almost went down, but recovered and continued on.

They came to a dark place on the river, where thick overhanging branches draped down almost to the surface, in some cases actually in the water. The stream was twenty feet across. The water broke around a big rock and flowed past on either side, the saplings and larger pines crowding along the banks.

Plato ducked low. Elizabeth felt the branches sweep over her buttocks and back, felt the sharp pine needles through her clothes. Plato gasped, 'I gots to put you down now.'

Before she could brace for the pain Plato swung

her off his shoulder, held her in his arms as if she were a bride at the threshold, and then knelt down in the deep spot in the wake of the rock.

The water was cold, blessedly cold over her ankle, dulling the pain. She gave a quick gasp as cold water seeped under warm clothing. Plato sank down, down, the water coming over their waists, their chests. At last he was on his knees, still holding her, the water up to their necks.

The pine boughs draped over the stream and it was as if they were in a little room, with the rock forming one wall and the tree branches the other three and the roof as well. Peering out through the clusters of green needles, they could see into the woods on the far shore, maybe fifty feet.

'I can kneel on my own,' Elizabeth whispered, and Plato gently eased her down. Her ankle was hurting a little less and the water was a buffer to the jarring and it was not so bad. Her skirts were heavy, wrapping around her legs, and they made her awkward movement more awkward still. But finally she was kneeling as well, on a flat rock right next to Plato, half floating in the dark water, staring out of their little room at the patches of sunlight and shadow that dappled the woods.

It was no more than a minute or two before they heard them, men coming up the trail, talking loud, voices of hunters who had no fear of being hunted themselves.

'Keep your eyes open, keep your eyes open, them Negroes is hard to see!' someone yelled, and then the sound of brush being beaten and then 'What's this! Mr Dunmore, over here!'

Elizabeth met Plato's eyes but neither spoke. The

hunters had found the tent and the dunnage. They knew they were on someone's trail.

'Come along, come along! Spread it out!' Dunmore's voice, and then men crashing through the undergrowth, coming closer. Elizabeth and Plato sunk a bit lower in the water until the stream lapped over their lips. Elizabeth was conscious of her breathing, aware of the noise it made, forced herself to take shallow, silent breaths.

They could see figures moving through the woods, following the stream, making a great noise as they went. They were on foot – the horses could not penetrate that thick wood – and they had no dogs, which was a relief. Elizabeth could see homespun coats, battered hats, and then the white coat and white breeches of Frederick Dunmore.

And another man. Elizabeth did not see him right off. Unlike the others he did not stand out in the woods, but seemed to blend into the browns and greens, squatting, examining something on the ground. Buckskin clothing, long black hair. Saquam, the one the whites called Powhatan. Better than a dog at tracking, less likely to be fooled. She felt her stomach sink, felt a flash of panic, willed herself to be calm.

'Hold up, hold up!' Dunmore roared, and the men stopped, no more than fifty feet from where the fugitives hid in the stream.

Dunmore pulled his long periwig from his head, revealing dark stubble beneath, and wiped his brow with his sleeve. It was the first time Elizabeth had ever seen him bareheaded. 'God damn your eyes, Powhatan, I thought you said we could surprise these niggers and take them in the field!'

Saquam stood, and with elaborate care turned to Dunmore. 'I said no horses. You ride horses through the woods, no surprise anyone.'

'Yes, well I say you did a damned poor job leading us to their camp. I can't say I'm certain where your loyalties lie, but I'll tell you this much. If we don't get any of those black bastards you'll see not another penny.'

Silence, save for the water rushing down the streambed, the breeze in the canopy overhead, the heavy breathing of hunters recovering their wind. Saquam turned and moved up the riverbank, slowly, stepping silently, looking at the ground as he moved. Thirty feet away, then twenty, and at last he reached the bank opposite them, ten feet at the most.

He knelt down, scooped water into his hand, drank, then scooped more and ran it over his head. He looked up at the trees overhead. Elizabeth watched, taking tiny breaths, motionless as she could be in the current. An odd expression came over the Indian's face, a puzzled look. He glanced up from the stream, his eyes sweeping along. And then he was looking straight at them, his dark eyes piercing through the tree boughs, searching into the dark. Fixed on Elizabeth, on Plato.

And then, to Elizabeth's surprise, he cocked his eyebrows, as if to ask 'What are you doing there?'

She looked at Plato. The black man gave a little nod of his head, gesturing upstream. And Saquam in turn cocked a single eyebrow. A hint of a smile played over his lips.

And then Dunmore's voice. 'Come along, come along, damn it!' Hats returned to heads, the tired

179

men huffed along after Dunmore, who was following after Saquam.

The Indian stood, and without a word headed off through the woods, upstream, leading the hunters away.

It was half an hour at least after the sounds of the hunters faded that Plato finally spoke. 'We best get out of here, we'll catch our death.' He stood, bending low under the overhanging branches, the water streaming from his shirt, and helped Elizabeth to her feet Her ankle was quite numb, and though there was a stab of pain when she put weight on it, it was not the overwhelming agony it had been. With Plato's help she hobbled to the far side of the stream and sat down heavily on the warm pine needle bed of the forest floor.

She sighed. 'Plato, I am absolutely useless to you people,' she said at last.

'Oh, no, Mrs Marlowe, that ain't—'

'Stop it,' she ordered, and Plato was silent. And then after a pause she said, 'Do you think you could help me get back to Marlowe House?'

'It would be hard. Hard on you, mostly, but yes, I could get you back.'

'Good. Then once it is safe we shall go. I am no more than a burden here. Perhaps in my own element I can be of some real help.'

CHAPTER 13

Madshaka sat on the quarterdeck rail, all the way aft. The three big lanterns on the taffrail were lit, as they were every night, because the Africans were not entirely comfortable with the darkness and the ocean all around, but he was in the shadows just below them.

He looked down the side of the ship, at the wake foaming white in the moonlight. He looked up at the sails, towering overhead, gray patches against the stars. Lovely, lovely, all of it.

Gone was the stinking hold, the smell of close-packed people and lingering death that had permeated the blackbirder. Gone were their worries over food and water. The French merchantman was stocked full of food and water, as well as clothing, wine, rum, and guns. Her hold was packed with silks and sundry other bolts of cloth, olives in barrels, hides, spices.

She was six days out of Havana, bound for Le Havre, or so they had learned from the mate they had taken hostage. Within those wooden walls were luxuries such as many of the people had never known.

It had been a nice day, a calm evening. They had stood on the deck for hours: James, Madshaka, and Cato, who had the watch, informal as it was. They said little. They did not have much to say to one another.

There was tension to be sure. No way to avoid that. James was no fool, he could sense the subtle shifts in power, but as long as he, Madshaka, was careful there would never be anything substantial enough on which to hang an accusation.

And even if James did suspect, who would he tell? Madshaka smiled at that thought. Cato? Good Boy?

From forward drifted the soft singing of the women as they finished their day's work. The people, the Africans, had no knowledge of ships, no prior framework into which they could fit such a thing as a sea voyage. For most of them their first view of the ocean had come when they were loaded aboard the blackbirder.

So rather than adjust themselves to life at sea, they adjusted life at sea to what they understood: the family units, the tribes, the rhythms of life on land, sleeping and waking and eating.

The women were up well before dawn, stoking the fires in the galley stove just as they might have in their own fire pits in their own villages. They cooked the strange food they had on hand, and fed their husbands and their children. In the late mornings they did their washing, singing their ancient songs while their children played around them, as their people had done for thousands of years in their native rivers.

And the men, rather than hunting or tending cattle

or clearing earth, stood their watches, trimmed the sails, laid aloft to fist canvas.

In the evenings they would build a fire in the portable cookstove and sit around it and sing and joke and tell stories, each to their own tribe, each in their own tongue. It was a genuine community, or a clutch of communities, a replica of their former life in Africa, only set on the alien, floating, wooden ship in the middle of the vast sea.

An hour before the sun set into the sea, the white mate came on deck, as he did every few hours, instruments in hand. He shuffled in his walk, head down, afraid to look at and possibly offend his captors. There were dark rings around his eyes, a few weeks' growth of beard. He had not bathed or changed clothes since his capture, and when he was not performing those duties for which he was kept alive he remained huddled in his tiny cabin.

As mad with terror as he appeared, he still went about his business confidently, as if having his familiar tools in hand allowed him to forget his nightmare circumstance. He laid his things gently on the deck, ran his eyes over the sails, glanced at the compass. He stepped to the weather rail and facing away from the setting sun manipulated his backstaff, measuring what, Madshaka had not a clue.

The others, the people dragged from the forests by the slave traders, looked on what he did as magic, as some kind of supernatural conjuring, but Madshaka knew that it was not that.

He watched the white man work his backstaff and heave the chip log over the taffrail and stick his little pins in the traverse board and stare at the stars with his nocturnal and he knew that they were just more of the white man's tools, the kind of inventions that were letting white men run unimpeded all over Africa.

Madshaka knew that the white man was directing their course to Africa, but he did not understand how. And though King James watched the man with a knowing eye, Madshaka suspected that he did not understand it either.

That was good. It was important that he did not.

At last the white man was done. He shuffled over to James, averting his eyes, as if James were some kind of real king, and muttered something that Madshaka could not hear. And then James turned to Cato and Quash and Good Boy and said something, and then finally said, 'Madshaka, we gots to wear ship. Get the people to their ropes.'

Madshaka nodded and trotted forward. This was the thing that made him uncomfortable. If the white man had said to him what he had said to James, would he have understood it? He could not 'wear ship' by himself. It was an unusual situation for him, to not be master of his environment. He needed James still, as much as he hated that notion.

Twenty minutes later the ship was turned and the white man had disappeared below and the black sailors had returned to their families and their dinners. The last vestiges of light disappeared in the west and along the deck drifted the soft singing of the women, each tribe to its different songs in its own language.

The embers burned low in the portable stove and the wind that blew along the deck and filled the canvas overhead was warm and steady and not a line needed tending. The clans sat together, the women

184

wrapped in the bright-colored silks and dyed cottons they had found in the hold of their prize, the children wrapped in cloth or running around the deck naked or curling up with their mothers, their shattered worlds secure again.

It was a comforting scene, a happy ship. When the sun went down and the manly shouting was done, then the women worked their influence on the people and it was peaceful again.

Madshaka did not know how long he had been sitting there lost in his thoughts. Long enough for James to fall asleep, long enough for the few people on deck to forget his presence.

At last a familiar form appeared on the quarter-deck, a man stepping aft.

'Anaka,' Madshaka called, softly. Anaka was the headman of the Kru. Madshaka's people. His word was law with them.

'Madshaka?'

'It's me. Come over here, Anaka, and talk with me.' Madshaka spent so much time speaking in so many languages it was comforting to talk his native tongue. Language was the bond here, the basis of trust.

'How are you doing tonight, Anaka?'

'I am well, Madshaka. Things are better now. The people are hopeful that we will see our homes again.'

'Yes, we will. I can promise you that. And we will be wealthy men.'

'How is that?' Anaka asked.

'This ship, all that is in it. She is full of cargo, you know, worth a great deal. We will sell the cargo and the ship too when we get to Africa, divide the money.'

Anaka was silent for a moment, considering this. To the people on board, the ship meant food, water, a safe vessel, one that did not stink of death. The idea that it could mean wealth had not occurred to them.

'How can we sell the ship?' Anaka asked at length.

Madshaka dismissed the question with a wave of his hand. 'I have spent many years as a *grumete*, you know that. I have learned the ways of these white men. I know how such things are done. That is why I tell King James we must take the ship, when he does not want to.' He paused for a moment and then said, 'How many Kru are on the ship? Kru men?'

Anaka thought for a moment. 'Twenty. About twenty.'

'Hmmm,' Madshaka said, but he did not continue.

'Why do you ask?'

'There is much more money to be made before we reach home, Anaka. Many ships on the ocean, and we have the warriors aboard that we could take them, take all of the valuable cargoes. Just think, after all the suffering we have been through at the hands of the white men, we could return rich, by taking back from them what they have stolen from us. It is a nice thought.'

A nice thought indeed, and in the dim light Madshaka could see that Anaka was thinking about it. 'Has King James said anything about this?' the Kru headman asked.

Madshaka nodded. 'We have talked of it. He is starting to think like me, that it is a good idea to enrich ourselves before we return. He knows a great deal about the ways of the pirates.'

'But he does not order it.'

'King James is a fair man. He does not want to

186

impose his will alone. He and I have discussed this at length.' Madshaka had to force himself not to smile. Lord, this was so easy! The ship was his to control, standing as he did between King James and the others, the only one who knew what both were saying, the sole conduit for communication.

Anaka was quiet for a long time as he thought about that. Madshaka knew from experience that the thought of easy wealth was hard for any man to resist.

At last he said, 'What should we do?'

Madshaka smiled. 'We are pirates now, you know? We vote on what we should do. We see a ship, we vote on whether or not we attack. King James will not order it, he wants to be fair, but he thinks like I do that we should enrich ourselves.

'Twenty Kru men, that is a lot, if they all vote the same. And you have influence over the other tribes as well.'

'That's true.'

'Will you talk to them? You speak other tongues, I know. Tell the others we can make the white men pay for what they have done to us. We can be free again, and we can be rich as well.'

'Yes, Madshaka, I will,' Anaka said, and there was determination in his voice. Anaka was now filled with thoughts of wealth. Anaka would talk to the others.

The headman hurried off and Madshaka remained on deck for a few minutes more, looking around, trying to see if there was anyone looking his way. The after end of the ship was lost in the darkness. No one around but the helmsman, and he was looking the other way.

He chuckled softly to himself. That had gone very

well. These others might not think of wealth, but he himself was no stranger to the notion.

He was an ambitious man, had once already worked himself into a position of real power and wealth before his ostensible partners had hit him on the head and sold him to the blackbirder. But he had not forgotten them. Their turn would come.

But first, pirating. By pure chance he found himself aboard a fast ship with a gullible crew of strong young men he could use as warriors. It was not an opportunity to be wasted.

When he was at last certain that no one knew or cared what he was about, he stepped forward and down the aftermost scuttle.

He was prowling now, hunting. He was aware of the power in his arms, his legs, the silence of his step, the strength that was there to be summoned instantly. He had seen lions before and they were the same, soft-footed, powerful. Nothing ostentatious, they did not need to be. When you were truly powerful you did not need to show it.

Down the after scuttle and down again to the lower deck, moving aft, crouched under the low beams, awkward for a man so tall, but still his motion was fluid. He was invisible in the dull light of the lower deck, his dark skin lost in the shadow. He did not expect to find anyone down there. The people stayed on deck as much as they could. They had had enough of ships' holds.

Aft, past the stacks of cargo, to the tiny cabins that lined either side of the stern section, one deck below where King James slept. It was all blackness there, save for the one feeble light that lit the white mate's cabin from within.

Madshaka stopped a few feet from the cabin door and listened. He could hear the man, breathing, making tiny movements. He could smell his unwashed body, the sharp smell of sweat, not sweat from exertion but sweat from fear. He wondered how long a man could live with that terror before his mind snapped. Perhaps he would find out.

He took a step forward, grabbed the latch on the cabin door and swung it open, slowly, slowly, letting the hinges give their menacing creak. Inside the mate lay on his berth, pushing himself back, back against the bulkhead, away from whatever new horror was coming to him, his bloodshot eyes wide.

Madshaka smiled, a broad smile, a look that he knew was terrifying under those circumstances. Reached to the small of his back and drew out his dirk. He let the light play off the long, thin blade, held it casually at his side as he stepped into the small space.

The white man shook his head in mute protest. Madshaka raised the knife, held the needle point under the man's chin.

'You don't want to die, do you, pilot?' Madshaka asked, softly, and the man shook his head again.

'I didn't think so.' He held the knife there for a moment more, letting the man consider the situation, then he withdrew the blade and sat back on his heels.

'Where you taking us, pilot?'

The man thought about it, as if the question were a trick. 'Kala—' he croaked, coughed, cleared his throat. 'Niger River Delta, Kalabari, like you say.' His English was heavily accented with French, but good.

Madshaka nodded his head, as if considering this

information. 'If I tell you to take us to Whydah instead, can you do that?'

'Yes.'

'And can you do it in a way King James don't know?'

The Frenchman looked confused, considered the question, then said, 'Yes . . . I don't think King James know the navigation. I don't think he know what I do.'

Madshaka nodded again. 'You take us to Whydah, then. You take good care with your tools, we have perfect . . . how you say?'

'Landfall?'

The smile spread across Madshaka's face again. 'Right. Landfall. You understand me, pilot. And you don't tell James, you don't tell anyone.' He raised the knife up. 'If anyone find out, I kill you, and I take a long time to do it. You believe me?'

The white man nodded, his eyes on the gleaming dirk.

'Good,' said Madshaka.

To Whydah then, and business to which he must attend. And when James found out who was really in command, it would be too late, too late by far for him.

CHAPTER 14

The night was black and still at that hour, somewhere around four o'clock in the morning, and it seemed as if there were no people left in Williamsburg, as if they had deserted the town, left it to the nocturnal creatures. It was the strangest sort of sensation, a floating, disconnected existence, something that Elizabeth was having difficulty adjusting to.

She slowed her horse to a walk when they reached Boundary Street at the western end of town and then stopped a block from the hulking shape of the Wren Building, that great brick edifice like an English country manor house. She listened, cocking her head this way and that, trying to discern any sound that was not crickets or frogs or any of the benign noise of the Virginia summer night.

There was nothing that she could hear, as if her horse were a raft on which she sat and drifted on a warm black sea.

Was it really necessary that she sneak into town this way? She had no idea. She had no notion of what was acting in the capital, what was being said about her, what accusations were being tossed about. She knew only that Dunmore had been able to run unchecked,

191

and neither she nor Marlowe had been there to counter anything that the man had said, and so it had probably gone hard for them.

It was possible that the law did not want her for anything, that there were no charges leveled against her, but she thought it unlikely enough that she did not care to be conspicuous. She had slipped out the back door of Marlowe House, kept to the shadows, moving, stopping, listening. She had no reason to think that the house was being watched, nothing beyond a visceral uneasiness, but such premonitions had served her well in the past and she took note of them now.

After a long moment of hearing nothing, Elizabeth climbed down from the horse, easing down on her still-sore ankle, and led the animal across the grass, far from the road, to the young trees that dotted the lawn in front of the Wren Building. The college had graduated its first class just two years before, and the trees had been planted just a year or so before that, so they were none too big, just big enough for Elizabeth to secure to them the reins of her docile horse.

She patted the animal's neck, then stepped back to the edge of the street and listened again, but again there was no sound. The two pistols she carried on loops inside her riding cape thumped silently against her hips as she walked; the dark hood masked her yellow hair.

She crossed Boundary Street at the head of Duke of Gloucester and hobbled east, keeping to the north side of that wide avenue. There was no moon, just a great dome of stars and the hazy Milky Way, and so every corner of the street was as dark as every other.

192

Still, she kept close to the buildings, close to the trunks of the trees, where movement would be less likely to be noticed, sailing along like a dark spirit.

She felt at ease, despite the need to be clandestine. It felt good to be back in a town, if such Williamsburg could be called. It had been a long time, a rough time.

The hike back to Marlowe House had been the worst.

Elizabeth and Plato had sat and rested in the cool forest for an hour, and their clothes were all but dry when they heard the hunters again, coming back down from their fruitless search. They had scrambled back into the thicker wood, pulling themselves into a dense patch of brush, wriggling forward as the branches scraped at their faces and hands and tore little rents in their clothes. They lay face down, watching as the men filed past, led by a visibly angry Frederick Dunmore.

Saquam trailed behind, his expression of indifference at odds with the scowls on the other men's faces. The Indian gave no indication of knowing they were there.

An hour after the sounds of Dunmore's party had faded in the east, Plato headed off into the woods, leaving Elizabeth alone with only a brace of loaded pistols for company. She spent a long time examining them, for lack of anything else to occupy her mind, holding them close to her face, studying every detail of the weapons, the muted colors of the flints, the ridges and valleys left where they had been chipped into shape.

When she could bear that no more she leaned back and looked up at the forest canopy, watched chickadees flashing through the trees in their frenetic bursts of flight, nuthatches hopping headfirst down the trunks, cardinals the color of fresh blood fluttering limb to limb.

Elizabeth secretly hated the woods, and all of her mental activity was calculated to prevent her from panicking at the realization that she was now alone in that wilderness. She was a city girl, born and raised in Plymouth and then a resident of London until the age of twenty-one. She felt more safe in those close-packed, filthy, crime-ridden streets than she did in the uninhabited forest. Tinling House – Marlowe House – was the most rustic living she had encountered and she was only now coming to embrace it. Being alone in the woods like that was too much.

The crack of a twig and she jumped, gasped, brought the cocked pistol around fast and only just avoided shooting Plato right through the heart at a distance of thirty feet. The black man stood, hands up, a look of surprise on his face. Behind him, George and Wallace. George carried two of Thomas Marlowe's fine muskets. Wallace carried what looked like a giant scroll, six feet long.

It was not a scroll, of course, but a litter: two stout pine saplings with a piece of number-two canvas lashed between them. Once Elizabeth had lowered the gun and eased the lock back down, Wallace laid the thing beside her and unrolled it and without a word he slipped his hands under her calves and Plato apologetically slipped his hands under her arms and they eased her onto the cloth.

Elizabeth wanted to protest, but that was pointless because she knew she could not walk all the way back to Marlowe House on her injured ankle. She tried to

194

find some position that made her feel like she was retaining some modicum of dignity, but there was no such thing. So she lay back, stiff, looking up at the trees overhead in the late-afternoon sun and tried to pretend she was enjoying the ride back down the trail.

Her arms were crossed under her breasts and she held a pistol loosely in each hand and that at least made her feel less like a helpless and pathetic child.

George scouted ahead, hurrying off down the trail, and they did not see him again until they came to the edge of the forest, three miles down. The hunters were gone. He had not seen anything that was worth warning them about.

They were actually on Marlowe's land by then, in the trees that marked the furthest point of clearing and cultivation. The big plantation house was a mile away and between it and their hiding place, and away to their left, were the former Tinling slaves' homes.

Wallace and Plato set the litter down and Elizabeth insisted that they help her to her feet. She stood on her good ankle and balanced against a mature oak tree and regarded her home in the distance. She cursed herself for not thinking to bring one of Marlowe's telescopes, but George assured her that he had approached as close as one hundred feet to the house and he could see no one there, inside or out.

They waited until it was dark, and while they waited Elizabeth insisted that they fashion her a crutch. Her dignity, which had been so under assault during the past week, would not allow her to be carried that last mile to the front door of her own home.

An hour after the sun set and it had gone full dark and there were no lights to be seen anywhere – no fires, no lanterns, no orange glow of pipes – the four of them emerged from the woods and covered the last mile back to Marlowe House.

Elizabeth had never in all the time she had lived there, as Mrs Tinling and as the widow Tinling and as Mrs Marlowe, been so happy to climb the steps of that porch and throw open the big front door.

She thanked the men for bearing her back home, asked them if there was anything more they might take back with them, but they said there was nothing they needed. She pressed one of Marlowe's telescopes on them, instructed them to keep an eye on the house, and they promised they would. She might be gone for a while, she told them, but when either she or Marlowe was back they were to send someone for news.

They would be able to return to their homes, she assured them, to their former lives as free men and women under Marlowe's protection.

The black men thanked her. They did not seem too certain.

For a full day she rested, let her ankle recover from its wrenching, let herself recover from her unwelcome sojourn into wilderness living. She watched from the window as Dunmore led his hunting party into the woods again, and then back out, with nothing that she could see by way of accomplishment.

They left Marlowe House unmolested They did not even approach. Even in his absence, Thomas Marlowe's reputation as a dangerous man threw a net of protection over his home, at least.

Around midnight she left Marlowe House. She had no notion of when she might return.

Nothing moved on Duke of Gloucester Street. At various irregular intervals buildings loomed up, square patches of black against the stars, inns and ordinaries, mostly, and taverns and a few shops and homes.

She looked down the length of the street. A light appeared, how far off it was impossible to tell, a yellowish, bobbing light. A lantern, carried no doubt by a man on horseback. The night watch, she imagined.

Elizabeth stepped into the side street that ran like a tributary off Duke of Gloucester, pressed herself against the high wooden fence that separated some private garden from the traffic. She stood silent, watching the light approach.

The rider went past on Duke of Gloucester Street, the light of his lantern illuminating his face from below. The night watch, on rounds. He looked bored, as well he might be on that uneventful night.

Once he was well past, Elizabeth stepped from the gate and hurried up the side street, past the back gates of private homes, past the blacksmith and the familiar brick wall surrounding the Burton Parish Church.

She turned again at the next corner and walked down that street, more of an alley, really, to where it joined with the streets bordering the long strip of village green. To her right, the church loomed high against the stars. To her left, and half a block distant, was the King's Arms.

She stepped quickly up the street to the front door

of the inn, looked up and down, saw nothing, and so stepped inside.

The King's Arms was not the finest inn in Williamsburg, but neither was it some mean hovel. Across the wide front room, scattered with tables and chairs, was a huge fireplace, clean and unused in those summer months.

A couple of candles burned in sconces on the walls, providing light for any of the inn's patrons that might come stumbling in at that late hour. They illuminated the place with a dull light and left deep shadows in the wake of the furniture. The ceiling was low and made up of heavy beams with wattle and daub between. The smell of pipes and roast beef and rum still hung in the air.

There was a desk in one corner, and on it an inkstand, paper, and a ledger that Elizabeth hoped would give her some idea of which room Billy Bird occupied, or indeed if he was still there.

She moved across the room and flipped the book open to the last written page, angling it so that the light of the candle fell across it. Names, rooms, receipts, all in neat columns. She squinted at the words, turned back a page, squinted again. There was Billy's name and 'Room Five' beside it and no amount yet received so she had to imagine that he had not yet left.

A footfall creaking on the floor and she froze, held her breath. Another, and the sound of a doorknob turning and she shut the book and stepped quickly back, finding the dark hall, stepping back and back into the shadows.

A door opened, another flickering light was added to the front room, and Elizabeth could see the proprietor in his nightshirt frowning and looking around. She pressed herself against the wall, silently pleading with the man to forgo making a complete tour of the premises.

What would that do for her reputation, to be found lurking around an inn at four o'clock in the morning? Whore. Whispers of Marlowe the cuckold. Would he believe her?

Then to Elizabeth's vast relief the proprietor shook his head and turned and went back the way he had come, satisfied that nothing was amiss. She closed her eyes and threw back her head and took several long and silent breaths, waited for the pounding of her heart to subside.

When at last it did she proceeded down the hall, the light from the front room reaching far enough that her now-accustomed eyes could see the numbers painted in white on the doors. One, two, three . . .

Four was the last on that floor and where five might have been there was instead a narrow staircase. Elizabeth climbed, slowly, easing her weight down on each tread to avoid creaking and avoid damaging her tender ankle. After what seemed a long time she came to the top of the stairs, the second floor, and there right across from her was a door with the bold number five.

She glanced down the hall, but it was dark and deserted, so she stepped across and paused at the door. She was not sure what to do, so she just stood for a moment and then gave the door the lightest of raps, not enough, she imagined, to wake Billy if he was asleep.

She listened, heard nothing from within, and then tapped again. Still nothing. She doubted that Billy had even heard her, but she did not dare knock louder. She shook her head, then felt for the latch on the door and slowly lifted it and swung the door inward.

A single candle on the washstand guttered in the last of its melted wax, but compared with the hall the room was brilliantly lit. A sleeping form lay under the cover of the bed, back to Elizabeth. She closed the door behind her, softly and slowly, then stepped across the floor. She put a hand on the shoulder, shook gently, whispered, 'Billy? Billy?' She did not want to startle him. It was never a good idea to startle a man such as Billy Bird.

Then the figure rolled over – long, thick brown hair, a pretty young feminine face, pert, milky white breasts – looked up through half-closed eyes, and said, 'Billy?'

Elizabeth jumped back in surprise. 'Damn,' she said, and then from behind, the click of a flintlock and Billy's voice saying, 'One move and I shall blow you away.'

She froze, knowing that Billy was quite capable of doing so. The girl in the bed pulled the blanket up over her, recoiled, began to scream, but Billy said, 'Silence!' and she bit off her cry.

'Let me see your hands.'

Elizabeth held her hands out from her side. She guessed that in the muted light Billy could see no more of her than a dark, hooded shape.

'Turn, slowly.'

She turned, saw Billy standing quite naked in the corner, the pistol held straight out. 'That is not the only gun you have been fooling with tonight, I take it?' she said.

200

Billy stared for a moment, unmoving, and then the gun dropped to his side and he smiled and said, 'Lizzy, dear, you are likely to get yourself killed, sneaking into a man's room like that.'

Before Elizabeth could answer, the girl in the bed said, 'What's this, then? Billy, what are you about?'

'Oh, Nancy, darling,' said Billy Bird as he snatched up his breeches and pulled them on, 'I fear you must be on your way, my love.'

'Now, see here—' the girl began, but Billy crossed the room quickly, clambered onto the bed, and pressed something into her hand. In the candlelight Elizabeth saw a dull flash of gold and Nancy became instantly cooperative. She climbed out of bed and began pulling her clothes over her firm and shapely body.

Billy met Elizabeth's eye and Elizabeth said, 'Very nice, Billy Bird,' and Billy smiled sheepishly.

In a minute Nancy was dressed. Billy gave her a kiss and a quick squeeze of her arse and said, 'We'll see you soon, my darling,' and then she was gone.

Billy turned to Elizabeth. 'Ah, Lizzy, I'm all but done in by that little bunter, but I think I can muster the energy yet.'

'As luck would have it, you need not even try. I'm here on other business.'

Billy stepped over to the little table in the corner, poured two glasses from a bottle of wine there, handed one to Elizabeth. 'Something involving that miserable Frederick Dunmore, I'll warrant?'

Elizabeth took a sip, sighed, said, 'Billy, I need your help. I am at a loss. I have no notion of what to do. My people are chased out into the wilderness and as long as that bastard continues his campaigning against them they shall never be allowed to return.'

'Not to mention that you are wanted as well for harboring them.'

'I am? What have you heard?'

Billy waved his hand. 'Oh, it's nothing. One hears rumors. But see here, you have come to the right place, as ever. I will take care of your little Dunmore. A tread on the coat, a few harsh words, a meeting arranged, and ten minutes after dawn he will never trouble you again.'

Elizabeth shook her head. 'No, Billy, you can't kill him. That won't help. There'll be more rumors, and surely someone will connect the thing to me. Not to mention the danger to you for killing a prominent citizen. No, there must be some other way.'

'Well, there are only two ways to stop such a man that I know of: kill him or disgrace him. You won't let me kill him, so I reckon we'll have to see what we can do to disgrace him.'

'You said there was something that happened to him in Boston.'

'Yes, but I fear I've not remembered any more than that.'

Elizabeth sat on the edge of the bed, suddenly very tired. Her ankle was throbbing. 'What can we do to find out what it was?'

'We shall go to Boston.'

Elizabeth looked up at him, taken aback. 'Go to Boston? Just like that?'

'Yes, go to Boston. My ship swims again now, in fine fettle, all predied for sea. There is no way we can find out what we need to know without we go and look for it ourselves. You couldn't do it through the post. You'd be an old woman before you were done, and even then I doubt you'd find out anything. No, we must go to Boston, discover the players in this drama, people who knew Dunmore, look them right in the eye, and ask them what is what.'

Billy's enthusiasm built as he spoke and soon he was carrying Elizabeth along with him, but still she was not certain. It seemed such a crazy thing to try.

'Oh, Billy—'

'No. Don't "Oh, Billy" me. It is Boston for us. That is how we will rout this foul demon out. After all our years of friendship, my dear Lizzy, I can do no less to help you.'

Elizabeth sighed again. It still seemed insane, but Billy's arguments were good, his enthusiasm infectious, enough so that she felt herself wavering, inching toward agreement. 'I will pay you for your services,' she said. 'Pay you in specie.'

'By which you mean that we will go together to Boston?'

'Yes.'

'Grand. But never in life would I have you pay for my services. Hell, you never made me pay for yours.'

Billy saw how unwelcome that joke was, and he stammered on. 'There are . . . a few considerations before we sail, but nothing of consequence. And now, my dear one,' he said, sitting beside her, 'will you not enjoy the luxury of my bed? It has been left quite warm for you.'

'Thank you, Billy, I will.' She unbuttoned her cloak and wheeled it off, catching Billy's glance down at her breasts as she reached behind her. 'And you, my dear friend, will comfort yourself on the cold and lonely floor.'

CHAPTER 15

A cannon fired some ways off, a puff of smoke, and a spray of splinters forward. King James looked up. The impact set up a great howling among the men clustered near the bow, shouting and chanting, like hitting a beehive with a stick, but it did not seem to James that anyone was injured.

It was a big Spaniard firing on them, a fat merchantman they had been chasing since sunup. It was not the way James had thought to spend the day.

First light and the lookout aloft had sung out and Madshaka said, 'He see a strange sail, right ahead of us.'

James's first thought was to turn away, to lose whatever ship that was below the horizon, but before he could say anything Madshaka was calling the men of the various tribes aft.

'What are you doing, Madshaka?'

'We vote.'

'Vote? On what?'

'On if we attack that ship or not.'

The men talked. They voted. Ten minutes later they opted for piracy. There was a surprising amount of unanimity in the vote.

James had not seen that coming, not at all. He felt as if he had been punched from behind. There had been talk behind his back, he knew that, and he did not doubt that Madshaka had been doing the talking.

For that matter, there may have been talking right in front of him. And even if he wanted to stop running the ship by vote, his explanation would have to be filtered through Madshaka, and James no longer trusted the *grumete* enough that he would try.

So pirates they would be, and all that James could do was to fulfill the peoples' wishes as best he could.

The Spaniard wore around again, presented a new broadside, fired, the iron smashing into the black pirates' ship.

She was well handled, or at least better handled than her attacker. She had tacked and wore around and fired round after round and skillfully eluded James's attempts to lay alongside and board her.

James looked down at the men at the tiller, yelled, 'Halloa!' They looked up at him and he pointed over the larboard bows and the men pushed the tiller to starboard.

'Madshaka!' James called forward, and when he had the man's attention he pointed aloft and Madshaka nodded and began to shout out orders for bracing around to the new heading. It was slow and awkward and by the time they were squared away on the new heading the Spaniard would no doubt alter course again, pelt them with another broadside, and gain a cable length or more on them.

James was standing on top of the quarterdeck bulwark. He could feel the warm oiled wood of the caprail under his bare feet, callused though they were. His loose sailor's trousers slapped at his legs.

Around his waist he wore a wide leather belt, his sheath knife in the small of his back, a vicious dagger hanging at his right side.

He was bare-chested, save for his leather jerkin, and two buff leather shoulder belts that made an X on his chest. Two braces of pistols were clipped to the belts. A cutlass hung at his left hip. His head was bound in red damask over which was a cocked hat.

He was a frightening sight, piratical in the extreme. That was the intent. He did not wish to kill anyone if he could avoid it. If the Spaniards could be frightened into surrendering, then they might be able to pull off a bloodless victory.

But it would do no good, in terms of frightening an enemy into surrender, if they could not close.

At first they had tried their *ruse de guerre*, acting as a ship in distress, the ensign flown upside down, the gun to leeward. The Spaniard had responded by flashing out more sail and bearing away. They had not been fooled.

And so it had devolved into a stern chase and the Africans had closed the distance, slowly, slowly, by virtue of their ship being the faster. But their ship handling, their sail evolutions, were so awkward and slow, thanks to inexperience and language barriers, that they could not capitalize on their speed.

In the bow, their own chaser went off but James did not even look to see where the shot fell. The gun crew had only just been trained. It took them five minutes to load and fire the gun. It was the first time that any of them had actually put their hand on a piece of artillery.

James recalled some story from the white religion like that, where men were trying to build a tower and none could speak the same tongue. He understood now the impossibility of it. The Spaniard had smoked their weakness and forced them into a game of sharp maneuvers rather than a flat-out race. Wear ship, pound them, and then sail away; wear ship, pound them, and sail away.

Tempers were getting short. There had been a fight already between warriors of different tribes. Madshaka had pulled them apart, using his great strength to shove them each to opposite sides of the deck where their fellows could hold them at bay. It was the first time that had happened since they had sailed away from Virginia.

James heard Madshaka sing out the word that he recognized meant 'belay!' and the braces were made fast. The bow chaser went off, the ball sent a water-spout aloft, not even close to the Spaniard. It was quiet again, settling into the chase.

It had been a long morning. James could feel the keen edge of his alertness growing dull. His mind began to wander and he let it go. Back, back to the *Northumberland* and the Chesapeake Bay and the simple pleasure of driving the sloop through blue-green water under flawless skies.

And then a shout forward and the Spaniard was wearing ship, turning her stern through the following wind, turning to bring her broadside to bear. One by one the guns went off, from forward aft, slowly. James guessed that each was being aimed by the gunner personally, who was walking aft from one to the other.

And a good shot he was. A ball smashed into the bow, sending a shudder through the ship. The next hit the fluke of the best bower with a thunderous clank like a bell dropped from a great height. Shrapnel screamed through the air and tore holes through the mainsail.

And just as the men on deck had recovered from the shock of it, breaking into raucous laughter with the ebbing of the sudden terror and pointing at the rents in the sail, just as they began joshing and shoving each other, a ball came straight through the forwardmost gunport and plowed into a knot of men standing by the foremast fife rail.

It happened so fast that some men were still laughing as those in the way of the ball were torn apart, limbs flung through the air, hot viscera pouring out of rent bodies onto the deck, blood pooling fast, running in streams for the scuppers.

Someone vomited, another screamed. James leapt down, hurried forward, and he and Madshaka met each other at the scene of the carnage.

James paused for a second to look over the damage. Four dead, three wounded, and one of those would not live. And the fife rail was smashed, the lines in a great tangled mess. The pull of the topsail and topgallant sheets on the shattered wood threatened to wrench the last tenacious bits of the rail right out of the deck, and then the chase would be over.

He was more worried about that than he was about the dead men. There was nothing to be done for the dead men.

He grabbed up the severed legs on the deck at his feet and hurled them over the side, yelled, 'Madshaka, tell them, clean up this!'

And then one of the Africans was shouting, pointing, waving a finger at James.

'He say, these Kru, his people,' Madshaka translated. 'They have death ceremony, don't throw in sea.'

James shook his head. 'Tell him this is a battle. No time for that,' and as Madshaka spoke to the man James grabbed the shattered body of one of the dead men, slick with blood, clothes saturated and still warm. He looked into the dark and lifeless eyes, and then with two steps was at the rail and the body was over the side.

And then the Kru warrior was there, his cutlass in his hand, waving it at James, screaming, and James jerked a pistol from his shoulder belt and held it out, straight-armed.

A ball from the Spaniard struck the side, just aft of them, made them stagger. The man stopped his advance, but his shouting did not diminish.

'Madshaka! What you tell him?'

'I tell him what you say, this a battle, no time for ceremony. He say, "Later, don't throw man in the sea!"'

James looked at the furious African over the length of his pistol and wanted nothing more than to squeeze the trigger. No time for damned barbaric ceremonies, not now.

He lowered the gun. Barbaric ceremonies? How had those words ever come to his mind? 'Tell him to do what he wants.' He turned to Cato and Good Boy, who were behind him, and said, 'Fetch up selvages and handy-billys and let us get these sheets squared away.'

And so it went on through the morning, with the big Spaniard wriggling further and further from their grasp. At noon the women, who had been taking shelter below with the children, poked their heads on deck, and seeing that there was no immediate danger of a fight, prepared dinner on the portable oven.

It was hopeless. James wondered if the others realized as much. He climbed down from the bulwark, stiffly, his joints protesting, and sat on one of the small guns aft.

One of the women brought him a plate of food and he was able to give a smile by way of thanks and then set it down on the deck and did not look at it.

They had to break off the chase. They would never catch this one, and there was always the chance of one of the Spaniard's shots doing real damage.

But what to say? Giving up was never good for maintaining the aura of command. James was intimately familiar with the pride of the African warrior. It had been his pride, once. He knew that admitting defeat did not sit well with them.

If he could only explain the situation, then they would understand. But he could not. He could only tell Madshaka and hope that Madshaka was accurately relaying his words.

His dinner grew cold and the turmoil in his mind grew more chaotic and the Spanish merchantman hit them again and again, but each impact was less devastating than the last as each was fired from a further distance.

Then he decided, he would just tell them. In a fight such as this he had the authority to break off the chase if he chose. No voting. That was the pirates' way.

He stood and sought out Madshaka, and as he did, the lookout aloft cried out and all heads turned to the main topgallant.

A pause, and then Madshaka stepped aft and said, 'He say there another ship, behind us, away off.'

James nodded. This would change things, in one way or another. 'Keep the ship on this heading. I'm going to go up, look myself.'

He grabbed up his telescope, jumped into the main shrouds, and headed aloft, glad to be leaving the quarterdeck below him and all its problems and considerations. Over the maintop and up, his weapons slapping against him as he climbed. They had a good, solid feel. He liked the weapons. They did just what he wanted them to do. Gunpowder and lead and steel did not dissemble.

At last to the main topmast crosstrees. The lookout greeted him with a smile and a nod and pointed right astern and said something that James of course could not understand.

James put the glass to his eye, pointed it aft. He found the newcomer right off, she was nearly hull up. Against the hazy horizon it would have been tricky for the lookout to spot, and James imagined that he was not looking too carefully in any event, with the excitement going on below and ahead of them.

He looked for a long time at the sails, not speaking, not moving, just looking.

It did change everything, that much was certain.

Now they would not just be letting the Spaniard go, they would be running themselves. How to explain to the pirates below that they were no longer the hunters, that now they were the prey?

How to explain what it meant to their hope of survival that Marlowe had found them at last?

* * *

211

The Elizabeth Galleys had heard the distant sound of great guns not long after first light, and it drew them like carrion birds to the smell of death. Mr Fleming had had the watch when the first dull thud came soft over the horizon. He had sent down to the great cabin to inform Marlowe and to ask his permission to crack on more sail.

Marlowe had come up on deck to find the men already aloft, already laid out on the yards with hands on gaskets, ready to cast off and let fall.

They had been under easy sail all night because Marlowe did not want to risk sailing right by King James in the dark, though only Marlowe and Bicker-staff knew that. He was not surprised to find the men so eager to spread canvas, but that was some damned cheek, he thought, laying aloft without orders from him, and decided they could wait a moment longer.

'Aloft, there! What do you make of yon ship?'

'Topgallants sometimes, on the rise, sir! Fine on the starboard bow,' the lookout called down, 'but there's not beyond that!'

Only one ship to be seen from that vantage. Could be a man-of-war exercising her guns, but Marlowe did not think so. Not many men-of-war bothered with such things.

'Very well, Mr Fleming, let us set all plain sail.'

Fleming stepped forward, called out the orders, the words flying from him like some great pressure had built up behind them. Canvas tumbled from the yards, men leapt to backstays and slid to the deck, sheets were tallied aft and belayed while others ran away with the topgallant halyards. The men fell to the tasks with a willingness and speed they had not demonstrated in some days.

'What think you of this?' Bickerstaff stood beside Marlowe on the quarterdeck as one after another the studding sails were hauled up and set to draw.

'Two ships in a fight of some sort. A running fight, by the sound. Men-of-war, perhaps, if this European war has reached this far already. Pirates? Privateers? One of those, I should think.'

'In any of those cases,' Bickerstaff observed, 'there is not so great a chance of one or the other being a legal prize for us. A man-of-war or another privateer would not care to share their spoils. A pirate might make more trouble than is worth. Do you think these fellows have thought on that?'

Marlowe looked at the men aloft and on deck, the fast, efficient handling of the gear, the high spirits, the absolutely piratical gleam in their eyes, the avarice that shone in their smiles. 'No, I do not think they have thought of anything but what they might plunder in the next few hours. Let us hope for the sake of ourselves that there is something for the taking. These men are eager for some reward. I would not put it past them to chuck us both overboard if there is not, like it was our fault.'

With all canvas set and drawing and trimmed with the skill of an eager and expert crew the *Elizabeth Galley* quickly overhauled the distant ships. It was an hour before noon when they were finally visible from the deck, an amazing feat, given that those ships were also carrying everything aloft that they could. But the *Galley* was fast, with a clean bottom, and everything about her was calculated for just this thing, running a potential prize to ground.

The men were crowded in the bows, craning their necks over the rail, and even those on watch found some reason to be forward, some work there that needed immediate attention. Marlowe would let no one go aloft who had no real business there. That kind of permissiveness led to chaos. That sort of thing was for pirates, not privateersmen.

Or, in their case, pirates who believed themselves to be privateersmen.

'Mr Fleming, let us clear for action,' Marlowe said at last. It had to be done and the men needed something to do. 'And when that is done let us serve out dinner and an extra tot as well.'

Marlowe shed his coat, took up his telescope, headed aloft. He had to go, though he dreaded what he might see. He felt like a man with a toothache, putting off his trip to the barber-surgeon, not sure what was worse, the pain or the cure.

He settled in the crosstrees and focused the glass forward. The furthest ship was still all but hull down. She was a big one and that meant she had to be a merchantman because a man-of-war that big would not be running from a pursuer.

The nearer one looked to be a merchantman as well. He watched her wear around, trying to dog the heels of the other. An awkward evolution, yards bracing around slowly, unevenly, fore, main, and mizzen not working with any coordination.

Marlowe felt unwell, unwell in the pit of his stomach. He felt a decision looming, one that offered no good choice.

'Mr Fleming!' he called down. 'Pray send one of those Frenchmen up here, one of those fellows we rescued!'

Five minutes later the Frenchman settled beside him. There was still a craziness in his eyes and

Marlowe knew it would be with him all his life. The unredeemable shock of seeing things his mind could not endure. He would die a drunken, broken wreck in some port town: Port Royal, Plymouth, Brest. They were all the same. Marlowe had seen it so very often.

He put aside such irrelevant thoughts, handed the man the telescope and pointed to the nearest of the two ships. The Frenchman put the glass to his eye and focused it with a practiced hand.

'*Est votre bateau?*' Marlowe asked with his modicum of French.

The man was silent for a long time, just looking through the glass. Marlowe could see his hands begin to tremble. '*Oui.*'

He put the glass down, looked at Marlowe. The two men held each other's eyes for a moment. Then the Frenchman said again, '*Oui,*' and without another word he swung himself into the rigging and headed back down to the deck.

Les pirates nègres. In an hour, King James would be within long-cannon shot. And beyond him, a merchantman that was no doubt a rich prize, just the thing that the Elizabeth Galleys longed for, indeed, the very thing that they required in exchange for their dubious loyalty.

And Marlowe would have to decide which to attack.

CHAPTER 16

By the time he set foot on the deck again, Marlowe knew that he just did not care anymore.

His apathy was not directed toward King James. He still cared very much about him, still wished very much that he did not have to kill the man.

It was privateering, pirating, all these fine points of Admiralty law. He was too tired of the whole issue to give one damn more. 'Sod them all, with their treaties and their laws and letters of marque . . .' he muttered.

He wondered at his own failings, his inability to hold the moral high ground for long, once he had taken it. What would Bickerstaff think, that he might so easily slip back into the amorality of the Brethren of the Coast? But his was a fatalism born of long years at sea, long years among the pirates, those most fatalistic of creatures, who cared about no man's life. Not their own, not that of anyone else.

'Well, set a thief to catch a thief,' he said to himself, then aloud: 'I reckon I'm the one to go after that pirate James. Mr Bickerstaff, pray, sir, a word?' Marlowe waved him aft, led him back to the taffrail, out of earshot of the helmsman or any of the others forward. Bickerstaff would still care. It was not fair that he should be led blind into this thing.

'So, Francis, it is quite a situation we find ourselves in. The far ship is some merchantman; English, Spanish, French, I know not. The nearer ship is King James and his horde.'

He let those words sink in, waited while Bickerstaff stared forward, looking at nothing, thinking the situation over.

'Will you attack King James?'

'I will not. We will fight, if James attacks us, but I do not believe he will. No, the governor's wishes aside, I fear I cannot let another prize go by. The men will not stand for it. And it will do no one any good if this lot turns pirate.'

'Indeed, they are a most piratical bunch, upon my word. And that Griffin is the worst of them. He does more damage to the crew than all the rich prizes we might ignore.'

'Yes, Griffin, well, we shall see about him. In any event, we'll let James sail off, for now, and if this other is a legal prize, then we are for them.'

'The thought of riches must ease your pain some-what.'

'Yes. Yes, it does.' Marlowe looked aloft at the fine billows of canvas against blue sky, then back at their long wake, foaming white under the counter and streaming off behind in a long, straight line.

Ah, how he loved the sea! How unfair it seemed that the perfect simplicity of this life, the steady rhythm of the watches, those basic considerations of conforming canvas to weather, the needs of the ship and her crew, should be polluted by such worries and considerations. Legalities and duplicity and petty negotiating were things for buildings on shore, not ships at sea. But like Bickerstaff he was not so naive as to think that being afloat made him immune to such intrigue.

He pulled his eyes from the wake, looked at his friend again. 'There is one other thing of which you should be aware. I do not, in fact, have a letter of marque and reprisal.'

'I beg your pardon?' Bickerstaff said, after the merest of hesitations.

'I do not really have a letter of marque. Nicholson would not give me one until I had brought in King James. I lied to the men about it, and to you as well.'

Bickerstaff said nothing. He looked away, then looked back at Marlowe. 'That is why you let that other ship go? There was some high talk aboard that she was a legal prize.'

'That's right. But I cannot do that again, and I certainly cannot tell the men that they have been deceived.'

'Good Lord, Thomas! But if you take yon ship, then it is piracy, no more.'

'Piracy, indeed. Funny how I keep falling into it. The sweet trade attracts some men like a lodestone. Men of a certain mettle, I suppose.' He hoped Bickerstaff would note the cleverness of that remark – mettle, metal – but Bickerstaff just sighed, looked outboard, shook his head.

'Francis, I told you this because I would never have you unwittingly do something you think immoral. The men forward, they don't give a damn and frankly neither do I any longer, but I would not have you join in this fight in ignorance.'

'Well, Thomas, it's a damned thing, ain't it? Will

you tell these men the reason I am not willing to fight, that you lied about the letter of marque, or just let them assume I am a coward?'

Marlowe nodded. It was a damned thing. 'You know, Francis, the sea is a dangerous place. Questions of right and wrong become . . . muddied. I fail to understand why you go to sea with me, me and all my moral failings. Why not stay home, at Marlowe House, with your books and your farming?'

'I do not know, Thomas, and I do not like to think on my reasons.'

The two men were silent for some time, and then Bickerstaff said, 'In faith, for all my high morals, I do believe I envy you and your pragmatic view. There is a certain excitement that the scholarly life lacks, and I fear that, like strong drink, when one gets a taste of it, it is hard to put it aside.' He considered his words and then added, 'The drinking simile is a good one, for I daresay that adventure such as yours is no more healthful or acceptable to society than being a wretched drunk.'

'Give me time, Francis, and I may be that too.'

'I would have thought that likely, but for Elizabeth, who is a better person than either of us, and who I trust will keep you sober and sane. And since by your admission we do all of this in order that she can enjoy her place in society, I suppose we can say that it is all justified.'

'Good for you! You see, just as you taught me to read and write, so I have taught you to justify any misdeeds you wish to undertake.'

'Yes, with the difference being that you can make yourself believe that nonsense, and I cannot.'

They left off their discussion of the morality of

what they were doing, which was fine with Marlowe, because he had already decided on his course of action and did not need his decision cluttered with such considerations.

And Bickerstaff, though he made it clear that he thought Marlowe was reprehensible for what he had done, nonetheless armed himself with pistols and sword and took his place in the waist, supervising the forward section of guns and backing Marlowe up in the boarding party.

Dinner, and an extra dram of rum, and the men were in a fine fighting spirit. They stood by their guns and leered at one another and worked themselves up to a high pitch as the *Elizabeth Galley* closed with the two ships distant.

King James maintained his heading longer than Marlowe would have thought likely. There was no doubt he would recognize the *Elizabeth Galley*. Even when she was hull down he would probably know her. No man alive, save for Marlowe, knew that ship as well as James.

They were within cannon shot of the former French merchantman and still James kept on the other ship's heels. Marlowe ordered the men at the bow chasers to give them a peppering, which they did, with great delight, and that at last convinced the black pirates that this was not their fight. They wore around, awkwardly, slowly, and headed off east with the wind over their beam.

The other ship was on a more northerly course and now she turned her transom to the *Elizabeth Galley* and made a race out of it, but it was a race she had no hope of winning, or even prolonging for very long.

There was half a mile of water between them when Spanish colors broke out at her masthead.

'Well, thank God for that, at least,' Marlowe muttered to himself. A Don, a legal prize for an English privateer. For the *Elizabeth Galley* she was close enough.

'Let us have Spanish colors as well,' Marlowe ordered the seaman standing by the flag locker, halyard in hand, and a moment later the *Elizabeth Galley* was showing the same bunting as her victim. But the real Spaniard was not fooled and did not alter course or take in an inch of canvas.

An hour of hard driving and they were looming up beside her, and there was Griffin on the foredeck, shouting curses and playing the big man, the fearsome pirate, rattling his saber at this pathetic merchant-man.

'Here, Griffin, lay aft!' Marlowe shouted, and with a suspicious look Griffin left off his bravado and ambled back to the quarterdeck.

'Now, Griffin, let us plunge into battle together, eh?' Marlowe said, filled with bonhomie. 'Comrades in arms? We shall board her side by side!'

'Aye, Captain . . .' was all that Griffin got out. He looked at Marlowe sideways, trying to puzzle out what he was about, suspicious, but there was nothing for it. He could hardly decline, so he took a position on the quarterdeck behind Marlowe and with the others he waited.

Stick close to me, you bastard, thought Marlowe, and I shall plunge a sword right through you, when things get hot.

They did not wait long. Ten minutes, and the *Elizabeth Galley*'s spritsail topmast was up with the Spaniard's stern and overhauling her. The two ships were charging ahead on parallel tracks, like two horses in a race, and separated by a strip of water one hundred feet wide.

The aftermost gun of the Spaniard's broadside shot off, the ball striking the *Elizabeth Galley* amidships with a great crash but doing nothing in the way of serious damage.

'Wait for it!' Marlowe shouted to the men hunched over the guns. The atmosphere was explosive, as if the men would blow apart from the internal pressure if they did not have at the Dons that instant. 'We'll give her a full broadside and then board her in the smoke!'

Marlowe looked back at the helmsman, gestured toward the Spaniard, and the tiller was pushed over, the bow inclining toward their victim.

Someone on the foredeck began to pound a belaying pin against the rail, slowly, rhythmically and the pounding was taken up fore and aft. And then another began to chant, 'Death, death, death . . .' and that built as well, built in a crazy, terrifying, hypnotic rhythm that sent a chill down Marlowe's spine, though he had heard the like before, though they were his own men chanting.

We are pirates now, he thought, pirates through and through.

He remembered the false colors flying at the masthead. He could not go into a fight under false colors; that was too much, even for him.

The sailor who had run them aloft was fully entranced with the chanting, and the enemy, growing closer, the gunfire, gun after gun blasting into the *Elizabeth Galley* from the Don's well-aimed broadside, so Marlowe spun the halyard off the pin himself and let the flag fall to the deck in a big, brightly embroidered pile.

Now, now, now. 'In the waist, stand ready . . . !' So close now, the chanting breaking down into screams, clashing of steel, but the Spaniards ready for them, not giving up, lining the side with weapons drawn, forty, fifty men perhaps.

'Fire!'

The *Elizabeth Galley*'s broadside went off as if it were one great gun, and the entire ship rocked away from the blast and the iron flew across the few yards of water and tore up the Spaniards' ship, smashing ornate carvings and strakes and wales, deadeyes and channels in one great devastating stroke.

Marlowe jerked one of his four pistols from his crossbelt, held it in his left hand, grabbed Griffin by the collar, and pulled him around until they were face-to-face.

'Ready, Griffin?' He leered at the man, wanted him to know that the time of reckoning was at hand. Saw the fear in Griffin's eyes.

And then they staggered together as the *Elizabeth Galley* smashed bowfirst into the Spaniard and there was the screaming and the wave of men over the bow and the pop-pop of small arms, the shriek of the first wounded and killed, just like so many times before, and Marlowe wondered that such horror could be so familiar.

Then the stern swung in, ground against the Spaniard, which was higher than the *Galley*. Marlowe let Griffin go, pointed to the quarterdeck rail, ten feet above their heads where they stood on the *Galley*'s quarterdeck.

'Let's go! Go!' Marlowe shouted, leapt up onto the quarterdeck rail, then stepped onto the Spaniard's mizzen channel and into the mizzen shrouds, up over the level of the rail and over the quarterdeck.

The officers were there, and several of the crew and passengers, all armed, determined to defend their ship or die in the process. Marlowe had his pistol aimed at the captain's chest, had the lock pulled back before the captain even saw this new threat. He shouted, twisted, aimed his own pistol. Both went off and both missed.

Marlowe swung around inboard of the shrouds and dropped to the deck and pulled another pistol with his left hand, his big straight-blade sword with his right. Felt a pistol ball whiz by his ear, turned a sword aside, thrust, felt the tip bite.

He was alone, and for a second he wondered if he had been abandoned, if Griffin had done for him, but here came more of the Elizabeth Galleys, up the shrouds and down onto the Spaniard's quarterdeck, and soon the space was crowded with fighting men.

Griffin was the last of them, the craven bastard, coming sheepishly up the shrouds, shouting like he was in the thick of it, looking around for a safe place to jump. Marlowe stepped out of the melee, took two steps over to the mizzen shrouds, grabbed Griffin by the coat, and pulled him to the deck.

Griffin's knees seemed to buckle under him and Marlowe pulled him to his feet, propelled him forward, shouted, 'Get in there, you cowardly bastard!'

Time for you to die.

One of the passengers came at Griffin, and Griffin

raised his sword and fended off the attack, pulled a pistol from his belt, and in his panic discharged it into the deck before he could even bring it horizontal.

Marlowe pulled pistol number three from his cross belt and aimed it at the man fighting Griffin, then swung his arm right three inches until the muzzle pointed right at the back of Griffin's head. He began to squeeze the trigger and then the Spaniard knocked Griffin's sword aside and Griffin stumbled and the Spaniard skewered him in a shrieking, bloody final thrust.

Griffin arched back, eyes wide, his scream cut off by the blood bubbling from his mouth. Marlowe adjusted his aim again, saw the Spaniard over the muzzle, pulled the trigger.

The ball ripped through Griffin's cheek and struck the Spaniard in the chest, tossing him back. He let go of the sword and Griffin fell squirming at Marlowe's feet and then was still.

Marlowe looked at the Spaniard, dead before he hit the deck. Thank you, sir, he thought, you saved me from having to be a murderer as well as a pirate this day.

And then he was back in the fight, his sword knocking aside whatever defense was presented, but the fight had all but ended even as Griffin was screaming his life away. Swords and pistols were thrown aside, hands raised over heads, calls for quarter in Spanish.

'That's enough! That's enough! Give quarter, there!' Marlowe shouted. He raced to the quarter-deck rail, shouted it down into the waist, and the powder-blackened, blood-smeared, crazed men

225

lowered their weapons, stared at the surrendering Spaniards, stood heaving for breath.

That was the difference, Marlowe told himself, the difference between the Elizabeth Galleys and true pirates, because true pirates would have continued with the killing, would have shed every drop of Spanish blood aboard in retaliation for the unspeakable offense of their fighting back, and because they were Spanish, which was reason enough.

They searched the ship and found hiding in the bread room a half a dozen women. A few were old, matronly, but the rest were young, the oldest of them perhaps twenty-three, and all lovely, olive skinned, with the untainted virginal beauty of the aristocracy's daughters. They were terrified, as well they might be, but Marlowe saw they were treated with great respect and set Bickerstaff, who spoke the lingo well, to look over them.

Here again, Marlowe assured himself, they were not pirates. He knew what the pirates would have done to them and he did not like to think on it.

It was a rich prize, as a Spaniard homeward bound from that country's American possessions was wont to be, and the Elizabeth Galleys were a happy crew once again. They worked with a will, emptying the hold, swaying its contents over and down into the *Elizabeth Galley*, tending the wounded, throwing the dead into the sea.

Marlowe spoke to the captain, who had survived the fight with no more than a vicious gash on his arm, which was bound in a blood-soaked shirt pulled from the body of one of his men. He had been in the far-flung settlements of the Spanish empire, had not heard of the war in Europe, would not have been in those waters if he had.

The war was fully involved, Marlowe told him. Land and sea, and they, the Elizabeth Galleys, were no pirates, but legal and legitimate privateers. Their behavior after the fight was proof enough of that.

The captain bowed, nodded. He was sensible to the fact that their treatment would have been much different in the hands of the Brethren of the Coast.

Mr Fleming stood to one side in obvious hope of attracting Marlowe's attention.

'Yes, Mr Fleming?'

'Sir, I wish you joy of your victory, sir,' he said.

'Our victory, Mr Fleming,' said Marlowe, nodding to the bandage around the first officer's hand. The blood that soaked it was dried and brown and only a little of the white cloth was visible.

'Oh, 'tis nothing, sir. But, pray, sir, these Dons has some spare sails that might well be worth the having, sir, but our haul has been so prodigious that we've scant room aboard, even now. I had a thought to start some of the water, sir, and break down the casks and then we could have the sails as well.'

'Hmmm.' Marlowe considered that. 'No, I think not, and let me tell you why. You may as well know, no point keeping good news a secret. You recall that ship with whom this Don was engaged? That took off and made easting when we came up with them?'

'Yes. Some of the lads was saying it was the Frenchies' ship, them Frenchies we rescued.'

'Yes, that is exactly the thing. Now this Don

227

captain had some knowledge of that ship and apparently she had quite a rich cargo aboard. The Frenchies won't tell you that, of course, but it's true. And those black pirates have been raiding all along the coast. Vast amounts of booty crammed in their hold. So how does this relate to the water? Well, sir, I've a mind to go after those heathens, take all that they have accumulated, a dozen ships' worth in one stroke, and by my reckoning they are bound away for the Guinea Coast, and we shall follow them.'

'Guinea Coast, sir?' Fleming did not sound so sure.

'Aye, I know, it's not a fit place for a white man, but think of the riches in that one ship! And nothing but a parcel of Negroes to defend it, which is like no defense at all.'

'Really, sir? That ain't how those Frenchies told it. I don't speak the lingo, but as I understood their story those black men were like mad dogs, sir, and twice as fierce.'

'Well, to a Frenchman I am sure they would appear thus.'

Fleming nodded. He could see the reason in that argument and he clearly understood the potential profit to be had in taking a pirate ship. And he would not be shy in spreading the word. 'Very good, sir, then we'll leave the sails be?'

'Oh yes, we are after bigger things than sails.'

Fleming hurried off to his work and Marlowe stepped aft, up to the high quarterdeck where the Spanish officers and the passengers were milling about. The women, now secure in the knowledge that they would not be raped, were talking among themselves and to Bickerstaff, whom they apparently found quite intriguing.

'Francis, how goes it here, sir?'

'Very well, Thomas. These people are very grateful for the gentle treatment they have received.'

'It would have gone easier if they had just surrendered, but they could not have known that.'

'I must say I am pleased as well. If you must descend once more into piracy, at least you are being civilized about it.'

'I thank you, sir, for those kind words.'

'Griffin did not make it, I see.'

'He did not. If you saw the body, you will have observed a bloody great Spanish sword thrust clean through him. I think that should leave no doubt as to how he met his end.'

'I was not aware that the matter was in question. Whatever do you mean?'

'Nothing, sir, not a thing. But see here, I think the men are quite mollified by this great haul we have made. When we are done here, it will be away to the east and hunting that rogue King James down.'

'You think the men will not object now?'

'I think they will be entirely agreeable, even if we must chase them clear to the Guinea Coast.'

Agreeable they would be, once Fleming spread his tale through the gunroom and it wound its way through the inferior officers' quarters and at last to the lower deck. The Lord only knew how inflated the story would be by then, the great riches carried aboard the Black Pirate, the treasures of the Orient, the plunder from the Spanish Treasure fleet.

Enticing enough to lure them clean across the ocean, to the shores of the Dark Continent. Sure, he could fool them into going; there was no more art in that than there was in driving sheep.

It was fooling himself that was the problem.

God, but he did not want to go there, did not want to do this thing.

Beware, beware, the Bight of Benin . . .

CHAPTER 17

Billy Bird settled the cocked hat on her head, flipped the long curls of the wig over her shoulder in a jaunty way, stepped back, nodded his approval.

'Not so bad, really,' he said. 'Bloody crude stitching, but what were we to do, on such a notice?'

'Humph' was all that Elizabeth said.

Billy Bird had told her, in all fairness, that there were 'considerations' to her sailing with him, and here was one of them.

'You see,' he had expanded on that comment, 'we've these sort of . . . rules . . . aboard the ship. Something we've all signed on to, and even me, as lord and master of the vessel, cannot quite get around them.'

'Pirates' articles?'

'No, no, dear Lord . . . pirates' articles! No, just some rules, you know, for fair governance of the vessel. In any event, one of those rules is that no women are allowed aboard, and the punishment is marooning, not a pleasant thing at all. But I should think we could get around that, with just a bit of the creative touch.'

Billy had left at first light, collected her horse from

where she had left it at the Wren Building, ridden back to Marlowe House. There he had gathered up a bagful of Marlowe's clothes, shoes, wigs, and hats. The clothes he carried to a seamstress who took them in significantly, but with no great art, since they were very pressed for time.

Now, back in his room at the King's Arms, they made Elizabeth's transformation.

'You would never pass for a foremast hand, of course,' Billy told her, 'one of these great hairy fellows. But you look every inch the foppish youth. Even without playing the man, you are more manly than some of the silly dandies I have seen prancing about this town. It was not that way a few years back, as I recall. There was a time when Virginia was a place of men alone, with little opportunity for these mincing dance masters.'

'Humph,' Elizabeth said again. She stood and regarded herself in the full-length mirror in the corner, assumed as masculine a stance as she could, one hand on her hip, the other resting on the hilt of her sword.

Billy Bird was right; she had to admit it. She would easily pass for a young man. The coat and waistcoat entirely obscured her breasts and her hourglass figure. She was not altogether pleased with that fact, that this disguise was so convincing, as if it made her somehow less of a woman.

It was late afternoon when they headed out, down the road to College Landing near the head of Archer's Hope Creek. Riding with them, bareback on a tired old mare, was a boy from the inn who took the horses back to town once they had arrived at the landing: Elizabeth's to be liveried and Billy's to be returned to the man from whom he had hired it.

At College Landing they hired a boat pulled by two big watermen. Evening was settling around them as they rowed down the creek to the James River and then down the James to the shallow mouth of a tributary on the southern bank called the Pagan River. Up the Pagan, as far as it might go without taking the ground, a solitary brig was riding at anchor. She was all but invisible from the James, her hull lost in shadow, her spars undetectable against the tall trees that lined the banks.

'Hoay, the boat!' a voice called from the brig's quarterdeck, called with a low, rumbling menace.

'It's Billy Bird, come back to you!' Billy called out, and nothing more was heard from the dark ship.

The watermen pulled alongside and Billy said to them, 'I would be pleased if you would forget all about the presence of this vessel.' And then he pressed into their hands two coins, pieces of eight, and from the look on their faces it was clear that Billy had just bought their undying loyalty.

Billy stood, tossed his seabag aboard the low-sided brig, grabbed Elizabeth's, and tossed that as well. 'Come along, then,' he said to her matter-of-factly, man to man.

Elizabeth nodded. Her palms were sweating and she knew if she held her hands out straight she would see them shake. She felt very exposed, as if her disguise was just the merest wisp, as if it should be clear to everyone that she was not a man. But the boatmen and the boy from the inn had not given her a second look, and she tried to take some comfort from that.

But again, the boatmen and the boy would not leave Billy Bird to die of thirst on some barren strip of sand if they found out, would not have their way with her until they were satisfied and then cut her throat, as the pirates would.

Billy stepped out of the boat and up the brig's side and Elizabeth stood and followed him, not nearly as sure on her feet as he, certain that her every move would betray her sex. She tried to step with a self-confident air, the kind of cock-first swagger she associated with men such as these, but that only made her feel pathetically obvious in her deception.

She took hold of the cleats mounted on the brig's side. Her leather gauntlets – Thomas's gauntlets – were ill-fitting, though Billy himself had restitched them with a care and delicacy that surprised her. Her shoes did not fit right either; handkerchiefs were stuffed around her feet to hold them in place. But despite these encumbrances, and the strange sword hanging from her waist, she managed to get aboard in a credible manner.

Bily was talking with a rough-looking man, a big man with a battered cocked hat on his head, a long, dark broadcloth coat, a cloth tied around his neck in the manner of seamen, all but hidden under a thick beard, cutlass, pistols thrust in his belt.

Elizabeth stepped through the gangway. The man glanced up at her; Billy followed his eyes, said, 'Ah, Mr Vane, this here is an old friend, who will be taking passage with us. William Barrett, younger brother of Malachias Barrett. Do you recall Malachias Barrett, from Port Royal, some years back?'

Vane frowned, then nodded, slowly. 'Yes, yes, I do.' He extended a hand to Elizabeth, and Elizabeth, who had anticipated that, grabbed it lustily and shook, squeezing back as hard as she could, which she feared was not very hard.

'I told William we would give him passage to Boston. He's just cargo, I fear, never the seaman that old Malachias is. William, Mr Vane here is quarter-master, runs the show, pretty near.'

Vane nodded, released Elizabeth's hand, and Elizabeth nodded back. 'Welcome aboard, William,' Vane said.

'Pleasure,' Elizabeth said, and Vane turned back to Billy and the encounter was done, and if Vane had any suspicions about their passenger's gender then, he gave no indication that Elizabeth could see.

She was tense, she realized, every muscle in her body taut. Now she forced herself to relax, to let her muscles loose, like untying the laces of a bodice. She crossed her arms over her chest in what seemed to her a masculine stance, and ran her eyes over the brig.

She had seen just one pirate ship before, the one that Thomas had captured at Smith Island back when he had command of the guardship, and she had heard his tales and Bickerstaff's of what others were like.

The deck she stood on now did not resemble those descriptions, she had to admit, nor did it remind her of the one she had seen. There were none of the empty bottles kicked into the scuppers, none of the tangles of cordage and discarded remnants of meals and men passed out in various places around the deck.

Rather, it was fairly tidy, shipshape, more like the respectable merchant vessels she had been aboard –

Thomas's guardship, the *Plymouth Prize*, or her namesake *Elizabeth Galley*. There were a few men on deck and they were working at something, talking quietly, and paying no attention to the business of their captain and quartermaster.

She heard Billy Bird say, 'Very well, then, three bells in the middle watch,' and she turned to him and he turned to her and he said, 'Come along, William, we have some hours before the tide turns and we can get under way. I shall show you your cabin and let us have a glass together.'

He led her aft, under the overhanging quarterdeck and through a door in a bulkhead that led to the after cabins, a series of doors lining a narrow alleyway dimly lit by a few lanterns swinging from the beams overhead. At the far end of the line of cabins, the door to the great cabin, the captain's domain. Billy opened the door, gestured her into his rather finely appointed quarters: wine rack, sideboard, polished cherrywood table amidships, various weapons mounted on the bulkhead and ceiling.

'Very nice, Billy. I had thought that pirate captains did not enjoy the full privacy of a cabin, that the others were free to come and go aft as they pleased.'

'Dear William, will you please stop referring to us as pirates? We are merchants, free traders, and as captain of the vessel I enjoy all the luxuries of any captain, including the absolute privacy of the great cabin.'

As he said that he pointed emphatically over his head. Elizabeth followed his finger, saw a skylight in the deck above, like a little raised house with glass ceilings. Those ceilings were propped open, allowing the night air into the cabin, allowing anyone on the deck above to hear whatever was said in the great cabin below.

Elizabeth looked down, nodded her understanding.

'Now, young sir,' said Billy Bird, 'as a favor to my good friend Malachias I shall allow you my own personal sleeping cabin.'

He crossed the day cabin, opened a door on the starboard side. Within was a small sleeping cabin, much smaller than the pantry at Marlowe House, fitted out with a hanging cot, washbasin, chamber pot, and a chest lashed to the deck.

'You may take your rest in here,' Billy Bird said, 'but lest you become too relaxed, be aware that on a ship one might be called out, day or night, at a moment's notice. You are free to sleep through any of the regular emergencies, but anything truly grave will require you to be on deck. So, pray, always be ready to appear on deck.'

Elizabeth nodded. The message was clear. No lacy shifts or feminine sleeping gowns. The disguise was to be maintained at all times.

'And when do you think we shall see Boston?'

'Ah, Boston,' said Billy, 'Boston I think will be no more than a week, perhaps ten days' sail from Charles Town, if the wind favors us.'

'Charles Town?'

'Yes, quite. I fear we have some business there, which we must attend to first. That is the other consideration.'

'Goddamnit, Billy, why are you telling me this now?'

'Well, dear Billy Barrett, I am kind enough to tell you while we are still affixed to Virginia's soil. If you

237

would rather go ashore and arrange another passage, then we can still do that. But where you will find simple merchants more discreet than us, I do not know.'

Elizabeth glared at him. He did not tell her about Charles Town because he wanted her aboard, still hoped for a casual fuck, she was quite certain of that.

'Forgive me, Lizzy,' Billy said, so softly that he would not be heard on deck, 'but in truth I did not want to discourage you, not when it was clear to me that you had no choice. We shall be in Charles Town and then up to Boston in less time than it would take you to find another vessel sailing direct from this dismal outpost, and that is not even considering the danger you face of arrest.'

'Humph,' Elizabeth said.

'And what is more, I could not let you face the dangers of Boston alone. I absolutely have to be with you in your quest. Knight-errant and all that.'

At that Elizabeth smiled, her defenses shot through. 'Damn your eyes, Billy,' she said, but there was no malice in her words. She had never succeeded in being angry with him, never for more than a few moments at a time. 'Very well, I'll wait patiently as you go about your no doubt honest business in Charles Town. And, please, tell me, I have forgotten to ask, what is the name of your honest merchant brig?'

'Why, she is called the *Bloody Revenge*. It is a name the men insist upon, though I daresay it is a bit . . . bellicose . . . for honest merchant sailors such as we.'

Frederick Dunmore reined the horse to a stop from a full gallop, braced with his legs to keep from pitching forward over the animal's head. Jumped down from the saddle, ran across the dark lawn, lit only by the stars, took the stairs to the porch two at a time, pistol held in one sweaty palm.

Bold man, when you know it is only the woman at home, and not even her, most likely, he thought. Coward, bloody coward.

He stopped at the door, listened. Nothing. Nothing from within, nothing without, save for crickets, the far-off screech of some night creature.

I am a night creature too, he thought. A hunter by night. I am the fox.

He crossed the porch with bold strides, seized the doorknob, the white sleeve of his coat a dull gray in the black night.

He was alone. Even his watchers were dismissed, the useless bastards.

They had come to him, heads down in deserved shame. 'She's gone again,' one had said. 'Didn't see her all day, so we got closer, looked through the windows even, but she ain't there. Might have gone back with them niggers . . .'

Of course she had not done that! Dunmore was furious, but he did not let any of that show, just dismissed the men with a 'Very well,' and a wave of the hand.

He had had Marlowe House watched from the moment the woman and the Negroes had fled into the woods. He knew she would come back, a delicate creature like that could never live like a savage in the forest. And he had been right. After their last raid, the one in which they had nearly taken them all, it was right after that that the watchers saw her again, saw her through the windows, moving about.

They had reported to him. He had been right. And that only reinforced his knowledge that he, Frederick Dunmore, was controlling events entirely.

Talking to the governor, talking to the burgesses, seeing what charges might be leveled against her: arming Negroes, aiding the escape of slaves. (How legal was it, what Marlowe had done? Really, now, are we to think of his people as freemen, able to come and go as they please?)

And those people, Nicholson, the burgesses, were listening. A day or two more, a few more carefully worded arguments, and the bitch would have been in jail.

It was something. It was all that was left. He could not catch the Negroes in the woods. He had realized that at last. The others had realized it too, had given up the hunt, left him alone.

No matter. The so-called free blacks were in exile, run off, pushed far from civilization where they might spread their poison, and that was almost as good as rounding them up and selling them off. Better, perhaps. And she was still within his reach.

He rested his left hand on the doorknob, readjusted his sweating grip on the pistol in his right hand.

What if I do find her home? What will I do to her?

He felt a surge of conflicting desires and passions, dark and ugly and secret things. He twisted the knob and pushed the door open.

It was blackness within, perfect dark, and he stepped into it and closed the door behind him.

In the foyer, he stood absolutely still. He let the tiny sounds of the house fill him, the sounds and the faint smells of past fires and past meals and traces of perfume, until he was as much a part of the darkness as they were.

When he was certain the house was empty, he stuck his pistol in his belt, fished in his haversack for his tinder-purse, and pulled that out. He knelt down, feeling for flint and steel and match and arranged them with practiced hands. He struck steel on flint and the sparks that drifted down to the match gave him a faint glimpse of black and white checks painted on the floor.

And then the match caught and flared and he picked it up and with it lit a candle. The room revealed itself in dull yellow light. A wide staircase up to the second floor, a sitting room opening up to the right, a hallway leading to the back of the house on the left of the stairs.

Against the wall nearby stood the tall case of a clock, silent, unmoving, like a dead man propped up there. Was that some indication of how long she had been gone? There was no way to tell.

He moved to the bottom of the stairs, looked up as far as the throw of the single flame would allow him to see.

Why am I here? To find out where she has gone. To bring her to justice, to help stop the spread of the plague . . .

Liar, liar, liar. Coward.

He stepped onto the first step, tried his weight. It did not creak; his shoe was silent on the plush runner that covered the center of the steps. The next and the next, he stepped up, thrilled, terrified, filled with righteous purpose and self-loathing. The storm battering his brain.

He was in Marlowe's house, inside Marlowe

241

himself, it felt like. Swaggering, self-assured Marlowe, who would step into a fight to the death with never a thought.

As would I, Dunmore thought. I am in that now, a fight to the death, and I will fight till my last breath to keep the pestilence out of these colonies.

But you are careful not to give Marlowe leave to call you out. Coward.

But is a coward worse than any friend of the black man? One who would see them all free if he could, populating his country with their little black babies? He felt his courage spread as it did with the first effects of an excess of wine.

Those few times he had had an excess of wine. Twenty-eight years as a Boston Congregationalist, from a long line of preachers, he could no more abandon certain habits than he could change the color of his eyes.

The top of the stairs, and at the far end of the hall an open door. He walked down that way, stepped in. It was the bedroom: a big canopy bed, dressing table, chest of drawers. A wardrobe, the doors gaping open, a row of wig stands, several empty. Signs of a rapid departure, but why would Elizabeth take wigs?

He stepped over to the bed, ran his hand along the smooth silk cover. Stepped over to the chest of drawers, a tall affair standing on fine carved legs, claws gripping balls on the floor. A lot of damned money this bastard has, Dunmore thought. Wondered if perhaps Marlowe was richer than he, an uncomfortable idea.

He stuck his candle in a candleholder on a side table, pulled open the first drawer in the chest. They were her things, underclothing, silky things, things that would cling against her naked skin. He ran his hands lightly over them, let his fingertips thrill to their silkiness, let the rustling of them release their perfume.

He grabbed a handful of silk, picked it up, buried his face in it, ran his tongue over the smoothness, let the sensations wash over him. His erection was pressing hard against his breeches. He wondered if she rutted with one of those black bucks, maybe while Marlowe watched. He pushed the silk into his face.

He thought about killing her, recalled what it was like to see the life go out of a person's eyes as he squeezed, squeezed her throat. He thought about his strong hands on that long and perfect neck, what she would look like as she fought him for her life.

And then the storm hit him from another quarter, the reality, the black despair at what he was and he moaned out loud, dropped the silk cloth to his feet, his cock wilting.

He shook his head hard, recalled that he was there ostensibly to find information. He looked around the room, at the windows set in deep cases, the long curtains that pooled on the floor. He stared at the curtain, then at the candle flickering on the chest of drawers. He watched the flame, the cleansing flame, dancing, dancing, as it might dance over those curtains, consuming all of Marlowe House in fire, purifying the ground on which it stood.

But he did not have the courage to do it, and he knew it, and he pushed the thought aside.

Where could she have gone? She had just disappeared, never a word from anyone in Williamsburg or Jamestown or Norfolk or Newport News.

Where would she run to escape from him? Or might she be plotting some counterstroke? Where would she go to do that? Where would he go, were he her?

Boston.

Dunmore felt a wave of panic break over him and he looked suddenly around, as if the threat were there in the room, and not just a fresh realization in his mind alone.

She might go to Boston. He thought he had left all that behind, washed it off him with a voyage to London and then a new life in Virginia, the fox losing the pursuing hounds over a long and convoluted trail. No one in Williamsburg knew the rumors, he was certain of it.

But Marlowe was a mariner, and he was friends with mariners, and those people did not stay put, they moved from place to place and they carried the ugly rumors and untruths with them. Could he know? Could she know? Might she be heading for Boston, looking for the truth of the matter?

'Oh, God!' he moaned out loud. He had to stop her, but he could not go to Boston. Impossible now. But he did still have people there, people whose reliability would cost him, especially for the task he would have to assign them.

Yes, but how would they find her, how would they know where to look for her? Boston was a big place, hundreds of people coming and going . . .

She would go to the old man. Of course, that would be where she would start, the only place she could start. What would the old man say? It didn't matter, she could not be allowed to see him.

They had to watch the old man's place, see who

was seeking him out there. He would describe her – a hard woman to miss. Yes, yes, if they watched the old man's place, then they would catch her up.

And with that thought came the warmth of salvation, the pieces fitting together. If she went to Boston and found out the truth, then he did not want her arrested in Virginia, he wanted her taken up there, far from the burgesses and his neighbors, taken and drowned in that city's already notable harbor.

CHAPTER 18

Madshaka stood on the quarterdeck, near King James, listened to the accusations shouted in the tongues of the Ivory Coast, the Gold Coast, the Grain Coast, the Congo, the Slave Coast. The words of each language passed easily through his head, as if together they were but one great language, so adept was he at speaking them.

He had joined in with the Kru funeral ceremony, singing with them their wailing song of death, because he was himself Kru, while James and Cato and Quash and Good Boy had watched, silent, ignorant.

Madshaka knew who the Kru would obey. He was their master now, master of them all. It was not hubris. It just was.

He turned to King James. 'They very angry.' He nodded at the representatives. They were standing, sitting, squatting on the deck, called aft to discuss their situation, to vote, like the pirates do.

Far forward, in the waist and the foredeck, the women and children looked on, apprehensive. They did not like how things were going, how their deliverance was changing before their eyes.

They, however, do not decide their fate, Madshaka thought. I do.

'What they angry about?' James was losing his temper, but it was too late for that to be a problem.

'They angry about running off, leaving that big ship. They think there much riches in that ship.'

'Did you tell them what I said? About Marlowe, how we be captured if we stay and fight? Did you tell them we trying to get home, not pirating all over the ocean?'

Madshaka shrugged. 'I told them.'

Actually, he had told them nothing of the sort. He had told them that King James was afraid of the white man, that King James was friends with the white man that came after them, that they had to vote as he, Madshaka, told them to or King James would steal all of their riches.

He had planted deep in their heads the idea of going back to Africa as wealthy men. The horrors of the Middle Passage were fading now, with the near certainty of returning to their homes. Now the thought of acquiring wealth before that return was finding fertile ground.

'I think they want to take back from the white man, after all they suffer,' Madshaka said to James. 'They think you too afraid, you don't understand. These men are warriors, not good to them to run from a fight.'

James scowled, looked away, and Madshaka waited, expressionless, for what he would say next.

This was so easy, now with Kusi gone.

'Tell them . . .' James began, and stopped and reconsidered.

James was becoming suspicious, but there was

nothing that he could do. Madshaka understood as well as James what his choices were. James could hope that Madshaka translated his words correctly, or James could kill Madshaka, if he was able, and then have no means whatsoever to communicate.

James would take his chances with Madshaka.

'Tell them, we are far from land now, we are halfway to Kalabari, not likely to see another ship. Tell them this was what we wanted, from the beginning, to go home, and that is what we are doing. Two weeks and then we are there.'

Madshaka nodded, turned to the gathered men, and called for silence. Then in one language after another he translated the words, translated them pretty much as James had said them.

There was no reason now for him to tell them anything different. Madshaka guessed that it was the truth, that they were unlikely to come across any more ships, this far out to sea. It was time to get back to Africa. He had business there as well.

As he spoke he saw expressions soften, heads nodding. For all he had inflamed these men with the lure of piracy, the great wealth to be had, for all he had told them about how rich-laden was the prize that they had abandoned, they were still men of the land, men of the African forest, and they would never be comfortable aboard a wind ship. The mention of home sat well with them. They, too, were ready for this voyage to end.

'There, I tell them,' he said to James. James looked out over the men who looked aft at them. They did look mollified, comforted. James nodded. Madshaka knew that there was nothing like the mixture of truth and lies to keep an adversary off balance.

'Good,' James said. 'Good.'

King James was a fearsome sight, with his pistols and his sword and his leather jerkin accentuating the powerful muscles of his chest and arms. Madshaka thought he would not like to fight the man, but of course he would not have to.

James was an enigma to him, and a problem. He was smart and bold. Killing the blackbirder's crew, sailing off with the ship, training those ignorant savages to be sailors – incredible. He wished that they could work together, he and James. What a team they might make, what wealth they might garner for themselves! But James would not side with him, he knew that, and so it was and so it had to be.

Destroying James was like destroying some valuable resource, like burning a ship full of rare cargo.

'Very good, Madshaka,' James said next. 'Tell them to have their dinner and then we stand our watches, like before.'

'Yes, Captain.' Madshaka gave James his big, wide grin. Turned to the men and translated the words, added that Captain James was not to be disturbed from his sleep, and the men nodded and then dispersed, back to their families, back to their tribes.

James had to be destroyed from the inside. A man like James could not be torn down, he had to be chipped away. And Madshaka needed him broken, because James, strong and confident, was not a man with whom Madshaka wished to tangle.

King James was not Kusi. King James would not be led to the little platform on the side of the ship and effortlessly shoved into the ocean.

No, James would take a lot of killing, when the time came, and he, Madshaka, had to start now.

He made his way forward, beyond the light of the three big lanterns on the taffrail, moving silently with his long strides, down into the waist and up by the knights' heads on either side of the bowsprit. In the dim starlight he could make out Anaka's shape, leaning against the knights' heads, waiting. He and Anaka now met there every night. There was much to discuss.

'Good evening, Anaka,' Madshaka said in his native Kwa.

'Good evening. How does it go?'

Madshaka shook his head. 'I am worried. I am worried about King James. I think he is plotting something.'

Anaka stiffened, and after a moment said, 'What?'

'I don't know. But I keep an eye on him. There is nothing he can do to trick you or me, but I am afraid for the others. They might be taken in by whatever it is he is planning.'

'Perhaps. But it is of no concern. The Kru are all with you. They understand you are their countryman. Not Malinke. Malinke that has been with white men for twenty years. We will stand with you and we have been talking to the others. It is your orders we will follow.'

'Good. It is safer that way.' Madshaka was grim-faced, though he wanted to smile, to laugh out loud. He had been robbed of everything, sold into slavery, and now he was halfway back. Now he had a ship of his own, filled with valuables. Now he had an army.

The two men were silent for a moment, taking in the ambience of the ship and the sea. Finally

Madshaka spoke, and his words were soft, like a parent speaking to his child, with not a hint of persuasion in his voice.

'In nature, Anaka, there are the strong and the weak. You know that. There is the lion and the antelope and the lion kills the antelope. It is the way of things.'

'Yes . . .' Anaka's tone indicated that he did not see where this was going.

'It is the same with men, have you noticed that? Some are strong and some weak. And with nations of men. The Ashanti are strong, the Nupe weak. The Kru are strong, the Oyo weak. We are the lions, they are the antelope.'

'That is true.'

'The lion is not blamed for feeding on the antelope, even though he kills it in order that he might be strong and well fed. I wonder if you think the same is true with men? With nations of men?'

'Well . . .' Anaka considered this. 'The strong nations have always dominated the weak. Like with the lion, it is the way of things.'

'Exactly. You are no fool, Anaka. The strong have always defeated the weak, taken them as their slaves, or sold them to others as slaves. It is the way of things.'

'Yes. But why do you say this?'

Madshaka was quiet for a moment, as if he was considering the question. 'I just want you to think on this, Anaka. We might have a great opportunity. We are a strong band, we Kru aboard this ship. We have fought together, we trust each other. In battle. And in our business. That is a rare thing these days. It may not be wise for us to part when we get to Kalabari.

251

Perhaps we should think of the future. Our future. Together.'

Anaka's face, his thoughtful, flattered, pleased, and curious face, was visible in the faint ambient light and Madshaka liked what he saw.

'Just think on that. That is all I ask. And talk to the other Kru. Not the other people, only the Kru, about what I have said.'

Anaka nodded. 'I will.' With that he left and Madshaka was alone in the bow with the great wind ship above and behind him.

He looked out past the bowsprit, out into the dark, toward Africa beyond the horizon.

They would not be going to Kalabari, of course, but it was not time to tell Anaka that.

One step at a time. That was how Madshaka would return.

CHAPTER 19

William Barrett, known also as Elizabeth Marlowe, sat propped up in the cot in the tiny sleeping cabin of the *Bloody Revenge*. She was still clad in breeches and waistcoat. On the small shelf over her shoulder a single candle guttered, and opened on her lap was Alexander Olivier Esquemeling's *The Buccaneers of America*, the second English edition from the Dutch original of 1678.

It was a hugely popular book and Elizabeth had read parts of it before, but it amused her to find it among Billy Bird's library. She wondered at his motive for owning it. To learn something of his trade? Hoping to see his own name in print? But of course Billy was no more than thirty-five years old, or thereabouts, probably younger, and the events and people that populated Esquemeling's book were from a former age.

The *Bloody Revenge* was all but motionless, riding at a single anchor, after five days of working her way south around Cape Hatteras and into Charles Town Harbor.

They were anchored in Charles Town Harbor, but not the raucous, lively, well-populated section, not anchored off the busy waterfront that bordered the Cooper River, with its several docks and crowds of shipping and boats pulling to and fro at all hours, its chandlers and slave markets and whorehouses, taverns and ordinaries.

Rather, they were tucked into a dark corner behind low, marshy Hog Island, across the river from the town, tide rode at the mouth of Hog Island Creek. In a town such as Charles Town, which trafficked quite openly with pirates, Elizabeth had to wonder what Billy Bird and his 'honest merchant sailors' were about, that such secrecy was required.

She could hear shoes and the soft padding of bare feet on the deck above. She stared up at the beams over her head. The rough cut marks left by the adze that had formed them stood out bold in the deep shadows of the single flame.

Billy Bird . . . She called him a pirate and he was not unequivocal in his denial. But still, his ship was not like what she had been led to believe pirate ships were. Billy gave orders and they were obeyed. Billy lived in the fine aft cabin, and no one entered that space without knocking first.

But Billy was polite to the men, and careful not to violate those 'rules' that governed their ship.

Well, there were pirates and there were pirates, and she imagined that Billy and his men had come to some understanding that worked for them all.

Billy Bird. He was handsome, wild, and reckless. Fun. If she were not married to Thomas, then this meeting might have been very different. But Thomas made her feel secure and safe, which Billy never could, and that was the thing she most craved now.

She wished Thomas would come back. She had no

idea of how long he might be gone, and she hated the uncertainty. She did not know if he was dead or alive.

She let her head fall back on the pillow, closed her eyes, sighed audibly. She knew fine ladies in Williamsburg who chafed under the boredom of their lives in their far-flung plantations, who dreamed of running off to London or Paris or being taken and ravaged by pirates, or what they thought pirates to be – handsome noblemen in disguise, like the highwaymen in their silly novels.

For Elizabeth, it was the boredom she craved, a simple life with her husband and her garden and not one damn thing happening out of the ordinary.

She sighed again, opened her eyes, swung her legs over the edge of the cot, and reached with her toes for the deck to stop the bed from swinging. She could hear that something was going on on deck, someone had come aboard, conversations taking place in low tones. It was none of her business, she did not even want to know what was happening.

She pulled out the chamber pot, set it on the trunk, reached down to grab the hems of her skirts, and only then recalled that she was not wearing skirts at all. She cursed under her breath and fumbled in the dimness with the buttons of the breeches, those damned irritating, awkward breeches.

She got the breeches down at last and relieved herself and then with even more difficulty pulled the breeches back up, buttoned them, and tucked in the shirt. She cracked the door to the day cabin, not wanting to carry the chamber pot past Billy, but the cabin was empty and unlit.

Through the aft windows, which were swung open in hope of finding some relief from the sultry night, she could hear frogs and crickets and mosquitoes and a host of other creatures that inhabited the swampy island under the brig's stern. Higher up, over Hog Island, she could see a few lights from the town of Charles Town, about one hundred perches away.

She picked up the chamber pot and stepped carefully across the cabin, letting her eyes adjust to the dark, not wanting to spill the contents on Billy Bird's fine furniture or the elaborate rug that occupied most of the deck underfoot. At the after end of the cabin she knelt on the lockers that ran athwartships under the windows, leaned forward with the pot, and poured the contents out the window.

She heard the liquid splash and then, to her complete surprise, a shout, a splutter, a curse, right under the window.

'Damn me!' she yelled, and with a start dropped the chamber pot into the dark. It did not hit the water but rather shattered on something hard. She leaned out the window. In the blackness under the counter she could see the vague outline of a boat, loaded with men, dark shapes against the water.

'Who are . . . what . . . what in hell are you about?' she shouted, more from surprise than anything, not thinking about who they might be, or why they were there.

And then, from the boat, 'Damn you!' and another voice, 'No!' and the flash of priming, the blast of a pistol and the window a foot from Elizabeth's head shattered. She felt the shards of glass prick her cheek and she fell back, fell back to the deck. Through the window, shouting, a voice commanding, 'Give way!'

256

Feet stamping the deck above, shouts of surprise and outrage, curses, the language of violence.

She pushed herself to her feet and listened. Overhead she could hear steel on steel, a pistol shot, then another, more shouting fore and aft.

'Goddamnit, goddamnit, goddamnit . . .' She said it over and over like a chant.

She snatched up two of Billy's pistols, thrust them in her waistcoat, two more in her belt, two more in her hands. She knew the guns were loaded, knew that Billy thought an uncharged gun the most useless thing on earth. She was not thinking, just acting, just knowing somehow that she wanted to be on deck, in the open, and armed, not trapped inside the cabin.

Through the door and down the dark alleyway, she bounced off the cabin bulkheads on either side as she ran. The door to the waist was ajar and she kicked it open and burst onto the deck, a pistol in each hand, stepping right into the fray.

The fight was fully joined in those few seconds it took her to grab the weapons and race out of the cabin. The men from the boat were pouring over the side and meeting the Bloody Revenges, steel clashing against steel, pistols blasting away the dark, and Elizabeth could not tell who were her friends and who were the enemies.

She took a step forward and with the edge of her left hand cocked the firelock of the pistol in her right.

A man coming over the side, a man she did not recognize. He turned, looked at her, brought his pistol around, and she knew he was not her friend and she shot him, square in the chest, blowing him back over the rail.

She flung the spent gun away, transferred the other

to her right hand, cocked the lock. The man fighting Quartermaster Vane, standing over his kneeling form, cutlass drawn back, she shot in the head from a distance of three feet, just as he was about to slash Vane's throat.

He tumbled to the deck and she saw his brains blown in a great red swath across another man's shirt and in the unreality of the moment all she could think was, will such a mess ever come clean?

She tossed that gun aside, pulled another from her belt. Billy Bird was standing on the main hatch, a long sword in his right hand, a dirk in his left, fending off a wild, savage attack, the tails of his coat swirling around his legs as he lunged, parried, danced side to side.

Then there was a sword in front of her, wielded by a man she thought was the *Revenge*'s gunner, and she tried to smile at him but he lunged at her, point first.

She pivoted, turned sideways with a dancer's grace, and the sword made a rent in her waistcoat as it passed and she brought her pistol up, the end of the barrel actually touching the man's forehead.

The man gaped at her, shocked that she had eluded his thrust, surprised to find that it was he who was going to die, and then she pulled the trigger and the face was lost in the smoke and when the smoke blew away the man was gone.

She tossed that gun aside. One of the pistols she had thrust in her waistcoat was slipping out through the gash cut in the brocade cloth, and she grabbed the barrel and pulled it out all the way, felt the flint scrape painfully across her breast, and then some great hulk of a man slammed into her, knocking her to the deck.

Her shoulder banged into a hatch combing and a shock of pain radiated through her neck and back. She rolled over; the gun was still in her hand.

The man who had run her down was fighting with one of the Revenges – the boatswain, she recognized him, he had been kind to her in pointing out the various aspects of the vessel's rig – and Elizabeth lifted the gun in her hand, pointed it at the center of the other man's massive back, and pulled the trigger.

The man pitched forward and behind him stood the boatswain, shocked, his adversary seemingly struck down by the hand of God. Then he saw Elizabeth lying on the deck. Their eyes met, he nodded to her, then turned and flung himself back into the fight.

Billy Bird was still there, still making his stand on the main hatch, sword and dirk working together, but there were two men on him now, and he was breathing hard and there was a heaviness in the way he wielded his weapons.

The enormity of the scene, growing more real by the second, was working on her head, and the noise and the shouting and the flash of guns were making it hard for her to think. She saw one of the men lunge at Billy, saw his sword catch Billy's shoulder, saw Billy twist in pain even as he used his dirk to knock the blade away.

Shoot them, Billy, just shoot them, she thought, and could not fathom why Billy did not do as she wished. She rolled over on her hands and knees and crawled forward, through pools of blood, warm and sticky on her palms. There were men looming over her, swords clashing in the air above her head, but she crawled on.

She came at last to the main hatch and sat up on her knees, pulled the pistol from her belt, cocked the lock, fired into one of the men fighting Billy Bird, and as he crumpled she thought, there, just shoot him.

She tossed the gun aside and pulled her last firelock from her waistcoat and cocked it and looked over the barrel. The man she intended to shoot had seen her and now he was turning from Billy and coming at her, his cutlass over his head.

Elizabeth's sense of reality began to waver. The man swam toward her. She could see his crooked and rotten teeth, his stained, filthy shirt, ripped from the neck down, broadcloth coat, his battered cocked hat, dirty red sash around his waist, all of that she took in in the fraction of a second it took for him to close with her and for her to discharge her pistol right into his stomach.

His cutlass came down as he pitched forward, and Elizabeth dodged to one side as the man fell past, the cutlass hitting the deck and the man falling on it. She felt the deck shudder as he hit and he made a gasping sound as the breath was knocked from his lungs and then he was groaning, gasping, gurgling blood.

'Bastard!' Elizabeth screamed, and then stopped screaming, and in the odd quiet that came with her stopping she realized that she must have been screaming continuously, for how long she could not recall.

She pushed herself to her feet, swiped the hair from her face, stepped away from the horrible dying man. She saw figures going over the rail, as if they were abandoning the ship, but it was quieter now;

the guns had stopped firing, she could not hear the clash of edged weapons, and when she looked again she saw that the fight was over, and she recognized the men on deck so she assumed that the Revenges had won.

And now Billy Bird was looking at her, his eyes wide, and she smiled at him.

'William, dear William, well done,' Billy said, stepped toward her quickly, dropping his weapons to the deck rather than taking the time to sheathe them. She saw his eyes dart down toward her chest.

She looked down. Her long blond hair was loose and hanging over her shoulders like she often wore it. Through the rent in her waistcoat and shirt she could feel the warm, moist night air on her breasts, but looking down she could not tell if they were visible through the tear.

Still, she grabbed the cloth and held it together as Billy stepped up to her, saying, 'William, bully for you, now let us go to the cabin and have a look at that famous wound you have suffered.' He spun her around and all but shoved her aft and through the door to the privacy of the great cabin.

Marlowe had thought they were right behind King James and company, had thought they would run them down easily, but after taking the Spaniard they had failed to raise those new-fledged pirates, or any other vessel for that matter.

For three weeks they searched, through more than sixty degrees of longitude, following roughly the fortieth parallel until dropping south of that and raising the Azores. Marlowe had come on deck every morning before dawn, expecting to see the French

261

merchantman, and each time he was greeted with empty seas all around.

Finally they had dropped the hook in Ponta Delgada on the Portuguese island of São Miguel. There Marlowe was able to sell, discreetly, some of the vast bounty taken from the Spaniard, since there were few among the Portuguese who worried overmuch about anything plundered from the Spanish.

That done, he was able to distribute some small amount of specie to the men, who were given leave to spend it all in as short a time as they could manage. That they did, with the famed abandon of sailors ashore, drinking to insensibility, fighting, whoring, venting all the pent-up aggression and passion that is by necessity held in check while aboard a tight-packed ship, the survival of which depends upon mutual effort.

Two days of that and the Elizabeth Galleys were sated, their money gone, their heads pounding, their cocks limp, and they were more than happy to lay into the capstan and drag the anchor up from the mud, cat it, let fall the topsails, and head off to the forced sobriety of the sea. As they staggered about the deck, some were moved so far as to claim they would never do the like again, some even to the point of believing it.

Four days after the Azores had dipped below the horizon, Noah Fleming approached Marlowe on the quarterdeck, fidgeting. 'Sir, beg your pardon, but some of the men, they wanted me to ask you . . .'

'Yes?'

'I know you don't countenance such things as secret meetings and votes and such things as the pirates are wont to do, and this is none of that . . .'

262

'I understand.' The Elizabeth Galleys were becoming quite the cooperative and unassuming bunch, now with gold in their pockets and Griffin dead. It was the singular bright spot in Marlowe's heaven.

'Well, sir, the lads was wondering about them black pirates. We're still after them, are we not?'

'Do the men wish to be after them?'

'Oh, yes, sir! And the prodigious treasure they have. Yes, sir, the men would like very much to pursue them.'

Ah, tales have been told belowdecks! Marlowe thought. 'Well, I had thought to give that up, Mr Fleming. It will be a hell of a task, finding them. I reckon they are heading for the coast of Africa.'

'I understand, sir. And, of course, this ain't no pirate ship. What you say is law, and no arguments. But the men would just like you to know, sir, if you was to pursue those men, well, that would be fine with them.'

Marlowe pretended to think about that. 'Very well, then,' he said at last. 'We shall start at Sierra Leone and run south. If need be we shall seek them out right around the entire Bight of Benin.'

'That's a good thing, sir. The men will be right pleased to hear it.'

'Good,' said Marlowe, and he meant it. He still had before him the herculean task of finding King James and the horrible job of killing him. But at least his own men were with him in that endeavor. It was a start. At long last, it was a start.

CHAPTER 20

It dawned on King James that he was not captain anymore. He still slept in the great cabin. The white pilot still showed him their position on the chart. He still gave orders to wear ship when necessary, to take in or set sail, but he was not in command.

There were subtleties going on, undercurrents running below the smooth surface of their daily routine, machinations taking place that he could not identify or understand for the differences in language.

They had been in stasis for a while, for three weeks or so, as they plowed their easting away, making for their homes in Africa, the waking at the end of sleep.

There had been a routine, of sorts, a nervous peace, between him and those few with him – Quash, Good Boy, Cato, and Joshua – and Madshaka and the rest of them, and around them nothing but the uninterrupted sea.

And so they sailed, south southeast, running before the wind as it curled south along the coast of Africa, like a stream of water butting up against a seawall. Over the larboard side and below the horizon, the continent, dark only to those who did not know it. What would happen once the anchor was down, James did not know, but he was desperate to be there.

Every day the Frenchman gave him the course, and if the daily headings did not seem to mesh with James's rough idea of where in relation to the ship Kalabari lay, James did not have the enthusiasm to question him. He looked at the chart, nodded, gave orders for changing course, trimming sail.

The puppet captain. He said the words, made the gestures. Madshaka pulled the strings. He knew that, and knew there was nothing he could do but wait for it to end.

Some time after their escape from Marlowe – two weeks, three, James did not know – they raised a headland, low and green, two miles away off the larboard beam. The people crowded the rail and stood in the shrouds and the tops, some jabbering, pointing, singing. Others quiet, just looking, silent tears streaming down dark cheeks.

Africa.

'Cape Palmas,' the Frenchman said. His eyes were wild, his face overgrown with an unkempt beard. He stunk.

James looked at him, nodded. If his own thoughts were somehow made flesh, James thought they might look like the French sailor, wild and unhinged. He picked up the glass and trained it on the distant shore.

He could see little. A strip of white sand that showed beyond the lines of breaking surf, tall palms with their burst of fronds on top, the green, green forest behind.

It was hot on deck, running as they were before the wind, the sun hammering them from directly above. African sun, less than eight degrees north of the equator. And on the breeze, the smells from the shore, the salt smell of the sea, the rotting vegetation of dark and tangled forests.

It was not the smell of America, not the smell of a new land, fresh and simple. It was the deep and profound smell of an ancient land, a land that had seen so much of humanity. It was a smell that James had not smelled in more than twenty years, a smell he had not understood when he had lived within it, but he understood it now.

He lowered the glass. 'Cape Palmas?'

'Cape . . . yes . . . Cape Palmas.'

James did not think so, but he could not argue the point. The sight of the African shore had spun his thoughts off on a whole new heading.

When he had first been taken from those shores he had thought of nothing but getting back.

Then he had despaired of ever returning, and then later he had thought only of escaping his bondage and finding a home somewhere in the New World.

Then, finally, he had thought only of the life he might make at Marlowe House, what happiness he might carve out as a free black man in the context of a slave society.

And now he was back.

Cape Palmas. Very well. If the pilot was right, then they were not above a thousand miles from Kalabari. A week of sailing if the wind held for them.

James felt his thoughts coming in a jumble, a disorganized heap. He was supposed to be giving orders to the people, but he could only give them to Madshaka and hope that Madshaka told the people what he said. He felt as if he had to break out of this pattern, but he could not see how. He could not figure what he might do to gain control.

It was like bondage again, like the shackles and the yoke that kept him from moving, but it was worse. Then, there had been a physical restraint to chafe against, something he could feel and understand. Now the shackles were invisible: confusion, indecision, an inability to speak.

James stared at the green headland and wished he could fling himself onto that beach, curl up on that land as if it were his mother's lap, let Africa comfort him the way he had not been comforted in so very long.

The point receded in their wake and the pilot said, 'Our new heading, it should be east northeast, a half east . . .'

James looked at him, sharply. 'East northeast?'

The pilot cleared his throat. 'The land, it tends away here, we must cross the Gulf of Guinea now. There are currents . . .'

Finally James nodded. The land did tend away, to be sure. Very well. He could not think about it. His mind was awhirl and he could not think. 'Madshaka,' he called, 'we must wear ship.'

The ship came around, settled on the new course. Lines were coiled down, the rhythm of the shipboard community resumed, and James wondered again if any of those dozens of people forward were aware of the silent drama, the lopsided struggle for dominance, going on aft.

He did not think so.

They knew only what Madshaka told them. Just like him. They followed Madshaka's orders, and if they thought that those orders originated with King

James, then they were mistaken, and there was no way for them to discover the truth.

Marlowe woke, and when he came to he realized that he had one foot on the deck of the sleeping cabin, one hand on the hilt of his sword, the other going for his pistol. Beyond the door, a light rapping, someone politely knocking to wake him.

I have got to bloody relax, he thought. These are not the mutinous villains of a month past.

He released the weapons, put both feet on the deck, stood, stepped out of the sleeping cabin into the great cabin, and called out, 'Come!'

Gosling, foretopman, stepped through the door. It was still sometime in the middle of the night – the stern windows were like mirrors with the darkness outside and the single burning lantern within.

'Sir,' said Gosling, 'Mr Fleming's compliments, sir, and we sees some lights, sometimes, on the rise.'

Marlowe nodded. His heart was still pounding from his coming suddenly awake and ready to fight. He worried that his mind was becoming unhinged by all of this. 'Lights, on the rise . . .' The thoughts began to organize themselves, questions formed. 'Where away? How many?'

'Right ahead, sir. Looks like three, right in a row. Looks like taffrail lights, sir.'

Thomas instantly formed a picture in his mind of the big taffrail lights on the French merchantman. Right ahead meant right downwind, right where he would expect King James to be. It was possible that they were not so very far behind that renegade band.

'Very well, I'll be up directly.'

He went back into his sleeping cabin, found a shirt, and pulled it on.

It was far too much to hope. The arrangement of three lanterns on the taffrail was hardly unusual. There was a plethora of shipping in those waters. Absurd to think it might be James.

But still he could not rid himself of that silly anticipation, and it was with a strange amalgam of emotions that he climbed up onto the dark quarter-deck and looked in the direction that Fleming pointed.

He had to wait a moment, but then there they were, like a little constellation, low down in the water, and moving with a rhythm different from that of the *Elizabeth Galley*. Three little lights, the center one a bit higher than the outer two. Taffrail lights, beyond a doubt. But whose?

'What time is it, pray, Mr Fleming?'

'Just gone seven bells, sir.'

Just past three-thirty in the morning. An hour and a half or so until dawn. No need to roust the men up from below, not yet. They'd be up soon enough.

'At the next change of watch we'll clear for action. Quietly. And let's have the watch below roused nice and gentle, too. Like mothers kissing their babes.' Marlowe was in fine spirits and he realized it was because he had already decided that this was King James and his outlaw band in whose wake they were sailing.

But that, he recalled, was an absurd assumption, and that realization cooled his ardor a bit.

The next turn of the half-hour glass signaled eight bells, though in the interest of stealth no bells were

269

actually rung. The watch below was called, quietly, and all hands were sent to quarters.

In the predawn dark the *Elizabeth Galley* was readied for a fight: guns cast off and loaded, temporary cabins under the quarterdeck broken down and stowed in the hold, decks sanded, linstocks supplied with lit match, tubs of water set between the guns, small arms distributed.

And when that was done the men fell to that most ubiquitous of combat duties. They waited.

The men knew exactly as much about the situation as did their captain, at least as far as the chase was concerned. There were three lights to be seen up ahead, steady now, not just on the rise, which meant they were overhauling whoever it was. That was all they knew. The rest was speculation, and it ran thick and fast along the crowded gundeck.

Marlowe and Bickerstaff stood all the way aft, in their familiar position back by the taffrail, where they could speak in almost normal tones with no fear of being overheard. They too knew only that there was a ship ahead, but unlike the men forward, they also understood the tricky political and legal issues involved, niceties that Marlowe had done his best to keep to himself.

'You hope that this is King James?' Bickerstaff said, his eyes on the three bobbing lights.

'I hope with all of my heart that it is him. I hope we are able to kill them all by dinner and have all their ill-gotten booty stowed down in our hold by the first dogwatch.'

'Indeed? That is quite an agenda for one day. But what if it is not King James. Will you let them be?'

'There are three other possibilities. The first is that

270

it is a vessel that belongs to England or Flanders or some such friend of ours, in which case we must bid them a fare-thee-well. The second is that it is a man-of-war belonging to one of our enemies and too much for us to handle, in which case we run like a dog. The third is that it is a legal prize, or would be for a ship with a letter of marque, in any event.'

'And if that is the case?'

'Oh, Lord, sir, I do not know.'

Since it was, by Marlowe's thinking, useless to worry about something he could not change, he didn't, and instead contented himself with a little breakfast for him and Francis and an extra tot of rum all around, to bolster the spirits of men whose spirits really needed no bolstering at all.

An hour after the ship had been readied, the first hints of dawn began to appear. Marlowe sent the sharpest pair of eyes aboard up into the main topmast crosstrees. He recalled a time when the sharpest pair of eyes aboard meant his. Not anymore. He felt decades older than he had just two months before.

A very long fifteen minutes passed and then the lookout cried, 'On deck! I sees her, sir, right ahead, with them lanterns still lit!' From deck the taffrail lights had been swallowed up in the gathering dawn.

Another long few minutes during which Marlowe forced himself to not call out. The lad up aloft was no fool, he would sing out when there was something to sing about.

Finally he did so. 'On deck! I can see her proper now . . . topsails and fore course, nearly the same heading as us . . . big son of a bitch . . .'

The anticipation hung like gunsmoke over a

battlefield. Every eye was trained aloft or forward. 'Breaking out colors, sir! Looks like a Frenchy, sir!'

Smiles, grins, hands rubbing in anticipation. A Frenchman was the best they could hope for, an undisputed prize for a privateer. Every man aboard knew that a Frenchman was fair game. It would all be spelled out in the letter of marque that Marlowe had shown them.

'French colors,' Bickerstaff said, let it hang in the air.

'Still might be King James. It was a French ship they took, after all. He'd have to run something up if he was playing at the innocent merchantman.'

'Yes he would. So in fact this ship yonder still could be the solution to your troubles, or a twofold increase in them, and we still do not know which.'

'Yes, very neatly put. I thank you for that, Francis.'

They plunged on, the *Elizabeth Galley* spreading more and more sail, as the gray dawn sky turned to the light blue of morning. Up ahead the ship in question was setting more sail as well: the main course, the topgallants, then studding sails to weather, but slowly, methodically. It was not the actions of a ship fleeing pursuit, but the routine setting of more sail with the onset of day.

'Well, damn him for an impudent bastard,' Marlowe said at last. 'Whoever he is, James or not, he seems none too concerned with having a well-armed privateer nipping at his behind.'

'Pirate,' Bickerstaff corrected.

'Perhaps. We have yet to see.' Marlowe took the big telescope from the binnacle box, climbed up into the mizzen shrouds to where he could see past the mainsail, and trained the glass forward. They were still too far to make out any of the finer details, but the big telescope told him something, and years of experience with ships and the sea filled in the unknowns. He climbed back down to the deck.

'I take her for an Indiaman. A French East Indiaman, and a damn big one. Of course, they are all damned big, and well armed too, like a man-of-war, really. That's why she ain't frightened of us, I reckon.'

'Well . . . she is a handful, to be certain. Will you run from her?'

'I am loath to give that order. It would not do for me to look shy in front of the men. They are still a volatile bunch, for all the good fortune we have had, Griffin's untimely demise and all. But they are privateersmen, you know, which means they are after riches and don't much want to risk their necks for them. So what I will do is let them vote on it.'

'You'll let them vote? How very republican of you. But is that not at odds with your insistence on absolute command? That sounds more like pirates' ways to me.'

'Nothing like it. See the clever way I frame the thing.'

Marlowe stepped up to the binnacle box where Fleming had stationed himself. 'Mr Fleming, pray have the men assemble aft.'

Five minutes of calling around the ship and jostling in the waist and the Elizabeth Galleys were all gathered, looking up at Marlowe on the quarterdeck like they were waiting for a Royal address.

'You men, listen here,' he began. 'If I'm not mistaken, yonder ship is a French East Indiaman. You people are not strangers to the sea, you know how

273

well armed the Indiamen are. Trained like men-of-war's men. You didn't sign on to attack an enemy that was so greatly superior to us. We're not a man-of-war, not under Admiralty orders to risk our lives. So I don't feel it's my right, in this case, to order you into battle, not when the odds are this much against us. I won't do it. So in this one situation, I am going to allow you to vote! Either we fight, and the odds be damned, or we're off seeking other prey. What say you?'

From forward the captain of number-two gun, a great burly fellow from Plymouth, called out, 'I say we're with you, Captain!'

Smart fellow, Marlowe thought.

And then another man added, 'Aye, hear him! I say the odds be damned! Let's have at them!'

His words were greeted with a great rolling cheer, up and down the deck, as the Elizabeth Galleys shouted their concurrence.

Bickerstaff stepped up to Marlowe's side. A smile was playing across his lips. 'Very cleverly framed, indeed. The men never suspected you. They seem not to have even been listening.'

Marlowe sighed. It was the sound of a man accepting the inevitable. 'You know, Francis,' he said, 'I envy King James and his piracy. At least for him it is a fate of his own choosing.'

CHAPTER 21

The *Bloody Revenge* had been five days under way, running north along the coast with the wind and the Gulf Stream under her coattails, before Elizabeth worked up the courage to ask even one of the questions that plagued her.

She had stayed in the great cabin for the chief of the time, and Billy Bird had not encouraged her to come out. After the fight on deck, after she was secured aft and Billy had taken his leave of her and ordered the Revenges to up anchor and creep away under topsails, she had sat, silent, waiting for the sounds of Billy Bird's men murdering him for having smuggled a woman aboard.

But after a while he had come back to the great cabin and she let him examine the slight wound across her stomach as she held her breasts in cupped hands.

'Whatever was that about?' she had asked, then gave a little gasp as Billy gently swabbed her cut with whiskey. 'Who were those men?'

'Bloody villains. We had an arrangement, you know, for certain goods, and those damned thieves were hoping to storm the ship and take it all. God's body, I don't know what is happening these days. Is no one to be trusted?'

'Humph.' There was more that she wanted to ask, but she was afraid, and more afraid of the answer, and so she remained silent and waited for the moment when Billy would be killed and the others would come for her.

But five days later it had yet to happen, and she could discern nothing but the routine operations of a ship at sea, the change of watch, the clanging of the bells, the men tramping below for their regular meals. So on that fifth day, when Billy stepped into the cabin bearing their dinner, she said, 'Billy, my dear, I am pleased to see that you have not been knocked on the head or thrown overboard.'

'As am I. But why ever woud you think such a thing would happen?'

'Well' – she spoke softly so that her voice would not carry through the skylight – 'you did tell me that there was a rule concerning the smuggling of women on board.'

'Oh, that? I suppose there could be some trouble, if I had brought a woman aboard, but you are the honored younger brother of Malachias Barrett. Besides, the punishment is marooning, and it ain't so bad, you know. The guilty party is given some water and a loaded pistol for when that runs out.'

'The soul of mercy, to be sure. But Billy, I fear that during the fight on deck I might have revealed my true colors, as it were . . . my hair and my . . . the tear, you know, in my shirt. And I believe I was screaming a bit.'

'Oh, nothing of the sort. You were the very picture of manhood. I was screaming as well, you know.'

276

'Billy, tell me the truth.'

'Ah, the truth . . . well . . . let me say first that those lovely breasts of yours were never for a moment revealed to those who should not see them, not even to me, in fact, who should. But the hair, and the screaming, that may have given you away. In truth, it did.

'But as it happens, we never suspected those rogues were laying for us. That's why the chief of my guns was still below. They had insisted on no fire-arms. Would have taken us quite by surprise had you not kindly dumped piss on them. And even with that warning the fight was going badly for us, damned badly. Without you had come on deck when you did and shot such a string of them we might well have been taken. You saved Quartermaster Vane's life, and he knows it. Saved mine as well.'

'Shot a string of them, you say? For the life of me I cannot recall but a few images. Well, in any event, I am glad to have helped.'

'You more than helped, my dear. I've been keeping a weather eye out for some grumbling amongst the men, but there is none. Not a word has been said. I do believe they are inclined to overlook the one little fact of your sex, in gratitude for the great service done them.'

'I am pleased to hear that your people were pleased. But they will not turn on you?'

'They will not. Though if I try to pull such a thing again, I must make sure the lady is of the same heroic bent as you. Now will you not come on deck and see Long Island? Long Island in New York?'

Elizabeth did indeed go on deck, gladly, for she was heartily sick of looking at the inside of the great cabin, even for all its fine appointments and grand store of books and wine.

The warm air that blew in through the after windows below was stronger still on deck. Her long hair would have plagued her, blowing forward and whipping her in the face, had it not been tightly clubbed, with a cocked hat shoved down on her head for good measure.

She was still dressed in a thoroughly masculine fashion, she and Billy agreeing that if the Revenges were inclined to be so charitable as to ignore a capital offense, then they should not push their luck by flaunting it. So she stepped up to the quarterdeck, awkwardly, in Marlowe's too-big shoes, her breasts and her feminine contours again hidden by shirt, waistcoat, and coat. She was greeted with enthusiastic smiles and nods – which she returned with what she hoped were manly gestures – and knowing smiles and lascivious stares, which she ignored.

'William, good day to you,' said Quartermaster Vane without the least hint of irony. He pointed with his bearded chin over the larboard side. 'That land yonder is Long Island, in New York. This wind holds, I reckon we'll fetch Boston in a day or two.'

Elizabeth nodded, smiled, a sort of crooked grin. She did not trust her voice, but neither did she feel she could remain silent, so she swallowed and said, 'I look forward to that, Mr Vane,' in as manly a tone as she could muster without sounding like she was trying to sound manly. Such an absurd charade! She would be glad to shed herself of it.

But she could not until they were in Boston, and then she would be faced with a new set of problems. She was going there to find out what secret Dunmore held in his breast, what truth she might reveal to the world to destroy him before he destroyed her and Thomas and all that they had.

It had seemed daunting enough in Virginia, but now, faced with the real question of how she would begin that search, the problem seemed insurmountable. And to make it worse, it was all based on a vague recollection of Billy Bird's, a fact on which she quite purposely did not dwell.

She turned her face into the breeze, cocked her head to feel the sun direct on her skin. It was warm and the air was fresh and the brig rolled along on a rich blue sea under a robin's-egg sky.

The Bloody Revenges were delighted with her presence, and it appeared that they would not leave her old, dear friend Billy Bird to die on a barren stretch of sand.

That was as much as she could hope for, and there was nothing she could do about Boston until she arrived, and with that realization she allowed herself to relax and feel content, more content and more safe than she had felt in a long, long time.

That feeling, and the fine weather that in part engendered it, held for the next two days as they raised, then left astern, the green hump of Nantucket and then followed the long, low arm of Cape Cod north and west. At last they left the sandy shores of Provincetown in their wake and headed across Massachusetts Bay, and with every mile of open water they covered, Elizabeth found herself growing more tense, more grim, more doubtful.

'Have you been to Boston before, William?' Billy asked, and in her pessimistic introspection it took her a moment to realize he was speaking to her, to recall that she was William. William Barrett, younger brother of the pirate Malachias Barrett, known also as Thomas Marlowe. Damn Billy Bird and his damned perverse sense of humor.

'No, Billy, I have not.' They were at the quarter-deck hances, Billy sitting on the bulwark, a hand resting on one of the main shrouds, Elizabeth leaning on the rail that ran along the forward edge of the quarterdeck. Beyond the *Revenge*'s bow the green hilly country of Massachusetts Bay Colony took up more than one hundred and eighty degrees of horizon. The shore with which they were closing, which an hour before had appeared as unbroken land, was now revealing itself to be a number of islands scattered across the entrance to Boston Harbor, like a blockading fleet.

'It's a bloody dreary place, damned Puritans with their somber faces and their black clothes. Any woman there shows the least bit of spirit they hang her for a bloody witch.' He looked around to see if anyone was within earshot and added, 'So you best watch yourself.'

'If I am accused I shall make a quick escape upon my broomstick. But as I hear it, they are done with that nonsense.'

'Perhaps. In any event, these Puritans have a bloody lot of money. They can hardly avoid it, they do nothing but work and pray. They are a serious, sober, chaste, and deeply pious people, which is why I find them such intolerable bores.'

'Then why have you spent so much time in Boston?'

'I just said, my dear. These Puritans have a bloody lot of money.'

The *Revenge* followed the ship channel between George's and Lovell Islands, winding her way northwest through island after island, pine tree-capped rock thrust up from the bottom of Massachusetts Bay. It was late afternoon when Governors Island and Bird Island passed along the starboard side and before them, two miles away, lay Boston, like a toy city, glowing in the rays of the late-day sun.

The city was arrayed along a tapered hump of land, not much above four miles across, beginning where low, narrow Roxbury Neck clung tenuously to the rest of the colony and running north to where the city ended in a great cluster of buildings and wharves and a tangle of masts at the North End. Rising above the town, like a great sleeping beast, Beacon Hill, with its tall tower, and beyond that, hills that were higher still, looking down on the city, hills that Billy informed Elizabeth were separated from Boston by the Charles River, which they could not see.

There were watercraft everywhere, boats pulled by oars or working under sailing rig, fishing smacks, sloops, brigs, heavy full-rigged merchantmen. The harbor was alive with activity, vessels working in and out, setting and stowing sails. After tiny, sleepy Williamsburg, and the relative peace and isolation of the past five days, this bustling, crowded scene was no little shock to Elizabeth.

And it was not just Boston Harbor. The city itself, rather than ending abruptly at the water's edge, seemed to ease itself into the bay with a complex array of wharves and shipyards and batteries. There were ships tied to nearly every inch of waterfront, so many ships that one could not tell where one left off and the next began, or which masts belonged to which vessel. Jutting out from the middle of the halfmoon harbor was Long Wharf, over half a mile long, and the center of the frenetic harbor activity.

Perpendicular to Long Wharf, and even longer, Old Wharf ran like a connecting street from the middle of Long Wharf north to where it touched the shore at the foot of Clark's Wharf. And all along the whole of it, ships, men, trade, and beyond that the city of two- and three-story buildings, shoulder to shoulder and rising one above the next as the city of Boston climbed up the hill at its center.

'Body of me, Billy, I had no notion that Boston was such a city!' Elizabeth said, and to her great annoyance Billy burst into laughter.

'Dear me, you have been too long out of London! Sure, by the paltry standards of America it is some great metropolis, but come now, have you really turned such a country bumpkin? This is no city, not by the standards of the civilized world.'

'Humph.' Billy was right, of course. Perhaps she was becoming a country bumpkin. She might not be fit for the backwoods, but the dozen or so houses and shops and ordinaries in Williamsburg were metropolis enough for her now. She was done with cities. She knew cities, and she knew that little good happened in them.

The sun was disappearing behind the distant hills by the time the *Revenge* found a clear anchorage among the vessels off Long Wharf and dropped her best bower into the Massachusetts Bay mud. Billy, for reasons that Elizabeth could well guess at, preferred to go ashore after dark in any event, so they had their supper in the great cabin and packed

Elizabeth's chest with those things she might need ashore, such as dresses and her toilet, and when the sun was well down they were rowed to the Long Wharf in the *Revenge*'s jolly boat.

The *Revenge*'s boatswain, Ezra Howland, and a foretopman whom Elizabeth knew only as Black Tom, pulled the boat's oars. In the bottom of the boat lay their swords, wrapped in canvas, beside her chest and Billy's seabag. Under their coats, mostly hidden, each carried a brace of pistols. It seemed a lot of weaponry for pious, Puritan Boston, but Elizabeth made no comment.

The jolly boat at last drew up to a worn and slime-covered ladder that ran from the Long Wharf, ten feet over their heads, down into the dark water from which it rose.

'William?' Billy gestured toward the ladder and Elizabeth rose on uncertain legs and grabbed the ladder and found one of the rungs with her oversized shoe. She could feel the slickness and she made certain of her foothold before stepping up and up again. The tide, by good fortune, was more than halfway through the flood and she did not have too far to climb before she stepped up onto Long Wharf itself, moving aside for Billy with his seabag over his shoulder and Black Tom with her chest.

The sun was gone, but night had not brought much of a lull in the activity along the wharf. By lantern and moonlight fishermen unloaded catches and cleaned their day's haul and packed it down in barrels of salt. Serious men hurried along the prodigious length of the wharf on some business of great personal import. Piemen and oystermen and women selling clothes and ribbons still paraded along, calling out the virtues of their wares, hoping to make one last ha'penny before retiring for the night. It seemed wild, frenetic, harried.

Elizabeth smiled and shook her head in wonder at what a naive, simple country girl she had become.

'Here, boy,' Billy snapped, and a young boy with a wheelbarrow grabbed up the handles and maneuvered the vehicle over to them with practiced ease. 'You know the Ship and Compass on Crooked Lane, by the Town House?'

'Yes, sir.'

'Take this dunnage there, boy, and be quick.' He pressed a coin into the boy's hand – Billy's usual excessive payment – which made the young man's eyes go wide. When the shock had worn off he lifted the trunk and bag into the barrow and hurried off with great alacrity.

'Good lad,' Billy called after him. He nodded his thanks to Black Tom and then, with a gesture as if he were welcoming Elizabeth into his home, he indicated that they might now proceed down the wharf to the town beyond.

They stepped over rough-cut planks worn smooth by the traffic. To their left, the wharf's single row of permanent buildings, big two- and three-story structures, surprisingly substantial, given that their foundation was just a wooden platform.

Long Wharf ran on to King Street and into the heart of Boston town. A block beyond, Crooked Lane intersected King. The Ship and Compass was two doors down from the corner.

Elizabeth paused, looked up at the sign that hung over the door, a bas-relief ship superimposed on a compass rose.

They had made it, had arrived in Boston at last. On Billy's urging she had agreed to come all this way, to try and root out Frederick Dunmore's darkest secret.

And suddenly all of the fine arguments Billy Bird had made in the inn in Williamsburg seemed insane, the task before them impossible.

Whatever had she been thinking?

CHAPTER 22

The closer they drew to the French Indiaman, the grimmer things looked. Marlowe had purposely sent no flags aloft until they had smoked the stranger's identity. Once they had, he ran French colors aloft, fore, main, and mizzen. It did not appear to have fooled them.

The two ships had closed to a mile or so when the Indiaman began to casually reduce her spread of canvas to fighting sail. The studding sails disappeared first, and though they were not doused with any sort of breathtaking speed, neither was the evolution the kind of slow and clumsy work that would indicate a small or poorly trained crew.

Topgallants after that, with hands sent aloft to stow, and then the mainsail was hauled up in its gear. It was all unhurried, almost leisurely, like a confident duelist who carefully removes his coat and waistcoat and sets them down with care, certain he will be putting them on again soon.

The Elizabeth Galleys watched this and they were not immune to the effect.

Not that the men who sailed under Marlowe were wanting in courage, not at all. But being ordered into battle was one thing, being able to choose one's fight was another, and the closer they drew, the bigger and more imposing the Indiaman looked, and the less certain they became.

'She is a monstrous thing,' Bickerstaff noted. He and Marlowe were at the weather rail on the quarter-deck and not aft in their private place. The time for privacy was past. 'Are they all so big?'

'Generally. Not much protection from the navy in the East Indies, and quite a bit of danger. There are the native pirates, of course, and the Great Mogul's navy. And now these fellows on the Pirate Round, sailing out of New York and Newport and such and taking whatever they can lay hands on. Thomas Tew's successes there in ninety-four have quite inspired those of an adventurous mind.'

'Sailors from the American colonies? Taking prizes with never a letter of marque?'

'Shocking, ain't it?' Marlowe agreed.

'Thomas Tew, if I am not mistaken, died while holding his guts in place with his own hands, trying to replicate his famous voyage.'

'True enough, but those of an adventurous bent understand that such things could not happen to them.'

Marlowe looked forward at the grim men standing by their guns. He wondered how many of them thought they were impervious to French iron. Not many, he imagined, not anymore. Given the chance, he reckoned a solid majority would now vote to turn and run, but none of them down there was going to be the one to broach the subject, and neither was he. The die was cast.

'How do you think she is armed?' Bickerstaff

asked. His was an active mind. Marlowe thought that if Bickerstaff was about to be shot in the head he would be wondering about the make of the gun, the merits of firearms over cold steel, the physiological aspects of a bullet tearing through flesh.

'Probably eighteen-pounders. Perhaps twenty-fours. I think I count twelve gunports.'

'Indeed? Heavy armament, to be sure. Much heavier than ours. Have they the men to work those big guns?'

'Good question. That might be their weakness. You see, for all their arms and man-of-war styling and such, East India companies – and this is true of all of them – are still merchantmen, which means they are parsimonious to a fault. They'll keep crews as small as ever they can to save on wages, so it is possible that their guns make a great show, but they do not have the crews to work them.'

'If that is the case, then, this should not be a bloody day for us. Either broadsides or boarding, we should have them.'

'We should. Unfortunately, the Indiamen are often used to transport troops. If that is the case she could be packed with men. Trained fighting men.'

'Which could explain her apparent disregard of the potential threat we pose.'

'Yes it could. And damned insulting it is, I might add. I think she should be quite terrified of us.'

If the Indiaman was in fact terrified, she continued to do an admirable job of hiding the fact. The *Elizabeth Galley*, with all plain sail set, and studding sails to weather, ran down fast on her, but she made no attempt to run, no attempt to gain the weather gauge, no attempt to defend herself beyond reducing down to fighting sail. It was making Marlowe's men very nervous indeed.

They were no more than a quarter of a mile apart when Marlowe saw something flash on the Indiaman's side. He put his glass to his eye. They had opened gunports and run out the great guns. Marlowe shook his head. Now what?

'Studding sails in! Clew up topgallants and mainsail!'

That was the first thing. Now what?

They had to exchange broadsides, at least two. That would tell Marlowe how well manned they were, whether he should consider boarding, or standing off in an artillery duel, or throwing up his hands and running for the horizon.

'Get those Frenchy colors down, run up the English,' he called. 'Sail trimmers, stand by. Gunners, a broadside on my command . . .'

He looked aloft. The French colors were coming down, those of Old England on their way up. Do this thing proper, he thought.

The English ensign hit the main truck. 'Larboard your helm!' Marlowe called, and the *Elizabeth Galley* swung off. 'Sail trimmers, meet her . . . fire!'

The larboard broadside went off in one great blast. The deck shook like an earthquake under their feet, the thick smoke swirled and rolled downwind, and the men, well trained by now, fell to loading again.

Marlowe saw shot fall around the Frenchman and two at least strike the high-sided ship. Now the Indiaman was turning to starboard as well, bringing her broadside to bear. More and more of her high side was revealed as she turned. Marlowe counted gunports. Fourteen per side, not twelve.

The Frenchman fired. Marlowe saw the smoke through the glass, spurting from fourteen muzzles, and he whipped the glass from his eye as the noise of the broadside and the whistle of iron and the heavy fusillade all reached the *Elizabeth Galley* together. Round shot whipped past, punched holes in the sails, slammed into the side of the ship, tore sections of bulwark free.

'Damn my eyes!' Marlowe said in surprise. Well aimed, and heavy shot. Twenty-four-pounders. They had to be.

'Frenchy's tacking, sir!' Fleming called out.

The Frenchman was still turning, her bow pointing right at the *Galley*'s waist, and the faster of the *Galley*'s gun crews were able to get off racking shots, but Marlowe did not think they would do much good.

The Indiaman's sails came aback and they hauled main and mizzen around, and despite Marlowe's fervent wish that they should miss stays and get hung in irons, they completed their turn through the wind.

The Frenchman's larboard broadside now came around to bear on the *Elizabeth Galley* and the two ships fired nearly at once, the *Galley*'s fire ragged, uncoordinated, with the crews loading and firing at their best speed, the Frenchman's all as one, the preloaded guns throwing out a wall of smoke and flame and iron.

A shot hit the ship's bell in a great clanking and screaming blast of metal. 'Damn it!' Marlowe shouted, and when he saw that none of his men had been felled by the spray of shrapnel, he added, 'Bloody thing cost thirteen bloody pounds!'

Two cable lengths separated the ships as they

passed, the Frenchman having tacked and begun clawing her way to windward, the *Elizabeth Galley* still running with the wind between two sheets.

'Now we shall see how well she is manned,' Marlowe said to Bickerstaff. 'See how quick she can load those fine, big guns.'

And then, as if answering that question specifically, the great guns rolled out again and fired, all fourteen at once. The section of bulwark between numbers five and seven guns was knocked flat and number seven was overturned, half the gun crew blown apart in the blast, the rest slipping on their mates' blood as they tried to flee from the loose gun barrel.

The stay tackle was severed, and the big fiddle block plunged down onto the main hatch and dropped one of the powder monkeys as he ran for the scuttle. The fore brace was likewise parted and the foreyard swung away at a crazy angle.

'Hands aloft! Reeve off a new brace there!' Marlowe shouted, and then in a low voice he said, 'Well, my dear Francis, they've no dearth of men aboard, it would seem.'

'I should say not.' The *Elizabeth Galley* was firing back, firing fast and true. Marlowe could see the wood flying in sprays of deadly splinters as the shot struck home, could see the holes in the sails, the bits of rigging hanging free. But it was still the *Elizabeth Galley*'s six twelve-pounders per side versus the Frenchman's fourteen twenty-fours. If the *Elizabeth Galleys* did not get lucky, they would not survive the day alive and free.

'Sail trimmer! Stand by to brace up, larboard tack! Starboard your helm!' The *Elizabeth Galley* began her turn, swinging her bow toward the Frenchman,

291

coming around on a parallel course. 'Gunners! Starboard battery!'

Marlowe paced the quarterdeck watching his men in the waist, the sails overhead, the enemy across the stretch of deep blue sea. How long had this battle lasted? Ten minutes? Was it just ten minutes ago that the two ships had been sailing in the lovely quiet of a ship at sea, just the water rushing down the side, the occasional squeak of a block or thump of the rudder?

Ten minutes and their whole world had changed. Now ears were ringing with the blast of cannon, decks ran red with blood, the air was choked with gunpowder smoke and the sound of flying metal and the shouts of the living and the screams of the dying. From one world to the next. And what would be the next world after that?

The forwardmost gun on the *Galley*'s larboard side came to bear and the gunners fired, and then the next and the next, but from the Frenchman, nothing. Their gunners were taking orders from an officer, and that officer chose to fire in broadsides, and he was waiting.

He did not wait long. The *Elizabeth Galley*'s bow came around, just past the midsection of the Indiaman when they fired again. It was the full broadside, shot almost down the *Galley*'s centerline, a terrible, racking fire.

Marlowe saw men flung into the air and come down in broken heaps on top of the guns. A ball plowed through the main shrouds and parted three of them like spunyard, and he heard the mast groan and settle. The number-one gun was on its side, on top of its swabber, but the man was happily dead.

And then Marlowe was spinning around and falling

and then he was on the deck, dazed, looking up. He breathed, breathed again, did a mental inventory of his parts. He was alive. Something had knocked him down but he was alive.

He rolled over, pushed himself up, shouted in agony, and collapsed to the deck again. He turned his head, looked at his right arm. It was still part of him, but the angle was not right. Just below the elbow. It was not supposed to bend that way.

Bickerstaff appeared above him, reaching down. 'Thomas, Thomas, are you all right? Are you hit?'

'Damned arm is broken. Here, help me up.'

Bickerstaff grabbed him under the arms, pulled him to his feet. He was as gentle as he could be, but still it was agony. Marlowe let his arm droop at his side as he surveyed the destruction on deck.

We can't take much more of this, he thought. We'll board. We'll board and take our chances. There is nothing else for it.

Then overhead came a low groan and Marlowe had the notion that someone was groaning in pain nearby. He looked up but did not see anyone. And then the groaning grew louder, higher in pitch, and with it came a snapping of wood, a popping of cordage, as standing rigging and running rigging were torn apart.

The fore topmast leaned heavily to one side, as if it was drunk or trying to peer around something. The sail collapsed, half aback. A backstay parted, whipped free, knocking a man to the deck, and then the whole thing – topmast, topsail yard, topgallant, and topgallant yard, with all their attendant rigging and sails and hardware – toppled forward and to starboard, crashing down half on the deck, half in the sea, a great tangled broken heap of detritus that draped over half the forward part of the ship and made her spin up to windward, entirely out of control.

'Larboard battery, keep firing!' Marlowe shouted. His arm was useless, throbbing in pain, but he tried to ignore it. 'Keep firing! Never mind the wreckage! Sail trimmers, cut that away. Cut those shrouds free, the fore topmast stay, cut it free!'

They were helpless now. If the Frenchman chose to stand off and pound them to kindling, it could do so. If they chose to board so as to not further injure their prize, they could do that as well.

We have to pound them, pound the bastards, Marlowe thought. Hit them hard enough and perhaps they'll lose their taste for the fight. Perhaps we'll score a lucky hit, like they did.

In the waist, furious activity. The gunners were working their guns like crazed men, swabbing, ramming, running out, laying, and firing. They knew the score. They knew how helpless they really were, how vital it was now that they show they still had teeth.

Men swarmed over the wreckage, hacking at the still intact rigging with axes, cutlasses, sheath knives, whatever they could. Even with the topmast shot away they might be able to sail the *Galley*, enough to keep their broadsides bearing on the enemy, but as long as the wreckage was dragging alongside they were immobile.

'I believe they have had enough.'

Marlowe looked up. Bickerstaff was standing beside him, hands clasped behind his back. He looked like he was addressing a rhetoric class.

'What?'

294

'The Indiaman.' Bickerstaff pointed with his chin.

The Indiaman had fallen off, turned back to her original heading, the one she had been on when they first spotted her, running before the wind.

'Hold your fire!' Marlowe shouted, and the guns fell silent and then all along the *Elizabeth Galley*'s deck the men were silent as they watched.

'She'll come around again!' Fleming interjected. He had taken a glancing blow on the scalp from a splinter and the blood ran down his cheek and matted in his hair, and though the wound was superficial Fleming looked like he might die at any moment.

'She'll come around, lay off our quarter, pound us to slivers.' There was no fear or anger or panic in the mate's voice. It was just an observation.

But it was wrong. The Frenchman did not turn, did not bring her other guns to bear, did not heave to where the *Elizabeth Galley*'s guns could not reach and pound away.

Rather, she settled back on her old heading. Her guns ran in; her mainsail tumbled from the yard and was sheeted home. Topmen raced away aloft and loosened off the topgallants

'The impudent dog!' Marlowe exclaimed. He tried to point at the Indiaman, for emphasis, forgetting his broken arm until he raised it up. He felt the pain shoot through him. He gasped and let it drop again. 'Can't even be bothered with us! Like we were some trifling annoyance.'

'If you would rather they come back and murder us all, I could go ask under flag of truce,' Bickerstaff suggested.

'No, no, I suppose we'll let him go.' Marlowe was feeling buoyant, despite the pain.

He watched as the Frenchman set her topsails once again. Lord, he thought, how long can luck like this hold out?

CHAPTER 23

The Ship and Compass was no strict-run Puritan boardinghouse, but rather a place that catered to visiting sailors, men who were not quite as firm in their piety as the citizens of Boston. That much was clear to Elizabeth.

Billy Bird, it turned out, had patronized the lodging so often, and spread his gold so liberally, that he was welcomed like the prodigal son, despite the late hour.

They spent the night in the inn's best room, Billy sleeping like the dead on the floor, Elizabeth lying awake on the wide bed, thinking, planning, fretting. When dawn at last made the cotton drapes glow with gray light, she still did not know how she would proceed, what she would do to find out Dunmore's dirty little secret, why, indeed, she had even come to Boston.

'Good morning, my dear,' Billy said, rising from the floor at the foot of her bed. Elizabeth pulled the sheets further over her.

'Humph.'

' "Humph"? Is that it? Do you appreciate how difficult it is for me to be cheerful after having spent the entire night with the most beautiful woman in Boston and having to sleep on the floor the whole while? I think some sympathy is due.'

'If it is so bloody hard being cheerful, then bloody well don't be.'

'Uh-oh. Someone has had a hard night.'

'Billy, whatever are we going to do? We have come here with no plan in mind . . . how ever are we to discover anything about Dunmore?'

At this Billy looked confused, as if she had asked him how they would find air to breathe. 'How? Why, we shall just ask.'

'Ask whom?'

'Dunmore's father, I should think. And people who know both him and Dunmore the Younger.'

'How shall we find Dunmore's father?'

'God, Lizzy, you are a bleak one in the morning. Dunmore's father is some kind of preacher. If we ask in any church, I should imagine they would know where to find him. Boston ain't London, as awestruck as you are by the size of this place. We'll find him. Now, I hope you can stomach cod for breakfast, because that is damned near all they eat around here.'

Billy's optimism did much to buoy Elizabeth's spirit, enough even that she was able to eat the breakfast of fresh-baked bread and cod's tongues that was served to them in the ordinary adjoining the Ship and Compass.

She was further amused to find that no comment at all was made about the fact that Billy had arrived with a young gentleman friend the night before and come downstairs the next morning with a woman of strikingly similar appearance. The absolute lack of

298

surprise on the part of the innkeeper and his servants made Elizabeth guess that the Ship and Compass was as much honored for its discretion as its room and board.

They headed out in the late morning, making their way through the crowded, narrow streets in the direction of the closest church they could see. In the daylight, and with the excitement of their arrival having passed, Elizabeth was able to make a more sober assessment of Boston.

It was big, by colonial standards, and crowded by any standard, save for that of the biggest cities. Brick buildings and timber buildings formed solid walls on either side of the cobbled streets, hemming in the people like the banks of a river; people on foot, people on horseback, people pushing carts and driving drays and wagons and carriages, all made their slow way through the city. It was as if God had taken up a small section of London, cleaned it a bit, thinned out the population some, and set it down in the New England wilderness. Being in those narrow, crowded, noisy streets brought back in a rush the memories of Plymouth and London, and she did not care for them.

'Do you see what a damned lot of Puritans they are?' Billy asked.

'Yes . . .' Elizabeth equivocated. There certainly were a number of men in their black clothes and white wigs and wide-brimmed black hats and capes, but not nearly as many as she had imagined. From Billy's descriptions she had expected the entire city to resemble a Congregationalist church service, but that was a generation or two gone. This was no longer John Winthrop's Boston.

But neither was it rollicking Virginia of Royalist birth, the Virginia of Raleigh and John Smith, with its hunts and horse races, its grand balls at the governor's house, and its raucous Publick Times. Boston was more sober by far than that.

They came at last to the church, called simply the Old Church, just across Cornhill Street from the Town House and Crooked Lane. It was a redbrick affair with a tall white spire and big wooden doors thrown open. With not the least hesitation Billy Bird climbed the granite steps and walked into the cool interior, Elizabeth trailing behind.

The church was empty. The tall, white-painted, uncomfortable-looking pews stood like soldiers in ranks waiting for the order to march. The walls were plastered and painted white; the arched windows rose high up the walls in regular intervals. Unlike the Anglican Burton Parish Church of Williamsburg, which flaunted its wealth and elegance with understatement, the Old Church displayed a genuine understatement, no more or less presumptuous in its conspicuous simplicity than the Puritan black coat and hat.

At the far end of the church, high in the pulpit, the minister stood flipping the pages of a book. He looked up at the sound of Billy's shoes on the wood floor echoing through the empty hall and climbed down the stairs to meet them.

'Good day to you, sir.' Billy gave an elaborate bow.

'Good day.' The minister was in Calvinist black, set off by his white wig and cravat fringed with a simple lace. His eyes flickered over Billy's fine red wool coat, his silk waistcoat, his hat with the gold trim, which he held under his arm, the sword at his belt. 'How may I help you?'

'We are just arrived from England to your country, sir, and we are seeking out an acquaintance of ours, a Mr Frederick Dunmore, whose father, I am told, is a man of the cloth in this town.'

At that the minister frowned, and if he wished to deny knowing Dunmore it was too late. When he spoke his tone said much more than his words. 'I have not heard tell of Frederick Dunmore for some years now. I had thought he was in London, but if you are just from there, then I suppose not. In any event, he does not live in Boston and I do not know where he now makes his home.'

'Then perhaps we shall call upon his father, if you would be so kind as to tell us where we might find that worthy gentleman?'

Butter would melt on Billy Bird's tongue, Elizabeth thought.

The minister cleared his throat and it took him a moment to decide what to say, during which time Billy smiled and waited, the picture of guileless innocence.

'Reverend Wait Dunmore is minister of the Middle Street Church, which stands at the corner of Middle Street and Cross. Do you know it?'

'No, sir, we are just arrived,' said Billy, too quick to be caught up in that snare. The minister gave directions to which Billy listened attentively, and then they bade him good day and left.

They made their way up Cornhill Street, across Dock Square to Anne Street and then down to Cross Street, Billy stepping with the authority of one who knows his way perfectly well, his request for directions notwithstanding.

'It is odd, is it not, that Dunmore's father should be a minister here? A Congregationalist minister?' Elizabeth observed.

'Why is that odd?'

'Well, Dunmore is no Congregationalist, nothing of the sort. Hell, he practically owns Burton Parish Church, or its minister, in any event.'

'Frederick Dunmore seems to have shed everything of his former life, so why not his church as well? He is an opportunist, from what I can see, and he gives not a tinker's cuss for God or the devil. But he is sensible to the fact that a Congregationalist would not go far in Virginia society. I suspect that his church attendance is entirely for social reasons. Not at all like your precious husband' – he grinned at her – 'whose piety is above reproach.'

'Above your reproach, in any event.'

At the corner of Cross and Middle Street they found the Middle Street Church, just as they had been told they would. It too was empty, but with the tall doors open, beckoning the faithful.

'Hold a minute.' Elizabeth grabbed Billy's arm and stopped him in his bold rush for the stairs. 'I must catch my breath.'

She stood on the cobbled square and looked up at the church. It was not just the exertion of the walk that was making her light-headed. Frederick Dunmore had been haunting her night and day for more than five weeks now, had sent her into flight to the woods, to Billy Bird's ship, and now to Boston. There was something unworldly about this, standing in this strange town, ready to confront Dunmore's past, ready to weed out that thing that she might at last use to destroy him.

302

Perhaps. Or perhaps this would all prove to be folly, a great waste of time. Perhaps the people of Marlowe House would have to live forever in the woods, form some renegade community out there in the wilderness, or join up with a tribe of Indians or come back to Williamsburg and be sold again as chattel.

I shall not find out standing here, she told herself. She took a deep breath, but that did not ameliorate the twisting in her stomach, the spinning in her head. She was never so grateful to have Billy Bird by her side as she was then. It was his very insouciance, his absolute disregard for anything that others might take seriously, that made him so good at games such as this.

'Onward, then,' she said, and together they stepped up the granite stairs and into the church.

Middle Street Church did not differ in any significant way from the first church they had visited, just a bit bigger. Once again Billy's shoes echoed in the cavernous space, but this time there was no one to be seen.

They walked slowly down the center aisle, stepping softly, not speaking, taken with the reverence that came naturally from being in a house of God, especially the strict, Old Testament God of the Puritans.

They were almost to the altar when a black woman appeared from a side door, a bucket of soapy water in her hand. Her dress was like that of any of the working-class women of the city: cotton mobcap, wool petticoat skirt, muslin apron. She looked to be in her thirties, perhaps a bit older. A slave or a free servant, there was no way to know.

'Can I help you?' she asked.

'Good day, ma'am.' Billy bowed, just as he might have bowed to the governor's wife. 'We would like to inquire of Mr Wait Dunmore.'

'Mmmm-hmm. What business you got with Reverend Dunmore?'

'We are here on a matter that concerns his son.'

That seemed to spark some interest, and the woman said, 'You wait here, I'll see if the Reverend can receive you.' She put the bucket down and disappeared through the door. A minute later she was back, beckoning them to follow.

She led them down a narrow hall at the end of which was a room, an office, with a desk and a couple of ladder-backed chairs, a big Bible on a stand, and several blanket chests, one of which was open, revealing itself to be crammed with papers – records of parishioners born, married, died.

Behind the desk was Reverend Dunmore. He was seventy if a day, but had about him that robust quality that comes with a life of hard work and prayer and no hint of debauch, a face whose natural resting position was a scowl, as if the man was too ornery to die or even grow weak with age.

He was scratching away with a quill and did not even look up as Elizabeth and Billy and the black woman stood patiently, and the black woman, at least, seemed to accept this as ordinary. At last he put the quill back in its stand, elaborately sanded the ink, tapped the sand off the paper, swept it away, and when that was completed looked up.

'Yes?'

'Reverend, these is the people come to see you,' the woman said.

'Thank you, Sally,' said Dunmore, and Sally curt-sied, turned, and left.

Dunmore scrutinized them, as Elizabeth in turn scrutinized him. This was Frederick Dunmore's father all right, there was no mistaking it. The son was more filled out, his face rounder, more fleshy, but around the eyes and the mouth, and the unpleasant expression, there was no denying the resemblance.

'Reverend Dunmore, how very good it is to see you again!' Billy gushed, and gave a great sweeping bow, thrusting his hat up with stiff arm into the air. 'My word, sir, it has been an age at least!'

Dunmore scowled and Elizabeth stared at Billy and wondered if he was making this up as he went along.

'I do not believe I have had the pleasure, sir,' said Dunmore.

'Oh, forgive me, Reverend, but of course you would never recall me. I was a child, nine years old, when last we met. Thomas Marlowe? I was a childhood friend of your son's. My family returned to England when I was nine, and I am only now coming back to Boston.'

'I am sorry, sir, but I do not recall you. If you wish to see Roger, I am certain his memory will prove more reliable than mine. He might be found in his offices near the foot of Clark's Wharf.'

'Roger . . . ?'

'Roger Dunmore, my son. To whom you claim this childhood friendship.'

'Oh, Roger, of course! But no, sir, forgive me but you mistake it! It was Frederick with whom I was playmates. Your son Frederick. Is he, too, still in Boston?'

This brought something close to the reaction that

Elizabeth had hoped for. The Reverend's ever-present scowl grew deeper, his white eyebrows came closer together.

'No, he is not . . . Sally! That will do!' Elizabeth turned in time to see that Sally had developed an interest in cleaning the wainscoting just outside the open door of the office. On Dunmore's bark she snatched up the bucket and hurried away down the narrow hall.

'No,' Reverend Wait Dunmore said again. 'He does not live in Massachusetts.'

'Oh. I am sorry indeed to miss him. I so hoped to introduce him to my wife, Mrs Elizabeth Marlowe.'

At that Elizabeth curtsied, but Dunmore just fixed them both with his unfeeling stare.

'What did you say your name was?'

'Marlowe, sir. Thomas Marlowe. Son of Joseph and Rebecca Marlowe, late of Salem Street?'

Dunmore shook his head.

'Perhaps you can tell me, sir, is Frederick well? He was always so . . . high-spirited. I hope he has found his way in the world, and not lost sight of Godliness.'

Dunmore stared, scowled, said nothing.

'I have feared for him, you know, all these years. So many times I took pen in hand to write, as if the Lord were telling me that Frederick was in need of what little guidance I could offer, but each time . . .'

'Frederick makes his own peace with God.'

'I am pleased to hear that. But how could he not, having such a pious upbringing. Might I inquire if it was business that drew him away from Boston? Has he gone to seek his fortune elsewhere, or perhaps to spread the true word?'

'You did not ask where he has gone.'

306

'Pardon?'

'I would think your first question would have been to inquire as to his whereabouts, not why he has left.'

'That was to be my second question, sir.'

'Get out.'

This simple statement took Billy aback. 'Pardon?'

'Get out, sir. I do not know who you are, or what you are about, but I want you to leave. Now.'

'Well . . .' Billy flustered. 'I have never . . . we are at the Ship and Compass, sir, if you wish to make apologies for this rudeness before my wife—'

'Get out!' Dunmore was on his feet, his chair flung to the floor with the violence of his standing. He pounded his fist on the desk. 'Get out!'

But Billy would not be flustered, not even in the face of such unfettered rage. 'Come along, my dear, let us go. This is just the thing I was warning you about, with the Dunmore family—'

'Get out!' He pounded the desk again.

Billy took Elizabeth by the arm and steered her out of the room and back down the hall, the way they had come. Billy held her back, despite her desire to break and run, forcing her to walk at a dignified, even leisurely pace. They stepped back into the church, past the wide-eyed Sally, down the aisle, and at last back into the bright midday sun of Boston, the crowded streets, the smell of the horses and brackish water, the close-packed houses and shops.

'Well, he was not as receptive to our inquiries as I had hoped,' said Billy, adjusting his sword until it hung at the desired angle.

Elizabeth took a deep breath, closed her eyes. Wait Dunmore's sudden violence had unnerved her, and now her shock was settling into despair. 'Oh, Billy, whatever will we do now? God, what a fool I was, thinking we could just show up here and discover some shocking secret. What have I done?'

'Lizzy, dear, I hope you never thought we would be simply handed what we want. Now at least we know there is something to learn. But it will take some ferreting, you know, and ferret we will.'

As usual, Elizabeth found some comfort in Billy's words, in the absolute assurance of his tone. 'But how? What will we do?'

'First we shall dine on the best that Boston has to offer. Cod fixed any way you like. And then we begin on the second part of the plan.'

'And what is that?'

'I do not know at the moment, my dear, but by the time our cod dinner is done I have no doubt I will. I myself am a master at cooking cod, did you know that?'

She looked at him, shook her head. This sounded like the setup of one of his idiotic jokes. She wondered whether she should encourage his sophomoric humor. 'No, I did not.'

'You didn't? Well, you do know there is none can stuff a codpiece nice and full like me.'

And despite herself, Elizabeth smiled.

CHAPTER 24

They were in among the shipping again, near enough to the coast of Africa that they could smell the land, even when it was not in sight.

Every day they sighted so many vessels that soon they raised no comment among the joyful, relieved, and optimistic men and women aboard the former French merchantman. Long dugout canoes, carved from a single tree and rowed by big crews of skilled paddlers, dark spots on the horizon, but the largest of these would on occasion paddle out to them, sometimes close enough to exchange a few words.

There were sailing vessels as well, the low-sided native craft with their great arching lateen sails, and brigs and snows and ships from Europe and America. On a few occasions those vessels passed to windward, and the revolting and frightening smell of a black-birder rolled down on them.

For a week their course had not changed, save to compensate for the baffling winds which during that time managed to come from every point of the compass. But most of the wind they could use, and the chip log spun out behind to show their progress as they closed at long last on their port of destination.

Then one morning James stepped onto the quarterdeck to find the pilot and Madshaka in conference by the helm.

He watched Madshaka's broad back, and the pilot, cowering slightly, and hunched. He could not hear what they were saying.

It was an hour past dawn and it was already hot, and the vessel, which had been motionless, was starting to catch some puffs and the slatting sails were starting to fill. The pilot said something to the helmsman, Madshaka gave orders for the yards to be trimmed around a bit.

Madshaka was armed. He generally went around with only a long dagger on his belt, but now, pirate fashion, he carried a sword, dagger, and a brace of pistols, as if he were readying for a fight.

The sky was pure, pure blue. On the puffs of air rode scents from the land, the nearby land, and James understood that he should be happy. Africa. Home. It was almost over.

Then Madshaka turned to him, grinned his sardonic grin, said, 'King James,' and jerked his head in a gesture meant to summon him over.

'The pilot, he say we make landfall, today,' Madshaka said when James had stepped over to him. 'I think, whatever you need to do to anchor, you better do it now.'

James just stared. 'You giving me an order, Madshaka? We not pretending anymore that I'm still captain?'

'No, no. I just make a suggestion. Captain.'

James nodded. Madshaka's sarcasm was the real answer. But if cockbilling the anchor and preparing it for setting would get them one step closer to being

310

done with the voyage, then James did not really care from whom the order came. He headed off forward, looking for Quash and Good Boy and Cato and Joshua. His men.

It took most of the morning to prepare the anchor, the best bower having been lashed in place for so long, and the gear stowed away in parts of the ship never visited, and James working through the clouds in his mind to make sense of it all, and in the end it was done.

A headland had appeared beyond the bow just as they were bending on the cable, low green hills rising out of the blue sea. The wide arms of land spread as they approached, and by the time the best bower was cockbilled and ready to let go, their entire northern horizon, from east to west, was shoreline. They had not seen so much land in many weeks. It seemed the oddest of sights.

Cato put a hand on James's shoulder, a bold gesture of familiarity, a transparent attempt to lift James from his mounting despair. 'What think you, James? Kalabari!'

James shook his head. 'It is not.'

Cato was silent and he looked uncertain as to how to respond. 'It's not?'

'I don't think so. The beaches, the trees . . . it don't look right. Kalabari should not be to the north.'

The two men watched the approaching shoreline in silence. Off the larboard bow they could see, emerging from the forest, a city of significant proportions, an African city of low buildings. It appeared as a stutter of white geometric patches against the green forest, a strip of white sand in front, crowds of shipping anchored in the exposed roads.

James turned to Cato, tried to smile, but the result was not what he had hoped. 'I'm wrong, I think. I've not been here before. I suppose this is Kalabari.' But James was in no frame of mind for lying and he did not convince Cato.

James left the young man at the cathead, made his way aft. The ship crept toward the shore and the white squares resolved themselves into individual structures, houses with dark windows and roofs thatched with *bere* as if they were trying to blend in with their background. Against the press of the green hills he could see the tall, spindly palms, waving in the same breeze that was drawing them in.

Along the line of the beach, the treacherous surf of the African coast flashed white. The surf through which only the skilled *grumetes*, like Madshaka and Kusi, could safely bring the big canoes, a skill that made them so invaluable to the white men there.

'Madshaka, we best furl courses and topgallants,' James said. Madshaka shouted the orders forward and the men raced aloft and the sails came in. He did not acknowledge James, did not even look at him, as if James's words had just been thoughts in his own head.

As the voyage was ending, so was the pretense.

They stood on under topsails until they were in among the ships, ships of every size, from two-man canoes to big English and Portuguese slavers, all scattered along several miles of shoreline.

There was some kind of settlement on the shore, and boats going in and out of the surf and plying between ships, but they were a mile or more to the east of the big city they had seen. The people crowded the rail and stared, silent. They were here, and words did not seem adequate.

The French pilot said to Madshaka, 'Anchor there,' and pointed, and this time Madshaka turned to James and glared, because what the pilot said was beyond Madshaka's ability. James turned to the helmsman and pointed to the patch of water that the pilot had indicated and the helmsman nodded and pushed the tiller over.

The ship turned up and up into the wind and the leeches of the square sails began to shiver and James said to Madshaka, 'Tell them to clew up the fore and main topsails,' and once again Madshaka stepped forward and gave the orders as if they had originated with him.

The fore and main topsails came down on the run and the mizzen topsail came aback and the ship stopped on that spot of water.

'Let go!' James called forward. Cato waved his acknowledgment and let the ring stopper fly and the best bower plunged into the water with a great splash and the ship, that floating community of disparate tribes, was fast by her anchor to the shore of Africa.

And then one of the men was coming aft, yelling something at Madshaka, waving his arms and pointing toward the shore. He stopped a foot from Madshaka, still yelling. His tone was accusatory.

Madshaka stepped back, held his hands up, as if to ward off blows, and with a quick word he silenced the man. He turned to the Frenchman. 'This fellow, he say this not Kalabari. Where you take us?'

The Frenchman shook his head slowly, side to side, stammered, 'Whydah . . . this is Whydah . . .'

'Bastard!' Madshaka's arm moved like a great black snake, too fast for anyone to react, almost too fast to see. He jerked a pistol from his belt, brought it up, drew the hammer back with his big thumb and shot the pilot in the forehead from three feet away.

It was too fast for the pilot to say anything, too fast for him to react at all. The blow from the .69-caliber ball knocked him off his feet and blew his skull and brain apart, showering the bulwark with gore, and he was dead even before he fell in a bloody swath across the deck.

'Bastard!' Madshaka shouted again, and he took a step forward and kicked the dead man hard, the smoking gun in his hand. He turned toward the stunned men and women and children who were looking aft at them and shouted something in one language then another and another, pointing at the shore and the dead man.

When he was done he turned to King James. 'This bastard,' he pointed at the dead pilot, 'he trick us. We tell him we go to Kalabari, he take us to Whydah. He have friends here, I wager.' He waved the discharged gun at James. 'You, you supposed to know this navigation, you supposed to watch him! How he do this?'

James scowled, shook his head. God, would it stop? He had only taken cursory looks at the chart when the pilot had showed it to him. The track marked there had been one heading to Kalabari, but there was no way for James to know if the course the pilot had marked on the chart was the same as the course that the ship was actually sailing. And here was the result.

Whydah. What would they do in Whydah, in the heart of what the white men called the Slave Coast?

Now Madshaka was shouting at the people and pointing to James and the people were looking at

James with hateful eyes and for once James understood completely what Madshaka was saying.

He folded his arms, looked at the crowd facing him. He did not doubt they would fall on him, beat him to death, but he could not seem to move himself to care.

But Madshaka stopped the tirade, paused, glanced over at the shore. He raced to the rail, leaned against it, seemed to be studying the buildings, the beach. There was something artificial in the performance, something contrived about his stance, his concentration, but James could not see on the faces of the others if anyone besides himself felt as much.

Then Madshaka turned back to the people. He pointed toward the shore and he spoke again, but this time his voice was pleading and sad with just a hint of his former anger and James could not imagine what he was saying.

He spoke for ten minutes and by then the other men were nodding in agreement and were themselves looking at the distant shore. Then Madshaka said something with a tone of finality and the men nodded again, their faces grim, and then they dispersed.

Madshaka turned aft, and in doing so caught James's eye. He stopped short and the two men stared at each other for a moment, then Madshaka said, 'This where I was taken. Whydah, where I was put into slavery, I tell them I know where the factory is, just there, where they keep the slaves. I tell them we go ashore, free them all, take them away.

'Tonight, we go ashore, free our brothers. You come too, King James? Or are you afraid?' He let the question hang, grinned at James, and his expression was gloating and victorious, not that of a man

315

selflessly risking his life to emancipate his brothers in chains.

'Yes, I'll come.'

He thought of that old sailor's rhyme. Beware, beware, the Bight of Benin . . .

The warning was supposed to be for white men, he thought.

CHAPTER 25

Madshaka walked fore and aft, fore and aft, like a lion preparing to charge. He liked the feel of the still-warm deck planks under his hard, bare feet, liked the slap of the cutlass, the slap of the dirk, the thump of the pistols across his chest. He had to remember not to smile with delight at it all. This was a solemn moment. The people believed that. He had told them so.

Before him, in uneven ranks, his army. The nucleus of his army. Sixty men. Well trained. Vicious. They had already followed him in enough attacks that he knew he could count on them. He had taught them how to be merciless, how to butcher any resistance, how to roll over any confrontation. They would do it again.

Of the sixty men before him, seventeen were Kru, like himself. It was too bad they were not all Kru, did not all speak Kwa, did not all have that loyalty that came of an ancient bond of kinship. Then he would really have something.

But they were not, and he had no use for the others, the Yoruba, the Ibo, the Bariba, the Aja, all the rest. He had no use for the English speakers, no use for the women. No use after that night's work.

'The factory, two miles from the shore,' he told them. 'I know the way. No sound until we there. The King of Whydah has army, he will fight us, because he is an evil man. We must not be discovered until we victorious.'

He saw grim faces. The men nodded their understanding as he spoke.

'It will be easy, if we surprise them. Not many men there. We overrun them, kill only who I say. I open the prison, we go in, help our brothers out, take the white men's gold, and come back to the ship.'

A noble cause and one that would further enrich them. He could see the effects his words were having, words he translated into the various languages of his army. English too, for he had convinced King James and the other Virginians to go with them on their righteous crusade.

King James. Madshaka could well imagine what a hell his life had been. Stolen from a noble family of the Kabu Malinke, forced to endure the Middle Passage, a slave for two decades. His bold, selfless act of saving all those aboard the blackbirder turning into such a nightmare. Madshaka knew that a man's mind could endure only so much, and he knew that James must be near the breaking point.

And after all that, King James's life would end here, on the African shore, on that night, in the slave port of Whydah.

Another man might have felt sorry for him. But then, another man might have found pity for those people stolen into slavery and forced on to the hellish

318

voyage to the New World, especially after he himself had just been made to endure its living death.

But Madshaka was not such a man, and he was proud of that fact. Every horror that he lived through made him stronger, every new circle of hell through which he passed made him more contemptuous of those who were broken by it. Some men were hunters and some the hunted.

He looked up at the moon, saw that it was settling toward the horizon. It would remain long enough to get them through the surf and then it would set, leaving them to approach in darkness. Perfect. It was time to go.

On his word the army, his army of pirates, dressed as they were in their plundered sailor garb, colorful swatches of cloth bound around heads and waists, climbed silently down the boarding cleats and into the longboat below.

Madshaka felt Kusi's loss for the first time since shoving him into the sea. It would have been good to have another *grumete*, another boatman who could have taken the gig through the surf, so the longboat would not be so crowded. But it was a small thing, and did not measure up to the convenience of having Kusi drowned.

Madshaka came last. He took the last steps down the ship's side and stepped into the stern sheets of the longboat. He unshipped the rudder, which was useless in the big surf, and took up a spare oweep, holding it at his side like a soldier holding a pike as he stood on the after thwart and called, 'Give way!'

The rowers were clumsy and inexperienced, save for James and his people, and the boat was so packed with armed men that movement was difficult, but with Madshaka calling cadence they managed to get it under way. Once it was clear of the ship's side Madshaka slipped the sweep into the tholes on the transom, using the long oar like a rudder, a rudder with considerably more leverage and turning power than the former one.

They pulled through the dark and they made no noise, save for the creak of the oars, the drip of water from the blades. All along the dark shore were spots of light, lanterns or cooking fires still burning at that late hour.

In the moonlight the surf flashed gray, and soon the pounding of the water on the beach drowned out the sound of the longboat's oars, despite their being a half mile yet from the first breakers. The smells of the forest enveloped them, the high-pitched cry of a bird or an animal occasionally piercing the roar of the surf. It was his home. He was back.

Madshaka grinned. He could no longer help it. He had never felt so alive, so happy, so hopeful in his life. He was the hero returning, the conquering hero. Come back with a ship full of plunder from clean across the Atlantic. Come back with an army.

He thought of his darkest moments, a month into the Middle Passage, when he was so near death, even with taking food from others. He had despaired then of ever arriving at the place he was at now. Foolish man! As if the gods would ever abandon their most perfect creature!

He felt the after end of the longboat lifting with the first effects of the surf. He spit on his hands, took a hard grip on the sweep, gave it a slight pull to starboard to get their bow aligned. Two more strokes and the big craft was starting to buck, the white water was boiling around her gunnels. He could see wide eyes staring out at the foam, frightened eyes.

'Stop!' Madshaka ordered, and the men froze, their blades in the water. The surf lifted them again, and then they fell, this time with a sickening motion.

Madshaka stood on the stern thwart, his ears attuned to the sound of the water, his eyes judging the frequency of the rollers, his legs feeling the rise and fall of the boat. He was the lion, timing his pounce, the cheetah knowing by instinct just the second to bolt. The stern came up, up, then settled, and Madshaka called with all the urgency he felt, 'Pull! Pull!'

And the men pulled, pulled hard and fast, and the boat shot ahead, all but keeping pace with the breaking water. Madshaka felt the stern slough around. He leaned into the sweep, using that great lever to haul the boat back in line.

The wave passed and another had them and their speed built as it lifted them and hurled them toward the shore and despite himself Madshaka could not help letting out a great whoop, a battle cry, an expression of pure exhilaration as he alone, through strength of arm and mind, took that overloaded boat and those frightened children through the surf, the surf that had killed so many weaker men.

Another wave, but they were through the deadly part now, and Madshaka felt the blade of his sweep grind in the sand and then the forefoot of the boat struck with an impact that made the boat shudder.

He began to order the men out, to tell them to haul the boat up the beach, and he was wondering how many of them would actually dare get out of the boat, when he saw James and Cato and Quash and

Good Boy and Joshua leap over the gunnel and take the boat in their hands, pulling it forward when their feet found bottom, letting the boat take them when they did not.

There was something disappointing in that, and Madshaka felt as if a part of his victorious landing had been sullied by someone other than himself displaying knowledge and bravery.

But it did not matter. James could have his last little moment before he died in battle.

The men in the water hauled the boat further and further onto the sand, aided by the surging water, until those others judged it safe to leap out. One by one they went over the side, lightening the longboat and adding their effort to pulling it along, until soon it was high and dry, beyond the reach of even the most powerful surf. And only then did Madshaka unship his sweep and step ashore, regal and dry.

He savored the feel of sand underfoot, the constant but subtle undercurrent of sound: surf breaking, wind rustling the fronds of tall palms.

The French pilot had brought the ship to just the spot. Madshaka knew that stretch of beach as well as any place on earth. The curve of the tree line, the well-beaten trail – all but a road, really – through the forest, the palm trees like columns in front of some stately home, it was as if it were all his.

He remained silent, let his army wait for his next word as he enjoyed the moment. He moved past them, up the beach, toward the trees. Then he stopped, turned back to them, raised his arms over his head.

He had their attention now, every eye locked on him. It was a moment of high drama and he held it, let it build, then turned and brought his arms down like twin axes, pointer fingers extended, gesturing toward the dark road. With a wave he began to trot off up the beach and behind him his silent army of black pirates surged after.

Once they were on the wide trail, once they were enveloped by the woods, Madshaka slowed his pace. It would be better to arrive at the factory fresh than to arrive quickly. There would be no pickets along the road, no guards until they reached the actual gates of the factory. Slavers felt perfectly safe in Whydah and took no more than the most elementary precautions.

The moon might have set; Madshaka could not tell. Little light would penetrate the thick canopy of the forest. But he did not need much light, because he knew that trail so well, and what little illumination he got from the stars was enough to tell him where he was, how far from the factory.

They walked for half an hour through the forest before they saw the first flash of earthly light, a lantern or a fire, glimpsed through a gap in the trees left by some quirk of nature.

Madshaka raised his hand. 'Hold up.' He said it in Kru but the others understood his meaning and stopped. 'I see to the guards. Wait until I return,' he said, translating it into each language, and then when he knew they understood, he slipped away down the trail.

One hundred yards and the trail widened out like the mouth of a river, opened onto twenty or so cleared acres of forest, and in the middle of that, an English slave factory.

It was not the only such storehouse for slaves in

Whydah, not even the only English factory, but the others did not matter. This was the one. These were the men who had betrayed him.

He paused for a moment and let his eyes wander over the familiar sight. This factory, where Madshaka the *grumete* had become Madshaka the slaver. Where he had learned that the real wealth was to be had by plunging into the forest where the white men dared not go and rounding up those sorry people and marching them here, where they could be sold to the white men who possessed unlimited amounts of money, rum, gunpowder, guns, swords, knives.

The lion and the antelope. It was the way of things.

He was better at that game than any, and soon he controlled nearly all of the slaves coming into that factory from the backcountry. The white men did not care for that. It made Madshaka too powerful by half.

The white men at the slave factory did not care to have a lion in their midst.

So they had hit him on the head and sold him as a slave himself. There would be others to take his place, others more easily controlled than was Madshaka. It was not the first time white slavers had pulled such tricks. But they were not to be pulled on him.

The factory's outer defense, if such it could be called, was no more than a mud wall built up to a height of six feet. The wall formed a great square, each side two hundred feet long, that defined the courtyard within. In the middle of the front wall was the main gate, two wood plank doors shut tight. The worn trail ran from under those doors in a straight line to where Madshaka was standing and then past, a trail beaten by the hundreds upon hundreds of people who had come through that gate and made the one-way trip down to the beach and the ships beyond.

Over the top of the wall Madshaka could see the tall thatched roofs of the guards' house, the factor's house, and the trunk, a big common prison where the slaves were kept, awaiting their turn.

Torches mounted along the wall every fifty feet or so threw wide arcs of light, discouraging any clandestine approach over the open ground between the forest and the factory. It might even have given Madshaka pause, had he not known perfectly well that the one guard making his desultory tour along the top of the wall was the only sentry on duty, that the factor and his men would be drunk at that hour, and that barring any cry from the man on the wall they would continue to drink in peace, as sure of their safety as a child abed. Slavers did not feel threatened in Whydah.

Of all that, Madshaka was certain, but because he was smart and cunning as well as bold he remained crouched at the end of the trail for a full twenty minutes and watched, just watched. The sentry – he recognized Higgens's slovenly form – continued his slow, lethargic patrol. There was no other movement.

At last Madshaka moved, swiftly, crouched low, making his way along the tree line, completely invisible to anyone staring out through the torchlight. He skirted off to the right, stepping carefully, keeping his eyes on Higgens, who was moving away from him toward the left end of the wall.

When he was at the point where the forest made its closest approach to the factory wall, and when

Higgens's back was turned, he raced across the open ground, powerful and silent.

He reached the corner of the factory and stopped himself with his hands against the wall, let his arms absorb the impact of his great momentum. He pressed his back against the dry mud and he waited.

Five minutes, ten minutes, and then he heard Higgens's sloppy footfalls on the crumbling wall overhead, coming closer, closer. Madshaka shook his arms, limbered them up, tested the spring in his legs.

The crunch of shoes was just over him now, a bit of dirt knocked loose, falling on his neck, and then Madshaka sprung like a snake striking out. He saw Higgens's startled face, his recoiling body, heard the beginning of a shout as he grabbed the guard by the ankles and jerked him off the wall. Higgens fell in a great, awkward heap, arms flailing out, his musket coming to rest on the wall where he had dropped it in surprise.

Madshaka pounced, rolling Higgens over, knees on his chest, pinning him, one hand over the man's mouth, his dirk flashing in the other. He could have killed him that instant but he did not, because in the last seconds of his life he wanted Higgens to know who it was who had killed him. So he held the man down and grinned at him, a horrible leer, and thought of how Higgens had once grinned at him the same way as he jerked the chain attached to the iron collar around his neck.

He saw Higgens's eyes, already wide with terror, register recognition, and then go wider still.

Higgens began to thrash, to try and dislodge Madshaka, but it was futile, like trying to push over a stone wall. Madshaka leaned close, whispered,

'That's right, Higgens. It's Madshaka. I'm back. And now, time for you to die.'

A muffled shriek under his hand and then he cut Higgens's throat, sinking the blade of the dirk down through soft flesh until he felt it grate on bone. He held the white man down as he writhed in his death agony, felt the hot blood pulsing over his arm and hand, and then Higgens was still.

Madshaka leaned back, looked around. No one else in sight, no indication of any alarm from within. He sat and listened to the silence for a moment more, until he was certain that Higgens's murder had gone unnoticed. He wiped the blade of his dirk on Higgens's breeches and sheathed it, then trotted back to the tree line and followed it back to his waiting men.

'I kill the sentry,' he whispered. 'Now we go, silent, silent, like the leopard.' This he said in all their languages, slowly, so they would understand the import of his words, then said, 'Follow me, stay close, yell when I do.'

He turned, headed back toward the factory, felt the powerful and dangerous presence of the men at his back. He moved along the wide trail, paused where it opened onto the clearing, but still he could see no sign of alarm. He glanced back at his men, their faces set and determined. Their blood was up, he could see. They were ready for mayhem and slaughter.

He headed off along the tree line again, the same route he had taken to get close to Higgens. Behind him, the padding of sixty pairs of feet made no more noise than the wind in the trees. Less, in fact. He arrived at that point where the tree line was closest to the wall and stopped again and let his men assemble for the final assault. He bounced on the balls of his feet, his whole body tensed, ready for this moment.

No one betrayed Madshaka and lived long to brag on it.

He drew his cutlass, and all along the line his men drew their edged weapons as well. He held the steel aloft, looked left and right, checked his men's readiness, then stepped out, leading the charge at the wall, and behind him the others followed. He picked up his pace as he moved over the open ground, the wall less than one hundred feet away, the madness building, building with his speed and momentum.

And then he was at the wall but it seemed as if it was no impediment at all. His foot found a chink in the crumbling surface and his legs carried him up and his hands were flat on the top and the next thing he knew he was standing on the wall, and the factory, that familiar factory, lay spread out below him.

It was time to announce his arrival. He could not hold it in a second more, for he surely would explode if he tried.

The war cry started in his gut and spread up and out, filled his lungs and his throat and finally burst from his mouth with a thunderous and frightening whoop, and on either side of him his men were gathered on the wall and they began shouting as well, the same terrifying sound of warriors ready for the fight, the fight with no quarter.

The doors to the guardhouse burst open, fifty feet away, the doorway framed in weak light from within, and half-clothed men stumbled out, muskets in hand, right into the face of the horrible shouting, and

Madshaka yelled, 'That right, gentlemen. Madshaka's back.'

Then Madshaka leapt from the wall down into the compound just as the first of the guards fired. He heard a scream from behind as one of his own men took the bullet, but the rest were behind him, leaping down, racing forward.

More muskets blazed away, flashes of light, the bang of the gun, and his men screaming, screaming, in fury, in fear, in agony. Madshaka felt a bullet whiz by but there was no chance that he might be struck down. There was a shield of pure energy around him that would not be penetrated.

And then he was up with the first of the guards, all of whom had discharged their weapons and now were helpless because they had no skill for fighting, they could only fire muskets.

The man in front of him, a fat man, white face sweating, terrified, saw death coming at him in the form of a huge, leering black man, the death he feared most. He swung his musket like a club at that face, but Madshaka caught the butt of the gun before it developed any force and with the other hand drove his cutlass through the man's fat white face.

His army was there, falling on the guards so fast that they were not even able to retreat to their guardhouse, but were flanked and cut off and hacked to death where they stood.

The door to the factor's house was open, just for an instant, and Madshaka saw John van der Haagen, the factor – lean, vicious, his eyes like a snake's – staring out, saw his assistant and some of the others behind him, and then he slammed the door shut, as if that would protect him from the slaughter.

Madshaka looked around him. The Kru warriors, the real nucleus of his army, were clustered there, as he had instructed them. He gestured to them and they followed him at a run, racing for the factor's house.

The closed door was no more an obstacle than was the outer wall. Madshaka hit it with his shoulder and it collapsed in front of him and he was in the factor's house, which was no more than a hut, albeit a big one, with a grass roof and a few rooms.

It was the main room they were in now, with its long table spread with bottles and pipes and bowls and playing cards. Two lanterns hung from a beam overhead, making the room the most brightly lit space in the compound.

As he had guessed, the factor and his cronies had been carousing, drinking and gambling and working up the courage to go and drag one of the hapless slave girls from the trunk. But now they stood against the far wall, in breeches and sweat-soaked shirts, as if they were preparing for execution. Madshaka pushed into the room and his men flowed in behind him. Stevens, who was the assistant factor, raised a pistol in a trembling hand and fired.

The bullet missed Madshaka by inches – he could feel its passing – and struck the frame of the door.

Madshaka stopped, looked at the splintered wood, looked up at Stevens.

The assistant factor's hand was shaking harder now, his mouth open, sweat standing out in beads on his forehead. Like Higgens, like the fat guard, he saw before him now the very thing that made him wake in terror in the night: a dangerous African, sold into slavery, come back for him. The gun slipped

330

pathetically from his fingers and made a thudding sound on the dirt floor.

It did not matter that Stevens had fired at him. He would have died regardless. They were all traitors and bastards, but Stevens was the worst and the most expendable.

'Madshaka . . .' said Van der Haagen, a Dutchman in English employ.

Madshaka ignored him. A demonstration first, to make certain they all knew his position, and then talk. He sheathed his cutlass, took two long steps across the room, grabbed Stevens by the collar of his waistcoat and jerked him closer.

'Madshaka!' Van der Haagen shouted, but Madshaka whipped out his dirk and drove it into Stevens's gut, held him there, pinned on the long blade, their faces inches apart, their breath mingling. He could smell the stale tang of dried sweat on Stevens's clothes, the rum and smoke on his breath, the shit and piss that he could no longer hold in.

Stevens gasped, his eyes bulged, and gurgling sounds came from his throat. Then Madshaka twisted the blade and pushed Stevens away and the assistant factor fell to the ground and blood erupted from his mouth. But he was not dead, and Madshaka knew he would not be for an hour at least, and his writhing and choking on his own blood created just the background he wanted for their discussion.

'Van der Haagen.' Madshaka grinned at the horrified, terrified Dutchman. 'You think you get rid of your partner by hitting him on head, selling him like a common slave?'

'Madshaka, no . . . it was Stevens who done that.'

Madshaka threw back his head and laughed, a

genuine laugh, because it amused him greatly to see Van der Haagen writhing, just like Stevens, even though he had not yet thrust a dirk into the factor's gut. 'You a worm, Van der Haagen, a low worm, and you sell me out just like Stevens.'

At that the Dutchman had sense enough to shut his mouth, understanding that denial was futile and only negotiation could save him now. From the compound beyond the factor's door they could hear the former slaves chanting, shouting, singing their triumph.

'Very well, Madshaka. Kill me, if you will, or tell me what you want.'

'Oh, no, I don't think I kill you. But I think we be partners again. But it be different this time, what say you?'

'I am certain we can come to some understanding . . .'

'I certain too. But I have business first.' He stepped to the far wall and took down a big ring of keys, then turned to his men, who were crowding the room near the door, and said, 'Look after these men. Hold them here until I return.' He spoke Kwa. There was no need for any other language because all of the men in the room were Kru, like himself.

Madshaka stepped out and he shouted to the rest of his people, a great bellow that cut through their voices of triumph. He congratulated them on their victory, their great victory, and they cheered him.

He told them that they were the chosen of the gods and they cheered again.

And then he told them that it was time to see to their brothers. He led them at a trot across the wide

332

courtyard to the big trunk that took up a good portion of the factory and would be filled with slaves awaiting buyers.

He waved his cutlass over his head, led the charge to that big, familiar door. He found the key on the ring, thrust it into the lock, twisted it, and felt the lock pop open. With a practiced hand he pulled it from the hasp and swung the big door open and called to his men, 'Go! Go and help your brothers from their chains! Fulfill your destinies!'

And with a great cheer the men poured in through the door, shouting in triumph, the final triumph, ready to free the others as Madshaka had freed them.

And when the last of them had passed through the door, and only Madshaka was left outside, he swung the big door closed again. It hit the heavy frame with a shudder, a deep booming sound, and Madshaka slipped the lock through the hasp again and clicked it shut, a sound of finality.

And then despite himself, he laughed again, a deep laugh, a genuine laugh, a laugh to release all the laughter he had suppressed for all these weeks of fooling all those simpleminded people.

It was the true final triumph, he knew, and it was his.

Crouching on the dry mud wall, lost in the shadow midway between two of the torches, King James watched the drama in the courtyard.

He watched the butchering of the white guards, watched Madshaka peel the Kru off from the rest of the people, watched him disappear into the big house. And then, some moments later, he watched

Madshaka lead the people into the trunk, springing his trap.

Beside him, Joshua, Good Boy, Cato, Quash, muttered their horror, their shock, but James remained silent, watching. There was no shock in his heart, no horror. This was just the way of things.

They had reached the wall with the rest, clambered up, but James had not let his people from the *Northumberland* go any farther. Instead, they had stayed on the wall, retreated to the shadows, and watched.

James had agreed to accompany Madshaka, had let Madshaka think he was swayed by the big man's goading. But it was not that. James wanted to know what Madshaka's real intentions were. He knew better than to let Madshaka out of his sight.

He had come ashore with Madshaka, had followed him into the woods. But he was not such a fool that he would follow him into this slave factory. And he would not let the people he loved follow him either. James had sensed that something was out of alignment. He had smelled the trace odor of a trap.

From where he crouched, a cable length away, James heard the sound of the heavy door slamming shut, even over the cheering of the fools who, on Madshaka's urging, had rushed right into a prison. He heard the deep sound of Madshaka's laugh and it was the laugh of a victor.

James shook his head. Did Madshaka think that he was in the trunk along with the others? Probably. He would not think his triumph so complete if he knew that James was still free.

Madshaka had played them all for fools, had arranged this, step by careful step. James cursed

Madshaka and his genius, and cursed himself for having not killed the man a month before.

But it was not too late. As long as he could still draw breath it was not too late. In his hand the familiar heft of a cutlass, beneath his dark skin, muscles that were tensed and ready, in his head a mind that was sharp and clear again. He was in command now, of himself, of his tiny force of men. He would call the tune, and Madshaka would dance.

But not there and not then. He would need more favorable odds to beat Madshaka, more favorable than what he saw in the compound below him.

He turned to the others. 'Come on.' From his crouched position he leapt down to the ground outside the factory wall, heard the thump of the others landing beside him. Half bent and running, they raced back to the tree line and James led them back to the trail.

At the head of the trail they paused and looked back at the factory. The shouts of triumph had been replaced with a caterwauling of dismay and anger and despair. They listened for a moment, and then they turned and disappeared into the dark shadows of the forest.

CHAPTER 26

It took Elizabeth half a day to see as much of Boston as she cared to, as much as she ever wished to see.

After a tolerable dinner, she and Billy Bird made the rounds of the churches, asking after Frederick Dunmore, meeting with the same reticence, bordering on hostility, that they had received from the very first minister with whom they had spoken.

Billy pointed out that at least their reception indicated that there was something in Dunmore's past that was too unsavory to speak of, at least for those they interviewed to speak of to strangers.

And strangers they were. She and Billy did not fit in, she could see that. The clothes that she wore were unremarkable, perhaps even a bit conservative, by Virginian standards – mantua skirt looped up to reveal the petticoat beneath, a Steinkirk cravat around her neck, a straw *bergère* hat – but by the standards of Boston she felt brazen, overdressed. Billy Bird was something of a peacock in any company, of course, and between the two of them their foreign look put people on their guard.

'Perhaps you are right, Lizzy,' Billy said when she made this observation over supper. 'Bloody Puritans.

Tomorrow I shall see about outfitting myself in their dreary black garb. Mayhap I will get me one of these minister's outfits, pass myself off as a man of the cloth. Do you think God would strike me dead if I did so?'

'I am surprised that God has not struck you dead yet. But no, I do not believe you could convince anyone that you are a pious Congregationalist minister, not for all the black cloth in Boston.'

Billy sighed. 'I reckon you are right,' he said, and there was a hint of resignation in his voice, a touch of pessimism that Elizabeth was not accustomed to hearing, and it made her gloomier still.

'Well, no matter,' Billy said, brighter now, 'damn these ministers and churchmen, I say. Tomorrow we shall go poking about the fellows that print the newspapers. I know the gentleman who prints the *Boston Gazette*. He is apt to be a bit more talkative than these morose preachers.' But Elizabeth knew that he was not nearly as optimistic as he sounded.

They went for a stroll after supper, down Cornhill Street to Winter and then up to the edge of the Common. Elizabeth viewed the city with a perverse fascination, as if she were afforded a glance at her own past life in London and Plymouth, the elegant and pampered life of an expensive whore. That was the life she escaped by coming to America as the ersatz bride of Joseph Tinling, but prostitution, she discovered, was only a little more horrific than the hell that Tinling put her through before he died.

Now that was over, done with.

But being in the narrow, crowded streets of a city, even a small one such as Boston, made all those memories and their concomitant emotions stir again, and she was able to step back and observe them, as if they were happening to someone else.

'Let us go back to the inn, Billy. I'm tired,' she said.

'Very well, my dear.'

Billy reversed direction, and with Elizabeth on his arm he led the way back. The sun was setting and the streets were in the shadows of the buildings that hemmed them in and the crowds of people had diminished by half. It was nearly dark by the time they returned to their room and Billy opened a bottle of wine he had brought with him from the *Bloody Revenge*.

'This was for celebration, but perhaps we will use it to ease the strains of a long day, what say you? We can get another tomorrow, when we shall no doubt have something to celebrate.'

'No doubt.' Elizabeth took the proffered glass, gratefully, drained the wine and handed it back. Even as Billy was refilling it she wondered if they might send down to the kitchen for another bottle.

An hour later they did just that, and soon Elizabeth felt the sharp edge of her disappointment and frustration dull, felt a warm optimism creep in around the edges, and though she told herself it was only the drink, she was happy to find that she did not care.

It was warm in their room, but a cool, gentle breeze was wafting in from the open window, carrying with it the tangy smell of the waterfront, and the occasional sound of a wagon rolling by or the muted conversation of men passing below on the street. The two candles that lit the room danced in the moving air, giving a dreamy quality to the place.

It was not at all the thing, of course, sitting in a room – a bedroom – with Billy Bird, drinking, laughing. She was a married woman. She wanted Thomas, she missed him. She wanted comfort, strong arms around her. Billy was not Thomas, not by miles, but he was handsome and charming.

And then a knock on the door, a rapping, soft, hesitant, and they both jumped. Billy cursed softly and Elizabeth wondered if he was angry with himself for being caught unawares or angry with the person knocking for having destroyed the jovial mood that just might have lured her into his bed.

Both, no doubt, though it was no sure thing that she would have treated him to her favors, nor was Billy caught entirely unawares. He snatched up the loaded pistol he had set on the small table by the window, eased the hammer back, and gestured for Elizabeth to move out of the possible line of fire.

He stepped over to the door just as the person on the other side knocked again, a bit harder. He put his hand on the iron latch and pulled it up and swung the door open, the pistol at his side, hidden but ready.

Standing in the hall, framed by the door, was a black woman, a familiar face, but it took Elizabeth a moment to place her.

'Sally?' It was the Reverend Wait Dunmore's charwoman.

'That right . . . Mis Marlowe?'

'Yes, yes. Please, come in,' Elizabeth said. She could not imagine being more surprised to see anyone. She had not given Sally another thought since leaving the Middle Street Church.

Sally stepped timorously into the room. Billy

closed the door behind her and then, with that flamboyant egalitarianism of his, lifted the bottle they had been consuming and held it up for Sally's inspection and asked, 'Wine, with you?'

Sally looked at the bottle, looked at Billy, and she seemed to be wondering if he was serious or if he was mocking her or if he was insane. After a moment's scrutiny she apparently decided that he was at least serious, if not a bit insane, and she nodded her head. 'That would be nice, Mr Marlowe. Thank you.'

Mr Marlowe? It took Elizabeth's wine-soaked brain a moment to recall that Billy had introduced himself to Dunmore as Thomas Marlowe, another of his irritating verbal pokes in the ribs.

Billy poured a glass, handed it to Sally, gestured for her to sit. He topped off Elizabeth's glass and his own. 'Whatever brings you here?' he asked, once Sally was settled.

'I . . .' she began, nervous and not a little frightened. 'I couldn't help but overhear . . . you was asking about Frederick . . .'

'That's right. Frederick and I were boyhood friends, dear friends, but I have not heard from him in many a year and I was interested in finding what he was about.'

Sally sipped her wine, regarded Billy Bird over the rim of her glass. When she was done she spoke, and her voice carried more confidence this time. 'My family been the property of the Dunmore family for three generations. I been with the Dunmores since I was born. My memory's a lot better than the old Reverend, and I don't remember no Thomas Marlowe, neither.'

A pause, and not a comfortable one, and then Billy

340

said, 'Is that why you're here? Has old Dunmore sent you to poke around, try and find some secret reason for my asking about Frederick?'

'No. The Reverend don't know I'm here. He thinks I'm abed and I reckon it'll go hard on me if he find out I ain't.'

Silence again, and Elizabeth considered whether she believed her. Yes, yes, she did. She did not think Sally was lying. And apparently Billy did not either, because he did not snatch the glass from her hands and kick her out. Rather, he said, 'Very well. Why are you here, then?'

Sally took another sip of her wine. 'You was asking about Frederick, and it didn't take no scholar to figure you know he done something and you was trying to find out what that was. Why you wants to know?'

Billy met Elizabeth's eye and he raised his eyebrows and she took that to mean he considered the telling to be her decision.

'My husband and I are from Virginia,' Elizabeth began, then looking at Billy, added, 'My real husband. This man is a friend.'

Sally registered no reaction to this utterly improper situation, so Elizabeth continued. 'My husband freed the slaves on his plantation and has allowed them to remain and work for wages. Frederick Dunmore, who now lives in Williamsburg, has been persecuting our freed Negroes, has forced them to flee into the woods for their safety.

'I came to Boston in hopes of finding some secret from Dunmore's past that I could threaten him with revealing, to dissuade him from his heartless campaign against our people. It is a craven plan, and

341

base. I am aware of that and I do not care. I am absolutely at my wit's end.'

Sally was nodding and staring thoughtfully into the flame of the nearest candle. 'Virginia, so that's where he end up. The rumor was he gone to London, but now he back . . .'

Billy Bird said, 'There, we have been truthful with you. Will you tell us what you know of Frederick Dunmore?'

Sally looked up, as if startled from her thoughts. 'I'll tell you. I'se the only one will tell you. It's so shameful you won't find no white person will talk about it, and Frederick being the son of that pious old Reverend Dunmore. You keep on asking around, you'll find yourselves run out of town on a rail.'

Sally paused, collected her thoughts, began again. 'Frederick left Boston five years back, left near everything, save his money. He was a merchant. One of the most successful in the city. Rich as a king and after only fifteen years or so in business, starting with the little money the old Reverend give him.'

'He left all that behind? His business?' Elizabeth asked.

'Left right before the sheriff was going to arrest him.' She paused again. 'They accused him of killing an old woman, an old slave woman, named Isabelle. In a rage. Killed her with his bare hands. Strangled her.' She swallowed hard, clenched her fists. 'She was my great-grandmother, and he killed her.'

Elizabeth sat motionless, watched the emotion tearing Sally apart, even after half a decade. It was incredible, this crime she was describing, it seemed too much to believe, even for a bastard like Frederick Dunmore.

342

'But why would he do that?' Elizabeth asked softly. 'Why would Frederick Dunmore murder your great-grandmother?'

Sally looked up, and now the tears were running down her cheeks. 'It was on account of what folks were saying. He couldn't stand it, couldn't stand the thought of it, and I reckoned he blamed her.'

Sally sobbed, wiped her eyes, swallowed hard. 'He found out, he heard, that she was his great-grandma too.'

Elizabeth and Billy were silent, trying to digest this. Sally sobbed, and through the tears said, 'He couldn't stand it, the bastard, the bastard, damn his black heart . . .'

Finally Billy spoke. 'Let me understand you. You are saying that Frederick Dunmore's great-grandmother . . . was a Negress?'

Sally looked up, nodded, then cleared her throat and straightened her back and forced herself into some kind of composure. 'I'm saying that was the rumor. Richard Dunmore, that was Frederick's great-grandfather, story was he had a child by his slave and that child, named Isaac, was almost white and so he raised it like his own. And that child was Frederick's grandfather.'

'And that's true?' Elizabeth asked.

'I don't know. Frederick, he always hated Negroes. I don't know why, but he always did. Some people is like that. When he heard that story, he went crazy. Went to my great-grandma, she the only one of them still alive then, demanded the truth. Then my great-grandmother kept saying it wasn't so, and he didn't believe her and he killed her, he was so mad. My cousin Mary, she heard the whole thing. Once they come looking for Frederick, he run off. Rumor was he gone to London, like I said.'

The three were silent for some moments. Elizabeth realized she was shaking her head. It was incredible, too much to believe. What sick passions must drive a man like Frederick Dunmore? How much of his persecution of Marlowe's people was driven by his own self-loathing?

At last Sally spoke. 'Now you see why I wants to help you.'

Billy nodded. 'This is more than we had hoped for, much more.' Even though he had no stake in this affair, Billy was quite involved. 'But we need proof of some kind. Going back with rumors is not enough.'

Elizabeth nodded. This story would destroy Dunmore, completely discredit him, but Billy was right. If they were going to blackmail Dunmore into desisting, they had to convince him that they had some proof of his crime, or at least of his mixed blood.

The law could not help them. The thought of having Dunmore arrested in Virginia for a crime he might have committed five years before in Massachusetts was absurd. The letters, the warrants, crossing back and forth from London – they would all die of old age before anything was accomplished. Elizabeth did not even know what the law was, regarding the murder of a slave. Marlowe's people needed help now.

But merely circulating old rumors would not do either. They needed something else.

'I don't know as there is any proof,' Sally said. 'I don't even know if it's true that Dunmore has Negro blood. But them papers in the chests in the Reverend

Dunmore's office, they's all the records of everyone was born or baptized or died, going back to when Richard Dunmore was minister. I ain't got my letters, so I don't know what they says, but it might be written there.'

'Perhaps,' said Elizabeth, 'but I don't think Reverend Dunmore will be inclined to let us look through them.'

'Oh, Lizzy, Lizzy,' said Billy, smiling for the first time since Sally arrived. 'I doubt that the good Reverend sleeps in his office. And I will wager, that if it will help destroy that murdering bastard Frederick Dunmore, Sally here might just be able to find a key that will get us in of a late hour. Am I right, Sally?'

Sally looked at Billy, then at Elizabeth, then she nodded her head.

CHAPTER 27

They made their way back down the trail in the dark, stumbling, cursing, following James. Twice he heard one of them fall, swear, get to his feet again. They gasped in surprise when some animal made a sound not so far off.

These men of his, Cato and Joshua, these natives of Virginia, could belay, coil, and hang a line in complete darkness, could lay out on a yard and stow sail with their eyes closed, could tuck an eye splice in under a minute. Good Boy could wield hammer and saw, and Quash could pound raw iron into whatever he wished, but they were not accustomed to this sort of thing, making their way through the forest in the dark.

James was not so accustomed to it either. He had spent most of his adult life as a field hand, working tobacco crops, and more recently as a sailor. It had been a long time since he had had to navigate the African forest in the dark. But the memories were embedded deep in him, in his head and his legs and his feet and his eyes, and they stirred now and awoke and allowed him to make his way almost as if his life among the Malinke had never been interrupted.

It took them two hours to arrive back at the beach, stopping every ten minutes or so, standing silent and listening, straining to hear any sounds of pursuit. But there were none, and that was proof to James that Madshaka thought he and his men were among those unhappy people trapped once more in a slaver's prison.

'James?' Cato's voice. Uncertain. James considered how shocked the young men must be by the rapidly spinning events.

'Yes?'

'What was Madshaka about? Locking them people up?'

'He going to sell them again.'

'Sell them? You mean, sell them as slaves? After all that?'

'That's what I mean.'

There was silence after that, and James listened to the sounds of the night, but there were none that might indicate men coming after them. Then Quash spoke.

'But Madshaka, he was a slave himself. He was sold out of that very factory, he say so. Why he selling his own people?'

'He's not.' These men – boys, really – were children of the New World. They did not understand the ways of ancient Africa. 'Madshaka, he's Kru. He kept the Kru with him. The rest – the Ibo, the Aja, the Bariba, all of them – them he lock up.'

James listened for a moment more, then continued. 'Madshaka knows that factory too good to have just been a slave there. I think he was slaver. I think the white people betrayed him, sold him, and now he take his revenge.'

More silence as the others digested this. 'Damn me,' one of them said. Joshua. Then Quash said, 'Now what we do?'

'Go back to the ship. Get her under way,' James said, and it was not a suggestion but a statement.

In the dim light from the stars that filtered through the trees, he could just make out the others' faces, and he could see there was relief there. They were glad that James was in charge again, making decisions, leading them. They were relieved that the James they knew was back.

They continued on down the trail until at last it opened onto the wide beach, a great stretch of white sand, dull gray in the starlight, that ran off east and west as far as they could see. The surf made a great thunderous roar, with the white edges of the breaking waves foaming high above the level of the sand, then crashing down and racing far up onto the shore.

The surf made James uncomfortable and it gave him confidence, all at once. It overpowered all other sound, made it impossible for them to hear anyone approaching, which was not to his liking. But on the other hand it was the ocean, his element, not Madshaka's, and it gave him an edge, despite Madshaka's overwhelming numbers and local knowledge.

But they would not get to sea that night, would not get further than the beach. As soon as they stepped from the trees he knew it. The wind was blowing ten knots and steady, right off the water. It was churning up the surf, making it more dangerous than ever to negotiate. And even if they made it through, there was nothing they could do with the ship. The five of them and a shipload of women to whom they could not speak could not hope to claw the heavy merchantman off a lee shore. They would have to wait for the morning's offshore breeze, which would blow them away from the land under whatever canvas they could set.

'We'll go into the forest, sleep for the night,' James said. Even if they could manage to get through the surf and out to the ship, they would be trapped there if Madshaka and his men followed. 'You men sleep; I'll keep watch.'

The others made no protest as they stumbled into the dense woods and flattened out a place in the undergrowth where they could sleep. It was not terribly comfortable, not for men unaccustomed to sleeping on the ground, but they were so completely exhausted that ten minutes later they were asleep and snoring, and James at last was grateful for the over-powering volume of the surf.

He left them where they fell, and moved to the edge of the clearing and squatted by one of the great arching palms and watched: watched the head of the trail, watched the beach, watched the dim white water breaking on the tops of the waves, watched the stars wheel overhead. It was his homeland, his Africa. Why did he feel such a stranger there?

He shook off such selfish considerations and turned his mind instead to what he would do for the others. A prince had to put his people before himself and that he would do.

Those poor people whom Madshaka had fooled, and he was one. He could not suffer them to be sold into bondage again. He had thrown away his own life in freeing them from the blackbirder, his life and those of the men with him. He could not allow their sacrifice to be for naught, could not allow his own life to be worth nothing in the end. He could not let those people endure the Middle Passage once again.

Madshaka would come for the women still aboard the Frenchman, would come for the rich booty filling her hold. But first, if the wind served, he and his men would sail her away. And then they would return for the others. He did not know how, exactly, or when, but they would.

For an hour and more he sat, thought, watched, but there was no movement beyond the eternally restless surf. He knew he could not maintain his vigil all night. He needed sleep as well. He had to be sharp and he could not be if he was exhausted, so he made his way back to the clearing where his men slept, and lay down himself, and in a matter of minutes he was deep in a dreamless slumber.

He woke a half hour before dawn. He had done so nearly every morning of his life, and his body was so accustomed to that rhythm that he stirred despite his weariness and his protesting joints and muscles. He was getting old; he felt it in every part of his body.

The others were still asleep and he did not wake them. They could have a few more minutes because the wind was still onshore, but lighter, and James guessed it would be another hour before it died away and then was resurrected as the morning land breeze that would lift the French merchantman off the coast.

He stood and stretched and worked each aching limb, then stepped quietly to the edge of the trees and peered out at the beach. He could see a bit farther down the stretch of sand, just past the breakers, but still there was nothing revealed that might cause him any alarm or make him lead his little band back into the woods where they might hide from those hunting them.

He remained in that place as the sky grew lighter; first white then the palest of blue and finally orange, and the light spread along the beach and the forest and the ocean. There was the multitude of shipping – the local traders and the blackbirders and no doubt a few pirates – riding at their anchors, their bows pointed generally out to sea.

The French merchantman was there, just where they had left her. And beyond her, just coming into focus in the gathering dawn, another ship, standing in under topsails.

James drew in his breath, quite involuntarily. The sight of her filled him with delight and terror and ennui and anger, all those emotions, all jumbled together so he did not know what to say or feel or think.

She was the *Elizabeth Galley*, in all her perfection, one that he himself had helped render. Marlowe had found him, hunted him down like a runaway slave. And now, once again, everything had changed.

Madshaka had had a tremendous time, but as the black night that made dark mirrors of the windows of the factor's hut began to grow gray with the approach of dawn, he knew that it was time to rest.

He and his men, the Kru, the core of his army, had spent the night in celebration. They had feasted on Van der Haagen's food, poured his wine and rum down their throats, smoked pipe after pipe of his tobacco.

Madshaka knew the place well. He had spent many

evenings in that house, sitting, eating, drinking with his white colleagues. He knew his way around the pantry and the liquor stores, knew well the trophies that decorated the walls: war clubs and shields and spears and massive iron swords taken from warriors killed trying to defend themselves and their clans. Several he had collected himself.

And all the while the Dutchman and his colleagues had been made to sit at table with them, to join them, to pretend to be celebrating as well. This they did to the best of their ability, but with Stevens's corpse growing cold on the floor, his eyes open, his hands clawlike in death, the pool of blood around him congealing where he lay in it, they did not feel any of the bonhomie of Madshaka and his men. Still, they maintained their forced smiles and even produced a chuckle or two.

To his credit, Van der Haagen did not even pretend to enjoy himself, and he did not yield to Madshaka's threats and entreaties that he should do so. Van der Haagen understood the politics of Whydah well enough, Madshaka guessed, and he knew his murder would not go unpunished. He, Madshaka, could get away with butchering the assistant factor, could take the actual running of the factory for himself, but Van der Haagen was still needed to be the nominal factor. The king of Whydah would not ignore the murder of a British slave trader.

'Now, Van der Haagen, why you don't celebrate with us?' Madshaka asked, pushing a bottle of wine toward the Dutchman, who glanced down at it but made no move to pick it up. 'Your old partner Madshaka is back now, and I brought you a whole

352

shipload of slaves. And these are slaves you already sold once! Now you get to sell them again!'

'You sent a band of heavily armed men into the trunk, you bloody fool. What are you going to do now, and them all armed with cutlasses and knives and God knows what else?'

'Ah, you, too much worry. They get thirsty enough, they trade weapons for water, you see.'

'You better hope you're right,' Van der Haagen said.

'Of course I right. Them, like sheep, and me, a shepherd, and I lead them right here.'

And that was true. He had led them right to that place, herded them into the trunk and now they were his flock to do with as he would. There were no leaders among them, none that might inspire them to rise up, to fight back.

Except King James.

Madshaka stopped in midlaugh, squinted, looked down at the table. King James. He had meant to kill him last night, during the fight, but it had slipped his mind. He must not have noticed James among the others, or he would not have forgotten to rid himself of that potential problem.

He turned and said to Anaka, now head of his Kru guard, 'Go to the trunk and get King James. If you cannot get him out safely, then take a musket and shoot him through the bars of the door.'

'Yes, Madshaka,' Anaka said. He ordered two others to follow and they hurried from the hut. They spoke in Kwa, as they had all night. Madshaka knew that Van der Haagen and the rest could not speak or understand Kwa and it unnerved them. They could speak a sort of pidgin Yoruba, the lingua

353

franca of that part of the coast, but they knew no Kwa.

Madshaka understood how effective that could be. He had used it to entirely usurp King James's command, and James had not even known it.

'What is the matter?' Van der Haagen asked. 'Have you forgotten something? I hope your plan has not run into problems.'

'No, no,' Madshaka said, and he realized to his annoyance that he had been frowning, so he forced himself to smile his big, embracing smile and said, 'No, Factor, everything is at last as it should be.'

But he was not so sure, and though he forced everyone to continue on with the celebrations, Madshaka grew increasingly uneasy. And the longer his men were gone, the more uncomfortable he became, until finally he was no longer able to hide his mood behind a false smile. The others sensed this, and became more and more quiet, until the celebration was no more than a few muttered words.

Then at last Anaka was back. Madshaka perked up as he stepped through the door, and then frowned to see the look on the man's face.

'Well?'

'Madshaka, King James is not in the trunk.'

Madshaka just stared at him, said nothing, so Anaka said again, 'He's not there. We separated the people out, looked at each man individually, looked at every face. King James is not there. Not him or any of the English.' For want of another term they referred to those slaves born in Virginia as 'the English.'

Madshaka frowned, stared out the door at the courtyard. How could James not be there? He had

354

been with them when they charged the wall, he had made certain of it. But somehow he had not been part of the group that had been tricked into the prison.

If he was not in the trunk, then he was out there, somewhere, hiding, watching.

Madshaka thought that he should be angry about this, should be raging and turning the furniture over in his wrath. Someone should die for this blunder, but he did not know who.

His plan had worked perfectly, as flawlessly as ever one did in an ancient story told by elders around a fire. And now, a kink, a flaw, and, of all things, King James, loose, out there. He was not so foolish as to doubt that King James was a dangerous man.

He should have been burning with rage at the news, but he was not.

Madshaka was not angry. He was afraid.

CHAPTER 28

Boston at night. The streets that seemed so narrow in the daytime crowds now seemed impossibly broad. A sharp report from the waterfront – a pistol shot or a dropped hatch cover. Raucous laughter, but small, far off, and it died away and the streets were quieter still. And dark. The pious people abed, the frugal Yankees did not burn their candles.

Only the night watch stirred, and his shoes could be heard some distance away. The night watchman and Billy Bird and Elizabeth Marlowe. They walked in the shadows, paused to listen, Billy Bird and Elizabeth, Elizabeth chiding him for his secretiveness because she felt foolish. The more effort they made to be stealthy, the more she had to admit they were doing a bad thing.

But Billy Bird shook his head, put his finger to his lips, pulled her into the deep shadows of an alleyway. A rat squealed, ran away on tiny scratching feet. A block away, seen through the narrow gap between buildings, and only for an instant, the night watch, moving in the other direction, slowly, bored. So little crime in Boston he was no longer on the lookout for it.

They headed off again, moving from shadow to shadow. The greater good, Elizabeth reassured herself, and envied Billy Bird, who had no qualms about it, or if he had, hid them as well as his black cape hid him.

They skirted the Town Dock, then went down Anne Street, paused, looked up and down the length of the wide road, and took a quick step across, into an alley. Nothing illegal about being abroad that time of night, Billy explained to her, but it would raise questions. Better if they were not seen.

They stepped down the alley, stumbling once in the dark, turned right into another alley and then across a courtyard to meet up with Middle Street. Billy seemed to know back-alley Boston as she knew her own garden.

And then, looming above them, a black place against the stars. Middle Street Church.

They paused in a dark corner at the edge of the courtyard. Billy put a finger to his lips again and Elizabeth was silent. They waited, listened, listened for anything, but there was no sound to be heard. Billy nodded and they stepped out of the shadows, around the far side of the church, to a side entrance under a small slate roof.

They stopped and waited again but they were alone. A minute passed, then another, and Elizabeth was about to announce that Sally was not coming when they heard a step behind that made Elizabeth jump. She turned and Sally was standing there. She looked tired, frightened. She held up a key for Billy, could not go so far as to actually open the door herself.

Billy took the key and fit it in the lock and turned

it and the heavy door opened with a creak of exaggerated volume. He pulled the key out, handed it back to Sally. Sally slipped the key into her pocket. Their eyes met and Sally made a move as if to speak, but she did not. She just nodded her head and Billy nodded back and she turned and was gone.

Billy glanced around once more, then held the door open for Elizabeth. She stepped through, into the darkness of the church's interior, the only negligible light being that which came in from the night sky through the open door. Then Billy came in behind her and closed the door and it was absolutely black.

'Just hold tight a moment, Lizzy,' Billy said in a whisper. The words seemed absurdly loud. She could not recall the last time either of them had spoken.

At her feet she could hear Billy clicking steel on flint and then a little trail of sparks spilled down on the dry tinder, which glowed orange and flared. Billy blew on it, gently, gently, and when it was finally burning with some legitimacy he used it to light a candle he pulled from his tinderbox.

The flickering light fell on the oak wainscot and crept up the white plaster, finally to be lost in the deep gloom that engulfed the upper reaches of the big church. The door they had come through had led them into the side of the church proper. To their left and ten feet away, the door they recognized as leading to the Right Reverend Dunmore's office.

Billy gestured Elizabeth forward with a welcoming sweep of his arm, the way he had done when bringing her first aboard the *Bloody Revenge* and again when welcoming her to Boston.

It occurred to her that Billy genuinely believed that

358

all of the world was his for the taking, that wherever he wished to go it was his absolute right to do so, and thus wherever he was, he was welcoming people onto his own property. That was why he felt justified in making that gesture.

It must be a fine thing, she thought, to be so damned sure of your place in the world. She smiled and made her way past Billy's pews, headed for Billy's office.

Down the narrow hall and back through the door through which Wait Dunmore had just that morning ordered them to leave. The office was unchanged, save for Dunmore's absence, but that one omission made the space look much bigger, as if the force of Reverend Dunmore's personality pulled the walls in to him when he sat at his desk, and when he was gone they eased back to their normal positions.

Billy found another candle and lit it, and a lantern as well, and the room was filled with a tolerable amount of light. Against the wall, the chests of papers that Elizabeth had that morning noticed. 'Let us hope these are organized after some fashion, some fashion we can discern,' Elizabeth whispered.

'You look there, Lizzy, and I shall look to this Bible. If it is the Dunmore family Bible, it may have something of Wait Dunmore's true parentage written there.'

Elizabeth nodded and took up one of the candles. She knelt before the first blanket chest as if it were a little altar and began to thumb through the papers. Records of births, records of deaths, records of marriage, just as Sally had said. They appeared to be a great jumble, in no particular order, and Elizabeth began to despair at the thought of going through all of the chests, paper by paper. She did not think there was time enough in one night to do it.

But as she made her way through the papers, a system, a kind of order, began to emerge, seemingly random clusters of papers resolved into rational groupings by name and date and she nodded as she began to understand.

She heard Billy close the heavy Bible with a dull *whump*. He stepped up behind her. 'The Good Book says nothing of this, just a legitimate line of succession, right down to Roger Dunmore's no doubt monstrous child William, born two years ago. Have you anything?'

Elizabeth nodded again. 'I have not found the Dunmore family, but I see how they have put this all together. What was the name and birth date of the first Dunmore in the Bible?'

Billy paused. 'I'll have to look again,' he said, and a minute later, 'Ezekiel Dunmore, born 1563 in Kent, died 1646, Boston. Father of . . .'

'That should do.' Elizabeth stood and opened the next trunk and the next, thumbed through the papers, not finding the Dunmore clan but seeing at least that they were organized the way she had thought. The next trunk, and her fingers moved confidently and there, at last, she found them. The Dunmore family, bound together with red tape. Ezekiel, died 1646, written out with the fine lettering and archaic language of a former age.

She pulled the papers out, put them down on Dunmore's desk, pulled off the red tape. Billy set his candle down beside them, leaned in close, his curiosity on a par with hers. She spread the papers out, arranging them like a family tree. Ezekiel, father

360

of Elisha and Zacharias and Benjamin. The last, father of Sarah and Jonah and Rachel and Richard.

Elizabeth's hands were shaking, and she shuffled quickly through the papers. Wait Dunmore, father of Frederick. Wait Dunmore, son of Isaac Dunmore. Was Isaac the illegitimate son of Richard and the slave girl Nancy?

The record of his birth. It was there, in her hands. Isaac Dunmore. Father, Richard Dunmore. Mother . . . Anne Dunmore, born Anne Hutchinson of Boston.

And that was it. No mention of the slave Nancy, nothing but a record of a legitimate child of white parents. Elizabeth looked up at Billy, who was still looking at the paper. She felt the tears of frustration welling up. 'Oh, Billy, damn it . . .'

'Well, I suppose it would not be likely they would make an official record of such a union . . .' he began, but there was frustration in his voice as well. Disappointment.

And then a creak, the creak of the side door, left unlocked, the same creak it had made when they had opened it. Billy's eyes met Elizabeth's and she felt no disappointment or frustration now, just fear, and a twist in her stomach, and on Billy's face, alertness; like a deer, he was motionless, listening.

A footstep on wooden planking. Billy blew out the two candles and clapped the shutter half over the open lantern and the room was almost black and he motioned with his head for her to follow.

Elizabeth snatched up the papers, the Dunmore family record, and she shoved them down the front of her shift, though she did not know why, for they would do her no good. Still, she took them, felt the

361

rough paper against her skin as she pushed them out of sight.

Billy stepped into the narrow hall, put the half-closed lantern down on the floor. It lit up the pine boards on which it sat, and threw a diffused illumination out toward the church.

They could hear them now, two men, footsteps, soft muttering. Billy stopped, held up his hand, but still Elizabeth nearly ran into him before she saw his dark shape. She could just make out his hands as he flipped his black cape back so that the cloth did not impede his arms, but he did not draw a weapon, as if he was still not certain these people were enemies.

Elizabeth did not see how they could be anything but.

An observation, muttered, but loud enough for them to hear. 'I sees light. Down there.' A pause and then another voice saying, 'Easy, now, easy. Cold steel . . .'

The floor creaked and that was followed by a long pause as the men approaching stopped, waited, listened, just as Billy and Elizabeth were doing. Step, creak, pause; it seemed to go on forever.

Slowly, slowly, Billy drew his sword from his scabbard. Elizabeth could see his hand moving as he drew, could catch the occasional flicker of light on the blade. There were no windows in the Reverend's office, no door save for that through which they had come. They had no route of escape other than that one hall.

At the far end, against the gloom of the church's darkness, Elizabeth could see a shape, a moving blackness. She heard the light tap of metal on metal, heard the shape gasp in surprise and then Billy Bird threw open the shutter of the lantern with the tip of his sword.

The light spilled out, illuminated the big man blocking the way: bearded, in the rough clothes of a laborer, a battered three-cornered hat on his head, a sword in his hand, a big, meaty weapon, the kind of blade preferred by a man who fights with brute force and little subtlety.

'God damn!' the man shouted in surprise. Crooked black teeth, gaps in places where others were missing.

Billy Bird sprang forward, his sword in his right hand, his left hand crossing his belly and then his dirk was in that fist, long blade and short. He came at the big man and lunged and would have run him through if the man had not all but fallen backward in surprise.

'God damn!' he shouted again, higher pitched, but he recovered fast and came at Billy with his big sword, swinging it with two hands like an ax, and Billy was just able to whip his own sword out of the big weapon's arc before the heavy blade struck and perhaps snapped his finer steel in two.

Billy Bird was fast, nimble, like a dancer, and he lunged as the big man was off balance and got a solid jab in the man's upper arm and the man howled and stumbled back again. Behind him, the second man, smaller, more wiry, teeth and clothes no better, stepped up and Billy engaged him with dirk and sword.

Elizabeth looked wildly around, looked for some weapon, something she could use to help Billy. She had nothing, no knife, no pistol. She had deliberately resisted carrying any weapon; to do so was to admit to herself that they were doing something wrong. And now perhaps Billy would be overwhelmed, and then what would she tell herself?

She snatched up the lantern, raced after him. The smaller man was more of a swordsman than was his partner and he wielded his weapon with some finesse, made Billy work at defending himself, not giving away openings like the other, who was staring dumb at the blood soaking through his sleeve.

The little man slashed down and Billy caught his sword with the edge of his own, twisted his wrist, locked their blades, just for that instant, and stepped into the man and thrust his dirk at him. But the little man was too fast for that and he turned sideways and freed his sword and stepped back, ready.

The other one, the bigger one, was done staring at his wound. Elizabeth heard a growl building in his throat and it turned into a shout as the man charged, lumbering forward, coming at Billy with his sword again in two hands, and Billy might have finished him off if he did not have the smaller man to deal with as well.

'Oh God, oh God, oh God . . .' Elizabeth said, again and again. She felt useless, worse than useless, but there was nothing for her to do but watch.

The big man swept his sword down as if he were chopping at a tree and Billy ducked, hit the floor, his cape making a great flourish, rolled with a grace that left Elizabeth gaping, the big man swinging at air, and the little man dodging his partner's blade. Then Billy was up and over one of the pews.

It took the big one a second to understand where Billy had gone, how he had vanished from under his sword. He looked over, surprised, as if

Billy had disappeared and rematerialized beyond the pew.

He came at Billy again with the same heedless fury, slamming his knees into the pew and slashing down, and this time Billy ducked to one side and the heavy blade shattered the top of the pew, embedding itself in the wood. Billy slapped the hilt of his sword down on top of the blade, preventing the man from lifting it up. Then with his dirk he lunged and this time he caught the startled man in the stomach, sunk an inch of steel into his flesh, made him bellow like a bull, but the reach was too far for Billy to deliver a more lethal jab.

The small man watched this, unmoving for the second or two that it took. He began to circle toward Billy, more cautious than his friend, when he seemed to notice Elizabeth for the first time, and when he did he seemed at the same moment to forget entirely about Billy Bird.

'Bitch!' he hissed at her, and then he was moving toward her, sword held out, off to one side, a position that would allow him to slash her no matter which way she turned.

Two steps, three steps, and he was all but on her. She shrank back, thought of the lantern in her hand. She held the only source of light.

She slammed the shutter closed and the church was all blackness again. She pulled her mantua skirt free, buried the lantern in the cloth to hide the light leaking around the door. Fell to her knees, ducked down, shuffling away to her left. She heard the man's sword slash the air above her head and again he said, 'Bitch!' but loud, a shout.

Elizabeth backed up, crawling away at an oblique

angle from the man. She could hear him kicking out, trying to locate her with his feet and his slashing sword and she crawled back until there was no place left to crawl. The lantern was resting on her thigh and through her petticoats she could feel it start to burn her. She did not know where Billy was, if he was still alive or not.

A step closer, and the man was flailing with the blade and with another step or another he would find her. She was up against the wainscot now. She gripped the lantern hard, ready to crash it into his knees when he took another step.

Then the side door burst open again and more men rushed in, making no attempt to be quiet, and Elizabeth froze and her attacker froze and no one knew who they were, or who they were for.

A voice in the darkness. 'Billy Bird? Where the fuck are you?'

Elizabeth jumped to her feet, broke left, stepping sideways, her back against the wall, and when she was sure she was beyond the reach of the man's sword she pulled the lantern out from under her skirt and flipped the door open.

The hot steel burned her fingertips, and the yellow light that flooded out revealed five men: Billy Bird, still behind the pew; the big man gripping his stomach; the wiry one who had come after her, now turned toward this new threat.

And between them, swords drawn, Black Tom and Ezra Howland.

CHAPTER 29

It might have been laughable, those five men standing frozen, motionless, trying to sort this thing out, were people not about to die.

And then the big man, heedless of his bleeding arm and belly, shouted, 'Sons of bitches!' and tossed his sword aside. It hit the pine floor with a clatter, banging into the far row of pews, and Elizabeth thought he was surrendering when he reached under his coat and pulled out a pistol.

He raised it, thumbing the lock, and then Billy's sword came down on his wrist in a spray of blood and the big man's hand folded into an unnatural angle and he howled, dropped the gun, grabbed his wrist. Billy slammed him hard in the temple with the flat of his sword and the man slumped to the floor as if his bones had turned to ash.

The small man had seen enough. He wheeled around, bolted for the door, but Black Tom stepped toward him, kicked him in the shins and the man fell forward, sword flying from his hand, and came down hard on the floor, spread-eagled. Ezra Howland was there and he kicked the man hard in the head and he too was still.

Silence again, and then Billy Bird leapt over the pew and, to Elizabeth's surprise, shouted, 'Where in hell have you been?' He did not sound grateful at all for the help. Grabbed Black Tom by the arm, pulled him close, face-to-face. 'Breathe!' he demanded, and Black Tom puffed a breath in Billy's face. Billy frowned in disgust and Elizabeth frowned in empathy. She would not care to smell Black Tom's breath.

'Been at the damned tavern, haven't you? When did it occur to you that we might go abroad again tonight?'

Black Tom stared at the floor, muttered something. He looked like a child caught in some infraction.

'Billy,' said Elizabeth, 'I should think it a miracle that these men arrived in time to save us.'

'They were supposed to be watching at all times, but instead I have to cut these bastards down' – he indicated the two men on the floor – 'single-handedly before they amble in. Good thing I am man enough to take on two or more at a time.'

'Well, now, it weren't like we done nothing,' Howland protested.

Elizabeth shook her head. 'You told these two to watch us? At all times?'

'Dear Lizzy, you would never believe me that this is a dangerous business. Lucky one of us was clever enough to see that our backsides were covered.' He glared at Tom and Ezra.

But Elizabeth, for her part, was far too relieved to be angry at the Bloody Revenges, late though their arrival may have been. She swept across the floor and gave each of the men a kiss on their hairy cheeks, as they in turn blushed and stammered.

'Right, well, let's see what these sons of whores has that's worth the taking,' Ezra Howland muttered, trying to cover his embarrassment. He knelt over the unconscious form of the smaller man, dug through the big pockets of his coat, while Black Tom retrieved the pistol and located a few coins in the pocket of the other.

'Nothing,' said Ezra. 'A few rutting papers, that's it.' Ezra was not the kind of man who could imagine a piece of paper being of any value.

'Let me see.' Billy Bird held out his hand, took the paper.

'Tom,' said Howland, 'come on, then, let's see if there's anything down there, what we should have,' and with a jerk of his head he led Black Tom down the hall to Dunmore's office.

'Forgive them, Lizzy, plundering is quite in their soul. I would no more wish to try and stop it than I would try and stop a rutting bull.'

He held up the paper that Howland had handed him, angled it toward the light.

Elizabeth watched him read, watched his brows come together, his mouth form into a frown. 'Son . . . of . . . a . . . bitch . . .' He let the words come out slow.

'What is it, Billy?' Elizabeth asked.

'Here. Read this.' He handed the note over. Elizabeth let the light fall on the words and read.

Mr Elephiant Jenkins
The Golden Rooster Tavern
Boston

Mr Jenkins,
  As you have been of Great Service to me in the

369

past, let me Now call upon your Good Offices again to render me aid in a situation most unseemly.

There will arrive in Boston soon Two People who mean to do me most Grievous Injury by means of resurrecting such untruths from my past as they might endeavor to discover. They are a woman named Elizabeth Marlowe, aged around twenty-eight, with yellow hair and fine of feature, and most probably a man accompanying her whom you will discover. I am in no doubt that they will endeavor to Speak to the Reverend Wait Dunmore, my Father, at the Middle Street Church, and if you were to keep watch there you would discover them.

I have enclosed a bank draft to cover your expenses in an amount that I think you will find is Sufficient Payment for the task I request of you.

The last part she read out loud. 'I wish that the said Elizabeth Marlowe and her companion should never leave the town of Boston, except that their immortal souls should join with their Maker in Providence. I think an accident of Drowning in the harbor the most conveniently understood demise. Your obedient, humble servant, Frederick Dunmore.'

She looked up, stunned. Along with the letter was a draft for one hundred pounds. The papers shook in her hand.

'How very kind he is,' said Billy, 'to wish our souls at eternal rest.'

' "Aged about twenty-eight"?' Elizabeth said. 'Do I look to be twenty-eight?'

'Lizzy, what a great kindness our dear Frederick has done us. Here we were, searching for incriminat-

370

ing papers, unable to find a one, and here he has had just the thing delivered right to us. Proof of his conspiring to see us murdered. I think we need look no further.'

And then from the dark, the click of a flintlock snapped into place. Elizabeth looked up, assumed it was one of the Revenges, but it was not.

It was the Reverend Wait Dunmore, standing in the door, just at the edge of the lantern's reach. He looked ominous, frightening, in the deep shadows and flickering flame. He was hastily dressed, his long shirt only half tucked in, waistcoat unbuttoned, no wig to cover the bristle of hair on his head. The light of the single lantern served to deepen and accentuate the lines in his face, the heavy jowls and folds of skin around his eyes.

Dunmore held the gun out, pointed at Billy Bird's heart. Behind him, sweating, looking nervous, the night watch fiddled with his short club.

Billy Bird sighed, shook his head, not the expression one might have expected from a man held at gunpoint. 'I have been to governors' balls that were not as well attended as our little affair tonight. Tell us, Reverend, is your church so filled with people when there is a sermon in the offing?'

'Shut your gob, you little worm,' Dunmore growled. 'I shall give you until the count of five to hand over everything you stole before I shoot you. If you cooperate then I shall do no more than have you arrested. Let the High Court see you hang.'

'Arrest me? Who, the night watch there? The poor man looks as if he'll die of fright.'

At that the night watchman stepped forward, chins waggling, and cleared his throat, and before he could speak, another flintlock snapped into position, and then another, and Billy Bird shook his head, smiled.

Standing five feet behind Dunmore and the night watchman, Black Tom and Ezra Howland stepped from the side hallway, leveled their guns at the newcomers.

'Honestly, Reverend, have you ever seen the like?' Billy was smiling. 'Now, you could shoot me. Probably should. But if you do, my fellows will kill you and this poor night watchman. So there is your choice. Pull the trigger and three men die, put down the gun and no one dies.'

The options were clear, but the choice was not as obvious to the Reverend as Elizabeth might have thought it would be. He stood for five seconds, ten seconds, grim-faced, pointing the gun at Billy, looking at him with such hatred that for a moment she thought he might well throw away his own life and that of the watchman just for the chance to put a bullet through the insouciant pirate before him.

But he did not, and at length he lowered the gun, eased the flintlock down. He seemed to sag, his face, his body, the stiffness gone. He seemed suddenly much smaller.

Black Tom and Howland stepped around, guns still trained. The night watchman was holding his hands in plain sight, unwilling to be shot on suspicion that he was trying to defend himself.

'I am afraid we must tie you up. We can't have an alarm sounded, you know,' Billy said, and Dunmore just stared, said nothing.

'Tom, pray, go find something with which we can bind all these gentlemen. There must be a rope of some sort attached to the bell.'

Tom nodded, lit a candle from the lantern, and headed off toward the base of the steeple. 'Ezra, you had best shut and bolt the door. We have had quite enough visitors tonight.'

Ezra did so, and Dunmore and the night watch stepped out of his way. Then Dunmore spoke, and his voice had none of the gravel that Elizabeth had heard before, and for a moment she did not even realize it was him speaking.

'It's not true, you know,' Wait Dunmore said.

'What? What is not true?' Billy asked. 'That your son murdered an innocent old black woman? Killed her with his bare hands?'

The words were like a slap to the Reverend's face. He frowned, shook his head slowly. 'That I do not know. He might have, the poor creature. The evidence was there that he did. Had he been tried he probably would have been hanged. Never was a trial, of course, but in my heart I fear it is true.

'No, the lie is about Frederick's blood, my blood. There was never a child by Nancy. My father, Isaac, was the progeny of my grandfather, Richard, and my grandmother, Anne, and never did my grandfather fornicate with a slave.

'That story, the thing about Frederick . . . me being in part Negro was made up by someone and it spread fast, as such a story will. You see, Frederick hated the Negroes. Always did. I don't know why. Some are like that. I think Negroes frightened him. It made Frederick insane to think it true, that he was . . . part . . .'

'Why would someone make up such a story?' Billy demanded, and at that Dunmore actually gave a weak smile.

'You two are acquainted with Frederick, that much is obvious. And it is just as obvious that you hate him. You have gone to great lengths to destroy him.

'Well, you are not the only ones who felt thus. Frederick was never one to make people love him. There were plenty in Boston who might have started such a rumor. Plenty who knew of the loathing Frederick had for Africans, what it would do to him to think he was part Negro himself. To have all of Boston think it.'

Elizabeth shook her head. Incredible. Frederick Dunmore moved to a murderous rage by a well-placed rumor, an untruth. She did not think old Dunmore was lying. Whoever had thought of that trick to drive young Frederick mad was more conniving than she could ever hope to be, leagues more.

'And so,' Reverend Dunmore continued, and this time there was a hint of the old iron in his voice, 'this burglary of yours has been for naught. If you were looking for proof of Frederick's blood, or his crime, you have not found it, because it is not there.'

'No, it is not,' said Billy. 'But your son was kind enough to have delivered to us proof enough of his murderous spirit. See here.' He took the letter from Elizabeth's hand, picked up the lantern, held the paper up for Wait Dunmore to read.

Elizabeth watched the old man's face as he read, saw the horror spread over his features, his mouth moving as he read but no words coming out. When he was done he looked up at Billy, as stunned as Elizabeth had been. More so, actually. He looked as if he wanted to speak but no words came.

And then Black Tom was back with the bell rope. Dunmore and the night watch were escorted back into the office, the still-unconscious murderers were dragged back, and all four men were bound tight where they would remain until morning at least. Enough time for the *Bloody Revenge* to be under way.

Elizabeth and Billy stood at the office door, took one last look around, one last check that the men were well bound. Out in the church Black Tom and Howland carefully opened the door – from the office they could hear that all too familiar creak – and checked that the streets were still empty.

Elizabeth met Dunmore's eyes and held them. They considered each other, the two of them, the minister and the lady of Marlowe House, the father of a murderer and the former whore. The old man looked much older than he had that morning.

Billy Bird turned, led the way out, and Elizabeth followed, turned her back on Reverend Dunmore, on Boston, on the lot of it.

Out into the church and out the side entrance. The big door squeaked closed behind her. Before it shut tight she listened for some sound, some reaction – sobs, curses – from the Reverend Wait Dunmore, but the church was as quiet as a tomb.

CHAPTER 30

Whydah.

Marlowe stood grim at the break of the quarter-deck, watched that city of slave traders emerge from the predawn black.

He had been up and down the African coast in his varied career at sea, from Cape Verde to the Congo. Mostly during his time with the pirates. Wealth bled from the continent's dark interior, streams of blood money that poured over the Europeans that gathered on her shores. And Marlowe and his former mates had been there to relieve them of some of it. Africa was a good place for pirates.

Yes, Marlowe had tasted Africa. Had eaten the spicy, peppered food of the Kroomen, had slept in the mud and grass huts of the fierce men of the Bissagos Islands, had lain with dark-skinned girls in Cabo Monte and Elmina and Brass and Old Calabar.

But Whydah. He had been there only once before, as a very young man. Thirteen, perhaps. Experienced enough by then to be rated ordinary seaman. He had been seduced into joining a blackbirder's crew. Good money, damned good money, and at thirteen he felt himself quite impervious to the fevers that struck down white men by the score along the Bight of Benin.

It had been worse than a nightmare, worse than anything he could have imagined. Those poor people, led down into the hold, terrified, beaten, wailing in their despair. And then the stink and the moaning and the rattling of chains. There was no escape from it, like being separated from hell itself by a few inches of oak planking.

And the bodies. Carried up every day and tossed overboard. Stiff, wide-eyed, covered in their own filth, body after body, and every day he had to help carry them up, had to go down into that place, look into the eyes of the living and fetch the dead ones up. Over the leeward side, to the trail of sharks that kept constant company with the ship.

They had arrived in Jamaica with half the number of Africans they had left with, and young Malachias Barrett had jumped ship, fled into the city, not even bothered to collect his pay.

A year later he was a pirate.

And in all his years with that marauding clan he had never sailed with a more depraved and soulless bunch as the crew of that blackbirder.

It was odd, he realized, that he had never once felt the same pity for the victims of his piracy that he did for those slaves he had helped transport. The Lord knew he had seen terror aplenty in their eyes, had seen atrocities carried out against them, was guilty of enough himself to see him damned many times over.

Perhaps he did not think of those people as helpless victims as he did the slaves. Certainly those who had not resisted the pirates' attack had not been harmed – they had that opportunity to save themselves – whereas nothing the Africans could have done would have spared them their awful fate.

He wondered if perhaps that experience with the blackbirder was the real reason he had freed his people at Marlowe House. But that would suggest an emotional rather than a pragmatical reason for his actions, and he rejected that outright. He had always scoffed at Bickerstaff's notion that slavery should be abolished the world over. The world, Marlowe knew, consisted of the strong and the weak, and the strong preyed on the weak, as it was in nature. Emotion could not be allowed to hold too great a sway.

But sometimes he found himself listening to Bickerstaff's arguments and finding some sense in them.

He had never told Bickerstaff about his having served aboard a blackbirder, never told Elizabeth or James or anyone that he could think of. The shame of it still clung to him, the way the stink of the ship had clung to his clothes until at last he had stolen a new set and burned the ones he had. He did not know why he felt such humiliation still for something he had done so long ago. Surely he had done worse since?

He shook his head. Seeing the whitewashed city of Whydah growing more distinct amid the thick forest was making his thoughts turn morbid and morose. He was not a man for such introspection, and the more he found his mind turning over such ideas, the more he told himself he was becoming an old woman, or a philosopher like Bickerstaff, and it did not suit him.

'Good morning, Captain,' said Bickerstaff, stepping up from the waist with two pewter mugs full of the fine, pungent black coffee they had picked up in São Miguel. Marlowe took the proffered mug gratefully, awkwardly, holding it in his left hand. His right arm hung in a sling around his neck. A clean break, no reason to think it would not heal, but it still hurt like the devil.

The coffee was hot, but no steam would rise in the warm, tropical morning air.

'Good morning.' The sun had all but broken free of the horizon, a blaze of brilliant orange off the starboard bow. The sky was a brittle blue, cloudless, promising heat. The shore that lay under their bows, running from horizon to horizon, was still mostly indistinct, a thick, dark shadow and only the white, white buildings were visible at all. Those, and the smattering of vessels that lay at anchor in the roads, no more than a few miles off.

'Whydah, is it?' Bickerstaff asked.

'Yes.'

'Have you been, before?'

'No.'

The two men were quiet, watching the rising sun reveal what lay before them: more buildings, with smoke curling up into the nearly white sky from a dozen, two dozen points among the trees, more vessels of all sizes. White sand and a line of white surf that ran the whole length of the shore, as far as they could see. Birds wheeling around overhead, seabirds, and occasionally the bright-colored natives of Africa

'It would be odd to find them here, would it not?' Bickerstaff asked. 'Whydah is notorious for its traffic in slaves. One would think it the last place they might come.'

'One would think. I have all but despaired of

guessing what is in King James's mind. If I can only go back and tell the governor that I have truly looked in every port they might have ventured to, then at least I will be satisfied. The world is a damned big place, even Nicholson must realize that, and they could be any damned where in it.'

He had not meant for his reply to be as bitter as it was, but as the words came out, they drew the venom with them. He was tired of this, tired of putting such superhuman effort into a search he did not think was his responsibility. A search that he did not want to be a success. But neither did he want it to fail.

James, damn your black hide . . .

The French East Indiaman, after blowing away the *Elizabeth Galley* fore topmast, had simply sailed off. They apparently had more important things to do than capitalize on their victory, or they did not think the cost in blood was worth whatever they might get from the *Galley*. Whatever their thinking, Marlowe was glad of it, glad to see the big ship disappear beyond the horizon.

It took the crew of the *Elizabeth Galley* a full twenty-four hours to repair the damage they had suffered in fifteen minutes of fighting. With the threat of being blown from the sea gone, they were able to salvage a great deal of the wreckage, and happily they had on the booms a spare topmast, so in the end there was little apparent damage.

Once things were squared away they set sail, again hunting for King James, the men still eager for the fortune carried by those fabled black pirates.

Two days later they made their African landfall at Cape Verde, the northernmost point to which Marlowe thought James might be heading. They had looked there and into the mouth of the Gambia, gone around to Cacheu and Bissau, poked into those few anchorages in the Bissagos Islands, and then southeast along the Guinea Coast.

The only thing in their favor was the sparsity of anchorages along Africa's west coast, the few places where they had to negotiate their way into a well-defined harbor. Most of the coast was open roads, great long stretches of beach where the treacherous surf pounded and pounded and vessels took their wary moorings far from the land, relying on the skills of native boatmen to get them to shore and back.

In that case they had only to sail by, to make their way inshore close enough to survey the vessels there and see if any were the French merchantman taken by James and his pirate band.

And none of them were.

Past Cape St Anna and Cabo Monte, southeast along the Pepper Coast, then northeast at Cape Palmas and along the Ivory Coast to Axim. They doubled Cape Three Points and stood on to the Gold Coast, Ashanti country, past the open roads of Shama and Komende and Elmina and Cape Coast with its great, looming castle, the best anchorage for a thousand miles and the least likely place to find fugitive slaves. And indeed they did not.

They checked the vessels anchored at the mouth of the Volta River and made their easting into the Bight of Benin, the Slave Coast, not a place that Marlowe had any hope of finding them.

Up until that point the search had been a simple matter. Once they passed Lagos, however, and entered the area of the Niger River Delta, then there would be hundreds of creeks and rivers and backwaters where they might have hidden, indeed where they probably had. He would have to check them all, all the fetid breeding grounds of yellow jack and black fever, and he dreaded even the thought of it.

Damn, damn, damn you to hell, James, for putting me through this! He was angry enough that the idea of James being hanged was not so terrible. When he thought of what they had been through already, what more they had to do, he was ready to hang the man himself.

The sun was fully up and the shore with which they were closing quite visible. Marlowe took the last swig of coffee, spit a few errant grounds over the side. The native canoes were starting to close with them. He could see the boatmen working their paddles, racing out to the new arrival. Some would be *grumetes*, come out to offer their services in getting the white men safe through the surf, some would be bumboats offering for sale those things that sailors long at sea hankered for. That would be rum, chiefly, and he would have to tell Fleming to see that the men did not get their hands on enough of it to cause trouble.

He ran his eyes over the ships and brigs and snows at anchor, more out of habit than any thought that he might find the one he was searching for. His eyes settled on one ship anchored further to the east, away from the central part of Whydah, and he stared at it but his thoughts were elsewhere, with Governor Nicholson, explaining how he had searched the entire coast and had found nothing.

And as he stared, and as his mind traveled back over the Atlantic, back over the water they had just crossed, an odd something began to gnaw at him, like a dream he had told himself in his sleep to remember but on waking could not. It was the dull sensation of knowing there is something one must not forget, but forgetting what that something is.

And so he stared and he mucked around in the silt of his mind, trying to find what it was under there. So much had he come to accept the fact that he would not find James's ship, it took him a good five minutes before he realized that it was the French merchant-man, or something very like it, that he was looking at now.

'Dear God . . .' He stood up straight, knocked the pewter mug off the caprail. It bounced once on the channel and then plunged into the blue water, but Marlowe spared it never a thought.

'Whatever is it?' Bickerstaff asked, but Marlowe turned and fled aft and picked up the big telescope from the binnacle box and trained it forward. He shook his head as he stared through the glass. The ship was a mile and a half away – he could see none of the little details that would give him absolute confirmation – but nothing that he saw told him he was wrong.

He felt the emotions crashing together like surf coming across either side of a sandbar: the thrill that he might have found them, the relief that it might soon be over, the fear of disappointment, the dread of finding King James and killing him or bringing him back to an even worse death, the confusion of conflicting loyalties and desires.

The more he tried to make his life a simple thing – a wife, a home, a planter's life – the more it eluded him, the more his problems grew in complexity, like a vine out of control, wrapping itself around him.

Bickerstaff was there, but too polite to inquire, so Marlowe said, 'I think perhaps that is the Frenchman, yonder. James's Frenchman.'

Bickerstaff cocked an eyebrow, which for him was tantamount to a shout of surprise. Marlowe handed him the glass and he trained it forward, though he did not have anything like the seamanship to pick out the tiny details that might distinguish one ship from another.

'Hmmm,' said Bickerstaff, thoughtfully. 'They fly no flag, and their sails are not stowed in any manner that would do a captain credit, if he were concerned about such things, and the yards all askew.'

Marlowe smiled. Bickerstaff was right, and it was a good indication that this was the right ship and he, Marlowe, had missed it entirely. He was too busy looking at the steeve of the bowsprit, the sheer, the number of black-painted wales, the somewhat archaic lift at the peak of the mizzen yard, to even notice the more obvious clues. Sometimes knowledge just got in the way.

'You think it is King James?'

'I think it might well be,' Marlowe said. 'I am sorry now we put those mad Frenchmen ashore in São Miguel, they could have told us for certain.' Then after a moment's reflection he said, 'No, I am still glad to be shed of them. But I think we will clear the ship for action and go to quarters and be ready when we come up with them.'

This order he passed to first mate Fleming who had it relayed in bellowing voices along the deck and below, an order that took the Elizabeth Galleys entirely by surprise. None of them were still abed; it being past dawn, the watch below had been roused and were making a clean sweep fore and aft and seeing to breakfast and attending to those many jobs that needed doing before breakfast and the change of watch. It was a steady routine that had gone unbroken for several weeks now, since their fight with the Frenchman, and there had been no indication that things would be different that morning.

For that reason there was more staggering around, more dumb looks, more questions than Marlowe would have preferred. But still the men fell to with credible speed, casting off guns, arranging tubs of match and buckets of water, fetching out cutlasses and pikes.

They were a good crew, disciplined, happy enough. Griffin's death had been like pulling a rotten tooth: painful at first, but in the end a vast improvement.

Fifteen minutes later they were ready, as the sea breeze carried the *Elizabeth Galley* inshore, closing, closing with the Frenchman. Marlowe kept the glass trained on the ship, but he could see nothing out of the ordinary. A few figures moved around the deck, and they looked to be Africans, though it was still too far to tell. A plume of smoke rose from just abaft the foremast, but it looked like nothing more sinister than a galley fire.

'Where there is smoke, there is breakfast,' Marlowe observed to Bickerstaff.

'Where there is breakfast, there is no fear of imminent attack.'

That was true enough, and it added to the confusion of the thing. And then overhead the *Galley*'s main topsail gave a slap as it collapsed and then snapped full again in a fluke of wind. They were losing the sea breeze. Soon it would be dead calm, and after that the wind would fill in right on their nose.

'Mr Fleming, let us see to the anchor. We'll carry on as close as we can.'

The wind held for ten minutes more, then came in puffs that began to box the compass, and then died away altogether, leaving the *Elizabeth Galley* to drift beam on to the incoming seas. She wallowed side to side in those swells that marched on under her keel and then flung themselves in breaking foam onto the beach a mile away.

The anchor was let go and the bow came around to point into the waves, making the ship pitch rather than roll, an altogether more comfortable motion. And when she finally snubbed to a stop at the end of the anchor hawser, they were no more than one hundred yards from the suspect ship.

Both ships were pointing into the waves and so were nearly in line with each other. Thomas stood at the taffrail, scrutinizing the other.

He could see that the people aboard were indeed Africans, but they appeared to be women. He could see no one that he could positively identify as a man. Perhaps all the men were ashore. That would explain the absence of alarm. But how odd. Why would they do that? Why would James go ashore in Whydah, of all places? It made no sense at all. The disparate parts could not be made to fit.

But that was all right. He did not have to understand everything. The facts were these: he had found a ship that looked very like the one James had taken.

Aboard that ship were African women. Not slaves bound in chains and ready to be stowed down but women walking the decks free, cooking, going on with life.

That was not at all what one would expect to see aboard a ship anchored off Whydah.

And that meant that he *had* found King James.

CHAPTER 31

James did little that day but watch and hide. When the others awoke, they crept down to the tree line and knelt beside James and watched the *Elizabeth Galley* coming to her anchor. They watched as her men brailed up the sails, laid out along her yards, and stowed the canvas as the ship finally came to a rest one hundred yards to seaward of their captured French merchantman. They said nothing.

Each one of the men crouching at the forest edge was intimately familiar with that ship. Indeed, so obsessed had Marlowe been with her fitting out that there was not one of his people who had not had a hand in it, from the men who had pounded home trunnels and drifts and stepped masts and hove out rigging gangs, to the women who had seen to making hammocks and outfitting the great cabin with curtains and cushions and even building some of the lighter sails, to the children who had been given tar brushes and buckets of slush and put to work at the messier jobs for which their juvenile indelicacy made them ideally suited.

The *Elizabeth Galley* was a part of their home, a fixture from the docks at Jamestown. After all they had endured, and all the miles they had sailed, there was something unreal about seeing her here. It was as if they had walked down the forest trail and come upon Marlowe House itself, transported whole and set down on that strange land.

Good Boy was the first to speak. 'Goddamn, I ain't never been so happy to see anything in my life.' A muttering of agreement followed.

James frowned, kept his eyes on the ship. The boys were reacting, they weren't thinking. They were so far from everything they knew, hunted by strangers with whom they could not speak, in a land such as they had never seen before. Of course they would be relieved to see something, anything, familiar, even if that thing had come to carry them all back to the gallows.

Or perhaps not.

He himself was a dead man, he knew that. Everyone knew him, the black man who had fought at Marlowe's side, the arrogant nigger who commanded the *Northumberland*. There would be nothing but the noose for him if he returned, and if the court did not deign to put it there, the mob surely would, and the white-suited Frederick Dunmore, Esq., leading the way.

But it was just possible that no one knew the identity of the young men with him. If Sam and William had kept their mouths shut, then Quash and Cato and Good Boy and Joshua might be able to return and blend back in with the others at Marlowe House and no one the wiser.

But the first step was begging Marlowe for his mercy, and that was asking a lot: asking a lot of Marlowe and of himself. He had never asked anyone for mercy before, and not surprisingly he had received little of it during his life. He would never ask for himself. But for these others, whose lives had been destroyed by his own unchecked rage, for them he would humble himself.

He was about to lead them out onto the beach when he saw movement on the *Elizabeth Galley*'s deck. 'Hold a moment,' he said. They remained where they were, crouched at the tree line, watching as the *Galley*'s longboat was swayed over the side, as a party of men climbed down and took their place on the thwarts. The sunlight flashed on the white oar blades as they were raised up in two lines, and then the boat was under way, pulling for the French merchantman.

It covered the distance quickly, the oars pulled by expert hands. It swept around the stern, circled, disappeared from sight around her bow, then re-appeared again.

'What he doing?' Joshua asked.

'Marlowe don't know it ain't a trap,' James said. 'He don't understand why he don't see no men on board. He going to take a good look before he goes aboard her.'

The longboat stopped under the Frenchman's counter, and though they were too far to hear any conversation, King James could well imagine the one that was taking place. Marlowe was looking for the white crew, trying to find out why this ship was manned by African women alone. Marlowe could speak a bit of the patois of the coast; he might even be able to communicate with one of them.

Five minutes of that, and then the longboat pulled up to the Frenchman's side and one by one the men

390

boarded her. James could not identify any of them in particular, but he had no doubt that one was Thomas Marlowe and another was Francis Bickerstaff.

Bickerstaff. He would be the key to this thing. He would be the calm voice of reason. If there was to be any cooperation, any mercy or forgiveness or contrition between two headstrong, arrogant, stubborn men such as King James and Thomas Marlowe, then it would be through the intercession of Francis Bickerstaff.

They watched for another ten minutes, but nothing of note happened, nothing at all that they could see. Marlowe and his men would be searching the ship, deck to keelson, moving carefully in case it was a trap.

It was time to confront him, time to prostrate himself before Thomas Marlowe and beg for the lives of his men. James looked up and down the beach, as far as he could see from their place of concealment, saw a dugout canoe pulled up in the sand. It would be a tricky thing, getting through the surf, but they would do it.

He turned to his men, was ready to order them forward, when he heard something else: voices, a number of them. They were not close, and were all but drowned by the crashing surf, but in the lull between the breakers he could hear them, talking loud.

'Come along,' he said, and rather than leading his boys out onto the exposed beach he led them back into the forest, deeper than where they had slept that night, to a place where the thick undergrowth hid them completely. 'Wait here. I be back.'

James headed off through the woods, moving fast,

despite the thick tangle of vegetation. He knew instinctively where each foot should fall, and the next, and the next. He moved silently, more silent than was necessary with the crash of waves a scant fifty yards away, following the line of the beach, moving toward the voices. He was amazed at how quickly the woodcraft he had known as a child came back, as if the knowledge of it was embedded in the ancient earth of that continent, and he needed only to be reunited with her to have all that dormant skill wake again.

They were standing at the trailhead, where the packed forest floor gave way to the fine sand of the beach. James could hear them clearly even before he could see them, and though he did not understand the words, he recognized the rapid, clipped sound of the Kwa language. They were Kru, Madshaka's elite.

Another dozen steps and he could see them at last, in glimpses through the foliage, but it was enough to tell him what he needed to know. They were heavily armed, a hunting party, eight out of about twenty of the Kru who had stood by Madshaka. Apparently his place at the slave factory was not so secure that he was willing to send off even a majority of his private army.

The Kru might have been sent to hunt for James and the rest, but they were not hunting now. Rather, they were pointing out to sea, talking fast among themselves, with wild gestures, and again James did not need to know the language to understand what was being said. They were discussing the arrival of the *Elizabeth Galley*, the significance of the longboat going over to her.

Despite the rudimentary seamanship that James had drilled into them, ships and the sea were not their world. They would not recognize the *Elizabeth Galley* from the brief encounter they had had on the other side of the Atlantic. They would not know how to interpret this new development.

James knew already what they would do – send two men back to inform Madshaka of the *Galley*'s arrival, post two to watch the ships for further activity, send the remaining four off to hunt the Virginians – and five minutes later they did just that.

The hunters split up and James receded back into the woods, moving diagonally until he could see a section of the beach. He had no fear of his men being found out. They would have been nearly impossible to discover in any event. And while eight well-armed men might have made a vigorous and effective search, the hunters now were outnumbered and looking for an enemy they knew to be armed with cutlasses and knives at least, and so they were not putting any great effort into the task.

James watched for ten minutes as they made their perfunctory inspection of the tree line, looking for where the Virginians might have entered the forest, and then worked his way back to his men.

They spent the remainder of the morning there, hiding, resting, eating what wild fruit James was able to obtain.

Noon, with the sun overhead, beating down on the beach but unable to penetrate to where they hid, and more voices drifted up from the shore: chatter, then the crash of surf, chatter, crash.

James made his way to the tree line once more. Madshaka and the eight hunters stood, feet in the swirling sea, staring out at the two ships that bobbed in unison like dancers and tugged at their thick anchor cables.

Madshaka was making wild gestures, twirling around now and again when his fury got the better of him. The Frenchman represented a fortune to him, stuffed as it was with booty and slaves for the reselling. Even the ship itself, sold at a fraction of its value, would be worth more than most Africans would see in a lifetime.

Twelve hours before, Madshaka had all that, plus King James's very life depending on a single word from him. And now, in just half a day, it was coming apart, and Madshaka was not the kind who would let that happen. There was no life that Madshaka would not expend to protect his empire.

James knew now who Madshaka was.

And he knew Madshaka was not stupid, and he was not rash. He would do everything in his power to get the Frenchman back, but he would not attack in the daylight and he would not make a headlong assault against an overwhelming enemy. The capture of the slave factory told James all he needed to know about Madshaka's tactical mind, and so he rested easy through the daylight hours, certain that no move would be made until dark, certain that Madshaka would not move until he thought he could win.

The sun went down in a great show of red and orange, filtering through the sands that were lifted off the African deserts by the steady winds and drawn up into the far reaches of the sky. And then it was dark and King James roused his men, led them slowly toward the beach.

Flickering light danced over the Frenchman's

lower masts and through her gunports. The women had lit their nightly fire. James could picture them gathered around it, sitting cross-legged, holding in their laps their children, or the children they had adopted out of the 'cargo,' rocking slowly to the rhythm of some sad song of the Ibo or the Yoruba or the Aja.

And from the *Elizabeth Galley*, a single anchor light forward, and the big stern lanterns, and below them, the brightly lit great cabin. Marlowe and Bickerstaff and probably Fleming drinking their port, the remains of dinner spread before them.

The five men waited, silent, for the most part, as the moon climbed higher and higher and first the fire aboard the Frenchman faded away to nothing and then the lanterns in the great cabin were extinguished one by one until there was nothing to be seen of either ship, save for the lanterns burning topside aboard the *Galley*.

'Time to go,' James said quietly.

'We going aboard the *Elizabeth Galley*?' It was Quash, and his voice was eager.

'No, not "we." I am.'

'Oh.' There was no attempt to hide the disappointment. Sanctuary, or so they saw it, within sight, and James would not allow them to enter.

'Listen here, boys. We still outlaws, you understand? Might be we goes aboard and they hang us all, right there. Can't take that chance.'

'So why are you going aboard?'

'Because I gots to see that you boys will be safe. So I'm going to go aboard first, and I'm going to have a talk with Captain Marlowe.'

* * *

Captain Marlowe was not asleep, had not been asleep, and did not envision being asleep anytime soon. He lay still in his cot, stared up at the blackness. He had tried to use his arm as little as possible, but he still was forced to use it a lot, and now it hurt like hell. On the deck above he heard the clanging of the bells, seven bells, half past eleven p.m. The sound was an underscore to his restlessness.

Boarding the French merchant ship had unsettled him. All those women and children. Not renegades, savage killers as he had pictured, but families, going calmly about their business.

Marlowe had picked up some of the coastal pidgin during his various adventures along that coast and with that he was able to talk to some of the women, after a fashion. They told him something about pirating and about Kalabari and Madshaka, though if that last was a person or a place he could not tell. They told him something about someone who sailed the ship being dead, but when he said 'King James?' they pointed to the shore.

In the end he was more confused than he had been before going aboard.

He thought about the ship. She had been full-laden when James took her. Rich fabrics, spices, tea, not an insignificant amount of specie. If the Elizabeth Galleys had begun to doubt his tales, they doubted no more. She was a rich prize, and the vessel itself was worth enough to make the cruise profitable.

He might not have a letter of marque and reprisal, but he carried with him a commission from Governor Nicholson to run these black pirates to ground, and Marlowe felt it was not an unreasonable assumption that he also had the right to keep for him and his men whatever stolen goods they might recapture.

And since it was too great a hardship to try to carry it all back to Virginia – dispatching a prize crew, keeping company, worrying about recapture – he reckoned they would just dispose of ship and cargo in Lisbon. There he could transform their great encumbrance into a more manageable chest of Spanish doubloons and pieces of eight, which would render the men much more cooperative and avoid irritating complications at home.

A chest full of specie and King James in chains down below. He tried to feel happy about it but he could not, at least not about the part that involved King James.

Well, perhaps James has run off into the forest and I will never find him, he thought, and rolled over and closed his eyes and wondered if he might sleep now.

He heard a creak from beyond the door, from the great cabin, and though the *Elizabeth Galley*, rolling in the ocean swells and pulling on her anchor hawse, was a cacophony of creaks, his mind separated that one from the others, singled it out as not being a part of the natural workings of the vessel, and before he had even had a conscious thought about it he was sitting bolt upright in his cot, his ear cocked to the door.

There was another sound, though hardly a sound at all, more like a warm breath on the neck. If he had been even half asleep, if he had not been tensed as he was, he would never have heard it. A foot coming down on the plush pillow on the after locker? The great cabin windows were open. It was not an impossible climb up the rudder and over the counter, not for a strong and nimble person.

Marlowe was up, out of bed, wearing only the old slop trousers he wore to sleep, and in the blackness his left hand fell on the hilt of his sword, his right hand on the loaded pistol he always kept in the same place for just that reason. A stab of pain shot up his arm. He clenched his teeth, grabbed the gun with his left hand. A silent step toward the door and with the barrel of the pistol he moved the little curtain a hair, peered out into the great cabin.

The lantern that always burned in the great cabin was out, but the light from the stern lanterns on the taffrail above the windows threw a diffused glow out into the night, enough to silhouette the figure stepping in through the window, moving carefully, stepping down onto the locker. Marlowe had no notion of who it might be and he did not care. Anyone making such an entrance was someone he was quite happy to shoot.

Marlowe took a step back, held the gun up, sword down, drew breath, and then lashed out with his foot, smashed the door open with a splintering sound, stepped forward, the gun coming down level as he did.

He could see the figure react, see him move, and he pointed the barrel of the gun at the center of his body and pulled the trigger. In the flash of priming and muzzle he had just a glimpse of white slop trousers, leather jerkin, loose shirt, leaping sideways, diving for the deck. He heard the sound of shattering glass as the bullet passed its target and smashed through the quarter galley windows on its way to plunging into the Bight of Benin.

'All right, Captain Marlowe, it's just me. James.'

Marlowe stood and stared into the dark. The smell of burnt powder was strong in his nose, his night vision quite ruined by the gunshot. He could hardly believe what he was hearing.

Then the door to the adjoining cabin burst open and there was Francis Bickerstaff, sword in one hand, lantern in the other, and though the one candle gave out just the merest flicker it seemed to illuminate the space like noontime sun.

'What the devil . . .' Bickerstaff said, his eyes flicking down to Marlowe's spent pistol. He followed Marlowe's gaze. Crouched on the aft locker, right by the open window, King James. Slop trousers, linen shirt with sleeves rolled up to reveal powerful fore-arms. Heavily armed, but his weapons hanging at his side, none drawn. Eyes alert.

Then there were hurried footsteps beyond the great cabin, pounding on the door. 'Captain? Captain? Are you all right?' It was Fleming, and there were others with him.

Marlowe paused, held James's eyes. If I had any brains at all, he thought, I would have Fleming in here and have him take this son of a bitch away in chains.

'Fine, Mr Fleming. Sorry for that gunshot. I thought I heard some damned thief coming up the rudder and took a shot, but it was nothing.' His eyes remained locked with James's.

A pause, and then, 'Very well, sir. You are sure you are all right?'

'Yes, fine, thank you. But pray tell the anchor watch to keep a bright lookout. You know these

Africans will steal the shoes from your feet, give them half a chance.'

'Aye, sir. It's a fact, sir.' Then with some muttered order to the others, Fleming shuffled away.

Marlowe turned to his visitor. 'So, James. Sneaking in here like the damned criminal you are?'

'I didn't know how me old shipmates felt. Thought it safer not coming up the side in the daylight, you know?'

'Safer? I damned near shot you, you stupid bastard!'

'No, not close. I know you sleep with the one gun only. I was ready for it. What happened to your arm?'

'Round shot. Attacking some bastard I took to be you.'

'If I known about the arm I not have been so careful.'

James was his same old arrogant, cocksure self. Marlowe felt the anger mounting, and not for the first time, but it was worse now. He tossed the spent gun aside, snatched a cutlass from the rack on the bulkhead. 'Not so careful, eh? Well you black whore's son, are you ready to take a sword through the throat, for all the damned trouble you've caused me? For sneaking in here like this? I can run you through with my left arm as well as my right.'

James remained motionless, his face set, frowning. 'You think you can get across this cabin before I go out the window? You that fast? You make that move and you never see me again, and then you can go back and tell the governor how you let me go.'

'Enough! Enough.' Bickerstaff stepped forward, set the lantern on the table. 'Thomas, if James has gone to the risk of coming aboard thus, I think we

400

can listen to him. James, you have put us all through a world of trouble and Thomas is quite justified in wanting to cut your throat. So since you are, both of you, the two great villains of the Western world, let us all at least don the mantle of civilized men.'

Marlowe looked at James, saw him visibly relax, felt himself do the same. He set his sword down, propped up in a corner. James stepped down from the locker, away from the window.

'I knew you'd come for me. Minute we cleared the capes, I knew you'd come,' James said. 'Knew you'd have no choice, and I never blamed you. I stuck a knife in my own heart the same moment I stuck it in that blackbirder captain, and I'd goddamn well do it again. But I am truly sorry for the hurt I must have done you.'

Marlowe took a breath. Nodded. Felt ashamed of all the anger and loathing he had directed at James. Reminded himself of a fact he knew well: in James's place he would have put a knife in the man's chest as well.

'I know you come for me, and here I am. Delivering myself to you. But I wants to make a deal. I got the boys with me, Quash and Cato and Joshua and Good Boy, and it ain't right that they should die just because they was with me.'

'If you are asking for me to leave them,' Marlowe said, 'I can. It is you alone that the governor demands.'

James nodded. 'I reckoned as much. But see here, you can't leave them. They strangers here, they don't belong to Africa, any more than you or Mr Bickerstaff. You got to take them back to Virginia, let them blend in with your people. Ain't nobody going

401

to recognize them, or know they was with the sloop. Sam and William'll keep shut. You do that and I'll come back with you, let them hang me.'

The words were startling in their frankness, in their unambiguous assessment of the situation, and they made Marlowe that much more aware of what James was sacrificing. He sighed. 'Francis?'

'James, I have always thought you a man of courage, but this is the most noble act I have ever witnessed. It would have been nothing for you to disappear forever in this country but you did not. And as to your plan, I think it could be done. I agree that the crew of the *Northumberland* was not well known, save for you yourself. Perhaps we could have the boys change their names. They should be safe enough. Though the Lord only knows what has been happening back at Marlowe House in our absence.'

'Good. Good,' said James, and he looked relieved. 'I thank you. I have peace with this. But there is one more thing I must demand.'

'Demand!' said Marlowe, but Bickerstaff silenced him with a raised hand.

'The people I saved from the blackbirder, they caught again, held in a factory a few miles from here. Again they will be sold. They . . . I . . . was played for a fool by one of them, a Kru named Madshaka.'

Madshaka. That was the name he had heard aboard the Frenchman. A person, then.

'Those people must be freed from the factory and taken to Kalabari. I told them they would be safe. They have suffered, more than anyone should. It is not right they should suffer more.'

'Now see here, you ask too much, too much by half!' Marlowe said. 'Are you suggesting we march

402

on a legal, authorized factory and set the slaves there free?'

'I not suggesting, I demanding.'

'Demanding! You impertinent little—'

'Thomas, please.' Bickerstaff raised a hand. 'James, while I feel that a plan to liberate a factory full of people about to be sold into bondage has much to recommend it, let me suggest you are not in a position to demand.'

'No? I still one jump away from that window. I go out and you never see me again, got nothing to bring back to the governor. I's willing to trade my life, Marlowe, but I ain't gonna trade it cheap. You can have the French merchantman, all the booty in her hold.'

'Oh I can, can I? How gracious, but in case you had not noticed, I have it now.'

The two men sat and glared at each other. Two men, pushed by so many contrary pressures, like ships acted upon by conflicting winds and tide and wave and current. Each with his future, his very life, hinging on decisions the other must make.

At last James spoke. 'It is a slave factory. There will be a great quantity of specie there. Gold, silver. There always is. It is part of their business.'

'You have seen it? The gold?'

'Yes.'

'Well, then.' Marlowe brightened. 'That is something else altogether. Now you have touched on Bickerstaff's good nature and my greed, and together they are forces to be reckoned with.'

'I had thought I could appeal to your mercy as well.'

'Then you do not know me at all, sir,' Marlowe

403

said. 'But more to the point, I must be able to convince my men of the benefit of risking their lives this way.'

He sat back, expelled his breath, felt the weariness of the ages, all the weight of thousands of years of accumulated history pressing him down. He was not old, not really. Was it at all reasonable that he should feel that way?

'We can have our men ashore in one hour. Will that be sufficient, King James?'

CHAPTER 32

Madshaka stood ankle deep in the ocean, the damned, damned ocean. How he hated it. He had been a *grumete*, sure, and a good one, but that was only because he understood that working the coast was the short path to riches. He had always loathed it. In his essence he was a man of the forest, and the night.

And now the sea, which had once taken him, had brought a new threat.

Around and behind him, the Kru warriors he had led down to the beach to help him in his work. His plan: off through the surf with a boat, out to his prize, and five minutes' work to cut through the anchor cable. The swells would drive the ship up on the beach. Most of the women and children aboard would make it to shore. Once the wreck was close in, he could send people out to take off what valuables they could.

That was the plan, but he was not happy about it. He was not happy about losing the ship itself, which was worth a great deal. He was not happy with the thought of getting a big boat through the surf with unskilled men at the oars. Landing was one thing –

the waves did the chief of the work – but getting back out was something else altogether.

He was not happy about losing however many women and children would drown in the surf. Every dead body was like a coin taken from his purse. He did not like the idea of having to do any of this just to retain what was already his. It was not right. But it was better than losing it all.

The sea crashed, further out, foaming white in the moonlight, raced in and rushed around his ankles, then receded. It felt like it was tugging him along with it, pulling him out to the dark water.

And then in the quiet between the waves he heard something, some new noise, like the noise made by a body of men. And then the next wave curled and broke and drowned out everything but itself.

What was that? He cocked his ear, ready for the lull in the surf. Yes, it was still there, a big sound composed of a hundred little sounds, coming from out there. He heard the clash of steel, the squeal of blocks, voices, someone shouting.

It had to be from the new ship. It could not be from his prize. What were they about? Were they going to take his prize, sail it away? There was no wind, not nearly enough to work the ship off the beach. Madshaka understood enough about the ways of wind ships to know that. And if not the prize, then what? Why would they be coming ashore at that hour?

King James.

Madshaka felt the panic working its way like a poison through his limbs and his chest, could taste it in the back of his throat. Panic like he had not felt since waking up in the blackbirder's hold.

King James. He knew the wealth and power that Madshaka had gathered for himself: the prize, the factory, the trunk full of slaves. He would want it for himself, and if he had talked those men on that heavily armed ship into joining with him, then he would have it.

No, no, no! He would not have it! Madshaka turned to the Kru, who, like good soldiers, were standing silent, waiting for orders. 'They are coming, the men from the ship. I think they want to take the factory for themselves. We will lie in wait for them, on the trail, take them by surprise.' Heads nodded. Silent agreement. They would do as they were told.

Madshaka turned. 'Come along,' he said, and the Kru followed. He headed back up the beach, his wide feet pushing aside quantities of the fine sand, and he hurried for the trailhead, hurried to get in front of the attackers, to lay his trap.

Marlowe was standing in the stern sheets of the *Elizabeth Galley*'s longboat, an oar in place of the rudder, but James had to admit that he did not have the same easy confidence, even exhilaration, that Madshaka had displayed. Marlowe was not a *grumete*. And to make matters worse, he was forced to use his uninjured left arm.

'Stand ready . . .' Marlowe said, looked over his shoulder at the set of the waves, pushed the sweep a bit to one side. The boat rose up on a swell, stern first, then the stern came down fast and the bow rose up with a sickening motion, and then Marlowe shouted, 'Now! Pull, pull!'

The men pulled, pulled hard, pulled with all they had, like panicked horses running away with a carriage. The big boat raced along with the surf, now surrounded by white water, curling, foaming, gunnel high. The oars came out of the water, forward, down. And in the undulating space between the waves, half of the starboard bank found only air.

James felt the boat slough around, felt it going over as it turned broadside to the surf. Marlowe was pushing hard on the sweep and shouting, 'Starboard! Give way! Give way!'

The aftermost man on the starboard side had fallen back, thrown off balance by the lack of resistance on his oar. James leapt up, grabbed the long sweep before it was sucked into the ocean. He wrenched it from the tholes, thrust it down into the sea, levering it against the side of the boat, trying to force the boat back perpendicular to the surf.

But it was too late for that. James felt the boat start to roll. One second he was looking at sea and then he was looking at the stars, sweeping by, and then the boat was over and he was tossed into the waves. He felt arms and legs striking him and when he thrashed to the surface it was black and the surf was a dull and muted roar and he realized that he was under the capsized boat.

And in the next instant the boat rolled again, flying away like a roof torn from a house in a hurricane, and he was in the full roar and fury of the waves, tossed toward the beach, tumbling, flailing uselessly with arms and legs.

He felt himself drop and he hit with a jar on hard-packed sand. He felt a surge of relief, but only for an instant, and then the surf grabbed him again, lifting him, tumbling him. His head hit something hard, his mouth was filled with salt water and gritty sand. He gagged, tried to spit, and then once more he was deposited on hard ground.

He scrambled onto hands and knees and crawled up, up the beach, crawled as fast as he could before the long arms of the sea could reach him once more. He felt the water swirling around him, but it was only the fingertips of the surf and it did not have the power to move him, so he rolled over on his back, closed his eyes, breathed.

A minute of that, no more, and he pulled himself to his feet, took a few faltering steps, and then composed himself, looked around. The longboat was flung far up the beach, capsized, lying at an odd angle. Men were staggering up from the water's edge, some walking, some crawling. Some were lying in the surf, flopping back and forth with the surge of the water.

'Come on,' James said to the few men around him. He led them down to the water's edge where they grabbed those men lying there by their coats or under their arms and dragged them up the beach. Some would be dead and some merely unconscious. They could sort them out later.

Then Marlowe's voice, calling the men to him, and James was relieved to hear it. He trotted across the sand with the others.

'Who have we lost?' Marlowe asked. Bickerstaff, looking at once bedraggled and composed, stood beside him.

'Johnson . . .' a voice called out.
'Llewelyn, but I don't think he's dead . . .'
'Starkey . . .'

Three more names after that. The first body count, and that was only fighting the surf.

'Very well,' said Marlowe. 'I don't expect anyone has a grain of dry powder left, so it's cold steel. James, lead on.'

James circled the crowd, stood for a second beside Marlowe, then waved the men forward. They had been told what the factory would be like, how they would attack over the open ground, what kind of resistance they could expect.

Their ardor did not seem in the least cooled by the fact that they would now be fighting without the advantage of firearms. The Elizabeth Galleys were a greedy bunch, and largely amoral, but they were not cowards. Or at least their greed quite eclipsed any hesitation they might have had.

They stepped across the beach and onto the forest trail that James was coming to know quite well, despite himself. They moved between the trees, and the light from the moon was all but blotted out, leaving just enough for them to see the difference between beaten track and forest edge. Every now and again one of the men would stumble and curse his misstep. It was not the silent approach that James had envisioned. If anyone was listening, they would hear the sailors approaching from a long way off.

They pressed on, and James turned that thought around in his head. The trail was the perfect place for an ambush. If Madshaka had left a man on the beach, watching, there would have been plenty of time for that man to race back to the factory and report and for Madshaka to set up just such a surprise.

'Captain Marlowe . . .'

'Yes?'

'I going to press ahead, see if I can smoke any trap.

Might be better if your men walk with weapons drawn.'

'Hmm, yes. Good idea.' It did not sound as if the thought of ambush had occurred to Marlowe, and now he did not sound too pleased with the possibility. 'Good, then. Go on ahead.'

James pulled his cutlass from the frog of the shoulder belt, more to keep it from slapping as he ran, then broke into a trot. He rolled with each step, heel to toe, listened for the sound of his own footfall but could hear nothing.

Soon he had left the Elizabeth Galleys behind, one hundred yards at least, and he slowed his pace to a brisk walk. He was part of the forest again. His nose took in the cumulative smell, his brain deciphered its many parts. He listened to the sounds and knew the rustle of leaves and the creak of tree on tree and the scurry of the tiny night hunters in the undergrowth.

He walked at the edge of the trail, right up against the tree line, as invisible as he could be. He thought of what Bickerstaff had said to him. 'It would have been nothing for you to disappear forever in this country . . .'

It was true, but that was all he could do. Disappear. Because his homeland was no longer his home. He had suspected it from the first mention of Africa, at the first meeting of the people he had freed from bondage. And now he knew. He had been gone too long. There was nothing for him there, not anymore.

Nor was he a part of the New World. Twenty years of slavery had taken everything but his life, had left him a floating entity, bobbing in the air, with no place left for him to come down.

And then a silent alarm rang in his head and he froze and all his introspection was whisked away. Something was wrong. He listened, but there was nothing for him to hear, save for a soft rustle. An animal, perhaps.

It was the smell. He caught it again, through the rotten vegetation and the warm dirt and the flowering plants. Human smell. Dried sweat on the soft breeze.

He crouched low, took a step back, wondered if the people to whom that smell belonged were aware of his presence. Back, he had to get back to Marlowe but he did not want to move, to give himself away.

If he was aware of them, then they, watching as they were, had to be aware of him. But why then did they not move on him? Because they knew he was a scout, and they were waiting for the main body of men.

He could hear the Elizabeth Galleys now, in their clumsy advance, somewhere down the trail. They were marching right into it.

Another step back. 'Marlowe! Ambush! Here!' he shouted with all his voice, the sound startling in the night forest, and then they were on him.

They broke from the brush like furies, screaming, swords raised. A gun flashed, the bullet passed close. Kru warriors, a dozen or more. They still wore their pirate clothes, the clothes they had pillaged on the high seas, but there was no mistaking them. And in the flash of the gun, Madshaka, hanging back, a grinning mountain.

James brought his cutlass up, caught a sword as it came down on him, turned it aside. His vision had been hurt by the flash, but he reckoned it had blinded the others too, and when the counterstroke missed him by a foot he knew he was right. Thrust, and the point of his cutlass caught flesh, penetrated. A scream, very close, and James leapt back as another man hacked at him.

Another pistol shot, wider than the first, and a glimpse of the men arrayed against him, and from down the road the sound of Marlowe's men running, shouting, cursing as they raced to the fight.

James stepped back into the tree line. Heard a cutlass swish past, searching him out. He jumped forward, slashed at the attacker, felt the blade cut, and then back into the trees.

Madshaka was shouting something in Kwa and his men were shouting back and James reckoned they were arranging themselves for Marlowe's assault. His vision was coming back, he could see the men on the trail, Madshaka behind them. They were preparing for the real threat, the armed brigands coming up the trail. They had forgotten about him, for the moment.

He moved through the tree line, just feet from the trail, but unseen by the men there, crashing through until he was behind their line of defense. And directly in front of him, Madshaka, his focus on the trail, on the growing sound of Marlowe's privateers hustling into battle.

James crashed out of the trees, cutlass raised. From his throat, a long, whooping battle cry, a Malinke cry, a sound he had not heard or uttered or even recalled for twenty years. Madshaka whirled, the look on his face shock, panic. He stumbled back, raised his sword just in time to prevent James from cleaving his skull in two. He shouted something in Kwa, took a step back, and then his dirk was in his other hand and he met James's fresh attack with crossed blades, caught the attacking cutlass in the V, turned it aside.

Madshaka circled around, both blades before him. He was too much the warrior to be shaken for long by the surprise rush from the tree line, and he was recovered now, tensed, a dangerous man.

James backed up, his eyes darting from Madshaka to the Kru and back, afraid to linger on either for a split second more than necessary. And then a movement caught his eye, a great surge, as the Elizabeth Galleys burst round the bend in the trail and fell on the Kru and in that instant of distraction, Madshaka attacked.

James did not see it coming until it was there, the dirk shooting forward like a snake, striking at his belly, catching him in the side as he twisted to escape. There was screaming on the trail, guns going off, two, three, four, Madshaka lit with the flashes of orange light. He drove the dagger blade home and James screamed with the agony of it and twisted further. The blade cut its way free as he jerked sideways to avoid the death thrust from Madshaka's sword.

The sword missed his neck, scraped along his shoulder, cutting through shoulder belt and jerkin and shirt and then flesh, a hot, searing pain. But Madshaka had committed everything to the lunge and now he was off balance and James grabbed the big man's wrist, pulled him forward, slashed with his own cutlass. He felt the blade bite, somewhere around Madshaka's waist, but the two men were face-to-face, too close for James to deliver any mortal wound.

And for a second, less than a second, they stood there, face-to-face, their breath intermingling, huge Madshaka looking down at James, as if they were telling each other secrets. Then Madshaka grinned his horrible leer, and twisted his wrist free. Strong as James was, Madshaka was stronger still and he broke the grip, pushed James away.

They stumbled apart, two bleeding fighters, ready to go at each other again, when they were swept away by a wave of men, Marlowe's men pushing the Kru up the trail, locked in bloody fighting. All the guns had been fired, and now it was steel on steel, and the Galleys' superior numbers were telling. James was knocked to the earth and he saw Madshaka look to his side, saw the surprise register, and then he too was knocked down by the press of men, the Kru yielding ground, first inches, then feet.

They would yield, but they would not run. They would hold that ground until they died, because they were Kru warriors.

Screaming, blades flashing in the dull light, cursing, shouts of fury and anguish in Kwa and English, men doubling over with wounds to the belly, hacked down by heavy blades.

James's cutlass was gone and he flailed around with his hands on the ground, searching for it, eyes up, waiting for Madshaka to appear, looming over him, his face in that grin, his sword dropping like an ax for the execution.

His hand touched cold steel. He put his palm down on it. Cold steel and hot, sticky blood – it was the blade of his cutlass. He found the hilt and snatched it up, pushed himself to a crouch. The cloth of his shirt pulled free from the wound in his side, sending a shaft of pain through him. He cried out in agony and in battle fury, pushed aside the man in front of him, and staggered through the combatants, looking for Madshaka.

Through the dark and the struggling men James could not see him, but he knew he had to be there. He saw him fall, saw him lose his sword. He could not have moved so far in the few seconds since they had been shoved apart.

But he was not there. He was not in the fight, not one of the handful of Kru still battling the privateers. Had he been, James knew he could not miss him. Madshaka was the biggest of them all, his great stature was the very thing that gave him the permanent aura of command, a quality he had used well. But he was not there.

James staggered back. He pressed a hand against the wound in his side, felt the hot blood oozing between his fingers, but the pressure felt good. The tip of his cutlass dragged on the ground.

The factory. Madshaka must have gone back there. He looked up the trail, as far as he could see. There was no sign of him. But there was no other explanation. James fought through the clouds of pain in his head. The Kru would all be dead soon, and if he, James, could see that, then Madshaka could see it as well. So Madshaka would be taking his leave, ahead of Marlowe's men.

No, he must not. That was all that James could think. No, he must not.

He took a stumbling step up the trail, found his footing, took another. With his hand pressed to his side it was not so bad. He could move fast, not a run but something like it. The sounds of the fight were behind him, already growing more distant, the trees staggering past as he moved at his best pace, his breathing loud in his own ears.

Madshaka. He would kill Madshaka. There was no other thought. That was all he had left.

CHAPTER 33

The slash wound in Madshaka's side was hot, searing, the pain shooting through him with each jarring step. The blood was pulsing down his leg.

No longer was his the lion's charge, or the powerful, silent lope of the leopard: it was the gait of a cripple, and it made Madshaka furious, his perfect body marred, his power sapped from him by one lucky stroke of King James's sword.

Damn him, damn him, damn him. Madshaka let the loathing flow with his blood as he raced for the factory, raced as best he could with the pain lashing him. James had ruined it all and now he, Madshaka, could do nothing but escape and take what little he could carry from the factor's hut.

A lesser man would have thought of revenge. A lesser man would have at that very instant been making absurd promises to himself to hunt the world over for the man who had brought him down and kill him.

Madshaka had heard plenty of broken drunks puking out such nonsense, but he would have none of it. He would survive. He would build himself up again. That was real revenge. And then, perhaps, when he was worthy again, the gods would deliver James to him.

The head of the trail at last, and the factory, low and ugly, sitting in the cleared acreage. No clandestine approach this time; Madshaka still ruled there, even if only for a few moments more. The factor and his remaining white toads were all locked in the little cell reserved for problem slaves that could not be trusted with the others. The only free men were the two Kru guards, Anaka and his lieutenant, whom he had left behind. They would be of greatest use in delaying the bastards on the trail.

Madshaka limped through the open gate. The wide yard was illuminated in patches by the torches that stood along the low mud wall. He paused, looked around, trying to think through the panic and the pain and the fury at having all this taken away so soon.

Then Anaka and his lieutenant were there, begging him for news, asking if he was hurt.

'I am fine, but they need you, down the trail! The others, they are all but victorious. Go now, both of you, throw yourselves into the fight and you will drive them back to the sea!'

The Kru nodded and hurried off and Madshaka watched them go. He watched long enough to be certain that they were really going. Incredible, such blind loyalty. Stupid bastards, they deserved the death that awaited them, if they were going to be so stupid.

He hobbled forward, made his way to the factor's house. A few things to tidy up and then he would disappear into the forest, and when he was healed, when the strength was back, he would return.

419

Into the factor's hut, past the array of primitive African weapons, the trophies, mounted on the walls, and over to the rack of muskets and pistols. Four of the white toads in the cell, so he loaded five pistols, stuck them in his belt, hobbled out into the night, across the compound.

The cell was no more than six feet by six feet, a cage really, with walls and a roof of iron bars, fully exposed. The four white men huddled in opposite corners and they stood as they saw Madshaka approach. None seemed at all afraid.

'Madshaka! Let us out of here, goddamn your eyes! What are you about, damn it!' It was Van der Haagen and his outrage was genuine.

Brave man, I have learned much from him, Madshaka thought. If only he had been willing to work with me rather than treat me like another nigger-boy, we might have built each other up to great wealth. It is too bad.

Madshaka grieved for nothing as much as he did for opportunities lost.

'Madshaka!' Van der Haagen was still in a demanding mood. Audacious for one locked in a tiny cell. 'Let me out of here, damn you!'

'I set you free, Dutchman,' Madshaka said. He raised a pistol through the bars, saw the flicker of panic on the man's face, pulled the trigger. The ball smashed into Van der Haagen's chest, flung him back against the bars. His eyes were wide, his mouth open, as he slumped down to the earth. Madshaka heard the death rattle, and then he was still.

For a second it was silent and Madshaka could even hear the insects in the forest, and then panic in the little cage. The three men still living rushed to the far

420

end, grabbing at the bars, pulled at them, for what reason Madshaka could not guess, screaming, for whom he did not know. He raised another pistol, shot one of them through the back and he fell. He tossed the pistol aside.

The two remaining men turned, eyes wide, shaking their heads, pleading. He raised the third gun, took aim. One man was cowering, half turned, arms crossed over his chest as if he could deflect the bullet, so Madshaka lifted his aim and put the lead ball through the man's skull. He crashed against the bars – the impact made the cell shudder – and then fell dead against the factor.

The last man knew what was coming and rather than cower he charged, flung himself across the cell, arms thrust through the bars, trying to get ahold of Madshaka, but Madshaka took one step back and was out of reach. 'Bravely done, Mr Adams,' Madshaka said, then up came the fourth gun, hammer back. He squeezed the trigger and Mr Adams became the fourth corpse in the cell.

Madshaka flung the pistol away, rested his hand on the one loaded gun still in his belt. The Kru would all be dead and all the white men of the factory were dead and so there was no one who could name Madshaka as the one responsible for this, for the taking of the factory, the killing of Stevens and the others. He was free. It was as if none of this had happened.

A few months in the backcountry and he would return to Whydah with a string of captives and begin again. Now he had only to get what specie he could find in the factor's house and be off into the night.

He made his limping way back across the

compound. He recalled the moment that the Virginians had rolled back the tarp on the black-birder's hatch and he had stepped on deck and seen the slaughtered crew of the slaver. From dark despair to a faint trace of optimism, a suggestion of hope. It was how he felt now.

King James reached the head of the trail and paused, stepped into the forest, ran his eyes over the factory in the middle of the open ground. The big gates were open but he could not see anything within, could not see Madshaka. But where else might he have gone?

Then through the gate came two men, Kru, running hard. The last two left behind? Judging from the number of men he had seen on the trail there could not be many more. He stepped back, one step, two steps, three steps into the forest, leaned against a big ironwood tree, let the shadows wash over him.

The Kru raced over the open ground and onto the trail and right past him with never a pause. James waited until he could no longer hear their footfalls and he stepped from the trees and started across the open ground.

It was no way to approach, he knew that. He should have worked his way along the tree line, raced to the wall, kept close as he moved along the perimeter, but he was too exhausted, too hurt, too far beyond caring to do that. So he half ran and half walked in full view across the clearing until he reached the gate.

There he stopped and pressed himself against the wall, then inched his way forward. He heard a voice, shouting, outraged and demanding, but he could not quite make out what was said.

Silence, and then a gunshot and James jumped in surprise. He felt the wound in his side throb. He pressed himself against the wall again. Screaming, panic, and another shot and another. He moved forward, peered around the edge of the gate. Madshaka was standing in front of a small cell and one by one shooting the men inside.

The fourth man flung himself at Madshaka but missed and Madshaka shot him too and tossed the last gun aside, observed his handiwork for a moment, then shuffled off toward the factor's hut. His walk was heavy, painful. James realized that his cutlass must have found more of a mark than he had thought. Good. In his condition he could not hope to fight and win against an unwounded Madshaka.

He followed Madshaka's labored movement with his eyes, saw his big form silhouetted in the frame of the door of the well-lit factor's hut, and then he disappeared inside.

James waited a moment more, then stepped from the shadows and hobbled into the factory's compound. He felt horribly exposed, vulnerable, as if someone he could not see was drawing a bead on him, following his movement with a musket barrel, preparing to shoot him from the dark corners. But no shots came, and he could see no motion anywhere: no guards on the mud walls or moving around the compound, no white slavers, no Kru.

The only living souls he could see at all were the captives in the trunk. Of those he could catch only glimpses, movement in the dark. He could see little beyond that and the people there made no noise. James knew what it was like to be in that cage. He knew they did not want to attract attention.

Across the open ground and as he drew closer he could hear Madshaka tearing the factor's hut apart, searching for something. James made it unnoticed to the hut's earthen wall, pressed himself against it, peered in the lower edge of a window.

There were several lanterns lit, illuminating the big room. A table in the center, the remains of a meal and numerous empty bottles strewn around. A sideboard, a desk, a blanket chest, all decently crafted bits of European furniture, very much at odds with the mud-built walls, and the various examples of native African weaponry that were mounted there.

Madshaka was at the desk, towering over it, tearing it apart. It looked like a child's play furniture in his hands as he pulled drawers out, emptied their contents, tossed them aside. Finally he picked the whole thing up, examined its underside, and then flung it away, disgusted. Whatever he was searching for, it was not in the desk.

He turned to the blanket chest, flipped open the lid, knelt before it, began flinging its contents over his shoulder.

James held his cutlass in his left hand, wiped his palm on his shirt, took a renewed grip on the weapon. He saw the pistol in Madshaka's belt. He knew he had to get within killing distance with his sword before Madshaka could pull it free and cock it.

He hobbled toward the door, stood for a second just beyond the fall of the light, clenched his teeth, then charged.

He raced into the room, the pain in his side forgotten, kicked a chair out of the way. Madshaka whirled, stood, grabbed at the pistol in his belt but James was there first, cutlass at arm's length, right under Madshaka's chin, the point pressed into the dark flesh, a little trickle of blood running down.

Madshaka struck at the cutlass like a snake, his left hand wrapping around the blade, pulling it aside. James pulled hard but could not break the big man's grip. He could see the blood running between Madshaka's fingers as he held tight on the vivious edge of the weapon. His eyes were wide, his teeth were set against the pain, but he did not loosen his grip.

With his right Madshaka went for the pistol, pulled it from his belt and James kicked him hard in the hand, sending the gun thudding to the dirt floor.

For a second they were motionless, then slowly Madshaka twisted the cutlass, twisted it back, in a direction that James's wrist would not admit. Then with a jerk he wrenched the cutlass from James's hand, tossed it aside, went for the gun.

James leapt back, grabbed the chair he had kicked aside. The pistol was in Madshaka's hand, coming up, Madshaka's big thumb on the flintlock. James could see the great bloody wound on Madshaka's side and he smashed the chair into it, hard. It shattered against Madshaka like hitting a marble statue, and James hit him again with the broken piece that remained in his fists.

The big man bellowed, doubled over, grabbed at the wound, but the pistol did not drop from his grip. James leapt back again, grabbed the edge of the table, tossed it over, tumbling it toward Madshaka, and Madshaka fended it off with his arm.

Madshaka screamed again with pain under the jarring impact of the table but James hardly noticed, because turning the table over had opened his own

wound again, like sticking a red-hot iron in his side.
His head swam with the agony, his eyes watered, and
he stumbled back, trying to clear his head, aware of
the pistol, of Madshaka, six feet away.

He hit the wall and the impact sent another wave
of pain through him, radiating from his shoulder and
his side and crackling through his limbs like Saint
Elmo's fire.

His hand went out and wrapped around the hilt of
a sword hanging on the wall and he jerked it free. It
was a great, heavy, iron affair, heavier even than the
cutlass he had carried, a long, straight blade, a hilt
bound in leather. It was a sword like the swords he
had been trained to wield as a boy, an African sword,
and if it was not Malinke, it was certainly from that
region.

He leaned back against the wall, breathing hard,
the sword held before him. He blinked the tears
from his eyes. Madshaka had fallen to his knees,
clutching his wound, but now he looked up, then
painfully regained his feet, as if he was aware that
James had recovered, as if he knew the fight was now
to resume.

The pistol was still in his hand. Madshaka straightened, as much as he could, leveled the pistol at
James, thumbed the lock back.

The two men stood there, staring at each other,
hating each other, breathing hard.

'You,' Madshaka said at last, and his voice was no
more than a harsh whisper, 'you are a sorry, sorry
little worm . . .'

James shook his head, slowly. 'No, Madshaka. No.
I am a Malinke prince, from the House of Mane. And
you . . . you are just a filthy . . . stinking . . .

426

blackbirder, and all the gold you steal won't change that.'

Madshaka flinched, he actually flinched, as if the words had physically struck him. He scowled, took a half step forward, the pistol held straight-armed before him, aimed right at James's heart.

A second more and the arrogant, defiant Madshaka was back. 'Well, Prince of the Malinke, I hope you got big magic that will make this bullet dance off you, because if you don't, then you going to be just another dead bastard. You think you can run that sword through me before I shoot you?'

James knew he could not. As close as Madshaka was, he could not cover that distance before Madshaka put a bullet through him. Very well. That was the way it was.

He shook his head slowly, lowered his sword, a gesture of defeat. He saw Madshaka grin, saw his straight-arm grip on the pistol relax, and James guessed that that was as good as it would get, and might even buy him a step or two.

He held Madshaka's eyes, felt his hands begin to shake, felt the war cry building silent in his gut, felt it creeping out along his limbs where before there had been only pain. He saw a moment's hesitancy in Madshaka's face, a wash of fear, and then he launched himself across the room, the big iron sword held shoulder high, point forward, aimed right at Madshaka's chest.

One step, two steps, a leap over the upturned table, and Madshaka's arm shot out straight. Over the table and the flash of the pan and the flash of the muzzle, those final seconds unfolding slow and dull, like moving underwater.

James felt the bullet tear into his chest, rip through his right lung, felt the searing heat of the heavy ball as it tore through his back, clean through, and then the tip of his sword was on Madshaka's chest, right on his heart, and he saw Madshaka's eyes go wide with surprise.

The momentum carried him on and the needle tip of the big iron blade pierced Madshaka's chest and kept on going, going, deeper and deeper. There was a scream, a high anguished scream, but James did not know where it was coming from. Everything was becoming dulled and soft to his eyes and he was aware that he was no longer running, just falling, falling, pushing the big blade before him as he went down.

Down, down he fell and then he knew he had stopped but he had no sensation of hitting the ground, or of jarring or of anything. He thought there might be other people in the room, or some great commotion, but he was not able to turn his head and look, so instead he closed his eyes and let the warmth wash over him.

He was thirsty. There was liquid in his throat but it did not sate his thirst. Thirsty, but beyond that, not uncomfortable, not in any pain. He felt ready. More ready than he had felt in a long, long time.

Then something was disturbing the comfort, forcing him back to the surface. He opened his eyes; the effort seemed impossible, but he did it. Swimming in front of him, a fuzzy image. Marlowe. He looked so concerned. A good man, Marlowe. He cared, he cared more than he himself knew.

'James, oh James, damn it, damn it . . .' Marlowe was saying. Silly. So hard to talk, why waste the effort?

428

James closed his eyes, tried to find the strength in his shattered and numb body. Had to tell Marlowe it was all right.

He opened his eyes. 'I'm going now.' So quiet. Could Thomas hear him? Marlowe leaned closer. 'I'm going to the only place I got left to go.'

He closed his eyes again. That was the last of his strength. He felt the soft darkness wash over him, the warm embrace, the gentle evening air, the warm water, the loving arms of Africa, his new Africa.

CHAPTER 34

He was dead. Marlowe laid his fingers gently on James's face, eased his eyelids shut, laid him back on the dirt floor. He stood and looked at the fresh blood that covered his hands. James's blood. He did not try to wipe it off.

The room was crowded with men: Bickerstaff, the Elizabeth Galleys. Less than a minute before, the Galleys had been a howling, blood-crazed mob, set on looting and tearing apart whatever fell in their path, but now they stood silent, respectful.

They all knew King James from the *Elizabeth Galley*'s fitting out. They had witnessed his final act as they raced for the factor's hut, had seen him fling himself headlong into the pistol's barrel, charging blade-first with such momentum that he had skewered his enemy and driven the sword right through him and through the mud wall of the hut, leaving the man pinned upright, even after he had suffered his mortal wound. The Elizabeth Galleys could respect such a man.

'A minute. A bloody goddamned minute more and we would have been here,' Marlowe said.

'And then what?' asked Bickerstaff. 'Prevent James

from dying thus, so that he could fulfill his promise to go back and be hanged like a dog? This thing' – Bickerstaff nodded toward the corpse pinned to the wall – 'must be the infamous Madshaka. We should all be so lucky as to die quick at the moment of our ultimate triumph.'

Marlowe smiled a weak smile. 'You are right, of course. As always. Now I pray, Francis, that you will be kind enough as to live until we return to Virginia? I shall tell the governor that we did indeed hunt King James down and we saw him dead, but I am not certain he will take my word on it. He will believe you, if you say it is so, but I am not convinced he would take my word alone.'

'I shall certainly endeavor to live that long and I will be happy to confirm your story. There is nothing in it that is not the truth.'

Marlowe looked around the wreckage of the room. A big ring of keys hung from a hook on the wall and he crossed the room, snatched them up. He turned to his men. 'I need ten of you with me, the rest are free to find whatever is worth carrying away from here. Francis, you will never object to our looting slave traders, I assume?'

Bickerstaff sniffed. 'I do not care to be involved with your moral relativism, Thomas.'

'Good, then come with me.'

They crossed the compound, approached the trunk carefully. To Thomas's great relief there was one among the captives there who had a small amount of English and a small amount of the coastal pidgin, enough that Marlowe could convey to him what he intended, and he to some others, and those to others, until everyone in the trunk was reasonably sure that they were not in for greater torment from these new white men. And when Marlowe was sure they were sufficiently mollified, he opened the iron door and let them shuffle out and knocked the chains and yokes off those who were still so encumbered.

They met up with the rest of the Elizabeth Galleys, who had found a small quantity of gold and some firearms worth the taking. They wrapped King James's body in a sheet stripped from the factor's bed and fashioned a litter from the tablecloth and carried him back down the trail.

On the beach they found the men who had not fared well in the surf; some of them were well recovered and some were not, and of those that were not, three were dead.

At the edge of the tree line they dug graves, four of them, eight feet deep and two wide, and in them they put King James and the three seamen who might have been James's shipmates but instead had died while hunting him down.

Francis Bickerstaff said a few words and they covered them over with the African soil.

The sun was just below the horizon and starting to light the eastern sky. Soon the land breeze would fill in to lift the *Elizabeth Galley* and her prize off the shore and out to sea.

Marlowe watched the last bit of dirt being thrown on the grave, took a deep breath, looked up and down the beach. The longboat had been hauled back down to the water's edge and his men and the people freed from the factory were milling about on the hard-packed sand.

'To hell with this damned place,' Marlowe said to no one in particular. 'Let us be gone from here.'

He turned toward the sea, marched off toward the waiting boat. James was not the first good man he had left to his eternal rest, not the first friend, and Marlowe did not think he would be the last.

Beware, beware, beware . . .

Billy Bird made the proposal to allow a woman, one Elizabeth Marlowe, to take passage with them to Virginia, and the Bloody Revenges agreed by formal vote.

They took their democracy very seriously, and though there was not one aboard who was not aware of the real facts of the matter, there was never a hint from one of them that he had ever set eyes on Elizabeth before. They all viewed Elizabeth as something between a talisman and a pet, which was their singular reason for agreeing to override an otherwise iron-clad rule.

They would take her to Virginia, but no more. Seven days down the coast and they hove to in Hampton Roads in the dark hours of the morning and took Elizabeth ashore by boat, depositing her amid the tiny cluster of homes that constituted the town of Newport News. And despite Billy's profuse apologies for such treatment, and his promise to return shortly for another visit, he seemed as anxious as the others to be back aboard the *Revenge* and gone.

A few hours later, when the sun broke from the water and burned off the late-summer mist that clung to the top of the bay like cotton batting, the *Bloody Revenge* was nowhere to be seen.

When the morning had progressed enough that she felt she could go abroad without arousing suspicion, she made her way into town and hired a horse and from there rode the twelve miles to Marlowe House.

She had no notion of what to expect after her five-week absence. Charred ruins, perhaps, or Frederick Dunmore living there, having found some way to lay legal claim of possession?

What she hoped more than anything was to find Thomas home, to ride up and see him sitting there on the big porch in his familiar position, booted feet kicked up on the rail, a glass or a pewter mug in his hand, engrossed in some philosophical discussion with Francis Bickerstaff, or goading his friend with silly banter.

But he was not there, no one was there, and the house was little changed. The garden was overgrown, and the grass looked wild, more field than manicured lawn, and the house itself forlorn, empty, musty, but still generally in the same shape it had been in when she left. The animals were still alive, and looked well fed, which meant that her neighbor had sent a boy over to tend to them, as she had asked he might in the note she had dispatched to him.

Tired as she was, and sore from the long ride, she built a fire and boiled bucket after bucket of water and took a long and luxurious bath in the big copper tub. She lay there for hours as the water went from hot to warm to cool, and finally she pulled herself out and crawled naked into the big bed that she and Thomas shared and then she slept.

She woke at dawn the next morning. She woke alert, ready. She dressed in a riding outfit, saddled a horse, and left Marlowe House once again.

It took her an hour to reach the big house that

Frederick Dunmore owned on the Jamestown Road, a mile from Williamsburg proper. She reined her horse to a stop on the road and looked down the long drive leading to the front door. She could see some people moving around in the fields beyond the house. They would be indentured servants. Dunmore kept no black slaves – an anomaly for a wealthy man in the tidewater – and now Elizabeth understood more of why that was.

She dismounted, tied her horse to a sapling on the edge of the road, pulled a leather pouch from the saddlebag. She did not want Dunmore to know she was coming until she was there, so she walked down the drive and stepped quietly onto the porch.

She paused, drew a breath, considered again what she would do, what she would say. Then she lifted the brass pineapple knocker and rapped it hard, three times.

Movement inside, and Elizabeth expected a house-keeper to answer, but it was Frederick Dunmore himself. He was dressed in a loose-fitting banyan of flowing silk. On his shaved head a sort of turban hat. He clearly was not expecting visitors at that hour, and judging by his expression Elizabeth guessed that he was expecting her least of all. His mouth fell open and he stared at her and tried to speak, and after a moment all that would come from his mouth was 'Damn me . . .'

'Damn you, indeed, Mr Dunmore. Does it shock you to find me alive?'

'What? Why should . . . What do you want?' He made no move to welcome her inside.

'Might I have a word with you? I have certain information . . .'

'Where have you been all these weeks?' His eyes narrowed as he regarded her, as if squinting might reveal something that direct sight could not. 'There has been some high talk, you know. Pirates raiding the public armory, making off with a great cache of weapons, their captain staying right at the King's Arms, spying things out, so the rumor goes. And you not to be found just a day later. Some mighty big talk . . .'

'Yes, well, talk is not evidence, is it? If you have evidence I would beg to know what it is,' she said, and in her mind she felt all the disparate and seemingly unrelated pieces fitting together: Billy Bird's appearance, the ship quite hidden in the Pagan River, Charleston, the Revenges' unwillingness to be discovered once more in the Chesapeake Bay.

Billy Bird. That bloody villain.

Frederick Dunmore was scowling at her but apparently had nothing more to say regarding her possible connection to the pirates that raided the armory. Instead he added, 'If you've come back to beg for your niggers you can forget it! If any of them show their faces in this town they will be arrested and sold, do you hear? Carrying arms against white people, running wild all over the countryside. They are a menace and they will be hunted down!'

'You do not give up easy, considering your less than impressive success so far. But see here. I have been away. I have been to Boston. You are familiar with Boston, I believe?'

She saw the flicker of anticipation and concern across his face, the subtlest of change in his expression, but he did not waver in his raw bluster. 'I lived once in Boston, there is no secret. Are you trying to imply something, you little . . .'

'I have here a document,' Elizabeth continued, pulling a paper from her leather pouch, 'that relates to your family. Your family tree, Mr Dunmore, do you know what I mean?'

Now the fear was in his expression, the uncertainty, eyes shifting from the paper to Elizabeth's face and back. He snatched the document from her hands, scowled as he studied it.

'This is a record of my uncle's birth . . . this means nothing. How did you come by this? You stole this!'

'That record means nothing, it is true. I show it to you merely to demonstrate that I do have your family records. I would not put the important one in your hand. The record of your grandfather Isaac's birth. The record of his father, Richard, and his mother . . . Nancy. The slave girl Nancy.'

Dunmore stared at her for a long time without speaking, then slowly crumpled the paper in his hand and tossed it away. 'It is a lie. It was always a lie. Do you think I'm such a fool that I would not figure it was a lie?'

'You do not sound so certain. Are you?'

'Yes, goddamn your eyes, you goddamned pirate's whore! It is a lie!'

Elizabeth shrugged. 'Perhaps. And perhaps not. Perhaps I have the document I say I do, and perhaps I do not. But pray, allow me to show you one more.'

She pulled another document from her pouch, handed it to him. 'It is in my hand,' she explained. 'I transcribed the original, which is signed by you. I see you are too rough with papers for me to trust you.'

Dunmore's eyes ran over the words. Elizabeth could all but recite them, having read the note so many times. 'I wish that the said Elizabeth Marlowe and her companion should never leave the town of Boston . . .'

Incredible. She was actually grateful for the letter. If there was ever a moment when she doubted the morality of what she was doing, she had only to think of that, and of the hired killers who had almost carried out those instructions.

Dunmore looked up at her. Again he could not speak, but this time his mouth hung open.

'The original was taken from a man who was trying most diligently to carry out your wishes. He had nearly one hundred pounds on his person. I am flattered.'

That wasn't true, of course, about the money; there was only the bank draft that Billy Bird, the villain, had insisted on cashing the morning after the fight in the church. They had nearly missed the tide, thanks to his audacity, and only just made it to the ship ahead of the sheriff. But the money, divided among the men of the *Bloody Revenge*, had done much to improve esprit de corps.

They stood there for a moment more, Dunmore unable to think of anything else to say, Elizabeth not feeling the need to.

Finally she broke the silence. 'I will take my leave, Mr Dunmore. I have enjoyed this talk, more than you will know. And now I have no doubt that my people will be allowed to return unmolested to Marlowe House, and that you will be their champion, and that I, in turn, will keep secret papers secret. Good morning.'

She nodded, turned her back on Frederick Dunmore, and walked away.

He stood in the door and watched her go. Tried to pin a thought down long enough to examine it, tried to calm the tempest so that he could see above the churning water, see what was beyond, what he might do, where he was, but he could not.

The storm was on him again, raging as it had never raged before, smashing him, smashing him as it had on the ship, sending him reeling off the cabin door, puking on himself, unable to stop. Just when it had been calm for so long.

It was the eye of a hurricane, a false calm before it hit from an entirely new direction, and worse than before. He felt the urge to bathe, to scrub his skin until it bled, as if he could wash the impurity from him. He saw his hands once more around the old woman's throat . . .

He turned from the door, staggered away, unseeing. He moved from room to room, trying to focus on something, anything, but he could not. He could not make his mind stop, could not even slow it long enough to have a rational thought.

Room to room he wandered, and back again. He bounced off a wall in the hallway, turned over a small table, sent a vase shattering to the floor, but he did not even notice. On his way around again he stepped on the broken shard, cut his foot through his silk slipper, left marks of blood in an even trail as he walked, but still he was not aware.

He paused, looked up at a big portrait of himself that stood above the fireplace. An epic work: he was on horseback, leading some fictitious charge, his great white wig flowing nobly down his shoulders.

He looked into his own eyes, rendered in oil, and as he stared the eyes seemed to stare back and he stood for some time, just looking.

And then a voice spoke to him. He did not know if it was the painting, or himself speaking out loud, or if he had just thought the words in his head. But no matter. They spoke clear, one sentence, that was all.

You are the fox.

Yes, yes, he thought. I am the fox. Quick, nimble. Vicious when cornered, able to fight with razor teeth. But that was rare, because the fox was too crafty to be cornered, too crafty by half. Doubling back, wading through streams, the fox knew how to elude capture, how to keep on the run.

Dunmore tore his eyes from the painting, raced up the stairs. In a back room, he found the old chest, pulled it out, dragged it to his bedroom, flung open his wardrobe, and began to toss suit after white suit into it.

There was money in the study, specie, quite a bit of it. He could send for the rest. Have the factor sell the house, the land, the horses.

But where?

He stopped in his packing, stood up straight, stared out the window. Where in that great world?

France. Yes, France, of course. England and France were at war, no one would find him there.

But would he be welcome in France? Of course . . . if he were a papist, seeking to escape from Protestant persecution at home. Of course. He had been a Congregationalist in Boston, Church of England in

440

London, an Anglican in Virginia, why not a Roman Catholic in France?

He was the fox. He could make them lose his scent.

He grabbed up his three best wigs and threw them in the trunk. The damned Romish church had all sorts of nonsense in its service, kneeling and babbling in Latin and eating its bread. But it was not so different from the High Church of England. He could learn all that. He could be a papist.

He slammed the trunk shut. Sent for one of the field hands to drive him by carriage to Newport News. A bit of business in Boston, he would tell them. And then, to France, by way of whatever route he had to take, with the dogs lost and baying further and further behind him.

Epilogue

It was all something of an embarrassment in the end. Frederick Dunmore had convinced some quite important men in the tidewater of the righteousness of his cause, of the need to stamp out Thomas Marlowe's example, and then he had disappeared.

An indentured field hand named McKeown had driven him to Newport News from which place, Dunmore informed the man, he was bound for Boston on some sudden business. A month later Dunmore's factor received instructions to sell everything and to send the money to an address in Flanders. The factor did as instructed. No more was made of it, officially.

The unofficial discussions, however, the whispered rumors, tales of mental instability, were widely disseminated and continued to be a favorite topic for some time after the event. And to judge from those remarks, it seemed that everyone in Virginia had known all along that Dunmore was a lunatic, unstable, though they had not wanted to say as much – not the thing, you know, to tell such tales.

All this Marlowe learned in the early autumn after the battered, weed-encrusted *Elizabeth Galley* worked her way up the James River to her old berth at the Jamestown dock and Marlowe and Bickerstaff walked the few miles up the road to Marlowe House.

It had been a long and uneventful sail. From Whydah they had made their way due south, then east, leaving the Niger River Delta to larboard and fetching Kalabari. They anchored off the beach and hired *grumetes* to carry the people ashore, those people whom James had rescued from slavery within the bounds of Chesapeake Bay, who had fought their way back across the Atlantic, who had been so terribly betrayed.

It was James's wish that they be carried to Kalabari, and Marlowe was happy to do it. They were not there three hours before the people were ashore and the *Elizabeth Galley* won her anchor again and left the Dark Continent astern.

For nearly two months Thomas had been dreaming of his reunion with Elizabeth, and she did not disappoint. Not in the matter of her enthusiasm at seeing him again, or in the matter of the feast of fresh food and physical comfort she provided, not in any regard did she disappoint.

The home that Marlowe returned to was little changed from the one he had left, save for the big empty place that King James had occupied. But the rest of the people were there, living in their quarters behind the big house, tending the fields and the gardens. Lucy, long convinced that James would not return alive, listened to the tale and accepted it with a stoicism unusual for her.

True to their promise, George and the others had kept a regular watch on the house, had come to speak with Elizabeth after her return, and once the news of Dunmore's shameful departure had been well known, the people returned. No one in the tidewater had ever said a thing. Persecuting them was Dunmore's obsession, and no one wished to be a part of that, now that Dunmore was gone and Marlowe had returned.

And so Thomas Marlowe and Francis Bickerstaff were not quite certain what they were in for, three days later, when they donned their finest clothing, strapped on their gentlemanly swords, took up their gold-headed walking sticks, and drove in Marlowe's carriage to the Wren Building and the office of Governor Nicholson.

'Marlowe, dear Marlowe! And Francis Bickerstaff, pray, come in, come in, be seated! A glass of wine with you? Good, good!' Nicholson did not seem put out at all by them, did not seem hostile in any way. Quite the opposite, really.

'Thank you, Governor.' Marlowe settled in a chair, the same he had occupied at their last and quite different interview, and accepted the delicate crystal glass. It seemed so fragile, insubstantial in his hand, after the heavy glassware and pewter mugs he had been using for months, vessels designed to endure rough treatment at sea.

'So, you've had a successful cruise, I'll wager? We've seen no prizes sent in here; I do hope you have not been entirely without luck.'

Marlowe cleared his throat, glanced at Bickerstaff, who gave him a cocked eyebrow. 'We have been entirely without a letter of marque and reprisal, as you will recall, Governor. We were sent out to hunt down those people who killed the crew of the slave ship. In that, we have been successful. We chased

445

King James to Whydah, on the Slave Coast, and saw him dead.'

'Well, excellent, excellent. Good job. I don't recall now why you had no letter of marque. Well, no matter, there is one for you now, if you wish. To your health, sir!'

And that was it. No further inquiry. Marlowe did not mention the raid on the slave factory. He did not mention the one hundred and fifty-odd captives they had freed and carried off to Kalabari.

He said nothing of the French merchantman that they had sailed to Lisbon and sold, along with the cargo of booty, for more money than the governor would see in all his tenure in the Colonies.

He did not mention the surviving members of the *Northumberland*'s crew – Cato, Quash, Good Boy, and Joshua – who had been smuggled back to Marlowe House in the middle of the night and had resumed their place among the people there.

Instead he simply thanked the governor for his courtesy and sipped the wine and inquired as to how things had been in Virginia during their absence. Twenty minutes later the interview was done.

It was a perfect afternoon through which they drove back to Marlowe House. The sky was a rich blue, like a blue jay's plumage, not an anemic robin's egg. A cool breeze flowed in through the carriage window as if trying to comfort the occupants. For a long time they said nothing, just watched the green fields and the stands of trees pass by.

'There will be no crop this year,' Bickerstaff observed at last. 'With your people in exile all this time the tobacco has gone to ruin.'

'No matter. Our pirating has got us enough money

to survive and keep out of debt and pay the people as well.'

'It is unfortunate for me that you use your ill-gotten gains in so honorable a way as paying your poor people for their labor. It makes the moral position that much more ambiguous.'

At that Marlowe smiled. 'Moral position? Do you still look for such a thing? Frederick Dunmore had the moral position, ask anyone, until he snuck away like a thief in the night. We chased poor James clear across the Atlantic in support of the moral position, and now there is no one gives a tinker's damn that we did.'

'There is such a thing as right and wrong, Thomas, the evil of such men as Frederick Dunmore notwith-standing. I will never cease to try to make you understand that.'

Thomas Marlowe leaned forward, put a gloved hand on his friend's knee. 'And I shall always love you for that, Francis. And I look forward to your constant company. Because, you see, when I think on men such as Frederick Dunmore and King James, and the fact that we were made to hunt the one in support of the other, when I think of how Dunmore has been discredited now for running like a rabbit and James lies dead and forgotten, on how a simple piece of paper separates the privateer from the pirate, when I think on all those things, then I realize that trying to make me understand something like absolute right and wrong will be, I assure you, a lifetime's occupation.'

THE END

**Continued in *The Pirate Round* –
to be published soon**

THE GUARDSHIP
by James Nelson

'A master both of his period and of the English language'
Patrick O'Brian

With the bounty from his years as a pirate – a life he intends to renounce and keep forever secret – Thomas Marlowe purchases a fine Virginia plantation from a beautiful young widow, Elizabeth Tinling. Soon afterwards, while defending her honour, he kills the favourite son of one of the colony's most powerful families in a duel. But in a clever piece of manoeuvring he manages to win command of the *Plymouth Prize*, the colony's decrepit guardship, and is charged with leading the King's sailors in bloody pitched battle against the cutthroats who infest the waters off Virginia's shores.

A threat from his illicit past appears, however, as an old pirate enemy plots to seize the colony's wealth, forcing Marlowe to choose between losing all – or facing the one man he fears.

Book One of *The Brethren of the Coast* trilogy, featuring Thomas Marlowe.

'Brilliant . . . Readers will gladly be swept along by a wonderful plot'
Publishers Weekly

'A master storyteller'
Sailing

0 552 14838 5